BOOKS BY ANNE MAYBURY
I Am Gabriella
The Moonlit Door
The Minerva Stone
The Terracotta Palace

The Terracotta Palace

The Terracotta Palace

Anne Maybury

RANDOM HOUSE

NEW YORK

The Terracotta Palace

I ⚭

IN THE PLANE ON THE WAY TO ROME, a picture haunted me. It was like a painting on a gauze curtain stretched across the changing scenes below, the flat fields of England, the white crested Channel and the Alps.

I stared at my secret picture as at a mirage, so absorbed and torn with longing that I was only vaguely aware of the movement and voices around me. The pretty stewardess with the high arched eyebrows held a tray of French perfumes toward me. I shook my head at her without really looking at what she had to sell. I knew that the fat man sitting at the end of the row of three kept flicking an eye toward me over the top of *Il Messaggero*, which he must have bought at London Airport. I felt the touch of Martin's arm as he reached to stub out a cigarette.

I was glad he didn't speak to me. I was too wrapped around by my memories to enjoy even Martin Kean's conversation, and the things surrounding me were not nearly as real as the picture fleeing by the plane's side across the cloud patterns. Malimbrosa—my "Terracotta Palace."

I wondered whether the walls were as deeply red as my child's-eye view had remembered them; whether the palms that made a frame for the great square house still stood dark against the ultramarine sky; whether the windows were as tall as they had seemed to me in those days. I used to think that they were like the many eyes of a sleeper, permanently shuttered as if guarding the ancient rooms from the thousands of tourists who peered through the wrought-iron gates, questioning, "Who lives there? Is their family old? . . . rich? . . . famous? . . ."

Nostalgia brought an ache to my heart and my emotions. For on this visit I would be one of those who looked at the Palazzo Malimbrosa from the outside. And if anyone happened to glance into the street from some opening in the shutters and noticed me, he would think I was just another tourist. Not one of them would recognize me and exclaim to someone in the room, "Oh, look. There's Juliet Holdroyd. Little Julie . . . grown up."

I had been eight years old when I had stayed there. Now I was twenty-two and the *palazzo* was a forbidden place. The memory of it during the intervening years had not dimmed. It was like a tale told to a child and lived by that child so vividly that the stresses of growing up had never entirely erased it.

MY INVITATION TO STAY AT MALIMBROSA in Rome had come as the result of friendships formed long before I was born and, later, of the deliberate bringing together of Vanessa and myself.

When my mother had been a student at Oxford she had become friendly with a brilliant woman with the unbelievable name of Amalia Dragon. After Amalia had left Oxford with a first class honors degree, she chose to teach, and eventually became head of a large and very well-known girls' school in the south of England.

My mother and Amalia Dragon had lost touch with each other over the years, but they had met again when my mother was married and I was seven years old. "The Fabulous Dragon," as she was subsequently called by us, had persuaded my mother to send me to her school. Mother, in order to pay the fees that would be a strain on my father's meager income, had taught French and Italian at a school near our home and because she loved languages, she taught me, too.

All through my childhood our conversations had been carried on in a happy mixture of English, French and Italian.

While I was at the school, Vanessa Malimbrosa came from Italy to spend a year there in order to learn English. She was an orphan, brought up by her grandmother at the family's *palazzo* in Rome. She swept like a dynamo into the huge Georgian house, defied rules with a flair, laughed at discipline, dismayed the teachers, and enchanted the pupils.

Vanessa and I didn't become friends by chance. The Fabulous Dragon herself drew us together. She found us in the grounds one day chasing a red admiral butterfly in order to study its lovely markings, and had told us that when she was at University with my mother, they had both met Vanessa's uncle, Roberto Malimbrosa.

Vanessa said, "I never really knew him. He lived in England most of the time and then he was killed in an air crash."

Miss Dragon looked at me and said, "I wonder if your mother remembers those days?"

When I asked her, I found that Mother did, but without much interest. "Oh yes, we were all three friends, but it was a long, long time ago."

It was such a small thing, just a few casual remarks in a garden, but it had drawn Vanessa and me together into a friendship that had led me to Malimbrosa for a three-week summer holiday. It was the first time I had been abroad and I returned to London in a state of ecstasy. For some time nothing in my own home seemed real to me . . . The reality was Malimbrosa, and I dreamed of my next visit.

On a windy morning in October, five months after that holiday, the telephone rang. I had been watering a cyclamen plant on the window sill when I heard my mother's angry voice. "I'll never, *never* agree to such a thing," she had stormed. "There's *no* argument . . . none whatsoever. Julie will not visit you and I hope—oh, how I hope—she will never see Rome again." There was a brief silence and then the final outburst. "Nothing gives you the right to say that to me. How dare you! You have no hold over my daughter or me. None, do you hear? And you can . . ."

"Go to hell," I murmured into the bright pink cyclamen blooms, delighted to remember my father's favorite outburst.

My mother's voice continued, loudly and angrily. ". . . forget all about Julie. She's my daughter and she's staying that way." The receiver crashed down.

When she returned to the living room, my mother's charming face was vivid with anger. I asked, eager and not a little scared, "Was that *Nonna* Allegra? Why were you cross?"

"Never mind."

I asked, terrified of a refusal, "I *am* going to stay at the *palazzo* for my holidays this year, aren't I?"

"No," she said. "You are not. I'm sorry, Julie, but there won't be any more visits to Rome and I'd rather you didn't ask me why."

"But *Nonna* said last year, 'You must come next summer.' She called me '*cara*' and touched my cheek, so I know she liked me. I didn't do anything awful while I was there."

Mother said gently, "You had a wonderful holiday, Julie. Be grateful. And if you ever speak of it to your friends, you will call Vanessa's grandmother Signora."

"But Vanessa calls her *Nonna* and I was told to"—"Vanessa is her granddaughter and it was a kindness to you because it was less formal for a little girl. But that's all over. Now stop looking sulky or I'll be too ashamed of you to take you out and buy you a new dress for Evelyn's party."

A new dress, a party in a friend's red-brick suburban house . . . panacea for a lost second visit to Malimbrosa. I stormed in secret, rebelling against God, who could so easily have answered my prayer, and had turned away.

ALL THESE YEARS AFTER that bitter childhood disappointment I was enjoying a small triumph, a compromise. I was on my way to Rome to stay with Vanessa. In the years since I had left school, she had paid occasional rushed visits to London. She had friends in all the capitals of Europe but she used to say, with a twist of irony, "They don't invite me to stay with them out of love for my beautiful character, but because they want to be asked to Malimbrosa."

When Vanessa was in London, she always came to see me. I loved her visits because she still had her extraordinary vitality that lifted those who were with her to a kind of permanent edge of excitement. She was not beautiful, for all her features had a strange upward tilt; her green eyes slanted, her mouth curved at the corners as if in perpetual amusement at the world. Her hair was red gold, curling like tongues of flame behind her longish pointed ears. She had been called "*une belle laide*." Yet to fit that description, her features had to be ugly and there was nothing ugly about Vanessa. She was an unusual-looking girl people would turn to look at in preference to the most beautiful woman in a room.

On her last visit to London only a few months ago, Vanessa had stayed with me at the wrong end of Chelsea Embankment, where the great houses had become apartments and artists collected to slash at their glaring abstracts; and where once Turner sat on his roof to paint the sunsets on the Thames. Our talks together would run on far into the night. Sometimes we spoke in English, sometimes in Italian, and I was eager for news of Malimbrosa. But it was clear that Vanessa had no idea why my mother had refused to allow me to visit the *palazzo* again.

She said, "I asked if I could invite you for the next summer holiday, but *Nonna* Allegra said, 'No. She will never be coming

· 7

here again.' When I asked her why, she said. 'It is Juliet's mother's fault.' And that was all there was to it."

During Vanessa's last stay with me in London, she suggested that if I hadn't already arranged my holiday for that year, I should take it in June and join her in Florence. "I have friends there and we'll have a marvelous time."

I had accepted without a moment's hesitation, afraid that if I said I would think it over and let her know, she might change her mind. I knew Vanessa's impulses and changeableness.

Then, two weeks before I was to join her, I received one of her rare long letters telling me that her plans were altered. She had quarreled with her grandmother and had left the *palazzo*. She did not tell me what her quarrel with *Nonna* Allegra was about.

She wrote: "Instead of Florence, you must come and stay with me in Rome. I have my inheritance from my father so I shan't starve, and I can promise you that I don't live in squalor. I have taken a little shop in the artists' quarter in Rome. There are so many painters round here and I shall display their work and take commission on what I sell. There's Mario who makes figurines in the green marble that comes from Sicily; Lorenzo's stained-glass panels and Artello's paintings—they're abstract and brilliant and angry. You'll meet these people when you come to Rome."

At the top of the letter she had carefully printed her address: 9 Via Prassodi. Rome. She added: "I live over the shop."

I wondered how she really felt behind the airy words she had written. Whereas *Nonna* Allegra's refusal to invite me to Malimbrosa had been an outsider's disappointment, Vanessa's banishment must have caused her far greater hurt, for the *palazzo* had been the only home she had known since her infancy, when her parents had been killed in a car crash.

Now, as I flew toward Rome, I was so absorbed in my thoughts that when Martin spoke, I jerked round as though I had been hit.

He asked, laughing, "What was that start in aid of?"

"I was a long way from here; I was thinking of Vanessa."

"She's not so far away. You'll be seeing her soon. I just wanted to bring you out of your daydream and tell you that we'll be landing in ten minutes."

I felt pricks of excitement up and down my spine. and took out my compact, peering at my reflection. A schoolteacher had once pointed me out to a colleague. Her voice carried and as I sat on the edge of the swimming pool, I heard her say, "The girl sitting near the diving board. The one with the honey-colored skin and the long brown hair."

There was nothing honey-colored about me now. My face was pale from the long hours I spent walking the corridors of Westminster in the shadow of an aging and demanding Member of Parliament. I had worked as secretary for Henry Mazarin for two years. He had now retired and after my three weeks' stay with Vanessa, I was returning to London to become personal secretary to my late employer's cousin, the elegant and rebellious William Mazarin, Member for Grays Magna. The color and ritual inside the Gothic walls of Westminster were very familiar to me. I loved listening to the debates and private arguments. I also loved the political gossip that wove like threads of a tapestry in and out of those somber, statued halls.

The plane suddenly hit a pocket of wild air. I hadn't realized that we had come out of sunlight into cloud but I did as I was told and fastened my seat belt.

Martin said, "I hate this restriction."

"I keep my fingers on the buckle all the time," I said. "I'll race you when the word comes that we can undo them."

We looked at one another and laughed. I thought again how good to look at he was. His fair hair was thick and carelessly arranged; his eyes were narrow and intelligent.

He said, "You know, I'm more Roman than the Romans and I'm longing to show you around. I wish I could find, when we arrive, that the whole of the British embassy, from the ambassador down to the youngest office boy, was on strike. Then I'd have time to take you to all my favorite places." His hand lay lightly over mine.

Immediately a feather of caution brushed through me and I edged away into my corner.

I wanted no emotional involvement. I was going to Rome to see Vanessa, to stay in this apartment she had over a crazy-sounding shop. I wanted to know about her quarrel with Allegra Malimbrosa and if she had found out, since we last met, the reason for my mother's anger against the woman that I, too, had been allowed to call *Nonna*. I also wanted to know what exactly was the relationship between Vanessa and my traveling companion, Martin Kean. He himself had given me no clue. He and Vanessa were, according to him, just friends; but as friendship was becoming an understated word between a man and a woman, I was more than a little dubious. I knew that Martin was half-Irish and that he worked in the British embassy in Rome. He described himself as utterly expendable —"A bit above an office boy and far below an attaché."

He had come to London on leave and had brought with him an introduction from Vanessa. "Look up my friend Juliet Holdroyd," she had said, and had given him my address.

It had become an easy, pleasant friendship. I liked Martin's gift of laughter. It was often impossible to take anything he said seriously, but he made the world a charming place when we were together. He had dark blue Irish eyes and fair hair. "My mother," he had said, "was a Rose of England—and I really mean that her name was Rose. She gave me my fair hair."

The first time we met, he told me he was nervous in case I should want to talk politics. "It bores me," he said.

"That's easy, then, we won't talk politics. What shall we do instead?"

"Bedazzle the town," he answered, and whirled me off to dance half the night away.

He explained that he had been born with two assets, a small private income and an uncle whose influence had got him into the Foreign Office. From there, he had been drafted to Rome.

"Are you ambitious? Would you like to be an ambassador?"

"Not in the least. I'm a clock-watcher. I have one small life to live and it's going to be good. Ambition is for those who don't know how to enjoy leisure."

On our last two meetings in London, I began to sense something more than a casual interest in Martin's approach to me and at once I wrapped myself in an armor of caution. There must be no plunges into an emotional life; no entanglements . . .

The image of Malimbrosa was gone. A distant cloud, shaped like a cornucopia, became a backdrop against which I saw two faces.

They were of the two men who had taught me to grow up. Their places in my life were as important as the lessons I had learned at school, or even more so. For I had loved them both. They were older than I; more sophisticated and ready to seize the pleasures of the moment with no thought of permanence. And, like some silly moth fluttering round lamplight, I had rushed with open arms, first to the one and then, after a period of heartbreak, to the other, living in each case in a few months of passionate excitement.

The pattern was the same. We talked about ourselves, and dissolved into violent emotional silences when we could not bear to draw away from one another. We listened to music; wandered with hands clasped along the Thames embankment, watching the old boats that plied the river. We lay in the warm grass on Surrey hills, greedy for each other. Yet for all the talking and the passion, lips and bodies one, neither man had loved me. As if I were Cynara, they had been faithful to me in their fashion.

I wept more bitterly the second time for, unlike the first, nothing had seemed to grow stale. We had had one last glorious summer night together and then he was gone—"abroad." I realized later that he was the type who finished a love affair before it began to drag. He liked his final memories to be beautiful.

My mother and father were both dead by this time, but a

friend of Mother's to whom I poured out the story of my star-crossed life, jerked me out of self-pity with a few apt words.

"You know, Julie," Ruth Warren had said, "a girl's first unhappy love affair is the result of inexperience; the second time it happens, she is a little fool. But if there should be a third time, then you give up trying to help her because she is just an emotional suicide and beyond help. Don't let this happen to you. Remember that your head is as important in a love affair as your heart."

I was determined to learn her lesson well. I had no intention of becoming a martyr to the mirages that I had called love. Nor did I, in time, any longer blame the men. They had acted honestly, by their own rules. It was just that I did not play the same game; I wanted constancy where there was none, and excitement where there was plenty. If only I had had less impulse and more worldly understanding; if only I had been strong . . . But when I said this to Ruth she was angry.

"If you're going to spend your time in regrets and indulging in memories of your failures, then you will *be* a failure. These were experiences. Learn from them."

I emerged with a new zest for work. It ceased to be just a job and became an engrossment. Westminster began to thrill me; I knew the halls as well as I knew my own small apartment . . . The Central Gallery and its statues; the Royal Gallery with its murals: the sound of tourists' feet on the gray flagstones. I filled the limbo left by my broken love affairs with my work. I was uninvolved, free. And I was going to Vanessa in Rome.

2 ❧

THE PLANE DIPPED TOWARD the baked earth. The storm over the Alps had not touched Rome. I looked down at the flat land of the Pontine marshes and the sun dazzled my eyes.

Martin said reflectively, "I suppose Vanessa won't be at the airport."

"She might decide to come and meet us if she has an assistant at the shop. Has she?"

"I don't know. I'd started my holiday in England when she broke with her family. I've never even seen the shop. Though—"

"Though what?"

"The Via Prassodi is a far cry from the Palazzo Malimbrosa," he said.

The plane landed on cushioned wheels and we flew along the airstrip like a skimming bird. As soon as I stepped onto the runway I was gripped by excitement. The air I breathed had a flavor of its own; the golden Roman light its particular quality.

Martin led me to a small car parked near the airport. I said, laughingly, as I got in, "Don't tell me your car has been waiting for you all these weeks!"

"I dropped a note to a friend and he brought it out for me."

"And didn't wait?"

Martin laughed back at me. "I didn't ask him to," he said, and started the engine and turned the car toward Rome.

To the right and left of us along the old Appian Way were groups of broken columns; fields of melon-colored grass; petrol stations. Then, as we entered the outskirts of Rome, there were the tall blocks of apartments with green festooned balconies, great ocher-colored houses, shuttered and remote; and high walls enclosing secret gardens.

I knew of such a garden. Fourteen years ago, as a child, I had played in one, reaching out my hand to cup the water of a Bernini fountain; chasing Vanessa round the stone urns where dwarf orange trees grew; plucking sky-blue morning glories from the walls, and seeing the blossoms wilt and crumble in my warm hands.

We had turned into a maze of side streets behind the Via del Babuino. The distance in mileage from the Palazzo Malimbrosa was relatively short; in every other respect it was a world away.

I read the names of the streets and Martin told me about them. "This is the Via Margutta and it's almost entirely occupied by foreigners." I looked obediently at the ancient houses propping up one another like old drunks. "You recognize that place, don't you?" Martin said, waving a hand. "The Piazza di Spagna and that's Keats's house at the corner. There are some art galleries around here, and lots of frame-makers. We're almost there."

"You mean Vanessa lives—?" I had no need to ask. I recognized an odd corner of a street we were passing.

On one of her postcards to me, Vanessa had drawn a rough sketch of this place. There was the old corner house with iron grilles over the lower windows and a broken flower urn filled with tired evergreen standing by the sun-blistered door.

Vanessa's correspondence with her friends usually consisted of postcards. Drawing had always been her one talent and Artello, of the angry abstracts, had given her a few lessons. She was too impatient by nature and too lazy by disposition to study hard, but she used her considerable gift to amuse her friends. She would make lightning pencil sketches of something she was seeing at the moment of writing. I suspected that to cover one side of a postcard this way meant that she needed to write less. She used very few strokes of pen or pencil, but those few were intensely telling.

I loved her cards but wished she would tell me more about herself and what she was doing. All her writing consisted of was a few words scrawled on the other side of the card and sent in an envelope lavish with stamps. She never bothered to find out just how many to put on, she just reached out and stuck on what was within her reach.

Sitting beside Martin, I watched as the car twisted through the narrow streets. I saw the untidy tables outside a *trattoria;* a wine shop with a partly boarded-up window; dusty gutters where lean cats lurked, and the tip and pitch of uneven paving stones. I had a pretty good imagination, but it did not extend to seeing Vanessa in these surroundings.

I sat stunned. A memory stirred of Vanessa as a child of eleven, walking under the great rotunda of Malimbrosa, wearing her best white nightdress like an evening gown, her grandmother's magnificent white furs trailing round her neck and onto the marble floor, and Allegra's Afghan hound at her side.

"Dressed to kill," she had laughed at my goggling eyes and had sailed in glory toward the double doors of the *salone.* She just managed to call in a small, imperious voice, "Open. Open in the name of Vanessa Malimbrosa," when her aunt Romola caught her and hustled her away from *Nonna* Allegra's probable anger . . .

"Here we are," Martin cried in triumph and slowed down at the curb.

When the sunlight touched it, which it did not do at this time of the afternoon, the shop might have glowed and aroused some interest. But now, in shadow, the little green nudes, the fury of slashed paint on canvases, the hand-made brooches and earrings, looked drab. I glanced beyond the window and into the shop. But the interior had a cavernous darkness.

Martin turned off the car engine. "Come on, let's find her."

I ran across the pavement, pushed open the door and called, "Vanessa—"

The girl who came forward could not have been any older than I. She looked at me with the hovering smile of someone hoping to make a sale.

I said in careful Italian, "I am Miss Holdroyd. The Signorina Malimbrosa is expecting me."

The girl's face changed, the smile faded into startled incredulity. "Signorina Malimbrosa? But I do not understand."

"This is her shop?"

"No"—her glance flashed to my left hand—"signorina, I am afraid you are mistaken. This shop belongs to my husband and me."

I said faintly, looking at Martin, "But this is Number Nine Via Prassodi?"

"Oh yes, that is right." She called over her shoulder, "Tino?"

He came from behind a brightly painted screen. He was black-haired, monkey-faced and very disarming. "Good afternoon, signorina . . . signore. You are lost? You are looking for some address round here?"

"For this address," I said. "This shop. It belongs to a friend."

The girl cried in sudden distress. "But you are mistaken. I am Carlotta Cotone and this is my husband, Tino. The shop is ours. We bought it—"

"So did Vanessa," Martin interrupted. "Vanessa Malimbrosa was her name—" He added sharply, "Why, what is it?"

Standing close together like two awed children, they whispered in unison, "The Signorina *Vanessa* Malimbrosa?"

"So you know the name?"

The girl nodded. "We know. Oh yes, we . . . know . . ." She was twisting her hands, her eyes dark and dazed. "But the signorina is not here—she cannot be here. You must know . . ."

"Know what?"

She shook her head. "Nothing; that is, it has nothing to do with us."

"It seems that it has," I cried. "The signorina is a friend of mine and she invited me here, to this address, to spend a holiday with her."

A car passed noisily outside. The Cotones seemed to be glad of the noisy interruption. When Tino spoke again his manner was more aloof. "There has obviously been a mistake. We cannot help you. I am sorry, but we took over the shop and the apartment from the last owner about two weeks ago. He was an old man and had retired from work."

Martin asked quickly, "Where does he live?"

"He is dead."

Martin murmured in English, "You couldn't be more off-putting, if you tried."

I asked, "Then what happened to my letter? I wrote about a week ago telling Vanessa—the signorina—what time I would be arriving in Rome."

The girl's face cleared. "So it was *your* letter. But the Malimbrosa family have no connection with this place. How could they—?" She gave me a sideways look. I immediately felt that she knew something but was afraid to tell us. I watched her pretty, plump figure running to the back of the shop. She disappeared for only an instant and returned with an envelope heavily stamped and covered with my own large handwriting.

The letter was unopened and I took it from her. "Why didn't you return it? My address is on the back of the envelope."

"We were going to readdress it to the *palazzo*. I am sorry, but in the efforts of moving in here and cleaning up the place, I am afraid I pushed it into a drawer and forgot."

I turned to Martin. He looked like a man who had just been told that someone he knew well had never been born.

I stared at the vivid crimson and violet patches of paint on a canvas propped on a table. At the corner was a signature,

"Artello Magnani." I gripped Martin's arm. "That painting. Vanessa mentioned the artist's name." I turned to the young Cotones. "Then if you don't know the signorina who was supposed to own this shop, you *do* know the man who painted this. He was a friend of hers. So, if you'll give me his address we'll go there and see him. He'll tell us—"

Carlotta Cotone said urgently, "Signorina, please. If you are looking for the Signorina Vanessa, then you must go to the Palazzo Malimbrosa." She flashed a frightened look at her husband.

I said firmly, "I'll have Artello's address." I couldn't explain to these young strangers that the last place I wanted to visit was Malimbrosa.

"But we cannot find it just like that," Tino protested, snapping his fingers. "Everything here is in a muddle. The old man from whom we bought the shop did not keep his records very well. We will have to look for it. If you will come back tomorrow, we will try to have found it for you."

Martin said, "You could look now, couldn't you? You don't seem busy." Then, as they conferred with one another, he whispered to me, "She has probably run away with a man—"

I only just heard what he said. My own conclusion leaped at me and was quite different from Martin's. I felt certain that I understood why the Cotones professed not to know of Vanessa's connection with their shop. When *Nonna* Allegra had heard of Vanessa's wild enterprise, she had been outraged that a Malimbrosa was running a business in a seedy little street, and she had forced her to give it up, had forgiven her and welcomed her home—and had forbidden anyone who knew of it to talk about it. And, typical of Vanessa, she had either sent a note telling me what had happened too late to catch me, or had been certain I would contact the *palazzo* if I couldn't find her here.

Martin, however, had not reached that conclusion. He shook his head as if a fog had obscured his thinking. "I don't know what to say. If she'd just gone off with some man, she'd surely have let *you* know." He turned his head slowly and looked at me. "I don't like it, Julie. Vanessa gives us this address and then vanishes. Why?"

"We'll soon find out. Come on." I dragged at his arm. Over my shoulder I said to the Cotones, "I may call tomorrow for Artello's address. It all depends on what happens today." Their faces were so young and touching that I added, "And I'd like to shop here for presents for friends before I go back to London."

When we were outside, Martin said, "We'll first have to find a hotel for you since you seem to be homeless." He reached for the door of his car. "The trouble is, the best ones are full at this time of year."

"A small *pensione* will do for me, but we'll think about it later."

He said with laughing exasperation, "My dear girl, don't you realize that I want to get you fixed up as soon as possible? The alternative would be a night on the hard, hot pavements or, of course, there's always my apartment . . ."

"Nothing is as important as where you're going to take me now."

"And where's that?"

"To Malimbrosa," I said.

3 ❦

IN THE CAR MARTIN PROTESTED, "You're not really going to the *palazzo?*"

"Why not? It's the obvious place."

"I doubt it. Vanessa wrote to me in London and told me that she'd quarreled with the family. She even said in her letter that nothing would induce her to go back."

"People say that kind of thing on impulse," I told him. "Vanessa probably took the shop in some mood of defiance and then when *Nonna* Allegra asked her to return to Malimbrosa, she went. I expect she soon got bored with the shop anyway."

Martin made no attempt to start the car. I watched him take a cigarette and light it. "I don't know," he said slowly. "Going back home as though she's defeated doesn't seem the sort of thing Vanessa would do. She's proud."

"But Martin, there's no other explanation."

"Except that perhaps someone took her away suddenly, unexpectedly."

"You mean—against her wishes? But they couldn't. People don't do these sort of things . . ." But they did. The newspapers of the world were full of the outrageous things people did . . . I said, and my voice sounded more determined than I felt, "I'm sure I'll find her at Malimbrosa. And if she isn't there, they'll know where I *can* find her."

He leaned forward and started the car. Then he put out his cigarette. "Funny, I never have a taste for cigarettes when I'm worried. It's like smoking dust." He drove smoothly and, for him, rather slowly and I knew that he was still preoccupied with anxiety about Vanessa.

"Did you see the way the Cotone's expressions changed when you mentioned Vanessa's name?"

"Yes." I watched the flower sellers at the Spanish Steps without really seeing them. "Perhaps *Nonna* Allegra warned them not to talk about what she would probably call 'Vanessa's escapade.' If everything is now forgiven and forgotten . . ."

"*If* it really is like that—" Martin said gloomily. "Oh, damn the traffic lights!" The car stopped with a jerk. He sat back and his fingers tapped the wheel. "Of course, I may be just a pessimist. Vanessa could be at Malimbrosa and the family may welcome you with love and prepare the royal suite for you—*is* there a royal suite?"

"I doubt if I'll get beyond the front doors," I said.

Back in the wider streets the sunlight reached us again. "Under the roof of blue Italian weather . . ." Shelley's words echoed from some poem learned at school.

The shop in the Via Prassodi had flung me into a bewildered depression. Suddenly I was lifted out of it. I was in Rome. There was no mystery about Vanessa. She would be waiting for me to call her at the *palazzo*. It was more than likely that one of her postcards lay inside my front door in London. I could even imagine the kind of picture she had drawn on it. A few strokes depicting a place—the steps of Malimbrosa, perhaps, and Vanessa and I running toward one another. She had occasionally drawn me on her cards, accentuating my long hair, my wide mouth, my smallness.

The way to the *palazzo* was very vague in my mind. But the

house itself was as clear a memory as if I had only left it yesterday. Five hundred years ago the family had lived on the rich plunder from the jewelled Indies. When they had amassed their fortune, they used it lavishly, with a kind of divine right to indulgence until, a hundred years ago, little was left.

It was Francesco Malimbrosa who in 1865 had saved the family from disaster. Stifling the pride which centuries of mixing with popes and princes had instilled into the family, he had entered commerce. A brilliant businessman by instinct but not upbringing, he had opened textile factories, one in Milan and one outside Rome. The family's products had changed over the centuries. Instead of textiles they now made chemicals in Milan and plastics at the factory on the autostrada that led to Ostia.

It was a rarity in Italy for old families to have contempoarry minds. But there were some, like the Malimbrosas, who combined business and money-making with private lives lived partly in the tradition of the past.

I wondered with awe just how many million million lire the Malimbrosas were worth, but it was beyond my imagination and, anyway, it was no real concern of mine. All I wanted to do was to find Vanessa.

The trees in the Borghese Gardens were quite still in the afternoon air. As a child I had walked with Vanessa and Gisela, her young nurse companion, through the Porta Pinciana, toward the tall pines and the pavilions, under the long cool shadows. I remembered how we had been taken to puppet shows there and the fascination, not unmixed with horror on my part, of the bizarre little figures, dancing and dangling out their dramas for a group of wide-eyed children. There, too, was the enclosure where riding was taught and small legs urged some semblance of spirit into sleepy ponies . . . The dream faded.

I saw Malimbrosa.

Under a northern sun, the place would have seemed garish, its hot color almost an offense. Here, with the ultramarine sky crowning it, it was spectacular, proud and shuttered and enclosed. Two leopards sat on pillars on either side of the wrought-iron gates.

The place looked deserted and I had one awful fear that the family might be away cruising or at their summer place in the Alban Hills: the rich Romans did not stay in their city in high summer. Then I realized that it was only June.

Or perhaps, even, they no longer lived at Malimbrosa. After all, who was left of the family to inhabit those vast rooms? Only *Nonna* Allegra and her daughter Romola; Leo, her youngest son, and his wife, Irena, whom I had never met. Just four people in a palace that would comfortably house fifty.

I was so absorbed in my thoughts that I hadn't realized that the car had stopped until Martin said, waving his hand at the red house and the tall palms, "You're not a bit happy about calling there, are you?"

"No. But I have no alternative."

"You have. I suggest we first go and find you a hotel. I know some pleasant small places. Then you can telephone the *palazzo* from there."

"I'm calling," I said firmly. "And we'll talk about hotels later. I know my mother quarreled with *Nonna* Allegra, but I can't believe that she'll refuse to see me now that I'm here . . . or let me meet Vanessa."

"*If* she's there."

"You don't think she is, do you?"

"I don't know what to think. I only know I've got one of those odd, primitive feelings—a kind of hackles rising sensation. I feel that something's very wrong."

"Then I'll have to try and find out what it is."

I turned the handle of the car door and Martin reached across me for a newspaper in the glove compartment. He tore off a corner and wrote something on it. "Here's my telephone number. When you're ready to leave, I'll come and pick you up, and in the meantime I'll look after your luggage."

"Can't you wait for me? I'm only going to the door to ask if Vanessa is there. If she is, she'll probably come out and want to say 'hullo' to you, too. Martin, please don't go."

He grinned at me, let in the clutch and drove off. "Damn him," I thought resentfully, "he might have waited."

―――――――――

WHEN I HAD COME TO MALIMBROSA with Vanessa as a child, I had dashed through the tall gates, up the steps to the great doors and triumphantly pushed the bell myself. Uninhibited, enchanted by the stories of the grandeur within the red walls, I had gone without awe into the *palazzo*, with Vanessa encouraging me and laughing. Now, I walked doubtfully, steeled for hostility.

I pushed at the gates, but they were tightly closed. Then I saw a bell on the right-hand pillar. I pressed it and waited, peering through the delicate lacelike design of the wrought iron.

No one appeared and I began to be quite certain that the family had gone to the country or their yacht. But, just as I was turning away, the gates began to open very slowly and then, when there was just enough space for me to walk through, they stopped. I went past them, turned and saw them close behind me. So someone in the house had operated the gates by remote control. I crossed the stone pathway and reached the steps that led up to the great, carved double doors.

On the third step I stopped dead, overwhelmed by a sudden nervousness. How strong was my pride? Suppose they turned me away . . . Well, so they turned me away. If the doors nearly closed in my face, I'd shout through the last inch into the hall, "I haven't come begging, if that's what you think. All I want to know is: Where is Vanessa?"

I hadn't moved from the third step, nor had I pulled the bell, but the two carved panels of the door broke away from one another, opening slowly. Then I remembered that Vanessa had told me that closed-circuit television had been installed in the kitchen. The staff could see, without going to the door, whether someone was approaching. I supposed the gates, too, were mechanically operated.

The man who stood just inside was tall and almost albino fair. He had the soft, petulant mouth of a dissatisfied moron and he obviously didn't think much of me. He wore a forest-green uniform. *Nonna* Allegra had once told me that for hundreds of years the Malimbrosa servants had worn the same color although, of course, the uniform had changed with the centuries.

The man was waiting for me to speak. He looked rather like a model posing, and his eyes were as cold as the pillars that glimmered behind him in the half light of the vast circular hall.

I gave my name and said in Italian, "I would like, please, to speak to Signora Allegra Malimbrosa. Or"—I added hastily because the sudden drop of his heavy lids over his eyes fore-warned a positive refusal—"Or the Signorina Romola . . . or Signora Irena . . ." I rushed on, establishing my right of entry by naming them.

Somewhere in that list I had managed to convince him that I had not come to steal the tapestries or Allegra's blue diamonds. I won. He drew aside and I entered.

For a quivering, exciting moment I was eight years old again and there was the column I had rubbed so hard with a licked finger because I couldn't believe the parma-violet tint of the marble wasn't painted on. There was the great gilded chair with the lions' claw feet and the faded ruby velvet where, it was said, Garibaldi had once sat. I remembered how I had been told that in the nineteenth century guests had held skating competitions up and down the huge corridors, crinolines wheeling, jewels flashing.

"Your business, signorina?"

I returned to the present with an uncomfortable jerk. "I am Juliet Holdroyd and I have come to ask for the Signorina Vanessa Malimbrosa's address."

The cold, impassive face changed very slightly. I had a feeling that a barrier of caution and suspicion had fallen between us. Oh, lord, I thought, was it common gossip even among the servants that I was an unwelcome guest here? But when he spoke his voice was quiet, with the beautiful poise of careful training. "I will see who can receive you, signorina. Will you please be seated?"

"In Garibaldi's chair?"

If he had had any doubts that I had a right in this place, that seemed to settle it. He very nearly smiled.

My heels rang as I crossed the marble floor. A little scared at the way I was breaking the majestic silence, I tilted forward onto my toes toward the tall chair underneath the thirteenth-century painting of "The Priest of Apollo." Even that I remembered. I sat quite still, my hands clutching the arms of the chair, and wished Martin were with me.

I was surrounded by the richness of long tradition, the spoils of opportunism. The Malimbrosas lived among the treasures of the past while they themselves had pushed forward into the present. The factories kept that magnificent sweeping staircase in repair; preserved the tapestries, the mosaic dome. This family which had begun as merchant adventurers had grown into a dynasty. And the power of money was still theirs, although it was no longer from jewelled plunder and services rendered to kings and favors to princes. The Romans are realists. And Allegra, the spinal column of the business, the French invader, was the most realistic of them all.

In an alcove opposite to where I sat was a bronze head of a beautiful woman. When I first saw it, I had cried, "That is *Nonna* Luciana."

Zia Romola had laughed. "Oh, no. This was sculptured two hundred years ago of an ancestor of ours."

Old Luciana Malimbrosa was dead now. She had been sitting in her suite at the *palazzo* laughing at something outrageous that Vanessa had done. Then suddenly she gave a little sigh; her head fell forward. She was dead at ninety-one.

I could still remember that charming, partially deaf old woman who was Vanessa's great-grandmother. When her only son, Ludovico, died it was his wife, Allegra—the woman from

Orléans—who had taken over the business. No one openly objected, especially not her own sons. Vanessa had told me that they must have been secretly relieved that the burden had not fallen on them. Roberto, the one who had died in a plane crash, had been the cleverest.

Vanessa had said, "Leo has brains, too. But not even he can stand up to *Nonna* Allegra."

So, old Luciana had sat quietly, watchfully, in her first-floor suite and had seen the Malimbrosa empire hold its power under Allegra's domination.

I had been shy of *Nonna* Luciana because it had been so difficult to talk to her, although she lip-read well. But I had instinctively liked and trusted her. I used to go and sit at her feet in her apartment with the cupids and the naiads painted on the ceiling and she would tell me stories of Roman history. She always smelled beautifully of some rose scent and her voice, unlike many deaf people, was soft—far softer than *Nonna* Allegra's.

I was looking at the pillars which upheld the first semicircle of the staircase when I heard a sound that had been so familiar to me fourteen years ago and, before I turned my head to see who was coming, I knew.

Changes of style in dressing, less clothes, more clothes— nothing could alter *Zia* Romola's love of rich taffeta under-skirts. Whenever she walked, her clothes set up a rustling as if tiny hissing snakes were secreted in the folds. She could never disguise her coming or going because her skirts were never silent.

"Juliet." She came toward me with her hands outstretched; a thin, haggard woman with a narrow face, black hair, and eyes that never laughed. She wore a silver-colored dress of some material that made her look scaly, like a fish. The dress made me realize that the hours had flown since the plane had touched down at the airport, and that the Malimbrosas always dressed for dinner.

When I was here before I had felt that she didn't like me; did not, in fact, like children at all and so I had not liked her. I used, also, to think her odd and ugly in the marvelous clothes that never suited her.

"My dear child . . ." Romola's dry cheek barely brushed mine. I felt that even this gesture cost her an effort to make. But at least she wasn't antagonistic.

"This is wonderful," she said in excellent English. "It has been so long since we have seen you." She held me at arm's length asking "What has brought you to Rome? A holiday? Or—?" She left the alternative in the air.

I looked directly into her eyes. They were opaque as if there was no light in her mind to make them shine. "I came because Vanessa invited me to stay with her. But when I went to the address she gave me, the people there didn't know her."

Romola's face changed in precisely the same way as the butler's had done. She half closed her eyes, watching me through slits. Her expression was blank and she had withdrawn from me.

"Vanessa is here, isn't she?" I asked.

"No." She hesitated. Then she said, "You must come in and see Mamma."

I said in surprise, "But *Nonna* Allegra won't want to see *me?* After her quarrel with my mother . . ."

Zia Romola said, "Dear child, that is a long time ago, and anyway, Mamma has told me to bring you to her."

It was as it always had been. *Zia* Romola would tell me nothing. Allegra, always Allegra who took control, not only of the business, but also of their lives.

I gave another swift thought to Martin and wished he had waited. I needed moral support as I followed Romola into the enormous *salone* I had once known so well.

4 ❧

THE LATE AFTERNOON SUN THREW a saffron light over the
brocades, the carved furniture, the golds and the greens of the
painted ceiling. The double doors that led into the next vast
room were closed, making the one in which I now stood as
cozy as anything so magnificent could ever be.

"Juliet."

"*Nonna* Allegra."

Another cool, dry cheek against my hot one; thin hands
holding my arms, rings hard against my flesh.

Allegra Malimbrosa was the ancient matriarch of a great
family, the Frenchwoman who had married Ludovico Malimbrosa and had become, when he died in his early forties, the
brains behind its vast industry, the final queen of its dynasty.

"Child, this is a great surprise." Now, with the light shining
on her, she seemed not to have changed at all. Her eyes
watched me from their deep sockets; her skin was like Victorian papier-mâché, cracked and crossed with tiny lines. She
had reached a kind of agelessness. "You are staying in Rome
and you did not let us know!"

It was a gentle but outrageous rebuke. Her clever, aquiline
face was severe; the blue veined hands were restless.

I said, "I thought Vanessa would tell you that I was coming. She invited me to stay with her."

There was a micro-second of silence. Then *Nonna* turned me round to face the room. "You know everyone here—or perhaps you were too young then to remember."

"*Zia* Romola," I said, "and *Zio* Leo. And—"

"*Zia* Irena," said *Nonna*. "Leo's wife."

I had one shattering thought: I have never seen anyone so beautiful. And then Irena Malimbrosa smiled at me and gave me her hand. She murmured words of greeting, but my glance had already moved from her beauty to a stranger standing by the mantelshelf.

Our eyes met across the distance. I had an impression of light irises, deep amber in color. I had seen such yellow brilliance only once before—in a tiger's eyes at the zoo.

Nonna Allegra said formally, "You must meet your countryman. Mr. Cornel . . . Philip Cornel. He is Rome correspondent for an English newspaper. Philip, this is Juliet Holdroyd. She was a friend of Vanessa's."

"*Was?*" Nobody chose to notice my single, battering word.

Philip Cornel asked politely if I knew Rome. I looked up at the dark, impatient face with the high-bridged nose.

"No," I said. "I'm almost a stranger. Do *you* know where Vanessa is?"

Someone in the room gasped. I turned quickly. Allegra said quietly, "You ask a question none of us can answer. Where is Vanessa? She has disappeared. We do not know where."

"You just do not know?" I heard myself giving every word the impact of a gunshot; my voice too loud, too harsh. The room was very still.

They were no longer people from a wonderful childhood world. They were Vanessa's family, ordinary people speaking with almost inhumanly cool control about a young girl's disappearance.

Allegra's hooded eyes watched me. "You have come to Rome to stay with her?"

"Yes. She wrote and invited me. She told me she had taken a shop and was living in the apartment above it."

Allegra pointed to a chair. "Sit down. Sit down." She turned. "Leo, fetch Juliet a drink. You do drink?"

I chose a negroni, quietly hoping that they would not make it too strong, for I needed my wits about me.

There were three people in that room whom I wanted to watch. *Nonna* Allegra, because her manner was impressive and suggestive of the infallible; Irena because of her flawless beauty, and Philip Cornel because he was the one stranger in the Roman household—and because, as if I had a built-in warning system, I felt he had a curiosity about me that I was certain, had I known its reason, would not be flattering.

The rest in turn chose their drinks and everyone seemed to be talking at once, asking me questions about myself, my flight, filling every second with their voices as if afraid of silence. The only person who never spoke was Leo's wife, Irena.

Once she caught my glance and we smiled faintly. Then, as I turned away I found myself looking directly into Philip Cornel's eyes. For one startling moment the room seemed empty except for the two of us. A question I had never before asked myself of anyone I had met for the first time flashed through my mind: What is his private world?

I was so shaken by my reaction to him that I missed a question *Nonna* Allegra was asking. "I'm sorry . . ."

"I asked if you had a comfortable journey."

"Thank you, yes."

Leo was saying that he hoped dinner had been arranged earlier because he had to catch the plane to Milan. "I must get there before the strikers' meeting tomorrow. Raphael will never be able to cope with the union leaders."

Nonna Allegra assured him that dinner would be half an hour earlier than usual. "You do not need to panic. Bruno will be waiting with the car, the plane will be there for you."

I had turned to look at an oversized portrait of a little boy that hung on the far wall. He had wide-spaced dark eyes and a down-drawn mouth and he seemed pathetically out of place in that great frame that should have rimmed a cardinal.

Nonna Allegra must have been watching me, for she said, "That is Pepi, the son of my daughter Teresa who died. You never met her, did you? I believe she was in Geneva when you were here before."

I said, "And is Pepi living here at the *palazzo?*"

"For most of the year, yes. But when he is away from school, he spends his time up at the villa at Grottochiara."

Because the portrait was blown up, over life-size, the un-childlike look in the eyes made an overwhelming impact. He was looking out at the Malimbrosas and his inheritance with the lost expression of someone finding everything too big for him.

"The fresh hill air is good for him," *Zia* Romola said. "He has been ill and we had to keep him away from school. But you can meet him, Juliet. Gisela brought him to Rome today to go to the dentist's. He is upstairs now. This evening he will be driven back to the Villa Sapphira."

I said with delight, "Gisela! Oh, I'd love to see her again."

Leo handed me my drink. It glowed deep geranium pink, flecked with ice. There was the second silence of the evening. I seized its opportunity.

"About Vanessa—" I began.

Romola dropped the little crystal goblet she was holding. *Nonna* Allegra scolded her as if she had been a recalcitrant child. A bell was rung and a woman servant came and cleared up the tiny, shattered pieces.

I looked across the room. Philip Cornel was standing by the fireplace looking at Irena. It was quite obvious that she knew he was watching her, but she ignored him. I turned from his alert, intelligent face to look at her. She had the features seen in classic sculpture—heavy lids, wide mouth, broad forehead. It had a brooding beauty that had a racial sadness in it, like the face of Nefertiti looking toward her golden Egypt.

While the smashed crystal was being cleared away, the conversation was impersonal. I was free to look, to study.

The three Malimbrosa women were all well dressed, but only Irena was really elegant. I had heard that the wealthy Italian women were alone among European nations in devoting their whole time to fashion and beauty. Certainly in her dusky crimson dress, with heavy sapphire earrings and a great ring as her only jewelry, Irena achieved a faultless glamour.

"Do you still live in the house in—Surrey, was it?"

I looked directly at *Nonna* Allegra and shook my head. "No. The lease ran out after my mother died and I moved to an apartment near Westminster. I work for a Member of Parliament."

"How long are you staying in Rome?"

"Until I can find Vanessa."

Every time I mentioned her name, there was the same imperceptible pause as if I had dropped a social brick.

Leo stood near one of the tall windows. His voice was cold and curiously disinterested. "We have told you, we can't help you. We have no idea where she is."

"But you must do something to find her."

"She has disappeared." It was like going round the mulberry bush, repetition getting nowhere.

I protested vehemently, "Vanessa wouldn't go away without telling you—or—or someone."

Nonna Allegra bent her head, obscuring her proud, cold face. "On the contrary, that seems just what she has done."

"She would have told me. *Told me*. She knew I was arriving in Rome today. I went to the address she gave and no one knew her there. Why? What happened since her last letter to me?"

Romola said faintly, "You are talking about the address of the shop she had . . ."

"That's right. Number Nine Via Prassodi. The young couple who now run it insisted that they did not know Vanessa. But their manner was odd, as if they knew something."

Nonna said quietly, "I think I can explain that. Her disappearance was made very public. We had our own detectives looking for her as well as the police. News travels fast in

Rome. Vanessa is missing and you arrive at their shop and ask for her. They could have been afraid that they would be drawn into some scandal."

"What scandal?"

Nonna Allegra drew her brows together. "Of course, there is none. But outsiders do not know that. They are always conjecturing about the wicked lives of the rich. And we do not want a scandal." Her English was careful; she spoke without contractions, as the Victorians did. "Do not" . . . "Will not" . . .

I said, "There was someone—an old man—who had the shop before these people who now own it. Who was he? Did he take the shop over from Vanessa?"

"I have no idea. She broke with us and went her own way."

"You mean, *Nonna* Allegra, you really mean that you never bothered to find out what she intended to do when . . . when she left here?"

"I mean exactly that." Her eyes flashed with momentary anger at the impertinence of my questioning her. I didn't care. I had no intention of letting people I would never see again embarrass me.

Glasses were raised, eyes were averted. *I* was embarrassing *them* . . . I looked across the room. Something in Philip Cornel's eyes, some pinpoint of thought coming through made me think to myself, You are my enemy, too . . .

I asked him, "You knew Vanessa, of course."

"Yes."

"And you can find out nothing?"

He met my challenge coolly. "I am not a detective, Miss Holdroyd."

"But newspaper men have . . ."

"Have a sixth sense for news?"

I was determined not to let him outstare me. "For one thing, yes. And you must know a lot of Rome reporters."

"What did you expect of me?" he demanded in his quick, cool voice. "That I bribe them to drop the work their editors hand out to them, to look for one girl who, for all we know, may have chosen to disappear?"

"Do you believe that?"

"What I believe is of no importance."

(I was certain that he added silently, "To you, Miss Holdroyd.")

We were like two people holding the stage. Again, I was oblivious of the family. My sensations were strongly and frighteningly personal. Between this man, Philip Cornel, and myself was an immediate contact that set off an alarm bell in the place inside me where emotion began. And the emotion was fear.

I turned deliberately toward *Nonna* Allegra. "I am going to find Vanessa." My words came clearly, like a speaker trying to carry a voice to the back of some hall.

Allegra moved slightly. The small blue diamond clusters in her ears flashed. Against their brilliance her face seemed very composed and very old. "If we cannot find her, how can you —a stranger to Rome?"

"I can at least try."

"We have tried, *cara*. But you cannot fight what will not be fought. There comes a time when one has to capitulate."

"I won't." It sounded reckless and childish and I knew it. "At least," I amended, and the rebellion went out of my voice, "I can try. Perhaps someone in the artists' quarter knows where she is. I shall begin there." I put down my glass and stood up. "Thank you for . . ." For what? For the drink? For the news that Vanessa might be dead? For the subtle closing of their ranks against me?

Nonna Allegra came toward me and touched my hand. "I'm sorry if we have shocked you, *cara*. But you had to know all that we know."

All? I asked myself. *All* that you know?

She asked, "What will you do now?"

"I have a friend in Rome who works at the embassy. He will find me a hotel. He *is* a friend of Vanessa's, too."

The fact that I had stressed the word *is* was obviously not lost on them. But no one said anything.

"Juliet." *Nonna's* voice had all the power and ring of a young woman's. I turned and waited. "You must not be allowed to leave us like this. You have come to Rome and you must stay with us for your holiday."

Perhaps it was her tone, making it a command more than a kindly invitation, that roused resistance in me. Or it could have been that they thought I had called with the intention of staying. I murmured that Martin would probably have found me a hotel.

"The young man from the embassy? Then he must cancel any arrangements he has made. You have his telephone number?"

"Yes."

"Then, Juliet, call him. After that Romola will show you to your room. Romola, you will first of all take Juliet to the telephone."

Philip Cornel opened the door for us. I avoided his eyes. I walked into the hall, my heels clicking on the marble floor, and into a little room behind a magnificent five-paneled screen at the far end of the hall. I dipped into my bag for the slip of paper Martin had given me, and after a moment's ringing his amused voice answered me at the same time that Romola's silk taffeta underskirt rustled away.

"Don't tell me, let me guess," Martin said. "I'm being sent for to pick up the pieces."

"Wrong. I've been invited to stay at the *palazzo*. But Vanessa isn't here and they don't know—" I stopped as I heard a faint sound like a footstep behind me. "I'll tell you more when I see you."

"Why not now? I'm not good at waiting—or at puzzles."

I craned round the screen and could see no one. "I've accepted the invitation to stay. It could be that they think I know something about Vanessa's disappearance, and they want to find out. By the same token, that's why *I'm* staying *here*. They may not have told me everything yet."

He said, "If you think I'm letting you give all your time to that family, you're wrong. We made a date for tonight."

"We didn't."

"Then we're making one now. You can have your luxury dinner with the Malimbrosas. Then I'm coming round and I'm taking you for a drive."

"I can't possibly—"

"You can. And there's no argument. Tonight at half past nine—"

"Martin," I cried as I heard the finality in his voice. "Martin, don't hang up. Listen. You've got my suitcases in the car. I need them."

"I'll bring them round and drop them at the door. And I mean drop them—I'm not going to be ushered in and risk a line of introductions to your lofty friends."

"Don't be so—"

The line had gone dead.

Zia Romola must have been hovering somewhere nearby waiting, for as I came round the screen I saw her standing there. I had lowered my voice when I spoke to Martin, so I doubted if she had heard anything I had said.

"Martin is bringing my luggage round."

"That is good. Come, I will show you to your room."

I followed her across the mauve-pillared hall. The elevator, with its gate of criss-cross gilding stood open, but I remembered how Romola had always ignored it. She was one of those women who seemed to feel that usage of physical energy magically recharged the batteries of her body.

So, I climbed by her side up the sweeping stairs that rose, curve upon curve, to the multi-colored dome. The first-floor rooms opened out of a semicircular gallery where four caryatids in the same pale violet marble looked down at the rotunda. I remembered that the main private apartments were off this gallery and I had a sudden memory of Vanessa and myself playing "dodge the cracks" along the marble floor.

Romola said, "You shall have the suite you used to have. Or would you prefer Vanessa's?"

"No." The denial came too swiftly. An involuntary shudder went through me as if I had been asked to spend the night in a ghost-ridden room. Then, without knowing why, I changed my mind. "Yes. Yes, please. I would like Vanessa's old suite."

We had crossed the wide gallery and Romola paused with her fingers twisting the knobs of the double doors. She gave me a long, intense look.

"You must accept, you know, that Vanessa will never come back."

"I can't."

She was giving furtive little glances to the right and left as if expecting someone with a gun to leap out at her. I reached across her and gave the doors a little push.

"We can talk inside," I said.

The family always said that Romola was too vociferous. Vanessa had once told me that *Nonna* Allegra had said that she had the instincts of a peasant whose chief joy was chattering in the market-place about the price of oranges and the virtues of pasta.

I followed her into the room. It seemed that I walked into haze of blue-hyacinth curtains; a carpet like a cut-out from the Mediterranean—deep, clear blue. A single portrait hung on the wall. It was smaller than the one of Pepi down in the *salone*, more sophisticated. The young, painted face looking down at me was neither lost nor pathetic. It was Vanessa. She wore a deep green dress and her hair was dressed simply with an Alice-band of pearls holding it back from her broad forehead. The artist had captured Vanessa's vivid quality; the wayward half-smile, as if she had some exciting secret she would tell no one about. Her only jewels were small pearl drops in her delicately pointed ears.

Romola was saying, "You remember the view?"

I joined her at one of the tall windows. There was a stone balcony outside and the view beyond reached across the Pincian Gate to the Borghese Gardens. The umbrella pines were drowned in late sunlight and a little girl, looking from this distance like a piece of scarlet confetti, was chasing a balloon.

I turned my head and saw Malimbrosa's great roof garden. Nothing had changed. There seemed to be a kind of timelessness about the whole place. There were the oleander bushes spread against the walls, and the urns of flowers. There was the fountain into which I had loved to dangle my hands, feeling the titillation of the dancing spray; the wall where the morning glory climbed.

Romola said softly, "About Vanessa . . . Leo thinks there could be a man—"

Martin had hinted at the same thing—a love affair so sudden, so violent, that Vanessa had set aside everything for its indulgence.

I asked, "And what do the police think?"

"They have done all they can. And, as Mamma told you, we have had our own detectives working to find her." She spread her hands. "The result is . . . nothing."

I turned to her so swiftly that she backed sharply from me. "Hasn't it occurred to anyone that she could have lost her memory; be in trouble of some sort; in need of help?"

"Do you think we haven't thought of everything? We have done all that is possible." She put out her hand to me in an odd, beseeching gesture, then before she actually touched me, she dropped her arm to her side. "You are here with us and that gives me such great comfort. I am sure it pleases Mamma, too, or she would not have asked you to stay. Enjoy your holiday, Julie."

"How can I?" I demanded. "Vanessa could be in some hospital far away from Rome, her memory gone. There *is* such a thing as amnesia, you know. It isn't just fiction."

Romola shook her head. "It's an easy explanation which I am afraid is all too rare in life."

"Then you think—?"

"Never mind." A closed look came over her face.

I said impatiently, "Don't hold out on me, please don't. Vanessa invited me to Rome; she gave me her address. She wanted to see me—" I watched Romola. Her face expressed a strange mixture of eagerness and dismay. "I am involved," I insisted. "You must tell me what you think."

We faced one another in the mist-blue room and my blood ran suddenly cold at the dark fear in Romola's eyes.

"Well?" I breathed at her.

"I believe that . . . Vanessa . . . is dead."

My cry of protest sounded loud in my brain, but it could only have been a whisper for my lips scarcely moved. "Oh, no. No!"

"You asked for my opinion, *cara*. In fact, it is more than an opinion because I do not believe Vanessa could possibly have vanished as she has without some clue to her whereabouts. But please, while you stay here, don't keep talking about her to Mamma."

"Why not? She can't have felt much love for her or she wouldn't have turned her out of her home. So, talking about Vanessa can't upset *Nonna*."

"Oh, but it does. The family—"

"She's afraid of some scandal. Is that it?"

Romola turned her face away. "The affair is closed."

"Not to me, it isn't."

"Juliet, please . . ."

I said furiously, "She could have been driving somewhere a long way away from Rome and been involved in an accident and be lying injured in some lonely place in the mountains. She loved swimming—perhaps she—" I put my hands to my face. I could not say *Perhaps she is drowned*. I kept thinking, "She can't be . . . she can't be . . . The sea gives up its dead and she would have been found by now . . ."

Romola said, "And do you see, Juliet, that until we know for certain that she is dead, we cannot even mourn. There must be evidence of death."

I said, "Oh, God!"

Romola turned away and picked up a celadon bowl. "I'll have flowers put in this for you. What would you like? Roses?"

I had a bitter desire to demand chrysanthemums—the flowers which in Italy festoon funerals. I pulled myself together. It was useless to let the flat acceptance that Vanessa was dead upset me; rage and hysteria helped no one.

Everything had its level. Besides, every shock has its moment of release when rock bottom is reached and there is only horror and acceptance. The Malimbrosas had gone through that period; I had only just reached it.

Suddenly, a thought occurred to me. "You say you tried desperately to find Vanessa. You knew she and I were close friends, yet you never wrote to ask if she had come over to London, to me."

"But Mamma did write. You didn't answer. I remember Leo saying, 'Shall I go over to England and find out if Juliet knows where Vanessa is?' And Mamma said 'No.' You see, by that time we had found Vanessa's passport."

"If *Nonna* Allegra wrote to me, then I didn't receive the letter."

"It was sent to an address at Woking."

"I had moved into London. But letters were always forwarded. There was no reason why this particular one should have gone astray."

"But it must have."

"An odd coincidence." I couldn't stop the irony that had crept into my voice. Had a letter ever been sent to me?

"That shop in the Via Prassodi . . ."

"We knew about it from other people. But Mamma would not allow any of us to visit her there. Whatever it was Vanessa did—and Mamma never told us—she never forgave." (Just as she never forgave my mother.)

"But you kept watch on her from a distance," I said. "*Nonna* couldn't quite let go. She must have, or how would she know she had disappeared?"

"It wasn't like that at all. It was because we knew she went out to dinner with . . . with someone one night—and no one saw her again."

"Someone who spied on her for *Nonna* Allegra," I said scathingly, "because although she was banned from her home, she was a Malimbrosa."

"No. This . . . this man used to see her, take her out . . ."

"Who is he?"

"You have met him."

I said, "Philip Cornel?" and waited.

Zia Romola stood, still holding the celadon bowl. "You may as well know that part of the story. Philip has been a frequent visitor here for some time. *Nonna* Allegra likes him and"—she added darkly, as if she enjoyed the drama of her inference— "so does Irena."

"And—Vanessa?"

Her mouth tightened. "He used to take her out on occasions. At one time—oh well, never mind that now."

"*I* mind," I said. "At one time—what? Please, *Zia* Romola, what?"

"We thought that there was something more than just friendship between them."

"And on the night she disappeared?"

"They had dinner together. Vanessa was going to stay up in the hills with an artist friend and his wife for the weekend . . . they had some terrible little shack up there. She wanted some of his work to show in her shop. She drove to meet Philip at a place midway between the hill village and Rome. After dinner, Philip drove her back to where she had parked her car. He saw her drive away, and the next day nobody knew where she was or where she had gone. The shop was not opened and there was no clue. It was . . . it was I who found that she had disappeared. You see, I cared for Vanessa and I worried about her. So, without Mamma knowing, I met her once or twice. I knew about this shop but Mamma had no idea that I did—she thinks that I am so ignorant of everything that goes on." She gave me a strange, narrow look. "I even knew that Vanessa had taken the shop under an assumed name."

"What name?"

"Maria Cyrena. I walked past it twice, wanting to go in and see her. Then, when I went a third time feeling more brave about it—don't look at me like that, Juliet, defying Mamma is not an easy thing to do." She drew a deep breath. "But I had to see Vanessa—I missed her so. And I found the shop closed and shuttered. I asked all round, in the other shops, everywhere, if anyone knew if she were ill. No one had seen her for days. I had to tell Mamma then. I said I had been in the district to try and find an old man I had heard of who was brilliant at restoring old picture frames—one of ours was breaking apart through age. I said I had heard that Vanessa had this shop but that no one had seen her for days. Mamma sent Leo round and he broke into the apartment and found that she was gone and there was no clue as to where."

"And Philip Cornel watched her drive away into nothing," I said. "Just like that! Which way? Did he say? Toward the artist's place or toward Rome? There must be only two ways in the hills—up or down."

"He says she turned the car toward Nemi."

"Into the Alban hills. And then, what? Did she drive round in a circle until he was safely out of the way, and then return to her own apartment in the Via Prassodi?"

"How do I know? How does anyone know? The apartment had a film of dust over it when we got there." She cried in exasperation. "Juliet, you are behaving like a counsel for the prosecution."

"I'd like to know how closely Philip Cornel was questioned. Or were they afraid to ask him too much? Did they fear an international situation—a girl from a famous Roman family and a foreign correspondent? Oh no, I can't believe—" I stopped abruptly. I was being unfair to *Zia* Romola. She looked unhappy and quite guiltless. "I'm sorry," I said, "but there's something very odd about this apparent disappearance. For one thing, where is her car?"

"It was found abandoned, three miles from Nemi."

I thought: There's a lake there, deep and dark . . . the volcanic sides are thick with woodlands . . . the lake shores are lonely. The Emperor Caligula had enjoyed festivals there; in the second century sacrifices were made at the lake to the goddess Diana. And Vanessa—my golden Vanessa—had she been sacrificed? For what? For love? For hate? . . .

Romola asked sharply, "Why are you looking at me like that?"

"I'm letting my . . . my imagination . . . run away with me." I brushed my hand over my face in an involuntary effort to clear mind and vision. I went on, "There could be a man—men *did* love Vanessa—" I thought: And she has fled from Rome and all the gossip and the scandal there would be if the family decided that he was unsuitable. For, banished from Malimbrosa though she might be, Vanessa would never be allowed to forget her name and her heritage. And she knew it. That was why she took the shop in the Via Prassodi under the name Maria Cyrena, and the young Cotones only knew her real identity when the story broke. *Zia* Romola said, "I have thought that there is probably a man involved. Perhaps she could not stand the thing that was happening . . ."

I jerked my eyes up to meet hers. She was hinting at something I had not thought of. "What do you mean? What couldn't she stand?"

Zia Romola withdrew from me almost visibly, hunching her shoulders, folding herself in. "The thing she found out, just as I"—she gave a great shudder—"I cannot tell you. I dare not. But *cara*, we have tragedy here. I only pray that you will not find out what haunts the family, because if you do . . ."

"If I do, what?" My voice was impatient. Hints always irritated me.

She shook her head. I saw that her fingers were working, clawing furtively at the sides of her scaly silver dress. "Just enjoy your holiday and don't ask questions."

"You're afraid of someone. Who?" I waited. Then I said, "Is it this man, Cornel?"

"I'm a silly woman and I'm full of fancies." She gave me a wide, meaningless smile. "Ah," she turned quickly. "Here is Alberto with your luggage. I will leave you to unpack. There is no hurry. We do not dine until eight o'clock." She hesitated then came close to me, whispering, "We have so much tragedy here, *cara*. Be careful, be very careful."

"Of what?"

"Tensions beneath the surface, Juliet. You do not know; you cannot possibly understand. You come here, fresh from the outside world . . ."

Her last words hovered on the air as she edged round Alberto, who had brought in my luggage. I had always been wary of melodramatic talk; it belonged to people who hungered for the excitement they couldn't find in their own lives. Now, for the first time, I didn't feel irritated by it. I sensed that it was as real as living and breathing. Romola wasn't being ghoulish for my entertainment.

She edged round Alberto and out of the room. I heard her heels on the marble of the staircase.

I unlocked my suitcases, opened one, and stood staring down at it. Outside I heard the thin, clear voice of a little boy. Then the soft clang of the elevator gates. I was quite certain that somewhere in my strange, tormented conversation with *Zia* Romola, she was trying to convey that Philip Cornel was the one most closely involved in Vanessa's disappearance. And from that came another thought. Did *Nonna* Allegra suspect the same thing, and was she keeping a watch on him, waiting for him to be betrayed into saying something that would give her a lead? She was a shrewd woman. But I doubted if Cornel would be caught that way.

An excitement ran through me. There was a faint chance that I might succeed where *Nonna* Allegra had failed. My first target in my search for Vanessa was Philip Cornel. As the old tag went, all was fair in love and war . . . and I could eliminate the first and concentrate on the second where he was concerned.

I began to unpack, choosing for the evening a dress the color of the sea. I left my heavy hair loose about my shoulders and wore, for jewelry, only a thin chain of small aquamarines. The first time Martin had seen me in the dress he had said, "You look like a water nymph." I hoped I would look equal to the splendor of Malimbrosa and not like a poor guest dragged in from the cold.

5 ❧

DUSK WAS FALLING OVER the umbrella pines in the Borghese Gardens and the swifts were diving with their little dark wings stiffly splayed as I took a last look from the balcony window before going down to face the family. Outside my room the long, curving gallery was deserted. I went slowly down the stairs and when I reached the hall I could hear the murmur of voices from the drawing room.

The door was ajar and I recognized Allegra's voice. I stood quite still, half concealed; an eavesdropper neither because I was shy, nor because I was inquisitive. I stopped short at the double doors because there was a question I wanted to ask myself before I joined the family again. Why had I been invited to stay here after so long a feud? Because *Nonna* Allegra had decided to bury the past? Out of courtesy, because I was alone in Rome?

Capitulation was not natural to *Nonna* Allegra, nor were such old Roman families given to casual hospitality. So, why the invitation?

". . . and so sentiment must not be allowed to enter into this." *Nonna* Allegra was sitting upright in her chair.

Leo said unhappily, "I don't know how I'm going to tell Filippo. He's a lifelong friend—"

"He can remain such if you wish. But he will no longer handle our advertising account. The last layout for soft plastics was almost amateurish. We have a standard of advertising to keep in the trade journals and Filippo Scribini no longer reaches that standard."

"His new fabric promotion was superb. Even you said—"

"One lion does not make a pride," she said.

"But Mamma—"

I stood listening and pleased that I could understand their language. I felt that I was watching a glamour film, and one so unusual in my country of impoverished castles and vanished magnificence that I needed to orientate myself before I could join them. It was not shyness, nor sensitiveness. Unease, perhaps . . . Ruth among the alien corn . . .

I looked for Philip Cornel and saw him again watching Irena. Standing concealed, I asked a silent question of him. What happened between you and Vanessa on that night she disappeared? What did you say to one another? I felt a sense of failure even before I could reach the kind of relationship with him where I could reasonably ask such questions. Cornel was obviously not a man to explain anything unless he chose. And he had the look of one who asks the questions, not answers them.

On the settee, like an elf on a green bank, sat a little boy. His legs dangled, the toes in his brown sandals turned in.

Pepi, of course. He was trying to stifle yawns, his eyes heavy, his black hair too neat, his face very clean. A little boy washed and brushed up for the formality of the grown-up's drawing room.

I remembered that Vanessa had told me of the quarrel between *Nonna* Allegra and Pepi's father, Count Fabrio Cassare Undino, when, six months after his mother, Teresa, had died, he had married again. The little boy, only three years old at the time, had been argued over as if he were a business involved in a takeover bid.

In the end, the Malimbrosas won. Vanessa had told me: "For

a huge, undisclosed sum, Pepi has been bought from Fabrio and has been given his mother's name."

My mind boggled at the thought of two young people existing as sole heirs to a great fortune. Vanessa and Pepi. Two? Or now only one?

I was so fascinated that I forgot I was an eavesdropper—in fact I was not, for I had stopped listening to the conversation in the *salone*.

How must *Nonna* feel, having produced four sons, two of whom were still alive and unable to give an heir to Malimbrosa? Teresa was dead and Romola, the surviving daughter, too old now ever to have a child.

This family had so much in life—wealth, success, lineage— but it lacked the ability to feed children into the jaws of the Malimbrosa Industries.

Roberto and Piero, Vanessa's father, were dead. The third son, Raphael, married and childless, ran the plastics business in Milan; and Leo, who lived at the *palazzo*, controlled the vast chemical factories on the road to Ostia, just outside Rome. Two remaining sons. And at their christening the witch had flung her curse. Sterility. And not the greatest doctors in the world had been able to help them.

So now there was only that bored, tired little boy leaning back on the great sofa, counting his fingers. And Vanessa.

I must have moved a little toward the opening in the door, for quite suddenly Philip Cornel looked straight at me. My secret scrutiny was over; I could no longer watch them as I would watch a stage play. I walked into the room.

"Ah, Juliet." *Nonna* Allegra smiled at me. "That is better. You look refreshed." She spoke in English and then said to the little boy, "Pepi, come here."

He obeyed reluctantly. Allegra extended her hand. "Juliet, this is Pepi, *Zia* Teresa's little boy. He should have gone back to the villa some time ago, but he wanted to meet you and I am afraid we indulge him."

I took the too-thin hand and said, "Hullo, Pepi. It was nice of you to want to stay and meet me."

He answered me in surprisingly good English, but with a slight stammer. "H-how do you do?" And then quickly, "Do you kn-know where Vanessa is?"

"I'm afraid not. But perhaps I'll be able to find her. I'm going to try, anyway."

"And now," *Nonna* cut in, "Pepi must go. It is a long drive back to Grottochiara and Bruno is waiting. Romola, take him to Gisela."

"I don't want—" His eyes flashed; his small fists tightened. I wondered whom he wanted to hit.

"What you want, *carissimo,* has nothing whatever to do with it." *Nonna* said calmly, "You are too young to stay up late. Sleep is necessary in order that you will grow strong."

"I don't care. I want to stay—"

Zia Romola tried to take his hand and he fought her. His small face was screwed up tightly, not with tears but with resentment and real anger. "I hate the villa . . . I want to stay here . . . I want Vanessa—"

But Romola's bony fingers were too much for him. I heard him still protesting as the door closed behind them.

Nonna sat imperturbably. "When Pepi is not at school, we always send him into the hills. I fear he is a little lonely up there but perhaps that will strengthen his character. In August he will come with us on the yacht. He will enjoy that. This year we go to Crete and Rhodes."

And what, I wondered, would there be to interest a small boy to whom the loveliness of the Aegean scenery would mean nothing? I wanted to ask if he were allowed to take some young companions with him.

Before I could speak, Leo said, "He has a number of friends in Rome. Not many, but they are all suitable."

They would have to be, I thought, watching the proud, angular Malimbrosa faces.

"And Juliet," *Nonna* smiled at me, "if during your stay you would like to go up to the Villa Sapphira, by all means do so. You are very pale. The air will do you good."

The conversation flowed round me and I was drawn into it

politely and charmingly. For the most part, however, I was content to watch and listen. And as I did, two things became very clear. One was their acceptance that Vanessa was gone from their lives. *We have mourned. Now we get on with living.* The second was Romola's acidity toward Irena. Hate seemed too strong a word; dislike too mild.

There was a possible reason for her behavior. Irena was beautiful and she was a nobody. On one of her visits to London, Vanessa had told me about the marriage between Irena and Leo, which had been a big social event.

"Leo was one of the very eligible bachelors of Rome," she had said, "and he liked it that way. He's an odd, rather withdrawn man and marriage was the last thing he wanted. But *Nonna* insisted. So Leo made a bargain: 'Very well, then, I shall marry the most beautiful woman I can find—entirely without loving her, without wanting her.'" Vanessa told me he had found Irena sitting at a typing desk in the Ostia office. Her parentage was unknown—she was one of the lost children of the last war and had been brought up by a porter and his wife who had found her, a child of four, lying in a roadway.

Romola, who had everything except marriage, must envy this lovely woman who had come, as she might put it, from the gutter. Or was I perhaps being unjust toward *Zia* Romola?

At dinner we ate Tyrrhenian shrimps and fowl cooked in cream; there were little wild strawberries from the hill fields and a dry white wine. All the time I was wondering how I could find an opportunity to speak to Philip Cornel alone.

The chance came after we had had coffee on the roof garden. *Nonna* Allegra had gone to speak a last word with Leo before he left for Milan; Romola was fretting about some dead goldfish in the pool. I wandered from her side, pretending to examine a cluster of roses, a vine, the oleanders and the dancing fountain. So, deviously, I reached Philip Cornel's side.

He turned as I joined him. "It's quite a view, isn't it?"

"If the ghosts of old Romans could rise from the Aurelian Wall, I wonder what they'd think of their city?"

"That's a question that will never be answered. There are no ghosts, except those we manufacture ourselves," he said.

"Have you any such ghosts?"

"Of course, haven't you?"

"I hadn't thought about it." I felt uneasy in his presence, on guard and out of my depth. I asked, "What are *your* ghosts?"

"Oh, no, Miss Holdroyd, we have only just met. We shouldn't tell our secrets to one another."

He was right about that. I changed the subject, trying to hold him by appearing interested in his work. "You're a foreign correspondent. I suppose you've traveled a lot?"

"India and Istanbul and now Rome."

"So you have no real home."

"No."

"Do you like your nomadic life?"

He laughed. "Oh, come, it's not as bad as that. I don't wear a burnous and ride on a camel. I may be here for two years or more. I can grow a few roots. And isn't that all any of us can settle for? The only thing we have always with us is ourselves. The rest comes and goes."

"You're being very profound."

He looked away over the starlit city. "On a night like this, who wouldn't?" He moved almost imperceptibly from me. I didn't want him to go before I had found out more about his friendship with Vanessa. Friendship?

Before I could speak, he asked, "What do you plan to do? Stay in Rome?"

It was a natural question, yet suspicion whipped up inside me. Why did he want to know? I said, "I'm not sure." I traced the line of a curlicue of stone running like a Greek motif across the balustrade. "You were—friendly with Vanessa. Didn't she tell you that I was coming to stay with her?"

"No."

I said incredulously, "You knew her well, yet she didn't say anything about me?"

He countered, "How well did *you* know her?"

It was like flinging down the glove at an adversary. I turned my head from the brilliance of his strange eyes that had caught the lamplight. "You saw her on that last evening. You were there when she got into her car and vanished."

"That's right, I was there."

"And what happened?"

"She was going to spend the weekend with some friends at Genzano, so we met at Frascati for dinner. We parted at about ten o'clock and Vanessa drove away up into the hills."

"These friends—?"

"Oh, they thought when she didn't turn up, that she had changed her mind about coming. When expected guests do things like that, you leave them. You don't run after them."

"So, she just drove into the night. But people don't disappear from choice—not, I mean, people like Vanessa. She had a passion for living."

"That presupposes she is dead. Who says she is?" His voice was—was what? Defiant? On guard? I couldn't make out. I only knew that antipathy stretched like barbed wire between us.

He asked, "Do *you* know where she is?"

I had turned away and was looking down onto the string of lights along the Via Pinciana. I pivoted round so quickly at his question that I nearly lost my balance. I clung to the balustrade. "*You* . . . ask *me* . . . ?"

"I do. Where is Vanessa?"

(A principle of battle! When cornered, take the fight into the enemy's camp.)

"She didn't come to London to stay with me, if that's what you're thinking." Then I remembered what Romola had told me. I said, "And since you're a close friend of the family, you must know that her passport is not missing."

"Oh yes—" he said nonchalantly.

The concealed lights among the oleanders lit up his face in profile. For all the quiet contours, I had a feeling that he was a paradox; that behind the façade lurked a mercurial mind; that whatever I did or said, he would be six steps ahead of me.

I was determined to not be disconcerted by his manner. "That night, when you and Vanessa had dinner . . . How did she behave? Was she upset? Excited?"

"Since you profess to know her so well, you shouldn't need to ask that question. Vanessa was always full of gaiety."

"She gave no indication that there was anything the matter; I mean anything on her mind?"

"No."

Yet, if she had intended to disappear for some crazy notion, her behavior would certainly have not been normal that night. I knew Vanessa. She could never subdue her own excitement. If Philip Cornel were speaking the truth, then Vanessa left him after their dinner together and drove into some adventure totally unexpected by her.

"So," I said, "she bid goodnight to you and walked out on her whole life."

"You put it rather dramatically. But yes, I suppose you could say that. She disappeared so far as her family and her friends were concerned."

"Deliberately."

"How should I know?"

That, I thought, as I refused to meet his eyes, was precisely what I was going to find out.

We stood there in a moment's silence, neither making any attempt to leave. I felt that we were both maneuvering for some position of enlightenment. I knew perfectly well why I was acting this way. But why Philip? Had my coming to Rome disturbed him?

I leaned against a stone urn, listening to the blurred noises of Rome and the tiny, flutelike sounds of the waters falling from the Bernini fountain. Then, a sudden picture came to me of other water, of the Tiber, sluggish and saffron colored; of the sea at Ostia . . . People were found drowned in rivers and seas . . .

Philip Cornel broke through my wild imaginings. "Why don't you accept the fact that Vanessa has chosen to disappear?"

"I can't because I don't believe it."

"So—?"

"I've got to do all I can to find her. I intend to question people who lived round the Via Prassodi, shopkeepers—"

"I suggest you leave it to those who know how to deal with such things."

I said angrily, "From what I hear, they're no longer dealing with it. They've shut their files on Vanessa. And if you think—"

He interrupted impatiently, "For sweet saint's sake, girl, don't you know what's already been done is a damned sight more efficient than anything you could do?"

" 'Girl'? All right, let that go," I said with a kind of tight anger. "So far as your second point is concerned, even the cleverest investigators can miss something an amateur might hit on."

He stubbed out the cigarette he had been holding but not smoking. "Sometimes amateurs get caught up in their own cleverness. Be careful, Miss Holdroyd. You've no idea where your amateur sleuthing might lead you."

"Are you warning me?"

"Of course," he said and walked away.

I stood against the still-warm stone, shaking as if a strong magnet had pulled me helplessly a way I didn't want to go. I hadn't come out of that little episode with particular triumph. I had forced myself into a situation before making a plan, and certainly before understanding my adversary. It was ridiculous, of course, to think of Philip Cornel as that, after only a couple of hours' meeting, but the sensation persisted.

I argued with myself that it didn't matter. We need never meet alone again; it would be better if our only contact was when the rest of the family were around. Yet I knew that it did matter. I wanted a relationship with him that was at least superficially friendly. It was only that way, by seeming to trust everyone and letting everyone trust me, that I could collect the most microcosmic detail that might give me a lead to Vanessa. And this became suddenly my main object for being in Rome. There is love in friendship and with love there has to be giving. I had to find Vanessa; to keep my search like some private operation, with Martin to help me—Vanessa's friend, my gay companion in London and the only one I could fully trust. His face swam before me against the background of the richly starred sky. I wished desperately that he were here with me with his cheerfulness, his matter-of-factness, for the problem facing me had suddenly become charged with difficulties, Little daggers of fear seemed to be stabbing me, and I needed my only ally very badly.

I walked away from the corner among the oleanders. Philip was standing by the fountain and *Nonna* Allegra came out from the lighted doorway. She must have seen us together a few minutes earlier, for she said. "I hope Philip was telling you about his life. It has been very full and interesting."

"We were talking about Vanessa."

With the soft floodlighting of the garden around her, Allegra's strong bones stood out, hollowing the cheeks of her gaunt face, stressing the sharp, French features.

Philip said, "Of course, it must be startling to come for a holiday and find no hostess to welcome you." He spoke formally and coldly.

"Juliet is going to spend her holidays with us," *Nonna* Allegra said. "If she happens to come upon anything that can solve our tragic mystery, then we shall bless her for it. But she must realize that everything conceivable has been done. Vanessa is gone. And Juliet must try to accept the fact and be happy here."

I turned my face away, shocked at the hardness and brusqueness of her dismissal of Vanessa. But then, *Nonna* Allegra would not have been the success she was had she been soft. She was old now, but the hardness and the strength would go with her to the end of her life. At seventy-five, Allegra must have suffered many tragedies and learned that survival comes only with a realistic approach; with a letting-go of sorrow.

But I wasn't sorrowing; I was being realistic, too. Romola

had said, "I believe Vanessa is dead." I was an outsider, a newcomer, and I was going to start with the presumption that she was alive.

A short exchange of comments on Roman affairs had been taking place between *Nonna* Allegra and Philip.

I heard him say, "If you will excuse me now, signora, I have a lot of work to do tonight."

She said with amusement, "The lights remind you, as usual. I know." She turned to me and waved her hand toward a building I could see across a belt of trees. "Do you see that narrow terrace with the lighted windows on the top floor, Juliet? That is Philip's apartment."

I said, "It looks all lit up for a party."

"The apartment is empty—at least I hope it is," he said. "I'm the lone tiger. But if I'm out enjoying myself anywhere around this part of Rome, I only have to look up across the roofs and I see those lights. They remind me that I have work to do, that's why I keep them on when I go out."

"It looks like a very large building," I murmured.

"It's really a run-down *palazzo*, which is now converted into huge and echoing apartments. Everything on the outside is cracked and peeling. Everything inside is patched and improvised. It is no Malimbrosa." He smiled at *Nonna* Allegra. "If you stand on top of a high ladder and hold a magnifying glass to the ceiling, you can just see the faded painted cherubs and their rose garlands."

Nonna Allegra said conversationally, "After her holiday with us, Juliet is going back to London to work for a Member of Parliament."

"William Mazarin," I said.

"The loquacious rebel," Philip said. "I once had to interview him for television. As you know, the questions are rehearsed beforehand. If you step out of the prearranged line with your answers, you risk throwing an inexperienced interviewer off balance. Well, your boss never once stayed on the question line."

"But he didn't throw *you* off balance."

"That's where you're wrong. He did. I was completely inexperienced and he knew it."

"And what did you do?" I asked.

"I lost my temper. There was an almighty row afterward."

Nonna laughed softly and began to move away like a queen, exercising her right never to be the one left behind. She called "Goodnight, Philip. You will come again soon."

I had thought he would behave in a very Latin way and kiss her hand. Philip did nothing of the kind. He just said, "Thank you, signora, for an interesting evening," and he and I stood together by the fountain watching her drift, in clouds of black chiffon, toward the doorway.

I moved, too. "We have already said goodnight, haven't we, Mr. Cornel?"

"We have. But, after I left you just now, I remembered an old Spanish proverb."

"Is it relevant?"

"Very. It goes, 'Glory on horseback, disaster sitting behind.' I am misquoting slightly, but that is unimportant." He turned on his heel and followed *Nonna* Allegra into the lighted gallery.

Once more, only the sound of the water dancing from Bernini's stone merman and Cornel's light footsteps broke the silence. I said the words of the proverb to myself and I knew why he had quoted them to me. It was a warning, spoken as a pleasantry.

All right, go ahead and search for Vanessa. And if you find her, God help you . . .

6 ❧

A FEW MINUTES LATER, as I walked down the short, straight drive from the *palazzo* to the gates where the stone leopards stood guard, I could see Martin sitting in his white car at the curbside. The lacework of wrought iron between us gave him a remoteness as if he and his car belonged to another world—as indeed they did. *My* world; my nice, ordered, unemotional world.

The gates opened for me and Martin turned his head, saw me, and climbed out of the car. "So they let you out?"

"What did you think Malimbrosa was? A prison?" I got into the passenger seat and flung a long green chiffon scarf round my shoulders.

"I'll bet that place was, to some people in the old days when they shut up their daughters against predators and married them to millionaires." He started the engine and pulled out into the stream of traffic. "Now, tell me what's been going on. Where is Vanessa?"

"I don't know, nor do they—at least I'm not quite certain what they know. I have a feeling they're keeping something from me."

"Then you'll have to find out what it is, won't you? People don't just disappear."

"But they do. People walk out of their lives and are never heard of again."

"Not someone like Vanessa. Her circle of friends isn't exactly small. By the way, I've got something to show you. One of Vanessa's cards—" I spun around so sharply that I jerked his arm. The car zig-zagged for a moment.

"Hey. There are enough ruins in Rome without you adding to them. You'll have to wait until we're held up, then I'll show it to you."

The traffic lights stopped us at the cross roads down the Via Nationale. Then Martin felt in his pocket and handed a card to me, saying, "The envelope was addressed to me but the note inside just said 'Give this to Julie.' Terse and to the point, no affectionate message for me, the brat! I found it waiting among the bills on my doormat."

I leaned over, trying to see the card by the mixture of dashboard and street lights. It was one of Vanessa's characteristic drawings. With a few swift pencil lines, she had drawn herself seated on an ordinary straight-backed chair facing a three-paneled mirror screen and in each of them I saw the vague outline of her reflection. The screen had vaulted tops and grotesque little figures, like gargoyles, perched on the top of each panel looking down, grinning as if mocking at vanity.

I turned the card over. Her writing was small and rather scrambling:

A lonely, eerie place. While I wait I am writing to a few close friends. Like sending out ribbons to hold them! Whatever you do, don't show this card to Nonna or the police. For my sake. I dare not—

There was no signature. The message broke off as though someone had entered and there was no more time.

Martin asked, "Is it Vanessa's writing?"

I remained bent over the note like a fortune-teller over a crystal ball. "I think so. It must be, mustn't it? It's a bit more untidy than her usual cards, but then she was obviously in a hurry and frightened. 'While I wait.' "

For whom? Philip Cornel?

I waved the drawing at Martin. "Do you recognize this place?"

"I haven't the least idea where it is. It's not particularly explicit, is it? I suppose it's a screen in someone's private house. But whose, and where, is your guess as much as mine. It's something we've got to puzzle out somehow—and you know, Julie, I'm not very good at puzzles."

"What happened to the envelope the card came in and the note addressed to you?"

"I threw them away. The envelope was a very ordinary one, cheapish, bought by the packet."

I looked at the card again. "I'm quite certain she was frightened when she wrote this."

"It struck me the same way."

"Martin, what can have happened to her?"

He said very steadily, "I think, whether it's bad or good, we've got to find out. Vanessa's impulsive; it could be that she's gone away with someone the family wouldn't approve of and she's scared."

"Do you really think that?"

He said unhappily, "No, I don't. God knows what she's got herself into!"

"And I suppose she sent the card to your apartment because she had no idea where I'd be staying. And she'd know I'd be worried and find some hotel to stay at while I made inquiries."

Martin turned his head momentarily and looked at me. "She also guessed I'd keep track of where you were. Having met you, she must have known I wouldn't let go of you that easily."

I let the implied compliment pass and stared out of the window at the Colosseum. I would have liked to have stopped there, climbed to one of the terraces to sit among the old stones, the ghosts of martyrs and the lean cats. I would have liked to remain there quietly with Martin and try to work out what had happened to Vanessa.

But we were past the huge, floodlit oval before I had a chance to suggest it.

"She asks us not to go to the police." I said. "That suggests kidnapping and a ransom, doesn't it?"

"Yet why hold her prisoner for so long before demanding the money?"

It was a point. I stared ahead at the patternless weaving of the people in and out of the shops below the towering mass of new apartment blocks. "Martin, what are we going to do?"

He said, "Heaven help us, I don't know. I just don't know . . ."

"Those last words of hers on the card. 'I dare not.' Dare not what? Tell us more? Do you think that's what she meant?"

"Why ask me? I'm as much in the dark as you are."

"I think she felt she had more time in which to write than she really had. The first sentences aren't terribly important. Perhaps if she'd known she had so little time, she wouldn't have written them, but would have kept to the more significant facts. And Martin—"

"What?"

"She was probably disturbed and so she hid the card until she could smuggle it out somehow. So there's someone around her who is on her side."

"It looks like it." He took a hand off the wheel and laid it over mine. "If we aren't careful we'll go round in circles. We're just guessing and that'll get us nowhere. We have to be practical and find Vanessa." He glanced momentarily at my fingers. "And if you go on mangling that card," he said, "you'll be destroying any evidence it might afford."

"Evidence?" I jumped like a startled cat.

"Well, you never know—"

I smoothed out the corner of the card and realized for the first time that when I was agitated, I folded and refolded edges of paper like the old Chinese playing with their patience beads of jade or ivory. Vanessa had a far more quirky characteristic when she was agitated or nervous. She would run her fingers through her hair, making the long strands flow like golden water. I looked again at the drawing. There was a line of one arm, one hand reaching up, fingers entwined in her hair. So, when she wrote that card, she had been agitated.

And where did that deduction lead me?

"Martin, think of something."

"That's just what I was doing all the time you were wolfing luxuries at Malimbrosa. I was eating pasta and drinking coffee and doodling and thinking. I can't even remember the surnames of any of her friends. She always kept them in tight little compartments. Or probably she just kept them away from me. After all, a junior clerk at an embassy isn't exactly a 'find' for the elegant tables of Roman socialites."

"*Nonna* must have known Vanessa's friends and made enquiries," I said unhappily and looked about me. "Where are we?"

"On the way to the Alban hills."

"When I was here before, Gisela took Vanessa and me to stay a few days at the family's villa. It's somewhere past Nemi —and so lovely. It's way beyond a village called Grottochiara, deeper into the hills and very lonely. I remember the vineyards and the shepherds and a goat that ate the blooms off a bunch of flowers I carried. Perhaps Vanessa—"

"Is up there? Then the whole village would know. Bury the thought, Julie. She could just as well be in Naples or Bologna or Genoa."

"That shop—"

"What about it?"

"People in the street must have known her. Even if she tried to keep apart from them, she must have bought food, wine . . . Someone might know something—"

"Which the police have already ferreted out of them."

We lapsed into silence. I put the card into my handbag.

The car's headlights raked the dark road that swept gently upward towards the hills. We had left the suburbs behind and the spreading landscape lay quiescent under the moon.

I said, "Do you know Philip Cornel?"

"No, but I've heard of him. He's some newspaper man, isn't he?"

"He's the Rome correspondent for the *Morning Observer*. He was at the *palazzo* tonight. *Zia* Romola told me that he and Vanessa had dinner together the night she disappeared."

I felt the tiniest resistant motion of the car as Martin's control of the wheel wavered. "Now that *is* something."

"Philip's story is that she was going on after dinner with him to spend the weekend with friends at Genzano. He said good-bye to her and she got into her car and drove away. That's the last anyone saw of her. But she's alive—this card proves it."

"It proves only that she was alive when the card was written. But when was that? I have no idea when it was put through my mailbox—"

"You didn't look at the post date?"

"It was delivered by hand. And I've been away for six weeks, it could have been delivered any time between the night she disappeared and today."

"You do believe she's alive, don't you? Martin, she must be . . ."

"Of course I think she's alive."

"But you said—"

"I merely said that the card proves nothing, since we don't know when it was delivered. Now"—he waved at the luminous hills—"shall we forget Vanessa and start to enjoy ourselves?"

"If only I could."

"I'm afraid you'll have to, *cherie*, or I take you back to your Malimbrosas."

So Vanessa didn't feature very strongly in Martin's life and he was beginning to find me a bore about her. I glanced sideways at him. In all the years I had known her, I had assumed that her flamelike quality, her vitality, attracted every type of man. It seemed I was wrong. Martin's concern for her was based on friendship, but obviously one that was not as deep and enduring as mine.

For a while I made light conversation. At least I could talk about the *palazzo*—and that amused Martin. It was like a museum inside, I said, except in the family's private apartments, which I had seen the last time I had visited there. The main rooms were full of treasures.

"Plundered."

"Probably, but so long ago. And the palace is built on the site of an old Roman villa. The dungeons are still there because they used the original foundations when they built Malimbrosa."

"And the skulls?"

"I didn't see any. They call them the cellars now and they're full of things they don't want but can't bear to throw away."

"So, no skulls?"

"You should know that the catacombs are all outside the city, that by ancient Roman law no one was allowed to be buried inside the walls. And telling you that," I added, "makes me sound like a know-all."

He laughed. "Oh no, not you."

Presently, as we reached deep into the hills, we grew silent. Martin began to whistle softly, always a sign that he was enjoying himself. I returned to thinking of Vanessa. She hovered against the backdrop of the dark road and the rays of the lights . . . Vanessa with her long red-gold hair and her vivid, laughing face . . . Vanessa and I in London, talking half the night away . . . Vanessa knowing, as only my close friends knew, of my two broken love affairs, and saying, "Love, for men, is merely desire seizing their imaginations. Why don't you accept love affairs for what they are and then marry for an entirely different reason?" . . . "What reason?" . . . "Oh, money; an attractive background; a sort of permanent escort. Or children." Vanessa with her slick wisdom and her enduring friendship for me. Oh no, she wouldn't have let me come all this way had she intended not to be here to greet me.

Martin stopped whistling and I said, "The Villa Sapphira can't be far away. It's past Nemi—"

"That's where we're going."

"Then let's call at the villa. Please, Martin."

"It may be closed."

"It isn't. Gisela is there with Pepi." I kept to myself the possibility that Vanessa might have confided something to Gisela which she did not dare tell the family. I shot Martin a pleading look which was entirely wasted because he was watching the road. "Please, let's call there."

"Do you know the way?"

"If you drive slowly, I may recognize it." I saw him glance at the dashboard clock. "I know it's late, but—"

"The Romans don't believe in that Victorian adage that two hours before midnight is better than four after it," he said. "All right, we'll pay a call there if it amuses you. Look—Nemi. Down there in the hollow."

I leaned over and saw the lake, the ancient Mirror of Diana lying far down in its woodland crater, the waters so still that the reflection of the round, risen moon was scarcely distorted. Vanessa had loved the stories surrounding it, part legend, part truth, and had told them to me, reveling in ghoulish details about pre-Christian sacrifices and the King of the Wood who guarded a certain tree on which grew the Golden Bough. Her stories were so vivid that Gisela stopped her with a little slap that made Vanessa laugh. I could remember it all so clearly . . . Suddenly I recognized a landmark. It loomed out of the darkness, jagged and pitted with the ill use of a thousand years; a broken stone arch lit by moonlight.

When, as children, we had first seen it on our way to the Villa Sapphira, *Zia* Romola had told us that it was so old its origin had never been discovered. "Some civilization," she had said, "that existed long before the Romans." The road to the villa lay beside it. I said, "Down there, Martin—"

He swung the wheel to the left saying good-temperedly, "I suppose it won't hurt me to feel a few stabs of envy at seeing how the rich live."

The road was narrow and twisting and the trees nearly meet overhead so that the moon was lost behind the abundant leaves. The car windows were down and I could smell a scent I had never forgotten—like a hamadryad's bouquet of rosemary and thyme tossed into the roadway under our noses. It brought a swift nostalgia for that enchanted past when, to my bemused child's eyes, everyone at Malimbrosa had seemed to love each other and be happy.

At the end of the lane was a small lodge. There were lights in a downstairs room and I cried, "Here it is," and scarcely waited for Martin to stop the car. There was an iron bell at the side of the closed gates and I pulled it. The door of the lodge opened and an old man came toward me, peering through the gates. The years dropped away and I recognized the lean, bent body, the jutting-out angle of the head. "Paolo," I called with delight.

My voice and what he could see of me meant nothing to him. Gnarled fingers clasped the iron curlicues as he squinted through at me.

I said in careful Italian, "I am the Signorina Juliet Holdroyd. When I was a little girl I came to stay at the *palazzo*. You were butler there in those days."

"The Signorina Julietta—" his voice rang with the delight of memory. "*Ciaio*." He fumbled with the lock of the gates and threw them open. I turned and beckoned to Martin. Then I took Paolo's hand and shook it.

"So," he said, "it is the little signorina."

"Grown up, and staying at the *palazzo* again."

"But that is good. So the past is over . . ."

As I waited for Martin to drive through the gates, I thought with wry amusement that he would have known of the breach with my mother; there were no secrets from trusted servants.

I took Paolo to the car and introduced him. "This is Signor Kean. We came out to the hills for a drive and, as we were so close, I thought I'd like to see the villa. I believe Gisela is there."

"With the *bambino*. She will be so happy that you have come. *Vieni, Vieni*."

I asked him about his family. Yes, his wife was well. Their one son worked in the local vineyards. La Signora was late coming to the villa this year, but that was because there was some trouble at the factory in Milan.

Martin was getting restive and I said goodbye to the old man and got back into the car. We drove past little serpentine walks and groups of pines and ilexes. We went along a path of cypresses that cast long shadows before us, past eroded statues standing in vine-covered alcoves, and then out again between terraces illumined in incandescent silver.

We rounded the last curve, and there was the house. The headlights lit its white façade and the beautiful central arch which led through to an inner courtyard.

Paolo must have telephoned from the lodge for the door was open and Gisela stood waiting for me. Fourteen years separated our meeting, yet she seemed not to have changed. There was nothing unusual about her. She had a square pleasant face and purple-black eyes. What I would always have known her by was the pretty short upper lip, the upward tilt of her nose, so rare in Romans, and the mole at the side of her mouth.

I held out both hands to her. She took them with a fierce, joyful gesture. "Signorina Julietta . . . Oh, come in. Come in. This is most wonderful. I never thought I would ever see you again. Sometimes I have wondered about you . . ." Her words fell over themselves as she led us through the square hall with its mosaic floor and the six branched candelabra standing in pairs on either side of the three carved antique *cassoni*.

Gisela's peasant-style skirt swung in a flurry of bright green, her breasts heaved in the tight white blouse in her excitement at seeing me.

Again, I introduced Martin and she smiled at him, murmuring a shy welcome. We entered a room hung with tapestries. I said, "Signor Kean is a friend of the Signorina Vanessa's."

The liveliness dropped from her face. "It is terrible. The police came here and Pepi heard them talking to me. After they left he wouldn't stop crying and he began to have nightmares. He loved her so much. She would play with him for hours and—" She gave me a doubtful, sideways look. "Even after La Signora sent her from the *palazzo*, she sometimes came here to see him. No one else knew except Paolo and Maria, who cooks for us. Pepi kept the secret very well. He was afraid if he told, La Signora would be angry. He is always either being harshly punished or too spoilt, so it is hard for him to know what he can and cannot do . . . Oh, but I should not have said that—"

"Don't worry," I reassured her. "I won't go running to the signora with tales."

Gisela said quickly, "But you must both have refreshment."

I said we would love coffee and when she left us to fetch it, I began to explain her to Martin. "Gisela has always been more than a servant."

He raised his eyebrows in amusement. "A pretty serf favored and petted by the family?"

"Oh no, Gisela is no plaything, but she has been entrusted with the care of Pepi and she is wonderful with him just as she was with Vanessa and me."

Martin had been leaning forward looking at a miniature of a woman with a pompadour hairstyle and a low-cut pink gown. He reached back and patted my hand. "I know all about Gisela. Vanessa told me."

I wandered away from him remembering nothing about the room except the overpowering tapestries that lined the walls. I was quite certain, though, that little had been changed during the intervening years since I had last been here. I thought of my own home and those of my friends. We rearranged our furniture—added, discarded. We liked to change color schemes; to freshen rooms for spring; warm them by richer colors for winter. But in such places as Malimbrosa or the Villa Sapphira, a carved table, a bronze head, a rare painting had been set in its place perhaps two hundred years before and, even when moved for cleaning, was replaced in the identical position. The pieces existed not out of sentiment, scarcely even out of reverence, but rather with a cold assessment of value.

"Gisela. Gisela . . ." The high, child's cry came from somewhere over our heads.

Martin said, with a faint mockery, "So the heir to Malimbrosa is awake."

I ran across the room. If Martin hadn't heard the sharp fear in Pepi's voice, I had.

Gisela was already in the hall. Coffee pots and cups were on a small gilt trolley.

I said, "Go to him, Gisela. I'll take this."

She began to run up the stairs. I called, "He sounds very frightened."

"It is the dreams I told you about." She called up, "I am coming to you, Pepi. Wait, *caro* . . ." Then she turned to me. "I think it is because he is so lonely. You see, signorina, when he is awake, he makes up wonderful stories to amuse himself. Then, when he is asleep, he . . . well, he goes on making up stories without knowing he is doing it. But they are horrible ones and he wakes up."

"*Gi–se–la* . . ."

She said, "La Signora says that he is too excitable and must be kept quiet. But he does not *want* to be kept quiet. Sometimes, signorina, I grow frightened for him when I think of what his future will be—"

A loud and prolonged scream broke through her words. Gisela turned and flew up the stairs, her green skirt billowing, her large, but very nimble feet flying from one stair to the next.

I wheeled the trolley into the *salone*.

Martin was smoking a cigarette. "It's odd, isn't it, that there are still people in Europe who live like this?"

I said, "If you think that about this place, you should see Malimbrosa," and poured out coffee.

He walked round the room holding his cup, peering at pictures, tracing the line of a piece of porcelain. "All of this to those who like it. For me, I'd trade the lot for a Bentley." He looked at me over his shoulder. "Aren't you going to see what's the matter upstairs?"

"I'll wait for Gisela. It would be better for her to see if she can get Pepi to sleep."

I had taken two sips of coffee when I heard her calling me. "Signorina . . . Signorina? Could you please come up here?"

I turned to Martin. "Will you come, too?"

He said firmly, "If he's been scared by having bad dreams, he won't want to meet a strange man. For all you know, I might resemble someone in his nightmare."

I took another quick drink of coffee and left Martin to his tour of the room.

Gisela was leaning over the wide balustrade. I ran up the stairs, past the line of portraits on the wall. "Can't you get him to sleep?"

"Pepi thought you were the Signorina Irena. You see, she said she would come tonight."

I exclaimed, "She's coming here?" And then wondered why on earth I should be surprised. The movements of the family were not my concern.

"The Signora Irena sometimes comes for a day or two when her husband has to go away on business. She says she loves the country. Also she likes to see Pepi and he gets very excited when he knows she is coming. I think she understands him better than any of the others, except the Signorina Vanessa, of course."

"And Pepi is staying awake until she arrives?"

"Perhaps if you would just come and see him," Gisela coaxed, "that will please him and he will sleep. He sees so few people up here."

We reached the softly lit room and Gisela pushed open the door. Then she hesitated, leaned toward me, and whispered agitatedly, "You must forgive him if he is a little sullen. He is difficult with strangers."

"He was very polite when we met at the *palazzo*."

"Oh, but that was in front of La Signora."

A long wail came from inside the room. "G-Gi-se-la, you are t-talking to s-somebody. Who is it? I w-want to see who it is. Gi–se–la."

It was like the wail of a beggar child I had once seen on a street corner in Morocco.

7 ✄

PEPI'S BEDROOM WAS LIT by a single pink shaded light. I had an
impression of heavy carved furniture, almost black in color, of
tall, shuttered windows, and of Pepi, sitting stiff and upright.
The bed was so large that he must often have felt lost and
lonely, wanting to reach out across that white space and touch
something warm and living. Did Irena come to him when she
was at the villa, and lie with him and hold him close, safe from
his fears and his nightmares? I couldn't picture her like that;
she seemed so detached, so queenly cool. Yet Vanessa had once
said, "Irena guards her emotions as if she were in a cocoon. I
doubt if anyone, even Leo, really knows her."

Back to Vanessa; always back to what she had done, what
she had said . . . as if she were my alter ego, my shadow ever
beside me. I sat down on the edge of the big bed and smiled at
the pale little boy. (Why, *why*, living in this sun-soaked place,
had he not become tanned?)

"Hullo, Pepi," I said. "We met earlier, didn't we?"

"D-do you know where V-Vanessa is?"

I shook my head. "Not yet." I wanted to reassure him, to
say, But she'll be back soon. I couldn't. Lying to a child was
too great a sin. I took his hand and was shocked to find that he
was trembling.

In the bed by his side was a toy tiger made out of dyed red muskrat. Its eyes were made of yellow glass cut so intricately that they glittered. I thought of lion's eyes; cat's eyes; Philip Cornel watching me . . .

"Have you c-come to s-stay?"

I shook my head. "No," and then in genuine surprise, "You speak excellent English."

"Vanessa taught me."

Gisela was hovering behind us. "She would come up here often and she would talk to him in English and tell him English adventure stories."

He gave Gisela a reproachful look over my shoulder. "You s-said *Zia* Irena was c-coming." He looked back at me as if he supposed I were a substitute.

"She will come," Gisela comforted him. "The signora does not break promises."

I didn't want to stay and perhaps excite him, but he felt my arms relax and clung. "*Zia* Juliet, don't go; don't go . . ."

I held him close. "Pepi, I must." I rubbed my cheek against his wild black hair. "But I promise I'll come back and, like *Zia* Irena, I always keep my promises."

He said with a childish sigh, "Everyone is always going back. Nobody ever s-stays . . ." He rolled over and hid his face in the pillow.

I picked up the red tiger and said, "He's very cuddly. What's his name?"

"Razullo." Then he turned his face up to me. "Vanessa g-gave him to me on . . . in . . ." He lay stiff-lipped, fighting tears.

Gisela explained. "On January the sixth it is a custom up here in our village for good children to be given a toy. Bad children find a piece of coal instead of a gift in their stocking. It is called 'The Night of the Kindly Witch.'"

Pepi was pulling at my hand, looking at the topaz ring I wore. "Is that a diamond?"

"A diamond as big as that would be like the Koh-i-Nor," I said laughing.

"What is a Koh-i—"

"A very special diamond that has lots of exciting stories about it," I said. "I'll tell them to you one day. But not now. You must go to sleep."

He shut his eyes pretending to sleep and he looked so like a shrimp in an ocean in the big bed that for all his great inheritance, I pitied him.

Gisela said softly, "He is quiet now. I will stay with him until he sleeps. But you, signorina, please have your coffee and . . . and wait. I would like to talk to you about the Signorina Vanessa."

Martin was sitting on the mosaic floor in the hall looking through the contents of the lower half of a heavy carved cabinet.

"*Che cerchi?*" I hissed at him.

He looked up and grinned at me. "I'm English, remember?"

"And I've been talking Italian to Gisela. All right then, what are you looking for?"

"Clues. A letter; a photograph. Something Vanessa might have slipped in here—it looks like the place where they stuff the snapshots friends take of them."

"I thought I was the one obsessed by what has happened to Vanessa."

"It's infectious," he said and as he scrambled up from the floor, his long legs skidded on the slippery surface. "Whoops!" He steadied himself and we laughed.

I walked past him and closed the cupboard door. "If you're looking for a photograph of Vanessa and some man, this isn't the place to find it. And anyway, the things people keep shut away are private."

He demanded softly, "Even when it's a matter of finding Vanessa?"

He had me floored. "You're impossible," I said.

He was quite unembarrassed. "While you were comforting the heir with the nightmares, I had a marvelous insight into his ancestors. There are boxes and boxes of old-fashioned drawings of women in crinolines and men in knee breeches. There's a terrifying painting of an old man wearing a red cloak like a cardinal. It's signed Giambattista Malimbrosa. Who was he?"

"I haven't the vaguest idea." I wandered down the hall, looking in doors. "Vanessa and I used to play in the cellars here when it was too hot to go out. It's a stone place and the floor was leveled and marked out so that we could have games of tennis there. I wonder if anyone has played there since? Come on"—I reached out for his hand—"let's go and see."

The staircase was in darkness. I felt along the wall for the light switch and flicked it on. Unlike the cellars underneath Malimbrosa which were a series of small cells linked by arches and damp stone passages, this was one enormous room, the walls planed and whitewashed. There were cupboards which contained sports things used by generations of Malimbrosas and never thrown away—skates and skis and tennis rackets. I remembered how Gisela had once said when we had opened a cupboard and a pile of old riding boots fell out, "Oh dear, this family hoards like squirrels."

Vanessa had said, "Let's make a heap of them and have a huge bonfire."

Gisela had been shocked. "You cannot do what you like with things that don't belong to you."

And Vanessa had laughed. "The people they belonged to are too dead to care."

Belongings . . . things chosen with joy . . . cared for . . . Vanessa had fallen in love with that red lacquer chest when she had seen it in a shop in the Fulham Road . . . The Madame Recamier settee which she had had specially covered in beige damask . . . *Vanessa's furniture*. I stood staring at it, recognizing the pieces she had bought in London at the time when *Nonna* Allegra had decided she was old enough to have her own sitting room at the *palazzo*.

"Martin . . . *look*. Vanessa's furniture."

"Is it?"

"You should know—"

"How, since I never went to the *palazzo* and was on leave in

London when she took the shop in the Via Prassodi?"

"I'd forgotten. But I *know* some of these pieces. I was with her when she bought them." I went to the lacquer chest and began pulling out the drawers. "I know this is hers."

It was full of sweaters, blouses, scarves—all of them expensive and typically Vanessa in the rich colorings she so loved. In one drawer I found a traveling clock and some table mats with a golden cockerel on a black ground.

"What was that you said to me about snooping around other people's possessions?" Martin asked softly.

"This is different. These are Vanessa's." I stared at the open drawer. "So when they found her gone, they must have stripped the apartment over the shop and dumped her things here. They didn't care . . ." I touched a navy and emerald Hermès scarf, letting the soft silk run through my fingers. It wasn't nostalgia that swept through me, but a compound of despair and fear. Despair because, in spite of my bravado in front of the Malimbrosas, I had no idea where to start searching for Vanessa. The fear was instinctive.

I shut the drawer and wandered across to the elegant settee. " 'Glory on horseback, disaster sitting behind.' "

"And what's that remark in aid of?"

"It was quoted to me as a sort of warning. By Philip Cornel."

"That newspaper chap? The last man to set eyes on her before she disappeared?"

"That one."

"Why?"

"It's obvious. If by some miracle I found Vanessa, I would be sorry for it."

"What's it to do with him?"

"That's what I intend to find out . . . Martin, *look*." I darted across the room and peered behind a table piled with books. "Her suitcases." I began to count. "Five pieces of matching luggage, dark red." I knelt on the floor and began opening them. They were all empty. I scrambled to my feet.

"Whatever she felt about furniture and things like that, she loved her dresses. If she hasn't taken those, then I'll know there's something sinister in her disappearance."

The two cupboards where the sports gear were kept were on the far wall. I went to them and dragged one open. The skis and the riding boots were gone. In their place, tightly packed, were clothes on hangers. My fingers tore through the long line, recognizing some. A black Quant suit, a rainbow chiffon kaftan; dresses of raw silk. Vanessa's clothes.

I leaned sickly against the cupboard door. "Now I know she didn't go voluntarily . . . No one goes anywhere for a length of time without taking their clothes with them."

"She could have had more."

"Then let's see what's here." I flung open the second cupboard. That too was stuffed with clothes swinging from velvet-covered holders. "She wasn't a millionairess. Even Vanessa, who adored clothes, wouldn't have had more than this. Martin, don't you see." I gripped his arm and he winced. "Someone forced her to go . . . with . . . him. She had no time to collect anything."

"She could have gone away with someone who insisted that she leave everything of her old life behind—you know, the romantic gesture."

"Do you believe that?"

"No."

The cellar seemed suddenly to be without air. "Let's get out of here," I said, and made for the spiral staircase.

Gisela was standing in the passage. "So, signorina, you have found it all. They brought everything here—"

"And dumped it and sold the shop to an old man who very conveniently died after he, in his turn, had sold it. It was all too easy. Perhaps they even paid him to take it over so that, when he sold it, there was no one to connect it any longer with Vanessa." I put my hand on Gisela's arm and led her into the hall. "Did *Nonna* Allegra arrange the transfer of the shop to this old man?"

"Oh, no. She did not wish to be involved; there would have

been too much talk and besides, she was so upset about the whole thing. And Signor Leo was away in Milan so—" She gave me a long, shy look. "It was Signor Cornel who made all the arrangements."

I turned swiftly to Martin. "You see. That man again."

"Well, someone had to cope."

"They didn't wait long, did they?"

Gisela said, distressed, "You must not think that they were without heart. Whatever the quarrel between the signorina and La Signora, she spoke so kindly about her after the disappearance. I think she wanted to close the shop so that when . . . if . . . the Signorina Vanessa was found, she would be brought back to the *palazzo* and everything forgiven. There would be no need for the shop."

I looked at my watch. "Nothing is resolved, is it?" I said to Martin, "It's late. I think we should go."

"Signorina, please, I would like to show you something."

She led us into a small room which I remembered as being the least formal in the villa. It used to be the dining room for Vanessa and me when the adults had guests. It was a long room with an arched doorway to a patio, and in the old days it had never looked so lived in. There was a sewing box and some brightly colored material beside an armchair. Some magazines were strewn on a table and a partly completed model of a ship with the rest of the pieces lying around it stood on a long sofa table.

Gisela crossed to a drawer, opened it, and took something out. "Read this, please."

It was one of Vanessa's cards. I translated the scrawled Italian into English.

"Please don't leave Pepi. And tell him I always love him. And do not, I beg you, show this card to *Nonna* or anyone. For my sake."

It was not signed, but on the other side was a very rough sketch of Vanessa. My memory of my childhood stay in Rome was vague, but certain small things were still vivid because of some unusual association. The slender broken columns in the drawing, for instance, were those of the temple of Apollo, where we had once been taken. I had seen a golden cat sitting on a tuft of purple flowers at the base of the column and had not understood why, since *Zia* Romola told us that it belonged to no one, I could not bring the lovely, wild-eyed creature back to England with me. So, Vanessa had been looking out onto the tall Corinthian columns of Apollo's temple when she wrote that card. Was she imprisoned then in one of the medieval houses near the Theater of Marcellus? I looked up and asked Gisela, "I suppose you haven't told the signora about this card?"

"Oh no." She was shocked. "How could I? Besides, they would have given it to the police and the Signorina Vanessa would be very angry. Perhaps this is a *scappatino*."

It was a word I didn't know. Martin said, "An escapade—a running away from things as they are. After all, she left her suitcases and everything that belonged to her behind as if she were going to an entirely new life."

"Where? With whom?"

"How do I know?"

For a few moments we all clung to silence. We had reached an impasse; no more questions to ask, no certainty; just wild guessing.

A car was coming up the drive. Gisela lifted her head sharply. We stood like conspirators, listening. Tires hissed on the gravel drive, then stopped. An engine purred and then it, too, was silenced.

Gisela whispered, "It is the Signora Irena."

There was no reason why we shouldn't stay to meet her, yet I heard myself saying in a hushed, hurried voice, "Martin, we must go."

Outside, the car door closed and I heard a man's voice. I knew it was not Leo because Bruno had already driven him to the airport.

Gisela suddenly became nervous. She ran to a french window at the back of the room in which we stood and pulled the curtains aside. "This way, signorina. If you do not want to meet them, go this way round the house."

Her need for our visit to be secret was far more urgent than mine. "Go that way?" I asked, staring at the window she had opened. "Like an interloper? But I'm not. I'm invited here when I like. I—"

Martin gave me a little push. "Outside, sweetie." He was grinning.

"Don't rush me." I turned to Gisela. "If you hear of anything that might help me to find the signorina, you'll let me know, won't you?"

"Yes. Yes. I will do that," she said hastily and her hands went on urging me through the glass door. She obviously did not want me to see who had come to the villa with Irena. She was in on some secret and I had no idea whether affection for Irena or a few bribes made her anxious that we should not know who the man was. I thought crossly, As if I'd go running to *Nonna* Allegra telling tales . . .

The curtain dropped abruptly into place, shutting us out of the room. The moon lay in a silver haze over the splendid cedar and the umbrella pines. Through the trees there was a glitter of water.

Martin laughed. "Well, well. The intrigues of Malimbrosa!"

"Your're jumping to conclusions."

"It wasn't a particularly high jump," he said. "You know, Julie, you're going to dine out on this Roman affair for years after you get back to London."

I didn't answer him. I was picking my way across the terrace between the Corinthian columns that supported the upper rooms and the little twisted pillars of the balustrade with their curls of wisteria.

Martin asked in a loud whisper, "Who do you think it is? A well-known politician or perhaps she has a liking for some handsome shepherd from the Abruzzi mountains."

I ignored him. He came up close behind me and put an arm round my throat, pulling me gently back against him.

" 'Cobwebbed with intrigue.' Where did I read that sentence? Anyway, it's applicable." He kissed the side of my head and let me go.

We went down a flight of steps and round the side of the house. The air was heavy and sweet with mingled scents, and on the walls camellias clung like white velvet brushed with moonlight.

When we reached the front of the house, I paused. It was not shyness that made me want to reach the car without being observed but a sense of embarrassment that, if I happened to turn my head in the direction of the lighted window as I passed, I might be a witness to something that was secret. Gisela's agitation had brushed off on me.

Martin slid an arm round my shoulders. "So this is a love pavilion."

"If you go around telling people at the embassy—"

"Don't be silly. The Malimbrosas are powerful. I'm enjoying my life in Rome too much to be bundled home in disgrace. I was just thinking, though—"

"What?" I asked cautiously.

He grinned at me. "Do they have the monopoly?"

I slid from under his arm and said crisply, "They do. Come on, make for the car and don't play Peeping Tom." I darted out of the shadow of the wall and across the patch of light thrown by the lamps in the unshuttered *salone* window. I opened the door of the car and climbed in. Martin followed more slowly. I sat staring ahead of me as he turned on the engine. Then, as the car slid forward, I looked back. It was a purely involuntary movement; I just turned my head.

My glance fell directly onto the lighted room. Irena was standing a little back from the window, but framed in it, still as a statue, his face highlighted by the moon, was Philip Cornel.

I looked guiltily away like a child being caught in some silly sneaking prank, and stared at the insects caught in the car's headlights. Perhaps Philip hadn't seen us cross the drive, hadn't recognized the dim white blur of my face in the car. But I suspected that, being Philip, he had.

Martin and I were very silent on the way back to Rome. For one thing, we had talked ourselves out concerning Vanessa; for another, it was late and he must be as tired as I. Yet, as the car flashed past the mirrorlike surface of the Lake of Nemi, past the woods and the silvered hills, my imagination clung to the threads of suspicion in my mind. This man, Cornel, the last to see Vanessa alive; a friend of the Malimbrosas and, very possibly, Irena's lover. These three threads seemed to make a pattern. What needed to be discovered were the pieces that linked them. That was what I had to find out. But for tonight, I had had enough. I felt uncontrollably tired. I slumped down in my seat and closed my eyes. Before I drifted into a slight sleep, I realized that I hadn't told Martin the name of the man who had arrived at the Villa Sapphira with Irena.

I CAME TO AS SOMETHING TOUCHED my cheek. The car had stopped and I saw that we were outside the gates of Malimbrosa. Martin said, "I kissed you awake. Wasn't that nice of me? But now you've had your sleep, what about coming back to my apartment? It's time you saw it and I've got a nice big bed."

I said laughing and stretching, "For such suitable occasions? Well, I'm sure Rome is filled with girls—"

"But not all of them have hair like yours. A man could feel gloriously imprisoned in it."

"All right. You've had your poetic moment. Now forget it. At three o'clock in the morning I turn into a praying mantis and I strangle men with my hair."

"It's only half past one. I'll watch the time."

"I'm watching it now." I touched his hand lightly. "Thanks for the drive. And now, goodnight."

He said as I got out of the car, "I hope you sleep badly."

He drove off as I rang the bell. Immediately the tall gates swung open and clanged behind me. The double doors of the *palazzo* opened and behind the kind face of an elderly man I supposed was a night watchman the lights glowed on the parma violet columns, the Apollo painting and Garibaldi's chair.

I bade the man goodnight and shut myself in the elevator. It slid silkily, with scarcely a sound, up to the gallery floor.

I switched on a dressing-table light and saw the room reflected in the mirror, shadowed, hyacinth tinted. A large white moth fluttered behind me, awakened by the light. It dashed its glimmering body against everything that was in its way. I opened the shutters and, with a piece of notepaper, made a flurry of air behind it so that it flew from me toward the window and freedom.

From the balcony I looked down onto the black mass of the Pincian Gate and the great Roman wall. There was still movement in the city and the floodlights made luminous patches against the starry sky.

By turning my head, I could see the roof garden. It was in darkness, but someone was there, walking to and fro among the flower urns. I knew by her tallness and erectness that it was *Nonna* Allegra, and wondered whether she was merely enjoying the quiet night or was torn by anxieties that would not let her sleep. I wondered, too, if she knew that Irena was not at home. At that moment she turned and walked my way. Immediately I dived back into the room and closed the shutters. I didn't want to be a guest who kept furtive watch on her hostess.

I had been tired only a few minutes earlier, but once in bed I couldn't sleep. My mind was as obsessed with the Malimbrosas now as it had been when I had visited the *palazzo* as a child. But then I had been unperceptive, seeing my Terracotta Palace as a child's fantasy dream come true. Now I saw it differently.

The Romans are a voluble people. But this family had an inbred introversion. In just one evening I had sensed beneath the closeness of their family life the tensions and the bitternesses that none of their money could alleviate. They were fighting to maintain a past solidarity. But in the end the whole delicate fabric of their lives would break because there was no promise of a future for them; no strength to come. Only a pale little boy demanding plaintively, "Where is Vanessa?"

8 ❧

I AWOKE NEXT MORNING to a satin-pink light flowing through the shutters. I blinked through mists of sleep, trying to orientate myself and, when I was more fully awake, I lay and made plans for the day. I wanted badly to see Rome, but there was a lot to be done before I went, renewing my old acquaintance with the Forum, the Colosseum and the fountains of Tivoli.

I had been told the night before that breakfast would be brought to me in my room. Punctually at eight o'clock an elderly woman entered and asked me whether I wanted an English or a continental breakfast. I was touched by the charming consideration and chose coffee and croissants.

"And honey," she said. "We have our own. It is made from bees we keep at Grottochiara."

"What is your name?"

"Caterina."

"Thank you, Caterina. I would love honey," I said.

Breakfast was laid on a table by the open balcony window. After I had eaten and dressed, it was still only a quarter past nine and too early to go out. In a drawer of the flat-topped writing table, I found a pile of notepaper with the Malimbrosa coat of arms on it. There were also some colored postcards of Rome—and even a little box of stamps. Where hospitality was concerned, the Malimbrosas forgot nothing. I sat down to write a few cards to friends in London but only to one did I give my actual address. She was a friend who was also a secretary to a Member of Parliament and I wanted, through her, to keep in touch with the movements of my future chief. I knew he was erratic and that he all too often made newspaper headlines. I didn't want to return to London to work for him in ignorance of what he had been up to while I was away, and I needed Laura to give me all the facts.

When I was ready to go out I paused on my way across the gallery and looked up at the great dome. I remembered that as a child, waiting in this same spot for Vanessa, Gisela had joined me and had pointed to the mosaic cupola high above us, saying, "You see, there's the red king and the green jester. Look, he has a balloon on a stick. And there's the female slave."

I had said, "She has nothing on."

And Gisela had laughed.

Now, as I stood leaning against the balustrade, a cloud cleared the face of the sun so that light suddenly blazed through four concealed windows onto king and jester and the slave's alabaster skin.

"Juliet—"

Zia Romola was coming toward me along the gallery. She gave me a bright smile, asked me how I had slept and if I had enjoyed myself the night before.

I told her that we had gone for a drive and that passing Nemi, had driven up to the Villa Sapphira. I said, "I hope *Nonna* Allegra won't mind, only we were so near and I did want to see it again."

"Mamma has told you to go there whenever you wish. Why don't you stay there for a few days? The air is so lovely it will do you good. And now, what are you going to do this morning?"

I said that I was going to the Via Prassodi to talk to the people who might have known Vanessa. "As Maria Cyrena," I added.

She gave me a long, sad look. "You will learn nothing that

we do not already know, Juliet. The police and our detectives have called at every possible place for information."

"All the same," I said obstinately, "I want to hear for myself what her neighbors have to say."

"They know precisely nothing about her as Vanessa. She never became friendly enough with any of them and so you see your journey will be a waste of your holiday. *Cara*, there is so much for you to enjoy in Rome."

"I know. But all that must come later."

She gave me a look of despair. I was being impossibly obstinate. I could read it all on her thin, dark, mobile face.

We went down in the elevator together, and in the hall she shook off her annoyance. "You must feel free to go anywhere you wish about the house, except, of course, into the private apartments. But you know that, don't you?"

"Yes. And thank you. You are being so kind to me. I'm sorry, *Zia* Romola, if you think I'm being difficult about Vanessa."

She watched me close the little gilded gate. "Not difficult, Juliet, just not really understanding. But you will, you will have to. Vanessa is gone. Perhaps she will come back in her own time, or perhaps—"

"What?"

"She never will. We must accept the inevitable."

"I won't believe that she is dead."

She said unhappily, "The shock is new to you, but we have had to learn to live with it. There has been so much tragedy even in my lifetime—my father died so young; then my brother Roberto was killed and now Pepi, the last of the line, is turning out to be a little weakling. Vanessa—" She reached out a hand as if to touch me and then withdrew it quickly. "Be happy, Juliet, and learn to accept. Now I must go to the clinic."

I knew that the place she referred to was a child-care clinic which had been founded by the Malimbrosas immediately after the last war, and I wondered how this woman, who so disliked physical contact, handled the mothers and babies at the place where she spent so much of her time. Perhaps she was different with them; perhaps she had depths of compassion which triumphed over her hatred of human contact.

I walked into the *salone*. The two sets of double doors that divided the huge room into three were flung open and servants were busy cleaning and polishing. When I had stayed there before, I remembered that on one night there was a ball. Vanessa and I had crouched behind the gallery balustrade and watched the guests arrive, peering and straining to see into the rooms. We had been forcibly removed by Gisela when Vanessa, fascinated by a woman whose huge bosom was enveloped with ostrich feathers, had climbed the balustrade and had almost fallen over in her efforts to see what happened when she danced.

"But the man she's with will never get *near* her," she had breathed with awe. "There's so much in the way."

I remembered the giggling little incident vividly as I walked through the rooms. The shutters were open briefly, and the sharp morning light glittered on the brocades, the crystal chandeliers and the settecento furniture. The servants smiled at me and bade me good morning. Miniatures, snuff boxes and rare pieces of porcelain stood on little inlaid tables; portraits and mirrors in garlanded frames festooned the walls. The spoils and acquisitions of hundreds of years were spread out under the three painted ceilings and I wondered if the family ever even saw them or whether such a feast of treasures was like a sunset to a blind man.

The doors at the far end of the third room opened out onto the narrow path that encircled the *palazzo*. I stepped outside and began to wander along the flagged stones, between the oleander bushes and the high wall.

Somewhere a telephone rang and was answered. I heard *Nonna* Allegra's voice and knew that I was near the room which she used as an office. There were only two things I remembered about it from my earlier visit; one was the huge desk that dominated the center of the room, with three impressive white telephones; the other, the chess set which stood on a small table by her side. The board was of mother-of-pearl and the chessmen were of jade and silver. Vanessa had told me that it had stood there for as long as she could remember and that often, when she was thinking out some business problem, Allegra would play some curious game of chess with herself, as player and opponent. "Just as some people doodle when they're talking," Vanessa had said.

The office had once been her husband's room. He had had a heart condition almost all his life and with the inborn Malimbrosa fear of outsiders in control of his empire, he had taught Allegra all that he knew of administration. Avid to learn, inheriting from her French forebears a delight in industry and a shrewd money sense, she had been a remarkable pupil, better prepared to take over the business than her three sons were when Ludovico died soon after his forty-second birthday.

I looked at my watch. It was after ten o'clock and time for my visit to the Via Prassodi. I went upstairs to fetch my handbag and found that my bed had already been made. There was also a Venetian glass bowl piled with apricots, purple figs, and Sicilian blood oranges with mottled skins and rich juices. I ate an apricot and then went downstairs, the tangy sweetness of the fruit lingering on my tongue.

A door to the right of the hall was open and sunlight poured through for a brief moment before Alberto closed the shutters. I told him that I wanted a taxi. His pale, immobile face took on some of the peach pink light from the walls of the room. He told me with implacable politeness that the chauffeur had taken the Ferrari to be serviced. La Signora would be using the Lancia but he could ask the signorina if the small car would be available for me.

"Please don't bother. I prefer a taxi. I don't quite know how long I shall be and the car might be needed. Anyway," I added, "it's a lovely morning, I may walk a little."

He bowed slightly. I wondered how many servants were quite as obsequious these days but then decided that Allegra would pay her servants well and, in return, would demand perfection.

I heard the distant peeling of a bell. I had no idea where it came from, but Alberto left me and crossed to the door. He stood waiting, apparently while the entrance gates were unlocked by someone watching on the closed circuit television in the servants' quarters. Then, with the gesture of a dancer, he put down both hands and opened the double doors.

Philip Cornel walked in, trailing a long scarf. Mine. He waved the strip of emerald chiffon at me.

"Good morning. You left this at the villa last night."

We faced each other in the hall and, as Alberto disappeared, the vacuum of silence was filled with my sudden, desperate thought. *The type that attracts me is the type that can destroy me . . .* This time, ironically enough, it would be Philip himself who would save me from the despair of wrongly directed emotions because his only interest in me was contained in suspicion and impatience.

He broke the too-long silence. "It *is* yours, isn't it?" He dangled the fragile length of chiffon in front of me.

"Thank you. I'm afraid I even forgot I had it with me. It was such a lovely warm night." I took the scarf from him and wondered if this were a deliberate attempt to let me know that he had seen me and that he suspected I had seen him at the window at the Villa Sapphira.

I had already noticed that Philip never covered silences with a spate of meaningless words. He let conversation flow at its own pace. He was too utterly at ease, his strange eyes too steady. I made no attempt to break the silence and, to my relief, he spoke first.

"Of course, it's too early yet to ask you if you're enjoying yourself in Rome."

"Much too early."

"You're going sightseeing this morning?"

Politeness? Curiosity? Or suspicion? I stood back a little so that I could look at him more levelly. "No. I'm going to the Via Prassodi."

"So persistence is one of your—virtues."

"I was trained to be a secretary to a Member of Parliament," I reminded him. "Persistence goes with the job."

A trace of a smile played round his mouth but his eyes remained cold and penetrating. "I'm afraid your search is going to spoil what might have been a wonderful holiday."

"Somebody has ruined Vanessa's life."

"You are making sweeping statements. She could be married and on her honeymoon for all you know."

I was quite certain he didn't believe what he suggested and I said quickly, "From the cards she sent, I'd say a honeymoon is most unlikely."

"What cards?"

Our voices clashed. His ease disappeared and he asked again, his manner suddenly alert, "What cards?"

I knew that I had said too much. Vanessa had written, "Don't tell *Nonna*," and the words hung on the moment's silence like a rebuke. I was fairly certain that anything I said to Philip Cornel would be repeated to *Nonna* Allegra, although I had no idea whether it would be out of friendship for her or in order to try and discredit me. I was full of suspicions for them all, the Malimbrosas and Cornel.

He was watching me, his disturbing, deep-gold eyes resting on mine.

I said lightly, to hide my confusion, "You know that Vanessa had a way of making rough sketches on postcards and sending them to her friends with little notes on the back. Well she . . . she sent me some. And she'd have told me if there had been anyone very special in her life."

"Would she?"

The question was softly spoken, yet it disconcerted me. I couldn't tell what lay behind it. Disbelief? Mockery?

I felt like an exhibit in some gallery, standing in that huge rotunda under the mosaic dome. I knew I must end our conversation before I made another unthinking remark which Philip Cornel might pounce on. I edged round him toward the doorway. "Thank you for bringing my scarf. I hope you didn't make a special journey just for that."

"No. I have to see the signora."

I paused for a moment on the top step, frowning into the dazzling sunlight.

"If you're wondering whether you have the strength to open those enormous gates, you don't have to worry." Philip was behind me, his voice light, amused. "They're operated automatically. You see, they have everything here."

Everything. Except a future . . .

"I know about the gates," I called back, and ran down the steps.

It was only when I was free of the house and its palm-fringed enclosure, that I realized my heart was thudding as though I'd been running for miles without stopping. I paused at the street crossing, waiting for the traffic streaming past the Aurelian Gate to ease. And as I waited, I took long, deep gasps of air. I felt as if I had come from some tremendous emotional scene—and all that had happened was that I had had a slight brush with a man I was growing more and more to mistrust.

I stood watching the darting cars without really seeing them; nor had I any idea how long I waited, because when the trembling ceased and I could think clearly, I was bewildered. It was almost as if Philip had exerted some strange influence over me so that I was seized with a complex of emotions so tangled, so bewildering, that not one was clearly defined. I was in a whirlpool of some strange manifestation that had begun the moment I had taken the green scarf from Philip Cornel's hand.

"*Immediate love is the touch of the enchanter.*" Behind all the confusion in my mind, these words, heard somewhere long ago, seared my mind with an almost physical pain. The touch of the enchanter—or a devil's trick to waste something precious on a mirage? The faces of the two men in my past swam before me. Their names taunted and echoed. Michael . . . Julian . . . Oh no, not again. And not a man who, if I knew him better would, I was certain, be everything I most disliked;

not a man who had nothing to offer me but a warning and a threat. "Glory on horseback, disaster sitting behind."

"Are you ill, signorina?"

A woman had taken my arm. I turned a startled face toward her. "Thank you, no. I was . . . day-dreaming . . ." I managed a laugh. "It's a good thing I'm safely on the pavement, isn't it?"

"You are not Italian—"

"Oh dear, is my accent so bad?" My laughing protest was shaken because I hadn't yet managed to steady myself. "I'm English. On holiday."

We crossed together and left each other on the other side of the road. I walked on down the Via Veneto and found a taxi.

As we drew near the Via Margutta, where I had asked to be let out, my conviction that I would find some sort of clue to Vanessa's disappearance among the people who must have known her or provided her with her bread and wine and groceries, diminished. It was so easy for imagination to have a conviction of success. Now that I was here, reality took over. I began looking for omens like some superstitious moron. I told myself wildly, If the sun comes through that cloud, I'll find a clue that the detectives missed . . . If that man leaning against the *trattoria* door watching me says "good morning" as I pass, it'll be a sign that I'll find someone who can help me. Making sun and cloud, people and things, symbols of fortune. Normally I would have laughed at myself, but I was so intent that I took every silly superstition seriously.

When I reached the little shop in the Via Prassodi, the monkey-faced Tino Cotone greeted me politely but without enthusiasm. He said, obviously anxious to forestall any barrage of questions I might hurl at him, "You have come for the artist Artello's address? I have it here." Then he led me to the door and told me how to get to the studio. He was obviously very anxious to be rid of me.

The girl called from the back of the shop, "Tino, the letter for the signorina. It's here . . ."

I wheeled round. She came, wearing a little red apron and

handed me an envelope. "You told us your name and so we kept it for you. We found it lying just inside the door when we opened the shop this morning."

It had been delivered by hand. I stood with the morning sun shining on the statuettes and the little pieces of costume jewelry, and slit the envelope.

Inside was, as I had expected, a card from Vanessa:

I so long to see you, Julie. I need help, but I can't tell you where I am. I daren't. That sounds melodramatic, but then it is—all of it. Don't tell Nonna.

I turned the card over. There was no drawing on the other side.

I thanked the Cotones and left, following the instructions to Artello's studio. As I went I took the address out of my handbag and re-read it. In my absorption I bumped into a little pavement table outside a *trattoria* and, almost immediately after, tripped over an uneven paving stone and was saved by a man with a blue chin and a grip on my arm like a vice. I said, "Thank you, signore. You probably saved me from a broken ankle."

"*Bella*," he hissed. "*Bellissima*."

I slid out of his grip and walked on.

The building where Artello had his studio was built round a courtyard. There were a lot of outside staircases reaching up to the various floors. The lower rooms had tall, weathered shutters, but just underneath the roof great studio windows were open to the light. There were pots of geraniums poking vermilion heads through the bars of lop-sided balconies. The whole enclosed square of buildings looked as if it were ready to collapse at the sound of a loud laugh.

Some very small children played among the dustbins. A tiny girl offered me a drooping carnation. I thanked her, took it and stuck it through the appliqué at the neck of my dress. We smiled at one another with innocent curiosity. Above us, the swifts teased each other, twittering as if trying to outdo the children's voices.

I hesitated, looking for the number of Artello's house. A man lolling against an open door asked if I were looking for someone.

"Signor Artello—?" The man jabbed a finger at one of the flights of iron steps.

I had always hated iron staircases. If I looked down, I felt that it was too flimsy a barrier between myself and the hard ground. So I climbed, keeping my head up, looking at the names on the doors of each small outside landing.

The top seemed a very long way away, but when I got there I went through the outside door and found myself in a large stone passage with three doors. Behind one, I could hear two people arraigning one another in Romanesco, that picturesque and bawdy dialect. From another apartment I heard music.

I peered round an open door and as I did so, a girl came out of the room with the music and told me that Artello was out.

"Leaving his door open?"

"We all do." She looked at me without interest and then turned her back.

"When do you think I could see him?"

She said over her shoulder, "It all depends what you've come for," and gave a clipped, cynical laugh.

"I want to inquire about a mutual friend. Perhaps you know her. Maria Cyrena."

She pivoted round and her eyes were very large and black. "Then you'd better stay away. He's had all the inquiries he wants about that one. He doesn't much like the police, anyway." Her door slammed.

I went back to the Via Prassodi and made systematic calls at the shops in the street that sold the *farfalloni* . . . *tagliatelle* . . . *tortelloni* . . . I questioned a woman over mounds of spaghetti, a fat man over a barrel of chianti. Oh yes, Maria had bought pasta, olives, oranges, wine. Everyone knew her and nobody knew her. In every case there was wariness in their manner and I knew that the police had already interrogated them.

At the end of an hour I had learned nothing. Frustration had tired me and with the sun blazing, I longed for shade and refreshment. I found a taxi in the Piazza del Popolo and directed the driver to the Via Veneto and the shade of the plane trees.

I told the driver to drop me at the junction of four streets, where there was a newspaper kiosk. Today was Tuesday and I had learned that Philip wrote his weekly column on Mondays. The English newspapers were usually on sale on the same afternoon but I hoped the tourists had left me a copy of the *Morning Observer*. I was lucky. I bought the paper, crossed the street, and found a table under a tree at Doney's.

9 ❧

WHILE I WAITED FOR MY COFFEE, I read Philip's article, grudg-ingly admiring the ease of his style, his perception and the occasional dry humor. When the coffee arrived, I read the column through again. Then annoyed by my growing absorp-tion in the man, I flung the paper down on the chair by my side and began to look around me.

Tourists; young Italians showing off; elderly Romans drink-ing their *cappuccino*, sleek cars . . . I glanced across the street.

And saw Vanessa.

She was standing quite still and seemed to be looking di-rectly at me. She wore a sky blue dress and her hair was an aureole of bright gold. I cried out her name, although the sound was drowned in the noise of the traffic and the voices around me. I flung some money on the table—probably enough for half a dozen coffees and ten tips, snatched up my handbag, and raced to the curb. As I did so, Vanessa turned and began to walk toward the Pincian Gate.

I darted into the road. Cars hooted, swerved to avoid me; heads leaned out of windows shouting at me. I was a mad-woman dancing to my own suicide. But I reached the other side of the street without being torn apart.

The deep blue of Vanessa's dress taunted me from some way

ahead. I began to run, but tourists hovering round shop windows, pausing to take photographs, and Italians stopping to chat, impeded my progress. At the moment that I had set eyes on her, I had been certain that it was Vanessa, but the thought grew that perhaps I had been too far away for certain recognition. I had to get close enough; I had to be certain that it was not just coincidence that a girl with golden hair and wearing a blue dress had seemed to be looking directly at me across the street. I kept my eyes on her as I followed, telling myself that it was unmistakably Vanessa's walk—light, swift, swinging.

The traffic curving round the wide streets at the Pincian Gate held me up again, and when I was able at last to cross toward the Borghese Gardens, she was a long way ahead. I passed the balloon man and reached the little lake. She took a path to the left. I walked under the peach trees, still a little afraid that she was just a mirage of my own wishful thinking and that if I took my eyes off her, Vanessa would vanish.

Then, with a startling unexpectedness, she turned and looked over her shoulder. As she did so, a man who had been walking between us for some time bent to light a cigarette. There was no significance in that. But I saw Vanessa put her hand to the side of her face. Then, as she dropped it, something fell from her fingers onto a seat she was passing. The object was so small that I couldn't see what it was, and her movement was so swift that she was walking on again before the man had lifted his head, blowing smoke into the still air.

Vanessa was walking more quickly and as the man between us sharpened his pace, I realized that he, too, had been following her. It seemed to me she had made certain that his attention was drawn momentarily to the lighting of the cigarette before she dropped whatever it was onto the wooden seat.

Some children ran across my path, scattering balloons, shouting taunts at each other. I extricated myself and began to run. Something glinted on the seat where Vanessa had paused. I stopped and picked it up.

It was an earring, a fire opal set with small rubies. I knew then for certain that the girl was Vanessa. She had shown me the earrings when she had last come to England. She had said, "Aunt Flavia gave them to me. But she told me not to tell *Nonna*." She had laughed. "You see Uncle Ludovico gave them to Aunt Flavia years and years ago and there would have been trouble if *Nonna* had found out. She suspected an affair between them at the time. Aunt Flavia gave them to me because she said her ears were too old and misshapen for such lovely things and she felt that it was a pity for them to be hidden away. But she told me never to let *Nonna* know I had them."

And now, one of those controversial earrings lay in the palm of my hand, the sunlight making minute tiny blazes of the opal's fire and little dancing flames of the rubies.

I looked up. I had wasted too much time. Vanessa was a long way from me and I fumed with impatience at my own smallness, which meant my steps were not so long or my stride so swift as hers. It was obvious that she didn't want me to catch up with her, but at the same time, she had sought me out and the earring was some kind of message; an assurance that she was alive, a demand for help.

The dark-haired man following her was also too far away. I saw his black shadow thrown across the grit path; I saw Vanessa turn a corner and become hidden from me by a belt of trees. The man turned also.

Two *carabinieri* crossed in front of me. I could stop them and tell them what was happening. I could say "The girl walking along the path at right angles to this is Vanessa Malimbrosa for whom the police have been searching. Go and stop her . . . I know she needs help." But I couldn't because this had been Vanessa's strict injunction: *Don't tell Nonna. Don't tell the police.*

I began to run, and my clothes stuck to my body in the heat, my face burned with the brash sunlight. It was like a game of laying a paper chase trail, using jewels. Only this was no game . . . I came to the corner where they had turned. Neither of them was in sight.

I searched the streets for so long and wandered so far that, in the end I knew I must find a taxi to sink into or I would end by lurching and stumbling out of sheer exhaustion.

Finding an empty taxi was my only real bit of luck throughout that blazing morning. And then, as I sank into the little dark corner and shut my eyes, I realized that, although I had lost sight of her, my great luck had been the proof of my own eyes—Vanessa was alive.

I felt the earring in my handbag as if it were a talisman. I wondered if Vanessa had seen me by chance on the Via Veneto, or whether she had been following my movements since I arrived in Rome and waiting for an opportunity to make herself seen by me; a moment, perhaps, when her follower's attention was distracted?

The earring must have some significance; somehow, it must be intended as a link to lead me toward Vanessa. Suddenly I knew what I must do. I leaned forward and redirected the driver to the Via Condotti. He asked which shop I wanted. I told him and he turned his head sharply and then looked at the road again just in time to save a collision with a bus. I gave a covert look at myself in my compact mirror and understood his surprise. Dishevelment and a shining face didn't go with visits to the elegant Juturna's, one of Rome's most famous jewelers. But I remembered that *Zia* Romola had once taken Vanessa and me with her when she brought a string of pearls to be restrung. All the Malimbrosas, she explained to us, went to Juturna's for their jewelry.

Inside the shop, I showed the earring to a young, aloof, but very polite assistant, and said that I believed that a pair had been made by his craftsmen many years ago. He examined the setting for a certain maker's mark and said that they had been definitely made by them. Had I lost the companion? I told him that I had found this one and that, by a coincidence, I was certain it belonged to a friend of mine with whom I had lost touch and wanted to trace. I saw that he didn't believe me. But, as he listened, he relaxed his hold on the earring in his hand and I reached out quickly and plucked it out of his palm. I had no intention of letting my only link with Vanessa go out of my possession.

He shot me a look of utter surprise and I saw him glance toward a closed door. I was afraid that there was a hidden bell under the counter and that he was going to ring for assistance. I met his long, suspicious look and said, "I believe that whoever has lost it will telephone you."

He watched me closely. "If you will let me have the earring, signorina, I will make the necessary inquiries. If there is a reward—"

"The reward," I cut in, "will be to meet this friend of mine again." I dropped the earring into my handbag and closed it with a snap. "Don't worry, signore, I have no intention of stealing it. I have a feeling that—that whoever lost it might contact you—"

"The police, signorina . . ."

"*You.*" I knew he thought me either a crook who had stolen the earring or an obstinate moron. It was impossible to explain to him that this visit to Juturna's was probably the very thing that Vanessa had intended me to do. She must have hoped that I remembered where the Malimbrosas bought their jewelery, remembered in particular this opal earring. In her desperation she was taking a chance that I would understand.

I said, "I'll call later, and see if the owner of the earring has contacted you. If not, then I'll come again tomorrow morning."

It was nearly one o'clock when I returned to the *palazzo*. Lunch was served to me alone in the long, crimson-walled dining room. I sat at one end of the black oak table, feeling as lost as a single sparrow in a strange forest. I was served by Nunzia who asked me, in a friendly way, if I would like cold *pollo arrosto* or *tonnellini*. I had never liked pasta, so chose the first. It was brought on a lovely green and white plate, the chicken thinly sliced, the salad tossed in rich dressing.

I wished I had brought a book to prop up against the Venetian glass dish, which held such a pile of fruit that I doubted if a volume of the *Encyclopaedia Britannica* would move it an inch over the polished surface of the table.

I ate in state, with only the dimmest sound of traffic seeping through the tall shuttered windows. I thought how ludicrous it was that I had brought my handbag into the dining room with me as if I were living in a hotel with a notice on the walls. 'The management will not be responsible for valuables left in visitors' rooms.' Yet Malimbrosa, for all its splendor, seemed to me to have that lonely formality.

I ate because I was hungry and the food was delicious. But I was depressed. All and everything floated across my mind. All the questions that had beset me since I had walked into the little shop on the Via Prassodi were like ghosts watching me as I sat at the beautiful, alien table.

I would have loved to have had someone else to talk to, but I was not, after all, a long-standing friend specially invited. I was an unexpected visitor, not important enough for the family to put themselves out for. Fair enough. I surveyed the fruit dish and again a thought struck me, as it had on the previous evening. Had I been invited so that they could keep an eye on me? Perhaps our suspicion was mutual.

I ate three luscious figs, folded my napkin and reached for the gold and enamel box that contained cigarettes. I seldom smoked, but I picked out a Balkan Sobranie and lit it. I had heard people say that a quiet smoke sometimes sorted out their problems. It did no such miracle for me. My thoughts continued to jockey for position in my mind and I could not find a good straight line to work on.

I stubbed the cigarette out, got up from the table and went to the window. I pushed open a shutter and took the earring from my bag and held it to the light. The chips of fire burned steadily . . . Vanessa's sign . . . the trail that was now begun —and was only for my following.

As I left the dining room, I heard Alberto close the shutters I had partly opened. Malimbrosa's rooms must be closed to the outside world; the source of life itself, the sun, must not penetrate the objects that had become museum pieces.

I hung about the empty *salone* until Alberto had left the dining room, and then I slipped into the little room behind the screen and telephoned Martin. He was my life-line, the one to whom I could talk, with whom I could plan and to whom I could express all my anxieties concerning Vanessa.

Someone in his office at the embassy tried to find him and couldn't. I thanked the girl and telephoned Martin's apartment. I let the bell ring for a full minute, telling myself that he might be at the door, putting his key in the lock, crossing the room to answer my call . . . afraid to hang up in case I missed him by a flash of a second. In the end, though, I knew I couldn't wait on the line indefinitely. I replaced the receiver and faced the fact that I was on my own.

Sometimes, when I lay down flat on my back, a tangle became unraveled, a dilemma resolved itself. In my bedroom I turned back the silken quilt and lay on the bed. One thing was clear to me. The dark man who had walked between myself and Vanessa had been following her and she knew it. For some inexplicable reason, she did not dare go near the *palazzo* or send a message to one of the family because they were all known to whoever stood between her and freedom. But I was a stranger; the man might even turn and see me, but he would not recognize me. I was merely a girl walking in the Borghese Gardens. So, she had been able to send me this obscure message which I was certain meant that a way must be found between us for contact.

The jeweler would not open his shop again until four o'clock. Between then and when he closed that evening, Vanessa might telephone him or even call and slip a message to him for me.

I watched the clock until I knew that the siesta closing-time was over. Down in the *salone* I was served tea with lemon and I sat alone again and drank it gratefully. Then I went out into the baking afternoon and took a taxi to Juturna's.

When I opened the door, the jeweler greeted me with far more warmth than before. He was obviously relieved to see me. He told me that he had a telephone call from a Signorina

Cyrena. "It is she who owns the earring you found and she has asked me to give you her address. If you would call on her this evening—*this evening,* she stresses—after half past nine, she would be very grateful to have the earring back. There will be a reward."

I pretended to be pleased about that. "The signorina is kind . . ."

"The earring is very valuable," he retorted, as if my gratitude belittled his precious commodity.

I made a note of the address he read out to me.

"Number four-three-four, Via Campisolo." He paused watching me. "You told me, signorina, that the owner of this earring was a friend of yours."

"That's right." I gave him a frank, open smile. "I have known the Signorina Maria Cyrena for many years."

He glanced at the piece of paper in his hands. I knew then that he had been testing me; that the Christian name "Maria" was written down and the fact that I had mentioned it, when he had not, convinced him that I was speaking the truth when I said I knew the owner of the opal.

A thought flashed through me that he might possibly remember the newspaper reports on Vanessa's disappearance and the name under which she might also be known. On the other hand, memory is usually short for facts read in newspapers and there was certainly no flicker of recollection on his face as he led me to the door and opened it for me.

I left Juturna's and went straight to a telephone booth at a hotel in the Via Veneto, stopped for a moment to look at my watch, and decided that Martin must be home. There was, however, no reply when I called his apartment and, with a sinking feeling that he was probably out somewhere and wouldn't be home until late that night, I telephoned the embassy without a hope of success.

To my relief Martin himself answered the call on the extension. I rushed my story out to him, scarcely pausing to take a breath.

He listened to it all without interruption. Then when I had

finished, he said. "It's the break you wanted, isn't it? But I still don't understand—"

"That makes two of us. Anyway it'll probably all become clear tonight. I've a strong feeling that I know what it's all about. I believe that someone is crazily in love with Vanessa and has more or less kidnapped her until she decides that she loves him. You know—or perhaps you don't know—Vanessa has always 'advanced and retreated' with men. Perhaps this one has decided to end the game and force her to be serious. But he can't keep her shut up all day in an apartment. So, when he lets her out he follows her. If she runs, he can catch up with her quite easily. And lover's tiffs in the street wouldn't cause too much fuss."

"Do you believe all that?"

"I don't know whether I do or not. I'm just arguing the possibilities."

"I wonder who the man was."

"I only saw the back of his head. Slim, dark-haired, wearing a blue suit. The only other thing I know about him is that he smokes."

"That's a lot of help."

"Perhaps," I said annoyed at his acid tone, "if you'd been there, you'd have run round and doubled back in your tracks and managed to come face to face with him. I don't walk—or even run—that fast. They both outdistanced me."

I heard him laugh. "*Mignon!*" he said softly.

I said, "Perhaps this man who is keeping her prisoner is out tonight and has locked her in somewhere. Even if we only talk through a closed door it'll be better than this awful doubt about her."

"She chose a rather risky way of getting a message to you, didn't she? Dropping a valuable earring onto a seat in public gardens. Anyone could have nipped in before you and picked it up."

"There was no one near us except some children who were running the other way."

"She took a chance, to, on your remembering Juturna's."

"Not really. Things from that shop are everywhere at Malimbrosa—the family jewels and a few old snuff boxes *Nonna* Allegra bought for her collection. Anyway, I'm sure Vanessa guessed that I'd recognize the earring from what she had told me about the scandal forty years ago."

"All of which may be very feasible," Martin said. "But it doesn't alter the fact that you're going to this place alone."

"What else can I do? Vanessa is obviously in some sort of trouble . . ."

"All right. All right. But ring me later when you've found out what it's all about. If you can't get me at home, I'll still be here. There's a reception for some foreign visitors and I've got to stay—not to meet the diplomatic lords, but just to be on hand for a while in case one of them wants to talk business. I'll be messenger boy to ferret some document in the filing cabinets."

"A glittering occasion."

"Not for me. I won't even be given a drink—that is, unless I'm slipped a couple on the side."

"I wish you were coming with me."

He heard the longing in my voice and said, "While you and Vanessa meet and gossip about all the things women gossip over?"

"If I *do* meet her . . ."

"You're not getting scared, are you? Oh, really Julie . . . you're the last person I'd have thought would ever be afraid of anything."

It was gently said but it roused me. "I don't scare easily. I just wish I weren't going alone."

"Well, you'll be in contact with me. I'll probably be here unless you're very late getting away from whatever pretty prison Vanessa's locked up in. Don't worry, Julie. I'll be around."

But with too much distance between us . . . I replaced the receiver and remembered my boast a few moments ago. "I don't scare easily." But I knew as I stared at the telephone that I was suddenly—and perhaps with good reason—afraid.

10 ✖

I MUST HAVE LOOKED AT MY WATCH at least twenty times until half past nine. *Nonna* Allegra, *Zia* Romola and I dined together at the long table. I thought again how ridiculously formal it was, three women eating with vast spaces of polished table between them, and attended by red-haired Nunzia. Alberto, it seemed, was only in attendance in the dining room on formal occasions.

Once during the meal *Nonna* Allegra mentioned that she was going to ask Irena to bring a fresh supply of herbs back with her from Grottochiara. She said, "And I shall suggest that she takes Pepi with her into the woods to pick wild strawberries. They will be just ripe now."

Zia Romola seized her glass, gulped down some wine, and said, "That won't please Irena."

"What do you mean?"

"Wasting her time picking wild strawberries. She has other things to occupy her at the villa."

"*What* other things?"

"You know perfectly well, Mamma, what I mean."

Allegra's voice was coldly formal. "Irena has gone to the villa to see Pepi."

"To spend her time with a *child?* Irena? Oh, Mamma, really . . ."

A knife clattered angrily on a plate. "If you have other thoughts, then you must keep them to yourself." *Nonna* Allegra rose from the table. "How you bore me sometimes, *figlia mia*," she said as she walked to the door.

Romola sat very still. She was looking down at her plate. Suddenly she lifted her eyes and looked directly at me. "Mamma has just received a shock." She spoke in a curiously complacent tone. "She does not know quite how much I know and how much I may be guessing, and when she is puzzled, she is angry." She gave an odd, dreamy smile. "It will be the first time in my life I have really bewildered her. There is something so gratifying about having power over someone who is stronger than oneself. It is like . . . like . . . ruling the waves . . ."

I waited, hoping that she would explain more clearly, but the door opened and Nunzia came in to clear the table.

Romola rose and her expression and her manner changed. She asked in a bright, social voice, "You are going out this evening, Juliet?"

"For a little while."

She nodded and smiled approvingly. "We want you to be happy during your stay here." It was said with a kind of parrotlike intonation and I knew she had other far more important thoughts on her mind.

I WAS IN MY ROOM WHEN *Zia* Romola knocked on my door, her voice calling me softly. I had an appointment to keep and there was no time for gossip and so, as she entered, I edged round her to the door.

She put out a hand and urged me gently back into the room. "I must speak to you."

"If you don't mind, some other time. I . . . I have to meet someone." I added unnecessarily, since she already knew that I was going out.

"I won't keep you." But she sat down on the edge of the bed as she spoke and I knew that she intended to take her time over what she was about to tell me. Her head was bent and she was looking down at her hands. They were so thin that the veins stood up like little mist-blue branches under her skin. She twisted her hands, looking at me apologetically. "You must forgive Mamma."

"I have nothing to forgive her for."

"It is not like her to be rude to one of the family in front of a guest. Only, you see, she is under a great strain."

She was protesting too much. "Of course I understand," I said. "Vanessa's disappearance must be causing her terrible anxiety."

"Oh, it's not that." She raised her head and stared at me. I glanced at the gilded clock.

"Why don't you sit down, *cara?*"

"I'm all right." I wandered to the window, turned my back on it and leaned against the sill, waiting.

Romola plucked at her dress. "You haven't been here long enough to realize the strains that we are under. And the biggest of all is—"

She was silent for too long. "Is—what?" I prompted her.

"Irena."

Again she paused and I had a swift memory of Leo's lovely wife as I had last seen her, standing well back in the tapestry-walled *salone* of the Villa Sapphira looking toward the window where Philip Cornel stood watching me . . . The memory was so strong, the faces of the two people so clear, that *Zia* Romola's voice startled me.

"Perhaps it is, after all, the answer to everything that has happened—Vanessa's disappearance; Philip coming here often; even Leo's absences in Milan. Perhaps all these things have to happen in order to facilitate this monstrous thing."

"What monstrous thing?"

She put her hands to her face. "I don't know what Mamma would say if she knew that I knew. But there it is, I do know. And I must talk to someone about it. I can't help it, Juliet."

Her eyes as well as her voice pleaded with me. "It's growing into an obsession. Do you understand how sometimes a secret you know and cannot tell can twist inside you until you can bear it no longer? But, no." She shook her head, clutching the collar of her dress round her thin throat. "No, you've probably never had to hold a secret you weren't supposed to know."

She looked so haunted that I softened my voice. "Couldn't you talk to *Nonna?*"

"Mamma?" she looked at me in shocked surprise. "Least of all Mamma. I have no one I can trust. But, Juliet, you are here and you are intelligent. It will not take you the three weeks of your stay to find out at least part of the truth."

She was obviously tormented by an anxiety she could not keep to herself and my determination to stay and listen was compulsive, although it might make me late for my visit to Vanessa. My intuition said "Stay."

When *Zia* Romola spoke, her voice was low and the words came slowly with pain. "Mamma tells me nothing. What I know of the things that go on here, I learn through artfulness, through deliberate listening . . ." She swallowed twice and the effort seemed to hurt her. "Mamma's office looks out onto the oleander bushes that ring the house and sometimes I go out and pretend to be looking to see if the bushes are healthy so that I can listen outside her closed shutters. The windows are usually open, except in winter, and so I hear . . ."

I waited as she broke off and thought: Her listening post— behind the oleanders!

"The morning that Mamma sent for Philip, I knew that it was important, so I went out. I heard Mamma talking, telling Philip that Pepi would grow into a nervous young man; that she was certain he would never be strong enough in body or in character to carry the weight of the Malimbrosa empire on his shoulders. She said, 'After Leo and Raphael, there must be someone strong. I could not rest if I felt that all that I had worked for was to be turned into some public company with strangers controlling it. But there is only Pepi. I eliminate Vanessa—' "

"Eliminate her?" I broke in.

"Very few women have Mamma's business ability—Vanessa certainly hasn't. And I sometimes felt that there was an active dislike between the two of them; a deep-down thing. I would not be surprised if Mamma had sometimes wished that God had not created Vanessa as her granddaughter."

"I can't believe it." I stared, frowning, at Romola, lean and erect, sitting uncomfortably on the very edge of the bed. "Vanessa is so full of vitality, she's intelligent and gay—"

"But it is a human frailty to envy those who have looks or talent—*and* a youth which we no longer have. I know I—" She shut her lips very tightly as if afraid of some impetuous confession of her own.

"And when you stood outside the window," I urged, "what was it you heard that so upset you?"

"Mamma said . . ." She shut her eyes, opened them again and turned away, speaking with her face averted in a plaintive, childlike gesture. "Mamma said, 'There will be no more children, Philip. There *can* be no more. My sons are—' And either she broke off, or she spoke so quietly that I couldn't hear her. There was a long silence and then Philip suggested adoption. Mamma would have none of that."

"Why not?" I had no idea why I suddenly felt so unreasonably apprehensive, as if what was to follow would affect me in some emotional way.

"Mamma is very proud. Leo must be seen to be manly—"

"So—?"

"There must be no adoption because it could never be kept a secret. The formalities before a judge, the medical certificates, the whole business would be too humiliating for a woman to whom the pride of a name is more important than anything else."

"And she told Philip all this? Why? Is he such a confidant of the family?" Illogical anger had crept into my voice.

Romola leaned toward me. "Don't you understand? Juliet—*don't* you?"

"No."

She took a deep breath. "Philip's wife died two years ago. We do not know the circumstances, because he never talks of her. But he is free, unattached." She waited, watched me anxiously. Her lips moved silently as if she were in secret prayer.

The silence was too long. I urged her again. "Yes, *Zia* Romola, Philip is free, so—"

"Irena wants a son as badly as Mamma wants one for Malimbrosa. Irena and Philip . . ."

I caught my breath. "Oh, a divorce from Leo, a marriage to Philip. But the name of their children would be Cornel, not Malimbrosa."

"There must be no divorce."

I refused to understand. "Then what—?"

She made a little hissing sound between her teeth. "Connivance," she whispered. "Philip has always been attracted to Irena."

"Con— Oh, *no!*"

"So now you understand."

I cried, "But it's outrageous that a mother should want another man to—" Why outrageous? It was a maneuver that had worked down the centuries. Why should I be protesting? Philip, Irena, the whole dynasty of Malimbrosa, was far outside my world. All the same, I lost my head and shouted, "Philip Cornel siring a child for the sake of some damned commercial empire? . . ."

Zia Romola recoiled from my unexpected fury. "Juliet, don't. It's horrible for me, too. You must know that what I have told you does not mean that I condone what is planned. We are torn within ourselves by jealousies and bitternesses. Oh yes, I resent Irena. I resent . . . But never mind. The point is that in times of trouble, we close our ranks, we are expected to be united."

"Then why have you told this to me . . . an outsider? . . ."

She got up from the bed and walked across the room. Then

she turned and faced me. "I am what Mamma says I am. A gossip; a woman who can keep nothing to herself. I over-spill. I cannot help it. It comes from a childhood in which I could never go to Mamma for gentleness, for sympathy. It has this effect on me now that I am no longer young. I cannot keep either joyful or tragic things to myself. But Juliet, you will promise me that you will never let anyone know that I have told you."

"You can be quite certain of that." I moved stiffly away from the window. "Did you actually hear Nonna putting this . . . this proposal to Philip?"

She nodded. "And I heard her repeat it. 'There must be a healthy heir. Philip, you understand. I want no child of inbred aristocracy. There must be good blood to strengthen the line.' And then she said again, 'You understand, don't you?'"

"And . . . and Philip said? . . ."

He said, "I understand." And then something that I could not quite hear. It sounded like, 'I care very much for Irena.' And Mamma said, 'That is what I hoped to hear you say.' I heard her so clearly that I knew she was very near the window, so I ran away."

I said, "But people don't do things like that these days." It was a hollow, foolish outburst. Romola's own helpless sincerity was proof that they did.

"The child could be a girl?"

"And after that, perhaps, a boy. Risks must be taken. And the word would spread round Rome. 'It has happened at last. Irena and Leonardo Malimbrosa have a son.' It'll no longer matter how Pepi grows up—strong or weak, they won't care now . . ." Romola was murmuring, "I shouldn't have told you . . . I should never have said—"

"You suggested just now that this—this 'arrangement' between Irena and Philip might be the answer to everything that's happened. Vanessa's disappearance . . ."

She lifted heavy eyes to my face. "Vanessa was fond of Philip. Fond? No; that is not the word. From the things she sometimes said, I believe they were in love."

"If that had been so, Philip would not have agreed to *Nonna* Allegra's monstrous suggestion."

"Men will do much for money."

I said, thinking aloud, "Philip is too proud."

"Do you know him that well, *cara?*"

I was stunned and silent.

She continued, "Philip has not been in Rome long. We know nothing about his life before he came except that his wife died very suddenly. Then, through Leo, he met us; he met Vanessa. They went out a great deal together, and I saw a change in her. She seemed so happy, so much softer. That little arrogant way of hers disappeared. And then"— she paused and shook her head—"then I overheard this terrible conversation. Soon after that Vanessa disappeared. Juliet, don't you see? Philip could have taken her to dinner on that last night and told her that he no longer cared for her. How do we know they didn't have a terrible quarrel? How can we know what happened between them that night at Frascati?"

But soon, now, I would know. I would be face to face with Vanessa . . .

Zia Romola was walking up and down the room. "I will tell you something else that makes it even more feasible. Philip told Vanessa that after his wife had died, he had drifted so far as his emotional life was concerned. Women were no longer important to him. And Vanessa said, 'But *I* will be, *Zia* Romola. You see, *I* will make myself matter to him.' And I thought, until I heard that conversation between Mamma and Philip, that she had."

A thought seeped into my amazed mind. I said, "But Vanessa is a Malimbrosa. If she and Philip had married and had children—"

"Oh, no. That would never have done. Vanessa would have had Philip's name and that wouldn't help the Malimbrosas. But if Mamma's plan succeeds, then everyone will be content—and proud." She made a sweeping gesture with her long hands; her mouth was down-drawn and bitter. "You have no idea, Juliet, how deep pride of family goes in Italy. An illusion has to be kept that all our menfolk are vital and handsome and virile. It is the men who are the wishful-thinkers; the women are the realists."

I glanced surreptitiously at my wrist watch. Romola didn't notice. Her fingers were busy pleating and repleating her skirt.

"And after the—the event," she went on, "Philip will probably leave Rome very considerably compensated for his services." Her voice became harsh. "He will find other fish, pretty ones. That's what women are to him, fish in mountain pools. He catches them and then lets them go—manhandled."

"You hate him so much . . ."

"For what he has done to Vanessa."

"But you don't know for certain that he has harmed her in any way. You only know—what you overheard between *Nonna* Allegra and Philip."

She nodded her head. "I know. I know it *in here*." She hammered at her chest and the small hollow sound she made filled me once again with a helpless compassion for her.

Outside, I could hear the burr of the elevator. *Zia* Romola heard it, too, and it seemed to jog her back into reality. She gave me a startled look. "I have a tongue, why don't I hold it? Juliet, you won't say a word—"

"You don't have to ask me again. I've told you I won't."

"I can trust you. I—can; I'm sure I can—" She was willing herself to believe it.

Outside, footsteps passed lightly along the gallery. Romola moved to the door and her fingers curled round the handle, her sharp chin stuck out over her shoulder as she watched me. "You are going out?"

It was a swift change of manner, an effort to wipe out our conversation with the normality of polite interest. "Ah, your young man, Martin—that is the name, isn't it? You must bring him to meet us one day."

I thanked her and she left me, rustling along to her own apartment. I had deceived her without lying to her. I ran to the door and flew down the stairs, my scarf trailing behind me. I hesitated for a moment, wondering if I should ask Alberto to get me a taxi. But I was afraid I would be offered one of the cars and I did not dare let Bruno drive me to the Via Campisolo.

II ✗

ON A MAP OF ROME I had already looked up the street where I would meet Vanessa and had seen that it was not far from the Piazza Barberini. In spite of the delay with Romola, I still had some time and so I walked down the Via Veneto on the side that had no café tables to impede me.

The sky was nearly dark but as I took the curve into the tall, gray lower crescent of the street I began to have a feeling of apprehension which, since I was never particularly intuitive, I put down to a mixture of excitement and nerves.

No. 434 was a huge, dilapidated building, obviously an apartment block, and I realized with a sinking heart that, in her haste and anxiety, Vanessa had forgotten to give me the number of the apartment. I went to the side of the huge staircase and looked up. How many doors must I knock on before I found her?

I went tentatively to the one to the left of the entrance and rang a bell. A big man with a belt over a bulging stomach opened the door to me. I asked for Vanessa under her assumed name. Did the Signorina Cyrena live there? No, and he had never heard of her. I described her; slim, with bright gold hair like—I sought for an expressive word—"*Miele*," I said. Honey.

The description meant nothing to him. The block was due for demolition. Already there were a great many empty apartments and he had no knowledge of a fair young woman. He was sorry. He gave me a broad smile and closed the door.

I called at the apartment on the opposite side of the hall. A girl came to the door holding a pan and a grubby cloth. No, she knew of no Signorina Cyrena. Most of the apartments were empty, anyway.

There were four more doors deep in the shadow of the building. I knocked on each of them and nobody answered.

I climbed to the first floor and worked systematically, going to the far doors first. I was becoming nervous. The emptiness of the place, my echoing footsteps, and the shadowy corners of the badly lit passages made me glance over my shoulder as if I felt someone were watching me from the black corners. As on the floor below, no one answered my knocks and rings in the apartments at the far end of the building and nobody in the front ones could help me.

It was on the next floor that I saw a door standing ajar. My dejection vanished. This was it, of course. Vanessa would be there waiting for me. I wanted to push the door wide and rush in, calling her name. Instead, I went cautiously, knocking first, peering round into a badly lighted hall and a dark room beyond.

"Vanessa?"

"*Avanti! AVANTI!*" The voice was a woman's, but I couldn't recognize it as Vanessa's, for it came from behind some closed door.

"Where are you?" I called. "Why don't you turn on the light?"

There was no answer. As I walked in, my foot touched a brown grocery bag lying on the hall floor. I glanced at it and saw the name of a place. Isolesi, and a trader's name, Guiseppe Tindari. I kicked the bag aside and walked into a dark room.

"Vanessa?" I waited. "I got your message through the jeweler. Why don't you turn on the light somewhere?" I stumbled against a table, felt the metal base of a lamp and switched it on.

The room was empty but I had seen a streak of light under a door ahead of me.

She was waiting there. But why didn't she come rushing to me in her usual impetuous way? Why wait behind a closed door? Unless she was literally a prisoner.

"Vanessa . . ."

I walked to the far door and listened. My hand was on the handle. I paused for one hair-raising moment and looked over my shoulder. Nobody lurked in the shadows of the room behind me. I opened the door to the next room and stepped forward.

It must have been I who screamed, as I flung myself backward into the room through which I had come. I lost my balance and fell with a thud onto the floor. For a moment I crouched there, twisted, not even knowing whether I had hurt myself or not; not even caring. My eyes were fixed with hot, dry horror on the emptiness beyond that door. The light I had seen was no warm lamplight from a welcoming room. It came through the window of a house opposite. And between that and where I crouched there yawned a great gap of nothingness.

I scrambled to my feet and, for a moment, stood leaning against the door looking sickly down at the jumble of stone and rubble below.

The reason no one had answered in all the back apartments on the floors below was now obvious. No one lived in them. At some time or other, the back portion of the building must either have crumbled away or been torn down because it was unsafe.

Some instinctive thought must have crossed my panicked mind that I must close the door to save someone else from falling. My hand shook as I reached it, and the bolts rattled as I drew one of them across to secure the door. The bolts rattled easily into place . . . because someone had oiled them recently . . .

I had never in my life before known real terror. I knew it in that moment. I leaped across the room toward the open door to the hall, my feet hammered on the bare floor of the passage. I took the curved staircase in a headlong rush. Sometimes my feet only just caught the edge of the steps as I trod on the narrow parts, so that I risked tripping and falling headlong to the dirty marble hall below. I made so much noise that I expected doors to open in protest or curiosity. None did.

It seemed that I took my first breath after opening that lethal door only when I reached the street again.

I was safe. I was among people. I paused at traffic lights, grateful for the enforced wait while the cars roared past. When I reached the far side of the road, I turned into the first restaurant I saw, sat at a pavement table, and ordered *caffè*.

I leaned back in my chair and tried to quiet my hammering heart and collect my thoughts.

Had I not heard the voice inviting me in, I would have believed that I had stumbled into the wrong apartment. Hunched in my corner seat, I faced the fact that I had assumed in the excitement of anticipation that the woman's voice was Vanessa's. Now I was equally certain that it was not. Vanessa wasn't evil; she wouldn't have sent me to the only room with a light under the door; wouldn't have been waiting, hidden, to watch as I was hurled to my certain death. Vanessa needed my help. So, somebody else had worked the ugly little plan to have me eliminated. Who had telephoned the jeweler? Vanessa? Or some other woman? Or even a man pitching his voice to a convincing falsetto?

I asked the young waiter who was hovering round a table where a pretty sulky girl was sitting with her parents if there was a telephone I could use. He took me into the dark little restaurant and led me to a corner kiosk.

I knew I had no right to call Martin at the embassy, but I was too shaken to care and surely a moment's conversation with me could not be held against him. After all, it was long past his accepted hours of work.

I had to wait a full minute before he came to the telephone, and without preamble I told him what had happened.

"Dear God in heaven!" His voice was explosive.

"I was nearly killed," I cried and saw, out of the corner of my eye, the head of the man behind the coffee urn lifted in alarm. I lowered my voice. "Martin, this is serious."

He said shakenly, "I'm sure it is. But I can't do anything about it—at least, not yet. Look, can you wait wherever you are for half an hour? Have another coffee, two if you must, but stay there."

"Very well. And—thank you. I'm sorry to have called you at the embassy."

"There's no harm done," he said. "I'm merely here as a favor to my boss. Where are you?"

"The first restaurant round the corner from the Piazza Colonna. I'm sitting outside."

"Right."

The line went dead and I left the telephone booth and returned to my corner table by the privet hedge.

Martin joined me after twenty minutes. I saw him park his car and cross the street. He sat down opposite me, ordered a coffee, and said, "Now, tell me again what happened."

I told him in detail from the moment when I had seen Vanessa. As my story developed I had a feeling that he thought I was exaggerating and I didn't blame him. Yet, in spite of myself, I became angry.

"All right. So you don't believe that any of this happened. But it *did*. Someone deliberately left the door ajar for me in that horrible building."

"It could have been that there was a woman in another room who was ill in bed and was expecting a neighbor to call."

"The only light came from under this particular door."

"But that doesn't mean that there were no more rooms. Some of the doors could have been very well fitting so that light didn't show."

"Why don't you come right out with it?" I demanded. "You doubt if any of it really happened, don't you? You don't believe for a moment that I saw Vanessa and that a man was following her; you don't believe everything was planned so that I should trace the earring and call at that house. You don't think that I was drawn to that particular door in order to be hurled to—to—my death." I checked my impatient fury because, by speaking aloud, I found it difficult to believe myself, but I couldn't bear the doubt in Martin's eyes.

"I'm not making any of this up," I said urgently and jabbed at the earring lying on the table between us. "This—this *is* Vanessa's."

"I can half believe that bit. I seem to remember her wearing something like it."

My despair lifted. "So you think that part of the story is true."

He said reluctantly, "If I do, then I'm choosing to believe in a most startling coincidence. You, a visitor to Rome, finding a friend's earring."

"But it happened deliberately. It wasn't coincidence." I thumped the table and the young waiter thought I was signaling him.

Martin smiled at him. "The lady needs a cognac. I'll have a green chartreuse." Then as the waiter left us, he said, "I don't know much about jewelery—I haven't yet had a chance to give a girl any." He gave me a sideways half-grin. "But I doubt very much whether only one pair of such earrings exists . . . All right, all right," he went on hastily, as I sat up ready for another hot argument, "If you say they're unique then they are."

"They are," I said belligerently. "And someone did say 'Come in' to me, and—if you choose to disbelieve me, then—"

"Julie." He leaned toward me and his hand reached out and covered mine as it lay on the table. "Julie, please, just don't fly off again. Let me be a sort of prosecuting counsel—you know, let me argue the case against what you believe."

"You're wasting time—"

"Just while you drink your brandy."

I looked down into the golden liquid and wished that Martin had let me choose my own drink. Brandy had always tasted like medicine to me. Very well, then; I lifted the glass, I'd accept it as that. Perhaps it would calm me . . .

Martin said, "You say the voice spoke in Italian. If it had been intended as a particular invitation to you, wouldn't she have spoken in English?"

"No. We're in Rome, not London."

"But if someone was expecting an English girl . . ."

"Vanessa would probably speak to me in her own language. And—and whoever called out to me knew that."

"Couldn't it have been a television or a radio program from the next apartment?"

"The voice was too clear for that and, besides, that really *would* have been a coincidence, and I don't believe in them."

"Then we'll return to the theory that someone spoke to you from another room—someone bedridden, an invalid welcoming the visitor she was waiting for."

"You can think again."

I saw the first shadow of doubt cross his face. "Well—"

"It isn't," I snapped back. "Not to me. It's *ill* . . . It's real; it happened—and I'm scared."

Martin stubbed out the cigarette he had just lit. "Then there's only one thing to do. We'll go to that apartment together and find out just who lives there and what happened. Finish that brandy."

I sipped a little, left the rest, and followed Martin to the car.

When we reached the house in the Via Campisolo we discovered from a man leaving the building that there was no longer a caretaker in charge.

"There are so few of us left here," he told us. "The place is to be demolished in a couple of months and the portiera received her notice. I think they felt that while she was making our lives so comfortable, we wouldn't leave and they wanted us out as quickly as possible. This building has collapsed at the back and the land is valuable."

I asked him if he knew the tenants.

"Most of them. There are just one or two, though, who have taken temporary apartments here because they're homeless."

A car outside sounded an impatient blast on the horn. The man grinned and explained that his wife was in a hurry; they were going to see their new grandchild.

We thanked him and went up the stairs. "There was a grocery bag on the floor," I said to Martin. "It had a place name on it. Isolesi. Where is it?"

"Somewhere in the hills, I believe. I've heard of it vaguely. A village."

"So whoever has rented this apartment here probably came from there."

"Not necessarily. But let's take one thing at a time." We had stopped outside the door. It was closed.

I stood back and whispered, "But Martin, I left it open."

"You probably rushed out and pulled it to and didn't hear it close."

"I didn't touch the door. I know I didn't. I just ran . . ." I looked at him blankly. "Now—what?"

"We knock," Martin said practically and knocked.

There was no answer, but I could have told him that.

"What do we do now?"

"We can't very well break the door down. Are you sure this was the apartment you came to? Was it perhaps on another floor?"

"This was the one."

He reached for the knocker again. I pushed his hand away and hammered more loudly. There was no sound behind the blistered, peeling door; no stir anywhere around us.

"Now what?" I asked again.

He took my arm. "Suppose we go and sit in the car and have a think?"

We went down the neglected stairs and when we were on the pavement, I turned and looked up at the building. An old woman with a shawl round her shoulders sat in a front window watching us. I hadn't noticed her when I called earlier, but she had the look of someone permanently settled there, cushions behind her back, curtains parted. I said to Martin, "Wait a minute," and dashed back into the house.

For a second time I knocked on the door to the right of the entrance and again the dark girl opened it for me. I apologized. "I have just seen a lady sitting in your window. I thought perhaps she might have noticed the fair signorina I'm looking for come in and out of here."

The girl gave me a strange look. "She sits there, but she sees nothing. She is blind."

"Oh, I'm sorry."

"You don't need to be. She has all her other faculties and is happy. She is my mother and she likes to listen to footsteps passing."

I wished I had some flowers from the over-luxuriant gardens at the Villa Sapphira to give her. Instead, I went with my empty hands back to Martin, who was waiting by his car.

"Of course," he said, "you had no luck."

I didn't tell him that the woman was blind, but I turned and smiled up at her as if she could see me.

"You know," he said as I settled in the car, "whoever said 'Come in' could have had just as bad a shock as you. She could have been expecting some man; it's my guess the apartment is a rather murky meeting place. And when the girl saw it wasn't the man she was expecting, she just kept out of the way."

"And undid the bolts of the back door? What for?"

"Perhaps she was absent-minded." He glanced at me, saw that I wasn't in the mood for absurdities, and said, "I'm sorry. You've had a shock and I'm behaving like a clown. But I still believe there's a very logical explanation starting with that girl you saw across the street. The Via Veneto is wide. I doubt if you could be absolutely certain of someone's features at that distance."

"I know it was Vanessa. And the earring proved it—"

"It proved nothing of the kind. Someone could have been impersonating her."

I swung round on him. I had underestimated Martin; he wasn't so unimaginative that he denied melodrama, after all. I said, "Impersonation, Martin, of course. It could have been . . ."

"In this fantastic world anything can happen. I've been arguing against you on principle. Now, I'll go along with you. Suppose someone worked out this elaborate plan in order to get you to that apartment in the Via Campisolo."

"But why? What have I done . . ."

"Come to that, what has Vanessa done? Of course, I don't wholeheartedly believe that someone lured you to that apartment—how would anyone know that you'd walk in without making certain that the person you'd come to see was actually there?"

"I was in a frantic hurry to find Vanessa."

He nodded his head slowly. "Which could have been their supposition, too, if they knew you and knew your impulsiveness."

"They? Who?"

"How do I know? Let's just say we haven't a clue what the meaning of it all is." He started the car and edged it forward. "Let's decide that in your haste, you walked into the wrong apartment."

But I knew as surely as I knew anything in my life that I hadn't and that he no longer thought so, either. The door was opened for me; whoever was in hiding and urged me in knew who I was; the bolts of the door to the vanished room had been pulled back for me . . .

Sitting there in the car with Martin, my eyes watching without seeing, the crowds and the lights, I was able to grasp the full, terrible implication of the past hour.

I heard Martin say, "Now we'll go somewhere and be gay. We might even dance. That'll banish the ghouls."

I answered in a small voice, "I want to go home." It was odd that I should be calling Malimbrosa 'home,' but this was not the occasion for meticulousness. I was grateful to him for not arguing with me. He must, at last, have understood some of the shock I had felt.

When we arrived at the *palazzo*, he came to the gates with me and gave me a light kiss. "It's no use my suggesting that you forget what's happened. But you work it out your way; I'll work it out mine. Perhaps, between us, we'll find the answer." Still holding my arms, he put me a little away from him. The street lamp under which we stood must have made me look like something between a scared rabbit and a be-numbed adolescent, for he said more gently, "I'll help all I can, Julie. We'll find Vanessa."

I pulled at the bell at the side of the gates. "Thank you for coming with me tonight."

"I didn't do much good, did I?"

"You're my ally." I said gratefully. The gates opened and I went through.

"Julie—"

I turned. He beckoned to me through the curlicues of ironwork. "I really do mean that we'll work this puzzle out together. I'm a bit tied up at the moment—there's a lot doing at the embassy. But I'll call you."

Alberto opened the door to me, closed it, and immediately disappeared. I was not one of the family, I was not even an important guest, therefore this young, casual visitor must understand that he had no intention of pandering to her caprices. I had none. All I wanted was my room and quiet.

When I was in the car, I had wanted only to get back to the *palazzo*. Now that I was here, the huge, empty rotunda gave me none of the sense of security that I needed. I leaned against one of the parma violet pillars and felt the cool marble against the back of my head. Only a few hours ago I had nearly died . . . I, Juliet Holdroyd, secretary to a Member of Parliament, young, strong and with no known enemies, had been urged to the threshold of death. Suppose I wrote it all in letters to friends in London? They would say, "Rome has done some-thing to Julie. It's all those stories of old violence the tourist guides have been telling her. Caligula and Nero and those racketing Caesars. She now thinks she's part of some plot.

She'll have to snap back to sanity when she returns to London." *If she gets back . . .*

The rooms opening out of the rotunda were silent and deserted and I was so alerted to danger that the light footfall behind me made me whip round like a startled cat. Irena was coming toward me from the passage that led to the servants' quarters.

"Ah, Juliet. I have just come from Grottochiara. Pepi was delighted that you went to see him. He gets so lonely up at the villa with only Gisela for company."

"I can well believe it. Why doesn't *Nonna* let him have some friends to stay?"

"He is by nature a rather solitary little boy. He doesn't make friends easily."

"If only he could be given the chance, he might learn," I murmured.

"It's a pity that he is an only child."

A great pity, I thought, and marveled at her clear, water-green eyes and the perfect arches of her brows. There were questions I longed to ask her. *Do you know whether it was Vanessa or someone impersonating her whom I followed in the Borghese Gardens? How much are you involved? And am I here to be watched because I'm too eager to know what has happened to her?* So, as I studied her face and listened, as though I were some third person, to our light, inconsequential conversation, I wanted to demand: Is Vanessa dead?

> *You have the face that suits a woman*
> *For her soul's screen—*
> *The sort of beauty that's called human*
> *In hell, Faustine.*

Was she evil? As we talked, I found nothing that betrayed an inner wickedness.

"I'm sorry," I said quickly, aware that she had been speaking and had broken off, looking at me in surprise, "You . . . you were saying—?"

She nodded, accepting the vagueness I must have shown. "I was only asking you if you had enjoyed your evening in the hills last night."

I said politely, "It is very beautiful up there."

We stood awkwardly, uneasy with one another, neither of us knowing how to continue the conversation. Then Irena glanced at a green malachite clock on a table. "I must go," she said. "I have to meet friends."

Friends, or Philip Cornel?

She said "goodnight" softly and smiled. *The smile, her soul's screen* . . . In beauty and in mystery she could so easily have been the inspiration for Swinburne's poem; she could be "Faustine" . . .

I went slowly up the staircase, trailing my hand along the balustrade, the silence around me vibrating with a kind of watchfulness that made me wonder if my suspicion that my enemy could be at Malimbrosa was in fact true. I reached my room, closed the door and leaned against it. The lights had been switched on for me; my bed turned down, my yellow nightdress laid out carefully with a little flip at the waist so that it looked as if it were already being worn by a flattened cardboard figure. I pulled off my clothes, tossing them onto a damask-covered chair. Just before I got into bed I went to the mirror. My face had lost its vitality; my eyes were tired. "Tread softly, Julie," I said to my reflection.

12 ❧

A WORD OR, MORE ACCURATELY, a name hovered in my mind.
Isolesi. Isolesi . . . Last night I had scarcely remembered it.
This morning it droned, small and insistent as a gnat. But a
grocery bag on an apartment floor was so unimportant that I
gave it a mental brush-off.

I sat instead, eating honey from Grottochiara, staring out of
the window onto the morning freshness of the Borghese Gardens and wondering whether Vanessa would try again to
contact me. Or whether whoever had intervened yesterday
and had led me to the partly shattered building in the Via
Campisolo would now guard her more carefully. And then I
came back again to the bag with the name Isolesi on it.

Where exactly was Isolesi and had the bag been blown there
by the draft of air from the open door? Or had it been
intended that I should see it? The questions were like the
threads of some tapestry of which the pattern was only beginning to evolve. I finished breakfast, bathed and dressed and
went downstairs.

Zia Romola was speaking on the telephone in the little room
behind the lacquer screen. I waited for her to finish and when I
heard the click of the receiver, I walked into the room, greeted
her, and asked her where Isolesi was.

She said in surprise, "It's a small village up in the Alban hills, a few miles from Grottochiara. Why?"

"I rather want to go there."

"But, Juliet, it's a very dull village, there's nothing even particularly beautiful about it. Now, if you want an interesting morning, why don't you go to Hadrian's Villa?"

I had the opal earring in my handbag. I could produce it and say, "Because of this," and go into a long explanation. But I had instructions to obey. Instead, I asked, "Do you know where I could hire a car?"

"You don't need to do that while you're here. We have three, although only Bruno is allowed to drive the Lancia and Irena has Leo's Ferrari. There is the small Dauphine. Would you like it this morning? You're very welcome to use it if, that is, you have your Continental driving permit."

"Yes, I've got that. Vanessa suggested that I bring it."

"So, *cara*, take the Dauphine. Bruno would have brought it round for you only he has already left with Mamma to visit our lawyers. I will get the key to the garage." She left me and came back with three keys on a ring. "You know, of course, where the garage is."

I knew. It was just outside the walls of Malimbrosa. "It's very kind—"

"We all want you to be happy while you are with us."

All of you? I wondered. But I smiled at her over my shoulder, pulled open the double doors before Alberto could appear, and stepped out into the sunlight.

The Dauphine was a woman's car, pale blue all over, as sleek as an elegant Parisian. I drove it out of the garage, locked the doors behind me, and returned the keys to Alberto.

I called first at Juturna's to ask if there had been another message for me. I received a new suspicious glance. No, but surely I had called last night at the address he had given me? I had, and found no one there.

He shook his head, puzzled.

I said, "I'll call again in a few days, just in case there was some mistake in the address."

He said with hurt dignity, "We do not make that kind of mistake here, signorina."

I escaped before he could demand the earring.

If Isolesi were near the Villa Sapphira, I had to make for Nemi. Fourteen miles out of Rome I found myself at Frascati. I slowed down, looking about me with interest at the beige-colored town and wondering where Vanessa and Philip had dined on that last night. I would have stopped and wandered a little, but the need to find Isolesi—the village *Zia* Romola had called unattractive—and one grocer whose name was Giuseppe Tindari, was too important.

I drove through Castel Gandolfo, past the Pope's Summer Palace, awed by its hugeness for one lonely man. At Genzano I saw an old woman sitting under a tree selling strawberries. I stopped and asked her the way to Isolesi. She pointed and gesticulated. "Nemi. Past Nemi and then left." She held out a tray of little baskets of strawberries. I bought one, thanked her for her help, and got back into the car. Presently I saw the gloomy hollow where the dark blue waters of Nemi lay still. I gave a random thought to what it must have looked like at the time when the ancient rites were performed there. Then I was past Nemi and climbing into the hot clear air of the Alban hills.

After another quarter of an hour of asking the way and twisting and turning, I found Isolesi perched precariously on the mountain side. It had a little tattered square and a fountain whose central figure was so chipped and eroded that I could not tell if the sparkling water spouted from a merman or a centaur's mouth.

The shop I was looking for sold everything from sausages to rice and matches. Giuseppe Tindari, who wore a striped apron, gave me a beaming smile that showed beautiful teeth. Yes, he always stamped his name on the bags his customers used. Special customers, he added, not the villagers. They carried their groceries back in their baskets or their arms. But the people from the villas, or the tourists—oh yes, he eyed me up and down hopefully, the tourists came a lot to his shop.

Pappardelle Isolesi was a local pasta; "Bella. Bella . . . "He kissed his fingers. And the Signora Batista's strawberry preserve. He paid another kissing homage to that, too. I said politely that I was sure everything he sold was marvelous but that I hadn't come to buy. What I wanted to ask him was—did he know the Signorina Maria Cyrena?

I watched him as I spoke her name and his expression was so blank that I was quite certain he spoke the truth when he said that he had never heard of her.

I described her. "She may have taken a villa in these parts recently."

He sucked the knuckle of his third finger, thinking . . . No. No, he knew of no strangers at Isolesi. The villas were owned mostly by Roman families who came out with their children in the summer months. There was no one except . . .

"Except?"

"The young couple who have recently taken the villa in the Dead Land. But they are only here on occasional weekends. Their name, I think, is Bitonto."

The name was unimportant; anyone could open a telephone directory and pick one out with a pin.

"What is the signora like?"

"Oh." He thought about it. "Very dark, like a Sicilian. I have only seen her once. She was sitting in the car while her husband came in for *pappardelle*." He looked hopefully at my handbag.

I kept it firmly closed. The girl was obviously not Vanessa. At the same time, there must be some connection between the apartment on the Via Campisolo and this little town, even perhaps with this strange new couple who had rented the villa in what he had called the Dead Land. I asked the way.

"But signorina, why do you want to go there? I am sure no friend of yours would be living in such a place."

"All the same, I'm very anxious to find the Signorina Cyrena. It is just possible that the people at this villa you might mention might know her."

"It is so desolate there."

"Some people like lonely places."

"This is not just lonely," he said with distaste. "It is as we call it, the Dead Land. A year ago there was a great forest fire. It devastated a large area and the elderly couple who owned the Villa Artemis fled. The house was of stone and was only scarred and not greatly damaged. But they never came back. Then, a little while ago, this young couple rented it. I think they must be newly married for they are seldom seen in the town, they do not yet need the company of others." He gave me a sentimental smile.

"What is the man like?"

He shrugged. "Ordinary, a little good looking, but not like any film star you would see out in Cinecittà, and dark."

Like the man who had walked between Vanessa and me through the Borghese Gardens . . . like a thousand, ten thousand other men in Rome . . .

"How do I get to this place?"

He said, looking through the window of the shop, "It will be a tough drive for your pretty car, signorina. The track is stony and the young couple's car is the only one that has used it for so long. Their car is heavy. *Phew!*" He spread his arms. "Like a tank. Yours is so delicate."

"It'll survive," I said and went to the counter and picked up a slab of Swiss chocolate and got out my purse to pay for it.

He took the money, showed me a pot of Signora Batista's strawberry preserve and, weak-willed, I bought some to give to Martin.

He came to the door with me and looked up at the ultramarine sky. "It is such a beautiful day, signorina, for a drive to such an ugly place. There is no green there, just brown trunks of burned-out trees and the earth is sour. It will be a long time before the sweetness comes back to the soil. They put the fire out, you see, with chemicals."

He kept two customers waiting while he watched me drive off, nodding and smiling as I waved back at him.

I was, of course, on a wild goose chase. Yet I kept doggedly on, following his instructions, turning left, farther into the hills, and pausing to ask of an old man scything a grass hedge if he knew the Villa Artemis.

He pointed to a narrow track. "But go carefully, signorina, the way is rough."

I thanked him and saw his eyes, narrowed with curiosity, watching me as I turned down the heavily wooded track.

I must have driven for about a mile, bumping and rocking over the broken road, between thick green woods, when I came upon a different world. It happened with such an uncanny suddenness that I stopped the car and stared. Before me was a burned-out world. Great charred trees stood in grotesque shapes bearing no sign of life in them; torn and discoloured fern tangled the banks. I put the car in low gear and drove on between the brown trees. Above me the stricken branches were flung out to the burning sun. The forest seemed to stretch for miles until it became a café-au-lait mist in the distance.

The track grew worse and I nursed the car as carefully as I could over the humps and hollows. The tenants of the Villa Artemis certainly did not encourage visitors.

The track turned a sharp angle and in a clearing ahead of me I saw a house of dull gray stone stained here and there with great rust-colored patches. There was a room on either side of the front door and three shuttered windows above. It looked as derelict as the land around it. Even the garden was arid, although here and there were little hopeful patches of green as if someone had thrown bowls of water over those places and an occasional dry seed had thrived again.

There was a very short drive, little more than a path, and on either side of it a thick stone gate post. I got out of the car and read the letters carved into the pillars. On one was "Villa," on the other "Artemis." There was now no gate between them.

I walked haltingly up the drive. Ferns, stiff and brown with death, tore at my legs; bushes that I could no longer recognize reached out claw-like branches and caught my arms. I walked toward the square, stained house, planning how, if anyone happened to be there, I would explain my call. I might say, "I am looking for a friend of mine—Signorina Maria Cyrena. I have a feeling that she may be staying in these parts. Do you happen to know her?"

It was a harmless enough question, and whatever answer I got I would probably act with an innocence bordering on naiveté because this was too lonely a place for bravado. If whoever opened the door admitted to knowing Vanessa, I would probably merely thank them and ask that a message be given her. I would say, "Tell her that I'm staying at the Palazzo Malimbrosa." Unless Vanessa herself came to the door, I wouldn't take a single step over the threshold—at least not alone. I needed Martin with me for that. But the pretty French Dauphine was my escape route. I glanced quickly back at it. The door swung invitingly open.

It was too late to regret the impulse that had led me to the Dead Land. I was only too glad that, if there were someone there, my question concerning Vanessa would not seem foolish. I could just thank whoever came to the door, and escape. After all, a grocery bag on a floor was a pretty slender link joining this particular villa with the wrecked apartment in the Via Campisolo. Or was it? *Nothing that has yet happened to you since you arrived in Rome has been casual . . .*

The last remnant of my courage left me and my limbs were curiously atrophied. I could neither lift my hand to knock on the door or find the power in my legs to make a dash for the Dauphine.

Oh, for heaven's sake, either knock or go. The rationality of my Scottish ancestors gave me the needed impetus. I raised my hand and hammered on the tarnished lion's head door knocker.

As I waited, the utter stillness hung heavily round me. I listened for footsteps behind the closed door, half turning, wondering if whoever lived here was perhaps out in the woods. But there was no rustle of dead fern fronds, no step on the path, no bird singing. I felt that even the ghosts had fled.

I left the door and went round the house. Here I saw more little clusters of green where life was fighting the sour earth for survival. All the windows were shuttered and every one had gaping holes. Quite suddenly there was a flurry of wings above me and a blackbird flew off. I watched it, thinking that it was like the dove set free from the Ark, the only living survivor in this dead world. It circled round me as if trying to scare me off, its wings like fans of black pearl in the sunlight. I looked down and saw fresh white bread crumbs on the window ledge. So someone had been here today, could be still here. At that moment I thought I heard a faint sound from the room behind the shutters, a scraping noise as if a chair had been pushed back. Someone *was* there; a woman, perhaps, nervous from being alone in so isolated a place. As the door of the house was enclosed in a small stone portico, she might not have seen who was knocking and might be afraid of some strange man—a tramp, perhaps. Did they *have* tramps in Italy?

Caution was not natural to me, but I was behaving with extreme caution, flattening myself against the wall (like someone in a television thriller).

Then, out of the endless silence came another sound. It was infinitesimal, little less than a disturbance of air somewhere near the half-closed shutters by my side.

My reflexes were swift. I ducked just one second before the far shutter swung open and something large and heavy hurtled out and crashed against the wall exactly where I had been standing. I didn't wait to see what had been flung with that fierce, sideways aim at my head. I tore back along the path, hurled myself at the car, and slammed the door.

I started the engine and turned the wheel, my heart hammering above the purring motor, my hands shaking. I drove over the rough ground, trying to find a clearing in which to turn, and could not. Twice I hit a high bank of tangled fern, twice the car rocked as though in protest and righted itself, and I realized that the only place where I could turn was between the two stone posts of the villa. I backed between them, constantly looking into the rear mirror. No one came out after me. For the second time I had been in danger from an attacker I had never seen.

I drove away over the track, not at all certain that somewhere down this dead brown road, there wasn't a path just wide enough for a car—a short cut along which my attacker could drive, to appear suddenly in front of me to stop my escape. Whoever lived in that villa knew the forest; I did not.

I seemed to have even greater difficulty steering the Dauphine than I had when I came up the track; the wheel jerked and resisted my guiding hands with an almost frightening will of its own to defy me. Because of this resistance, I drove at a snail's pace, my thoughts more concerned with the attempt, if not to kill me, then at least to knock me out.

The salient question was: Why had I been attacked? Because someone in the Villa Artemis was afraid of strangers? Or because I had reacted to the paper bag with the name Isolesi on it as it had been intended that I should?

With a growing unease I realized that even the possibility that I might somehow escape from the fall planned for me in that horrible apartment had been considered. They—whoever "they" were—had agile minds. The nets were being tossed for me in all directions.

The odd behavior of the Dauphine needed all my attention. I stopped asking questions I could not answer and steered a straight course over a vicious hump. The wheel jerked out of my hands and we hit a bank of ferns; I swung onto the track again and the car shot toward a huge tree trunk. It was fortunate that my foot was barely touching the accelerator, for even at my snail's pace the right fender of the car struck the tree and I was jerked forward against the steering wheel.

I turned off the engine, sat back and faced the fact that the very first time I had taken a Malimbrosa car out I had damaged the steering by driving along a track I had been warned was bad for a car.

I got out and examined the fender. Two small scratches marred the smooth gentian blue but I knew that it wasn't safe to take the car back over the lane. I climbed into the driving seat, reversed as best I could, and then drove on to a small clear patch of brown earth. Even that was a test of wills between the demon wheel and my determined hands, but I managed to get off the track. Then I got out, locked the doors, and faced a long and treacherous walk. I tried to recall how far I had driven out of Isolesi and guessed that I was about two miles from the village. Above me the sun seemed to be a blinding white light and my open sandals were no protection against the petrified roots of the trees, the stones and hollows.

All that was bad enough. What was worse was the fear that someone was watching me, had perhaps seen me park the car, and would stalk me through the thick cluster of dead trees.

I kept stopping, looking round and listening. If anyone followed me, he walked lightly as a ghost over the tangle of dry bracken. I quickened my step. A mile of track under the unrelenting sun, then another mile to Isolesi, would probably take me nearly an hour at this pace. My fear was like a fever, adding to the heat the sun already poured over me; my clothes stuck to my body and my hands were clammy. Even so, I began to run. Immediately my toe became caught in a twisted root of ivy. I stumbled and grabbed at a tree trunk to save myself from falling. Dry bark came away in my hand; I scattered it and leaned for a moment against the dead oak. I took a few deep breaths and noticed the air hadn't the pure quality of hill places; it was heavy and in it I imagined I could smell the ghost ashes of a million fire-consumed leaves.

13 ✣

I HAD ONLY TAKEN A FEW MORE STEPS when I heard a sound over my own footsteps. It was so faint that I thought it was a car passing on the distant road from Nemi, but as it grew louder I knew that it was approaching me. Someone was driving down the track.

Relief bounded up in me, I didn't care who was driving; he could be a thief, a rogue, a vagabond. I was reckless with joy that I could get a lift out of the Dead Land. In my brown linen dress I could be taken for part of the sepia landscape unless I made myself conspicuous. I stumbled into the middle of the track. It occurred to me a moment too late that if the car were coming this way, it could only be going to the Villa Artemis and that my need for help could be an impulse I would quickly regret. A walk to the village might be uncomfortable, but at least I would get there in the end. For all the macabre brown magic of the wood, I doubted if it housed dragons or demons or even if the mad ghost of Caligula walked up from his dark lake . . . I made a sudden dart into the trees, but I was too late. The car's tires hissed to a stop on the track, a door opened, and a man leaned out.

"Oh no . . ." It was an involuntary cry inside myself and

yet, there it was, bursting out into the forest, splitting my ears. I backed to a tree and clung to it, watching as the man opened the door.

"What in the name of Julius Caesar are you doing in this place?" demanded Philip Cornel.

I took a gulp of hot air. "The same question could apply to you. What are *you* doing here?"

"Following you." His voice was coolly deliberate; his eyes without kindness.

"Why?"

"Because sooner or later on your drive out here, you'd have had an accident and I was sent to pick up the pieces and—"

"Little mangled pieces of me? But I don't understand."

"You never will if you interrupt." He looked about him in amazement. "What a place you chose for your morning's amusement."

"Why did you come after me?"

"Because the steering of the Dauphine is slightly faulty. Bruno had taken the signora to a meeting at the Ostia factory, but she had forgotten some papers and sent him back for them. It was then that he learned that you had been lent the car. He had no time to come and find you, and as Romola was in a state of semi-hysteria, I said I'd come out after you."

"She telephoned you?"

"No, I had just arrived at the *palazzo* to deliver some English technical magazines Leo wanted."

"How did you know where I was?"

"Romola told me you were planning to drive to Isolesi. I just followed. I didn't come across you stretched out in the road, so I gathered that you had already been picked up and were being put together again in a hospital and the Dauphine towed away, or else the gods had favored you and you had reached Isolesi. When I got there, I found an old man scything a grass hedge. He told me you had asked the way to what the locals call the Dead Land. And so you made it! Congratulations. What are you intending to do? Picnic among the tree stumps?"

"I came because I had an idea that I might find Vanessa here."

The pause was just too long; his eyes were too wary. He asked, "And why?"

"It's quite a story."

"You'd better tell me. But not here. Let's sit in the car and talk."

I turned too quickly and caught my foot in a tangle of fern. He reached out and took my hand. I tried to snatch it away, but he held onto my fingers. "Have you got the car key?"

"Yes."

"Let me have it and I'll try and do a rather neater job of parking."

I stood a safe distance and watched him try to maneuver the car toward a clearer space off the track. The pretty blue nose went straight for another tree. Philip stopped, turned off the engine, and locked the door. "Saints have mercy, how did you get this far?"

"I must have been lucky," I said with exaggerated modesty. "Or the car's steering wasn't that bad until I drove it along here—and that put the finishing touches to the damage."

We'll have to drive until we find a garage to tow it away." He held the door of his car open for me. "Come on. Get in."

I said, "There's a villa at the end of the track. Perhaps they have a telephone."

"In this jungle?" He looked round him. "If there ever had been, the fire that raged here would have destroyed wires and posts." He started his car, backed it expertly, and managed to turn on the narrow track in three attempts. "Now what's this about coming here to find Vanessa?"

"Just a hunch I had."

"For a stranger to Rome, you go a long way to carry out your hunches. What—?"

"It doesn't matter."

"What? he said again, more firmly.

I thought quickly. How involved was he? He could know

everything that happened last night at the house in the Via Campisolo. He could even know about the grocery bag that had led me here. Why would he take the trouble to drive all this way unless he had a personal interest in what was happening to me? Another possible answer flashed across my mind. Of course, if the Malimbrosas had asked him to find me, he would come. He would dance to their tune until payment was made . . . I looked at him and hated him. It would be wise to tell him nothing more, but I had barely come to that conclusion when something reckless and intensely curious took over. On the other hand, it would be interesting to watch his reaction to what I might say.

"The house up there is called the Villa Artemis. I went there and knocked but there was no answer. Then I went round the house and I thought I heard a sound behind a shuttered window. I stopped. And that's when it happened."

"What happened?" He was nursing his long, beautiful Lancia over the ruts and hollows.

"Someone pushed open the far shutter and threw something at me. I ducked just in time. It was some very heavy object because I heard it thud against the wll and then fall to the ground."

"That'll teach you to go trying to find a way into an isolated house in a God-forsaken spot."

"I wasn't. I just wanted to know who lived there."

"Don't tell me you thought Vanessa could be hiding in this place."

"She could be."

At a particularly vicious part of the track, we bumped so much that I clung to the door handle so that I wouldn't be thrown against him; I was as nervous of contact with him as a gazelle scenting a tiger. And at any other time the thought of likening myself to a gazelle would have seemed irrepressibly funny. At that moment nothing was funny.

Philip stopped the car with an unexpected jerk, sat back and offered me a cigarette. I refused and he lit one for himself.

"Can't you put a check on this overdeveloped curiosity of yours?"

I said angrily, "It isn't that. You don't understand, do you? Vanessa is in trouble."

"And what do you think you can do about it?"

"Help, of course."

"Instead of which, you nearly get concussed—"

"Killed," I murmured, shuddering at the remembered force of that vicious object.

"Let's be practical. You came to Isolesi believing, for some reason you haven't explained to me, that Vanessa is hiding here. You walked round this villa and whoever was there, probably a woman, was afraid of strangers. So when she heard you at the window she naturally hit out at you."

It was too feasible; too glib.

"She—or he—nearly killed me. You call that a natural reaction?"

"I have a more rational mind. You were trespassing and she was alone and lost her head."

I withheld from Philip the fact that the same reason had occurred to me. I sat quite still, not looking at him, letting the difficult silence enclose us. I was half-ready to dismiss the significance of the grocery bag on the floor of the apartment in the Via Campioslo. Perhaps the draft had just blown it there and I was seeing too much significance in such a small thing. Once the imagination starts revolving, logic has to apply the brakes. I switched my mind to another question: How great had been the complications that had arisen when Philip had forced a break between himself and Vanessa in order to carry out Allegra's dynastic dream? What had been said at that last dinner at Frascati before Vanessa had disappeared?

I was afraid of Philip; afraid of the stillness that enclosed us. Yet, with a sense of incredulousness, I felt a strange terrifying excitement creep over me. I locked my hands in my lap and turning my face away from him, said "Shall we get on? We must find a garage."

He made no move to start the car, and asked, "What led you to believe that you would find Vanessa up here?"

"We can stay here all day, and I won't tell you." *Because I'm too afraid of you to confide in you, and, whatever you may say, I don't believe you came all this way just to help me* . . .

I wasn't prepared for his sudden movement. He seized my shoulders, turned me round to face him, and said, his eyes hard, his mouth tight with anger, "You utter little fool. Why don't you stop trying to probe into what doesn't concern you? I've warned you once. Now I warn you again. Go and look at the Colosseum, Tivoli, Hadrian's Villa—whatever you damned well like. But forget Vanessa. Understand?"

He let me go and I fell back into my seat. His vehemence pointed to a personal involvement. Yet it was not that which shook me as he restarted the car and drove down the track under the archway of dead branches. I was trembling for a reason that shattered and dismayed me.

Two years ago, after the second broken love affair, I had said "Never again." Yet, my guards had left their posts and, without warning and without armor, I was exposed again. I sat rigid in my seat, watched the sepia world ahead of me, and told myself that if I kept a cool head I could fight this strangulating emotion. I was suffering only the first murmurings of infatuation, that mirage that spells out the word "love" on the horizon and which, when reached, turns out to be the avenger of truth. If I were sane, and I believed that I was, I could not love a man I both mistrusted and despised.

Breaking the silence would help. I said, "Of course you know that Vanessa took the shop under the name Maria Cyrena?"

"Yes."

"And it was you who arranged for all her furniture to be moved to the Villa Sapphira?"

"Yes."

It was like tossing a ball to someone who refused to throw it back. I gave up and sat staring ahead of me, aware that Philip's hands were light and gentle on the wheel, treating the Lancia with a tenderness he certainly did not feel for me, nursing it over the cruel snares of the track.

In some obtuse way I resented that gentleness. I didn't want to think good of him. I wanted to hold on hard to hating him.

We found a garage in Isolesi, reported breakdown and arranged for the Dauphine to be collected. Then we drove on, past Nemi, past Castel Gandolfo, in the blazing morning.

I wondered what Philip would say if I showed him Vanessa's earring and told him how I had come by it. But I had a feeling that the less I told him, the less danger I would be in. Besides, I had to be guided all the time by Vanessa's request for secrecy. Martin and I were the ones she trusted. Not Allegra Malimbrosa, not Romola, not Philip—certainly not Philip.

There are moments in life that, brief though they might be, are never forgotten. They are our personal highlights, like the conquest of Anthony by Cleopatra; the meeting of Heloise and Abelard; like a woman postmistress shaking hands with a queen; a child being given an award for bravery for saving the life of some beloved pet . . . Hunched in the car, I hoped desperately that the moment when Philip had seized me by the shoulders and turned me round to face him, and so metaphorically touched me with an enchanter's wand, would not be such a moment for me. I wanted to be able to forget him as easily as I had forgotten the ticket I gave up at Rome airport. I didn't want to have to hold on even to hatred for him.

He said, turning off the main road, "It is getting late and I'm hungry. We're going to lunch here."

I asked faintly, "Is this Frascati?"

"Yes."

"Where you and Vanessa—"

"Dined before she drove off into the blue—or rather, the black. It was a very dark night." We seemed to go in a circle round the little twisted streets, passing a baroque cathedral and a line of caves cut into the rocks.

"Wine caves," he said briefly. "White Frascati wine." He slowed down outside a terrace restaurant, parked the car in a central square, and urged me out.

The restaurant had a low, russet roof and a fringe of palm trees. We walked into an airy room with wide floor-to-ceiling windows opening onto a terrace where tables were set.

"Go and find a place," he said. "I want to ring the signora. She must be back at the *palazzo* by now and will have been told about the car. I'd better tell her I've found you and also where I've left the Dauphine."

I found a place at the terrace edge. Vines climbed the pillars, casting a deep shade over the tables. I leaned over the low wall and looked out across the Campagna toward Rome. It hovered in the heat haze like the faded tapestry of some medieval city, towers and domes cutting the gilded skyline.

I didn't want to lunch with Philip; I wanted to get back to the isolation of Vanessa's lovely blue room; to lie on the bed and argue myself clear of emotional involvement. I had a presentiment that this was only the beginning of a private war I was going to have to fight within myself and I wanted to get it over, to win through and then forget it, for I needed all my energies for my search for Vanessa. Although I knew, as I stood there with the sun on my face, that my fight against whatever magnetism Philip had for women would be a hard one, I didn't doubt for one instant that I would win. All I had to do was to keep my head; to fight emotion with logic . . .

"Signorina?"

I looked round. A young waiter had brought me a drink. He set it on the table where I had laid my handbag and smiled at me. I thanked him, sat down at the table, and opened my handbag and looked at myself in the mirror of my compact. My face shone, my hair was tangled. I looked like nothing that would give a man pleasure to sit opposite. I picked up my drink and thought resentfully how typical of Philip to have ordered me what he chose for me instead of asking first what I would like. Why a negroni of all things? Because, on my first evening at the *palazzo*, this was the drink I had asked for. And

Philip had remembered. He might have remembered, too, I thought crossly, that in the middle of the day many people liked a less potent drink.

I took two sips, then I got up and asked where I could wash. I spent a long time looking at myself in the cracked mirror over the basin where only the cold water tap worked. I made up my face, did my hair, and put on a pair of sunglasses. I had strong eyes and scarcely needed them, except for moments such as those to come when I wanted to use them for deception, as a shield against Philip's watchfulness. Eyes can't lie, and I had no intention of letting that perceptive man see what he had done to me. I stared at my reflection and play-acted, grinning at myself. "Yes, thank you, dear. I had a most wonderful time. I was nearly hit over the head with a huge dark object that might have been the Venus de Milo for all I know. And then, dear, I had lunch with my enemy . . ."

I turned and walked out of the dark little washroom.

"And what," Philip asked, rising from the table, "are you laughing at?"

"A silly thought."

"Can it be shared?"

"No." (And it isn't really funny at all . . .) "This is a charming place," I said, and sat down.

"I thought you'd like it."

"Aren't I keeping you from your work?"

He lifted his drink. "Oh, I have to eat, too, you know. And hours, as such, mean nothing to me except when I have to rush a story through to London. Otherwise, I can work at any time of the day or night."

We were making conversation and it was less disturbing than our silence in the car.

"You enjoy being a correspondent?"

He gave me an exasperated smile. "Now would I be one if I didn't enjoy it?"

"There are people who hate their jobs."

"Then they should change them," he said shortly, and took one of the menus the waiter held out to us.

I said, "You chose my drink, now will you please choose what I shall eat?"

He did so without argument. "You'll like the chicken here. It's cooked in white wine and milk, and we'll have *paté di fegato.* You like paté?"

I said meekly that I loved it.

"Then *pollo alla ghiottona.* And for the finale, strawberries."

"Oh heavens, I bought some and left them in the car."

He laughed. "The mechanics at the garage will enjoy them."

Over lunch I talked a great deal. It was easy. He asked me questions and I answered them. I wanted to keep the conversation flowing because it was the only way to achieve any ease between us. Talking relaxed tension.

"Are you like your parents?"

"They were both fair," I said. "Father used to call me changeling child. He used to look through the personal columns of the newspaper pretending to see if anyone had lost a little dark-haired girl. I remember once I cried and said I didn't want to be sent back to where I might belong. And he said he'd build a tower round me so that nobody would ever take me away. He said, 'Of course, you could always let down your hair for someone to climb up and help you to escape if you wanted to.'" I was chattering like a schoolgirl and *gaucherie* didn't suit me.

"You have very beautiful hair," Philip said.

We talked through the paté and the chicken. Then, quite involuntarily as we ate strawberries, I mentioned Vanessa's name in connection with a play we had seen together in London. The shadow that had lifted with the potency of a negroni, the sunlight and the sweet Alban air, dropped onto me again like a dark wing.

If Philip noticed my plunge into a different mood, he made no comment. Instead, he changed the conversation, talking to me about life on a newspaper. Yet, by the time coffee came, I knew no more about him than when I had first set eyes on him at Malimbrosa.

I heard him mention Katmandu and Delhi and Istanbul; I had a feeling that he talked about the ruins of Ankor Wat and of nights he had spent in the jungle. Had I listened properly, I might have learned a great deal about the world of a newspaper correspondent who had spent most of his time in the East. As it was, his words touched only a superficial hearing. I was wondering how he and Vanessa had behaved toward each other on their last evening.

"Talking to myself," he said, "has never been one of my idiosyncrasies."

I said, startled, "I wasn't thinking that it was."

"No, but you were thinking all right. And your thoughts had nothing to do with what I was saying."

"I'm sorry."

"Oh, no you're not."

I saw that he was shaking with silent laughter and it floored me. I watched the swifts dive around the terrace; saw a girl at the next table reach out to the vine and pick a grape, bite into it, make a face, and hurl it over the terrace edge. I heard quick laughter . . . animated Italian . . . the sharp protest of a child.

I drank the last of my coffee and the thought that was so strongly in my mind came out in a rush of totally unbidden words. "Were you ever in love with Vanessa?" I sat back horrified. "Oh, but I had no right to ask that."

The light of amusement had left his face. "No, you had no right."

"I'm sorry, I don't know what made me ask . . . I mean . . . sometimes words just come out . . ."

"Then you should close your lips more firmly so that they can't, shouldn't you?"

I deserved to be crushed. I sat, still as stone, looking down at my splayed hands on the table. I knew that he lit a cigarette; that he was far more master of the situation that had held my impulsive question than I who had asked it.

The silence between us became an embarrassment to me, and I was certain that it was to him also, for, as if he found it unendurable, he rose and went to the terrace edge. I watched him stand between two slender poles that held the trailing vines, looking out over the Campagna.

He said with his back to me, "Why can't you take the moment and enjoy it? What's the use of all this beauty if you harp on darkness?"

"So you admit there *is* darkness?"

"Maybe I'm only admitting that you are seeing it."

He evaded the straight answer every time. I saw the three people at the next table watching us, trying to understand our English, sensing a quarrel, and I got up and went to his side.

"What you're trying to say is that what has happened is in the past, and I should forget it. But I can't. Vanessa is a friend and I believe she is in trouble. What am I supposed to do? What would anyone else do in my circumstances? Say, 'Oh, to hell with trouble. I'm going to enjoy myself.'? Well, I can't and that's quite, *quite* final."

He was looking away over the great plain toward Rome. "Did you know that I have been married?"

Again, a question for a question. I traced the outline of a little bunch of unripened grapes with my finger. "Yes, I heard."

"My wife died suddenly two years ago. Since then, women as people to love haven't meant much to me. When you've had perfection you don't get serious about second-best. You shut pain out and get on with superficial pleasures. You learn what compromise is."

Vanessa—a superficial pleasure; Irena a superficial pleasure. And before them, how many others? He had answered the question that had started this peculiar tract. Although *Zia* Romola had said that Vanessa had loved him, Philip had probably had her as an amusing distraction, and that was all.

"Do you know what my happiness is now that Marian is dead?" He turned and looked at me. "It is my freedom. I am utterly and absolutely free to choose what I want to take from life. Now—" he moved away from the terrace edge. "I think we'd better go before we get too profound."

While he paused to pay the bill, I walked out of the restaurant into the sunlit square. The fountain was tossing up spurts of water, making little hiccuping sounds. I sat on the rim of the basin and stared into the ruffled pool.

I probably looked like a girl tourist resting hot, tired feet. I was in reality fighting for inner control over the idiocy that seized me. I was filled with a longing I loathed for Philip to come to me, to make even the most casual gesture, to take my hand, to put an arm round my shoulder, even to give me one of his rare smiles. I stared into the water and conjured his face, trying to project hatred into his image. I was quite certain that he knew far more about Vanessa's disappearance than he told and his cool, almost arrogant dismissal shocked me. *I am utterly and absolutely free to choose what I want to take from life.* Carve that on your tombstone, Philip Cornel . . .

"Someone," he came up behind me, "has just taken a photograph of you. He probably thinks you look decorative crouched there. You do look rather like the Little Mermaid at Copenhagen . . . Only with clothes on."

I uncurled my legs and got up. A big man with a camera smiled at me and waved a thanks as if I had been a conscious sitter. "I like this square," I said. "I shall come again."

"Only next time, make certain you've got a car that is not likely to send you swinging into a wall at fifty miles an hour."

"Did you speak to *Nonna* Allegra when you called the *palazzo?*"

"No. Romola. She wept with relief into the telephone that you aren't lying mangled in hospital."

We walked together to the car and I watched him as he crossed in front of the car's hood to his own seat behind the wheel. Against the background of soft golden brown buildings, his face was exciting—or at least I and several other women found it so. It was seldom evenness of features that gave a face its stimulus, rather it was the contrast. Philip's face was strongly paradox. It was a mixture of harsh, uncompromising lines, arrogance and a curious overlay of gentleness.

As he sat beside me and turned on the car's engine, I realized that analysis was only strengthening his image in my mind. I had better stop caring what he looked like and how he behaved. In less than three weeks I would be back in London and I would never see him again. But it seemed that if I continued to search for Vanessa, I would very likely never see England again.

14 ❧

Philip delivered me at the *palazzo*, accepted my thanks for
the rescue with a brief, "Think nothing of it."

Zia Romola was in the hall. Her expression was almost
comic in its relief. "*Cara*, I'm so thankful you're all right. How
could we have been so careless? You could so easily have been
killed."

I said cheerfully, "Well, I wasn't. And the car behaved
perfectly until I drove on a bad track."

"Bruno tells me that the fault in the steering might not even
be noticed on good roads."

"That's exactly what happened. But that awful track in what
they call the Dead Land did the final damage. I'm sorry—"

"*We're* sorry," she said.

We had drifted, as we talked, into the *salone*. *Zia* Romola sat
down, got up immediately and crossed to another chair, settled
herself and then rose again. In her agitation, no chair seemed to
suit her. She gave up and stood by the carved fireplace. "Why
did you go to Isolesi, Juliet?"

"I wondered if Vanessa might be there. I thought—"

"Oh," she interrupted me, "because our villa is near there?
Was that it?"

It was a way out of the dilemma of having to start on the long story that had led up to my visit to Isolesi. I said nothing, implying that she was right. *Zia* Romola said, "It's only a quarter of a mile if you go through the forest. But if Vanessa were anywhere up there, the people at the villa would know. In these hill villages, nothing is secret."

"Except," I said, "any knowledge about a young couple who live in a small villa right in the middle of the Dead Land. No one knows about them; they come sometimes at weekends and keep to themselves. The people at Isolesi say they are a young married couple from Rome."

Zia Romola actually laughed. "You *can't* have imagined that the girl was Vanessa, surely! I've seen that house. Nothing would induce her to live in such a place. Vanessa is used to luxury and even without Mamma's help, she still has enough money of her own to indulge in it. No, Juliet, you must face the fact that Vanessa is probably—"

"I believe that she is alive."

Romola passed a hand across her face as if she had walked into a cobweb. She gave a small, distressed sigh. "If I could think that . . ."

I wished I could have taken her into my confidence. She was garrulous and in a way pathetic, but I trusted her. I turned away, going toward a table on which stood little settecento snuff boxes. I picked one up. I was rather like some go-between in a kidnapping. I knew something the family did not know, yet, for the safety of the hostage, I could say nothing. Hostage? Vanessa? But what did they want in exchange for her safety? Why, if she could smuggle out cards and contact me; if she could walk in the Borghese Gardens, didn't she go straight up to a *carabinieri?*

Romola was saying, "Philip offered to go and find you. I wished it could have been someone else, but there was no time. All kinds of dreadful possibilities flashed through my mind. There was no one else but Philip. Irena was out and I do not drive."

I said gently, "It's all right, *Zia* Romola. None of them happened. Let's forget it."

She said, "And then he gave you lunch at Frascati—the place where he and Vanessa—"

"I doubt if it was the same restaurant."

She seemed not to hear me. "How *could* he? But then, he is so without conscience that I doubt if that would have worried him." She began to walk to and fro across the room. "He comes here so much. This morning, for instance, he came with some excuse that he had some English newspapers for Leo. He knows Leo is in Milan and that the papers could wait. He is establishing a right to come and go here as he likes. And this morning, by sending him to find you, I aided that arrogance of his; that right to be involved with us. How could I? Oh, how *could* I?" She turned and stared into a great gilt framed mirror that was sixteenth century and imperfect so that her reflection looked blurred, as if she were unreal.

"He is getting such a hold over the family. It is terrible. Mamma is a clever woman but she is willing to pay the price of such a hold for the sake of Malimbrosa." She walked to the table I had just left and picked up one of the snuff boxes, opening and closing it, her fingers clawing at it, her dark-ringed eyes burning in her sallow face. "Why couldn't I have been the one? Years ago, when I was young, why couldn't someone have wanted me?"

I stood silent, distressed by the naked loneliness in her eyes as she turned to me. "I would have persuaded the man I married to change his name to mine and everything would have been all right. I would have had children; sons . . . the women in our family are not barren. Malimbrosa—" The little snuff box slipped from her fingers and hit the corner of a table before it fell in three pieces onto the Aubusson carpet. Romola dropped to her knees, snatching at the broken porcelain. "Now look what I have done . . . Why did I have to be made as I am?" She looked up at me with bewilderment and hurt. "Why clumsy . . . ugly . . ."

I knelt by her side and put an arm round her bony shoulders. Gently, I took the pieces of the box from her hands. "Stop thinking of yourself like that. You aren't ugly or clumsy. We all make awkward movements when we're upset. I know I do. I crash into things, spill things . . . Now, tell me where I can take this and get it mended and we'll say nothing to anyone."

"Do you think Mamma won't know?" she demanded. "She misses nothing."

"Then we'll just tell her that it broke. Do you think she has never broken anything in her life?" I looked at the marvelous room, at the mass of objets d'art. "There's so much stuff here that *Nonna* won't notice that one small thing is missing."

"She'll see there's a space where something should be."

I walked to a far corner where a table stood laden with miniatures and glass cases holding fans of painted silk and mother of pearl. "Let's take something from here and put it in its place."

Romola seemed not to hear me. She was speaking, as if to herself, in a queer, slow, lamenting voice. "We have so much . . . boxes and boxes of things in the cellars . . . things that we never even see . . . nobody sees . . ."

"Then I'll go down and look at what's there. Here, take these pieces and see if you can get the box repaired. And while it's being done, I'll find something in the cellar to take its place."

She stood in front of me, like a helpless child with an old woman's face. "Go on," I urged her. "Go and find somewhere. Do it now."

"It's too early. The shops will be closed."

Of course. The siesta.

"But as soon as I can, I'll take it to Juturna's."

My heart did a somersault. If by any chance the assistant there had looked up the old order books, he would have discovered that the opal and ruby earrings, one of which lay in tissue paper in my handbag, had been made by them for a Malimbrosa. He would probably mention the fact that a young woman had called to say that she had found one, but had refused to leave it. There was nothing I could do to stop this unfortunate possibility—only cross my fingers and hope that the earrings had been made too long ago for the assistant to have found the records.

I said, "I'm going down to the cellar to see what I can find."

"There's a dark oak chest with a carved front," she told me forlornly. "You might find something like this in there." She was opening and closing her hand over the pieces in such a way that I was certain she would cut herself.

"Wrap them up quickly," I said, "before *Nonna* sees them."

"She is resting. Or that is what she likes us to think. I doubt if Mamma ever really rests. She lies on her big day sofa and works out her problems."

I left her and went through the door to the servants' quarters, trying to remember which of the maze of doors there led to the cellars. But as soon as I saw it I recognized it. It was enormously heavy, very old and barred with iron strips so that I had to use both hands to drag it open. I stood for a moment at the top of the spiral staircase and remembered how, as a child, I had felt a fearful excitement as Vanessa and I had gone down there together and she had told me, giggling, how the cellars had been early Roman prisons. Once she had made my flesh crawl, telling me that they were really part of the catacombs that honeycombed ancient Rome. *Zia* Romola had told her sharply not to be silly, there were no skeletons down there.

Vanessa had said, "But people were imprisoned and some of them must have died, so there must be ghosts."

Zia Romola had said, "The ghosts live above ground, *cara*."

But neither of us understood her and we had played ghoulish tricks on one another until our shrieks had brought Gisela down to stop us before we terrified one another into hysterics by our infectious imaginations.

The cellars became a storage place and we opened great trunks and found old ball dresses, plumes and feathers and laces with which we dressed up. Vanessa even carried a heavy mirror down there, so that we could see ourselves, muffled and struggling in the dusty yellow and crimson and emerald satins;

the flattened sables, the bird-of-paradise head-dresses, everything smelling of some moth deterrent.

In spite of the coldness that seeped through the ancient stones, there was something almost friendly about the conglomeration of old chests, pieces of unwanted furniture, stacked paintings. There was a dust-covered lute and a spinet that still had patches of marvelous sheen on it. I had switched on the lights, for without them the only illumination came from a small grille across which the oleanders spread, poking pink blooms through the gaps in the heavy ironwork.

Irena's sleek Abyssinian cat, Loyolo, sat with unblinking eyes watching me. I went up to the high grille and called out, "If you want to come in, you'd better go somewhere else. I can't let you in this way." The cat blinked at me. He was so sleek and proud and beautiful.

I wandered through the high cellars with their vaulted roofs turning on lights, looking for the carved oak chest. I found it at last in the darkest cellar of all. The lid was a great weight and I had to heave it up. Inside objects lay wrapped in black tissue paper, in special boxes, even in wads of rotting silk. I found a few old snuff boxes and chose one that had a painting of a shepherdess enclosed in scrolls of gold. It was very similar to the one Romola had broken.

I closed the chest and went back through the great arches to the first of the cellars. Loyola still sat facing the grille, dreaming in the sunshine. I couldn't resist going to the *cassone* in which Vanessa and I had found the once-lovely clothes. Heaven knew why they were kept since the Malimbrosas had no sentiment. I bent and looked inside, putting my hands out, lifting the velvets and the satins. They seemed more faded, more dusty, than I had remembered them, but no moth had attacked them. I thought how some museum of costume would have loved to have had them and would have preserved them in something of their original beauty.

Next to the *cassone* was another chest which I seemed to remember was full of books. They were old and leather bound, mostly of the Italian classics, but I found a few small red-bound books with the Malimbrosa crest embossed on them. I picked one up and opened it. It was a diary dated some fourteen years ago and on the first page, written in a spidery sloping hand, was "Luciana Malimbrosa."

I was surprised that the diaries had been discarded by the family. But then Luciana, who died a long time ago, had been for years just a quiet, charming, deaf old woman. The diary would probably contain rather dull things that had happened within the household from day to day and so would not be considered important enough to be kept upstairs in Leo's library with its valuable first editions.

I opened the book and began to read the spidery writing with difficulty. There were little vignettes about people whose names meant nothing to me. But the observations were sharp and penetrating and although Luciana had been deaf for many years the pages of the diary seemed vibrant with the life of a woman who missed nothing of what went on around her.

Although I didn't know the names of the many friends about whom she wrote, her descriptions of them were amusing, sometimes touching and, as far as I had read, entertaining. I tucked the book under my arm, closed the chest, picked up the little snuff box and left the cellars, putting my whole weight against the heavy door to close it.

Zia Romola was waiting nervously for me in the *salone*. I set the little snuff box in the gap on the table.

"The painting on the lid isn't much like the broken one, but I doubt if anyone will notice."

She was looking at the book I held. "What is that?"

"A diary," I said. "One of *Nonna* Luciana's. I thought nobody would mind, after all this time, if I glanced through it. Or do you think I shouldn't?"

"Why not?" She was without interest. "I doubt if you'll find anything particularly absorbing in it. *Nonna* Luciana was stone deaf; I can't imagine that she knew much about what was going on. She probably lived in daydreams."

I kept quiet about the few vivid passages I had already read. I doubted very much if it were one of those diaries that would change the course of history—even Malimbrosa history.

Romola said "Thank you for finding the snuff box, Juliet. Let us hope that Mamma never notices." She picked up the broken pieces which she had piled on a piece of crested notepaper and smiled at me. I left her watching the clock for Juturna's to reopen.

Irena was crossing the hall and her scent made an aura around her—sandalwood, jasmine—I didn't know what it was, but it was rich and disturbing and I guessed that a man would find it so. In her arms she held her cat, who was looking over my shoulder with a golden-eyed arrogance.

15 ❧

THE SUN FLUNG AN UNREPENTANT GLARE at the roof garden and I found a chair in the shade of some small trees, swung my feet up onto the foot rest, and opened the diary. Vanessa had told me that Luciana had never loved her daughter-in-law. Here it was set out in the spidery handwriting.

"Allegra has been born out of her generation. She belongs to the past; to the medieval queen-dictators. She is hard and calculating and quite brilliant. I suspect that if my son had been a strong man, physically, she would not have married him. When I am dead she will probably destroy these diaries without reading them. I am sure that what I think does not interest her in the slightest. Even if she reads what I have written and learns what I think of her, it will not upset her."

I turned the pages. Someone came to luncheon; there was a dinner party; the family were going to the opera. "Oh, how tired I am of Cosi Fan Tutti!" . . .

Then on a page halfway through the year, Luciana wrote: "Romola is a sad and disappointed woman living in the shadow of a mother who has no compassion." . . . of Vanessa: "She is like a flame. I hope she will not burn herself out."

I turned to the next day.

"This morning I went to visit Flavia and Consuelo. They are

so like a little pair of their own twittering birds. I do not know how much Allegra has told them but I have a feeling they know nothing. It is all so wrong, but my protests are useless. Allegra goes her own way. They say that every age gets the government and the scandal it deserves. By the same token, my family must get the tragedy it warrants."

I frowned into the mauve shadows under the bushes. I could only guess that Luciana was thinking of some family secret that must never be spoken of. It could, of course, be nothing of importance. Luciana had been old; she had led a quiet circumscribed life so that a very small incident would be of tremendous importance to her. At the same time, the thought occurred to me that I might visit the aunts, who must be very, very old by now. I remembered their kindness to me when I was a child and I had been taken to their overstuffed house near the Vatican.

A few pages further on, I saw my name. "The little Juliet. She moves like a child enchanted. But she is very vulnerable. She will be hurt and this grieves me for I have grown fond of her. Why is it that the good God lets the dearest people suffer the most?"

I closed the diary, shaken by the comments on myself. I had seen so little of *Nonna* Luciana when I had stayed in Rome. She had occasionally called me to her apartments and had told me stories about ancient Rome. The two things I remembered most clearly about her were the beautiful solitaire emerald she wore on her thin hand and the scent of roses that always pervaded her room.

I stared ahead of me at the stone balustrade with its curtain of roses and jasmine. An incense smell hung about the garden, exciting rather than soothing; bees droned among the flowers; far below cars raced to beat the distant traffic lights. I had wanted to lie here indolently and read, but something of the restlessness of the city awakened from its siesta stirred me. The diary filled with the thoughts of a long-dead woman could be read at leisure.

I got up and went to the terrace edge. From there I could

look down onto the roofs of the surrounding houses. I saw the old *palazzo* where Philip had his apartment. Long, red-striped sunblinds came down over the windows leading to the terrace and as I looked, two people came out of the shadows and into the sun. A man and a woman. I could not recognize the man from this distance but I had seen the white dress with the green edging only a short time ago. Irena had worn it when she had stood in the hall with her cat.

I watched them, feeling as much an interloper as if I were actually hiding behind one of the big geranium-filled urns on Philip's roof. I wanted to turn away and I couldn't. I held onto the hot stone balustrade and saw Irena turn and say something. I saw Philip's hand go out to touch hers. For a moment they stood very quietly together. Then they moved into the shade of the awning and disappeared.

I turned at the same moment and fled to my bedroom, put the diary on the bedside table, walked to the mirror and began combing my hair. My angry face stared back at me. I was ashamed of my own feeling of betrayal. I was nothing to Philip Cornel and, by all logical argument, he should be nothing to me but a suspect who knew more about Vanessa's disappearance than he had told. He could, for all I knew, be my active enemy, the one who sent me to the apartment in the Via Campisolo; the one who knew who had hurled a lethal object at me outside the Villa Artemis. And, if he were innocent of all these things, it still didn't give me any reason to be angry. The plan concocted by Allegra was nothing to do with me, an outsider to Malimbrosa, here by luck—or ill luck.

I walked the room, wondering what to do next. The tourist attractions of Rome could wait. I fidgeted with the zinnias in the celadon bowl, folded a scarf, took out Vanessa's two cards and reread them. Then returning to the diary, I made up my mind to visit the two aunts, Flavia and Consuela, whom *Nonna* Luciana had so often mentioned.

I doubted if they would be out; Vanessa had once said that they never went anywhere except to church. But they might not remember me or agree to see me. Rome was not like easy-going London; outsiders did not make casual, unplanned visits to such people as the Malimbrosas. But the very idea of going down and looking up their address in the leather bound book in the little room behind the screen, the act of getting to their house, gave me the absorption in something other than myself which I needed.

As I sat in the taxi driving to the Papal Quarter near the Piazza Farnese, I looked at my watch. It was half past five. The day had been full and shattering; I wondered what the evening would bring.

The Malimbrosa sisters lived in a gray villa without any protecting wall. If the shutters were open then passers-by could look straight into the rooms at street level. Each of them however had heavy iron grilles.

I rang a bell and was admitted by a tall, gaunt woman who looked English. She neither smiled when I introduced myself nor gave any indication that I would be seen. I was shown into a small anteroom cluttered with heavy black oak furniture and old photographs. She would inquire if the signorinas would receive me.

She returned almost immediately and asked me to follow her. As I went along the wide passage to the back of the house, I remembered Luciana's words in the diary. "I have a feeling they know nothing." But perhaps they did know; and perhaps I would find out what it was. And if I did, would it help? Was there something in the past history of the Malimbrosas that linked Luciana's comment in her diary with what had happened to Vanessa? It was too wild a hope; there were too many years in between for what had been important then to be joined to what happened today . . .

A door was pushed open and I entered a room that was so dim that it took me a few minutes to recognize the two tiny women who came forward with little running steps to greet me. They put their arms round me, kissing my cheek, declaring that they remembered me well, exclaiming at the wonderful surprise in seeing me again. And all this to the twittering of a huge cage-full of budgerigars. Violet and yellow, dusty pink and sky blue, they darted from their tiny swings to their see-saws like some unplanned ballet of the birds.

Questions were tossed at me from the two little women who sat in straight-backed chairs facing me. Turning my head from one to the other, I answered all their questions, feeling, for once in my life, too large, too robust, and wondering what the friends who teased me about my own smallness would say if they saw these enchanting doll women.

When had I arrived? How long was I staying? At Malimbrosa! Really? They shot startled looks at one another, and Flavia gave an almost imperceptible shake of her head. I wondered what it was she didn't want her sister to say.

Had I had tea? I shook my head and said that I didn't need any. Half past five o'clock, I decided to myself, was not my idea of teatime. It was, however, theirs. Like many Romans, they dined late. "And," said Flavia, "we always have an English tea at this time."

"It was a habit we picked up when we came to England—"

"And we couldn't exist without it."

As I watched them pull the old-fashioned bell at the side of the fireplace, I remembered how amused I had been as a child when Vanessa and I had visited them and they had talked in this way, one starting a sentence, the other finishing it, as if they were one person.

When tea came, Flavia poured and I was handed a delicate green cup. "It's China tea, *cara*—"

"Scented with jasmine flowers."

I sipped it, said it was delicious, and refused a little cake. "I really wanted to know if you could help me to understand why Vanessa has disappeared."

Again they exchanged swift, questioning looks. Then Flavia said, "It's a complete mystery to us. I am sure everyone has done their best, the police, the detectives Allegra hired—"

"The last time Vanessa came to see us, we were troubled," Consuela said. "She seemed so over-excited and yet so nervous. We thought—"

"We thought that she was perhaps having some love affair

· *165*

that we might not approve of. The silly child. As if we would ever condemn."

"Condemnation. 'Judge not, that ye be not judged' "—

"We try not to," said Flavia. "But we wondered who the man was she had been seen with."

I said, "Vanessa knew lots of men."

"Ah, but this one was different—"

"You see, Juliet, when the daughter of a friend of ours in Geneva came to stay with us, we asked Leyla—that is our servant and friend, the one who let you in—to take her to the Vatican Museum. It was there, on the terrace, that she saw Vanessa. She said there was a man with her and that Vanessa was looking very distressed; she was sure that she was crying. Then, a little while later we sent Leyla to the *palazzo* with a gift for Allegra's birthday. Leyla said that as she left this man arrived."

"Did you tell *Nonna?*"

"Oh yes, we were so worried about Vanessa, you see—"

"But Allegra was not concerned. She just said that the man was a friend of the family, a Philip Cornel, an Englishman."

Their news wasn't particularly helpful. *Zia* Romola had already told me that Vanessa had been in love with Philip. Although I was happy to see them again, I knew that so far as hoping they could tell me something that might give me a lead to where Vanessa was, my visit was a failure.

I thought of the earring in my handbag but decided not to show it to them because it would demand the explanations I could not give and also cause Flavia unnecessary distress. After half an hour I rose to leave. They sent for Leyla to order their car to take me back to the *palazzo* and they both came with me into the hall with its curious Victoriana of potted palms and marble busts.

Consuela kissed me first and then, holding my arm, turned to her sister. "Do you think, perhaps, we ought to tell her?"

I asked quickly, "Tell me what?"

Flavia said, "We shouldn't."

"Why not." Consuela looked slightly rebellious. "Allegra need never know."

Flavia took the initiative. "You know, of course, that Vanessa was sent away from the *palazzo;* that Allegra would have nothing more to do with her?"

"Yes, I know all that."

Consuela said, "More than once, since then, Allegra has expressed a desire to see *you* again. Only last week she said that she was thinking of writing to invite you to Malimbrosa."

I whispered incredulously, "She was going to invite *me?* But why?"

"She grew very attached to you," Flavia said softly.

"As attached as Allegra can ever get to anyone—"

"And you see, when—"

"Consuela . . . !" Flavia flashed her a look.

"Signorina, what were you going to say to me?"

Consuela opened her mouth to speak, but Flavia got in first. "Oh, just that when you arrived at the *palazzo* so unexpectedly, Allegra must have been delighted. Is that no so, Consuela?"

She nodded, her lips tightly closed.

"Cara," Flavia said and kissed me on both cheeks for the second time. "You must come and see us again."

I was dismissed gently, without the real answer to my question. Outside, their chauffeur waited with a huge, old-fashioned car. I sat and brooded all the way back to Malimbrosa, wondering what it was Consuela had not been allowed to say and intrigued that it had concerned me.

16 ❧

"I HAVE ACCEPTED AN INVITATION for you to go to the Lyangente ball on Thursday."

Allegra had called me to her office and watched me as if the name Lyangente must mean something to me. It didn't. I repeated it softly, questioningly, and she said: "The *principessa* always gives a ball, one of the last before Roman society leave for their summer places and their yachts. It will be an experience for you." Her long fingers played with the pieces on the mother-of-pearl chess board. "Irena and Leo will be going, and Philip has been asked to partner you."

The thought flashed through my mind, "You call the tune, and Philip dances . . ." Allegra made it an order but I had the power to refuse to obey. In the frantic moments while I wondered what to say, I was divided into two people, one wanting desperately and shamefully to go with Philip and, like some mindless lemming, dance to its own destruction; the other part seeking, just as desperately, for an excuse not to go.

I said, "Thank you, *Nonna*, for suggesting it. But I—I can't go."

"And why not?"

"I haven't brought anything . . . anything . . . sufficiently formal to wear. Clothes, I mean . . . I . . ." I stumbled over my excuse.

"That is no problem. Romola will take you to Fernanda Guiscarda for a gown."

"But I don't *want*—"

She waved a hand at me. "You have been invited as a gesture to me, and you will go. Is that clear, Juliet? I wish you to go." She must have seen the mutinous look on my face, for her voice softened. "We have done nothing as yet to entertain you. Please allow me this gesture."

"You have given me hospitality, *Nonna*. That is more than enough."

She reached out and lifted the little jade knight and set him one place nearer the queen. The chess board glimmered in the subdued light of the room. I watched her, thinking, and I'm another pawn you're playing with. I'm to be used in order that Irena and Philip can be together without gossip. He was to be my escort; Irena was going conventionally with her husband. But why was all this maneuvering necessary? Had some whisper got around of the secret plans made inside Malimbrosa? And was I to be used to defy the rumors? "There's nothing to all that talk. Philip Cornel is with the English girl."

"Tell Romola I want to see her," Allegra said.

"I really think . . . if you could make some excuse to the *principessa* . . ."

She looked at me coldly. "You have your mother's ridiculous pride. Please, Juliet, don't be tiresome."

She knew she had triumphed. More refusal on my part would be just bad manners. I capitulated. "Very well. Thank you, *Nonna*."

She turned back to her desk, picked up some papers and, without looking at me again, said, "Now, do as I ask and send Romola to me. She must take you to the couturière."

The elevator carried me up, smooth and silken as an eel in movement, to the gallery. I knocked on *Zia* Romola's door and gave her the message. She said, "Oh, how I love going to Guiscarda's, although I never look nice in the dresses I buy."

She stopped my protests. "I have no figure; I am like a stalk. Never mind; I shall take great pleasure in looking at the gowns."

That last word accentuated the world of difference between us; the clothes I wore were "dresses" to me . . .

I paid her an elaborate parting compliment. "Whenever you walk, you make me think of the old French courts—the sound of all those rich clothes rustling through the chateaux must have been marvelous."

Her gratitude for my rather circuitous compliment was touching and as she rustled down the staircase, I went to the roof garden.

The sun's heat struck me full in the face as I walked out from under the blue awnings. The flame flowers against the stone archway, which divided the garden more for artistry than necessity, dazzled my eyes and I bent and dipped my fingers in the fountain basin as I passed. I went to the side of the *palazzo* that faced the huddled houses and wondered whether, among all that vast stretch of buildings—the villas and the palaces and the terraced houses—by some chance I could see the roof of the place where the three-paneled screen stood. Who owned it? Who lived in the house where Vanessa had sat and waited?

"Ah, Juliet, so here you are!"

I had been wrapped around in a haze of unclear thought, the sun mesmerizing me into a kind of vacancy, so that Romola's voice startled me.

"I am to take you to Fernanda Guiscarda to select an evening gown. Mamma has already telephoned and Signora Simionato is expecting us." She shook her head in sudden annoyance. "Mamma tells me that Philip is to take you to the *principessa's* ball. I asked her if the Conte di Mettrivesi could not perhaps be persuaded—he is a very elegant bachelor and an excellent dancer. But Mamma has decided upon Philip. I do not like it at all."

Nor do I, dear Romola . . . Aloud, I said brightly, "Well, so far as I'm concerned, Philip can leave me as soon as we get inside the doors of wherever we're going. I'll be perfectly happy just watching and lapping up all the glamor . . . there isn't that much glamor left in the world, is there?"

She sighed and looked about her as if to remind me that she was surrounded by it, yet it gave her no pleasure. "You must get ready, *cara*. We have an appointment."

———————

FERNANDA GUISCARDA's salon was in a gray house on a gray street. Its exterior was not in the least imposing, so that I was not prepared for the splendor inside. The décor was biscuit-color and gold, the floor of the main salon was covered with leopard skins and incense burned very faintly in censers. Here was luxury without guilt; unembarrassed splendor.

The gowns paraded before me bewildered me. I committed the initial sin of asking the price almost before I had looked at them. *Zia* Romola gave a little darting movement toward my arm, whispering, "The price is not your concern, *cara*. You are here to choose a gown, not to speak of cost."

By the end of the performance—for that was how I saw it—I owned a dress of white silk jersey with what the hatchet-faced Signora Simionato described as having "exquisite Grecian lines." I wondered, a little hilariously, as I stood having it pinned for shortening, whether it would come in useful one day as a wedding gown; I could see it otherwise lying as neglected as the gowns in the cellars at Malimbrosa.

A plain gold band was placed round my neck. "That is all you should wear, signorina."

It was heavy and beautifully simple. I fingered it, asking the cost. Behind me Romola gave an exasperated sigh. Signora Simionato told me as though she were tossing off the price of a tin of peanuts. I said politely that I had something that I thought would do just as well, and when *Zia* Romola began, "But, Juliet—" I stopped her.

"I have a gold necklace," I said. Which wasn't quite true

since gold and gilt weren't even brothers under the skin. I felt hilarious. The hushed pomposity of the place, the unwritten law that I had twice broken by asking the price, the elegant superiority of the very plain Signora Simionato, who behaved as if she were conferring a favor in selling all these things, aroused in me a bitter amusement. So much money was being spent in order that I might go to a ball with a man who was, in all probability, taking me for the sole reason of stopping any possible rumors about himself and a beautiful married woman.

I wondered as I sat in the car whether perhaps a servant had overheard something here or at the Villa Sapphira, and had risked dismissal by repeating it. Or perhaps someone had seen Irena and Philip together on his roof garden, as I had seen them.

The gown was delivered the next day. And, to my dismay, there was also the plain gold necklace. I said as Romola watched me open the velvet-lined box, "But I didn't order it."

"I told Mamma that Signora Simionato had suggested it and so she telephoned and gave the order that you must have it."

I submitted as graciously as I could and hung the dress in Vanessa's small, flamingo-pink dressing room, put the leather case with the gold necklace in a drawer, and went downstairs to thank *Nonna* Allegra.

The telephone bell was ringing as I came out of her office and when it stopped Alberto came into the hall to tell me that there was a call for me. I took it in the little room behind the screen.

The voice was strange, husky and cautious. "Signorina . . . Signorina Juliet?"

"Speaking."

"Ah!" The voice changed. "This is Gisela. If you were out I was going to pretend that it was a wrong number."

"What is it?"

"Pepi. I am very worried."

"Then hadn't you better speak to the signora?"

"I cannot. Pepi has had a card from the Signorina Vanessa, and she says on it that La Signora must not know that she has written. He is so terribly upset and I cannot quiet him. I thought perhaps you could come out here . . . I mean—"

"Of course I will. It's a little late to start for Grottochiara this morning because if I'm out to lunch the Signora may ask me where I've been and it's better that she doesn't know. I'll be along some time this afternoon." Though what, I thought, listening to her profusion of gratitude, I could do, I had no idea. At the same time I owed Gisela something for all her kindness to me years ago and I wanted to see the card that had been sent to Pepi. I doubted if I would have any soothing influence on the little boy; I was too much a stranger.

I wondered if anyone in the house was listening on an extension and, when Gisela rang off, I waited a moment, anticipating a click that would indicate that someone in the house had listened in to the conversation. If they had, they were cannily waiting for me to replace my receiver first.

The Dauphine was now in perfect running order and I was told that I could use it whenever I wished. I began to think of some small gift I could take to Pepi. I thought, perhaps, a book in very simple English would please him since I had been told that he had a flair for languages and loved speaking English. I would call at the bookshop in the Via del Babuino on the way.

The telephone bell in the room rang softly.

It was Martin. "Can you lunch with me?"

"Yes, please. I've got things to tell you."

"And I've got a rather nasty suspicion to tell *you* about. I'll come and fetch you about half past twelve."

It occurred to me as I rang off that, for a man working at an embassy, where caution was paramount, he was being a little reckless and indiscreet on the telephone. He should know that in a place like Malimbrosa, there must be a dozen or more extensions.

It was easy to explain to *Nonna* Allegra that I was having lunch with Martin, but I was very aware of the fact that she wasn't interested in meeting him; she wasn't even concerned with his friendship with Vanessa. He was a nobody at the British embassy and even if he hadn't been, I doubted if she would ever have invited him to the *palazzo*—the Malimbrosas did not seem to entertain much. But then, Allegra's reason for inviting me to stay was still a mystery, for it was obvious that my personal life, my friends, even my likes and dislikes, were of no interest to her.

Martin called for me and took me to a hotel in the Via Nazionale, where we ate on a terrace looking over a square garden with a very white nymph poised over a pool. From the opposite side of the garden, which was the wall of the Opera House, we heard the sonorous notes of a tenor practicing his part.

I reminded Martin of the grocery bag lying face upward on the floor of the apartment in the Via Campisolo. I said, "I went to Isolesi yesterday," and told him what happened.

He sat back and grinned at me. "You drive to an isolated house, walk round it and creep up to a shuttered window. What did you expect, a hand held out in welcome? 'Do come in and steal the family silver. It's all in this drawer. I'll give you something to wrap it in.'"

I said stormily, "You're just like Philip."

"Oh, so you told him?"

"Since he came and rescued me, I owed him an explanation."

"You mean he drove all the way into the hills?"

"Yes."

"It was an odd thing to do, wasn't it, when, if you'd had an accident, you'd have been in hospital and if you hadn't, you'd have telephoned for help."

He was being as logical as I would have been in his place. I said, flatly, "Well, he came. Perhaps he liked the idea of a run into the country."

"With you at the end of it?"

"No. Unless—" I paused, and then realized that Martin had to know even my own suspicions. "Unless he knew who was at the Villa Artemis and wanted to see if I had made inquiries in the village and had somehow found my way to the Dead Land."

"It sounds to me altogether too pat for Romola Malimbrosa

to send Philip after you. And he is on too friendly terms with Vanessa's family. I wonder why. Romans in their social bracket don't usually keep open doors for strangers. Where's the link?"

That was something I couldn't tell him.

He persisted. "This man Cornel. What if the Malimbrosas suspect him of having something to do with Vanessa's disappearance, since you tell me he was the last to see her? What if they're conducting a little private investigation?"

"It could be." I played with the grilled sole on my plate. Delicate herbs flavored it; the wine in my glass was pale gold like winter sunlight.

Martin said, "This brings me to the nasty suspicion I told you about."

"Part of me doesn't want to hear it," I said. "But go on."

"Suppose there was a quarrel between Vanessa and this man Cornel. Suppose in fury he struck out at her and she fell and hit her head."

"And then—*what?*"

"And she died in some place in the mountains where no one has yet found her. Or—he buried her."

My voice seemed to be locked up in my throat, and when I managed to make it audible, all I could produce was a croak. *"But I saw her—"*

"Or someone impersonating her? You only saw the girl's face from across the street, remember, and the Via Veneto is fairly wide."

"And . . . and the . . . cards?"

"It would be easy enough to copy her scrawl and even her type of drawing."

I looked at him with horror. "*Zia* Romola thinks she's dead, too, but I won't . . . I *can't* . . . Martin, she's too vivid. Vanessa and . . . and . . . death don't somehow go." I jerked out my broken sentences, aware that to deny mortality to Vanessa was like denying the changing of the seasons. All the same, I found another protest. "But if she were dead, then why is someone trying to harm *me?* Why not leave me totally in the dark, do nothing? Why encourage me to go on searching?"

"Perhaps because he—or they—know that you have a streak of obstinacy and you intend to find out all you can. So they're leading you a dance."

"A dance of death—" I shuddered.

"That's why the best thing you can do is to let everyone believe you've stopped looking for Vanessa."

"I haven't."

"I know that, but let's keep it our secret. We've got to go on searching, and we're in this together. But someone around is her enemy—and ours. It could even be someone in the family, or closely connected—"

"Cornel?"

"Perhaps."

We raised our wine glasses simultaneously. As I drank it seemed as if we were indulging in a macabre toast.

17 ⚹

LATER THAT AFTERNOON I DROVE to the Villa Sapphira. It was the hottest day yet and the monumental ruins brooded over the energetic new Rome as I passed on my way.

Old Paolo opened the gates for me and I drove down the long avenue of umbrella pines, ilex and cedar, to the house. There was a moving patch of bright green in the distance and instead of going up the steps to the door, I skirted the house and could see Gisela seated below me in the shade of an evergreen oak. I went down the flowering terraces between the box hedges and past the small white pavilion with its tendrils of gray-green wisteria climbing the three supporting Doric columns. The sunlight laid liquid trails of gold over the great garden and the scent of sweet herbs was heavy as if the air breathed it.

Gisela's head was bent over some sewing, so that I was quite near her before she heard my footsteps. She looked up, dropped the sewing onto a white wrought-iron table, and cried my name. "Oh, signorina, thank you for coming. I felt that I should not have asked you, but you made me promise . . ."

"Yes, I did."

"Please sit down. I will have coffee brought out. Or would you rather have it in the house?"

"Here," I said, and sank gratefully into a chair. "Where is Pepi?"

"He is somewhere with his tricycle. He was so dreadfully upset and Maria said I should telephone La Signora. But I did not want to do that. So, after a time we managed to comfort him and he slept for a while; he was so exhausted. Now, he is playing—but not happily. I will fetch coffee now and the signorina's card."

Pepi had seen me from some corner of the grounds and was cycling toward me. I got up and went to meet him. He dropped his tricycle onto a path and held out his hand politely. "Good afternoon, Z-Z*ia* Juliet."

I wondered whether he had remembered from the other night that I was English or whether Gisela had reminded him. I took his hand and walked with him to the little group of chairs, sat down and began to talk to him. Was he going to the sea for part of his holiday? He replied without enthusiasm that they would all be going on the yacht in July. "We shall be away for w-weeks and w-weeks."

"That'll be lovely."

"Yes—"

"You don't sound very excited about it."

"Excited?" he frowned.

I explained in Italian.

"Oh, I do not like b-being on the s-sea." He spoke clear but stilted English and moved away from my encircling arm and sat down cross-legged on the grass. "I like being *in* it. At Ostia I s-swim, but *Nonna* does not m-much like me going to Ostia."

"Why ever not?" I looked down at the small bones of his neck and shoulders that stuck out like a little frog's.

"It is crowded there in the s-summer and *Nonna* says w-where there are lots of people, you c-catch things from them, bad things that make you ill."

I thought that contact with a few common germs might bring him far more immunity than being kept away.

"Why have you c-come to see us?" He asked it indifferently, as if he had been taught the social lesson of keeping a conversation alive, but wasn't relishing it.

"It's a lovely day, I thought I'd like the drive."

"I wish Vanessa would come."

Gisela brought coffee and set it down on the table. "Pepi, *caro*, go and play. Look, be a kind little boy and take this sewing indoors for me, will you?" She held it out to him.

But Pepi watched her as she dug into the huge pocket of her skirt with her other hand and pulled out a card. "No. *No.* I will n-not go and p-play." He came to sudden blazing life. "That's my card. Vanessa s-sent it to me." He tried to snatch it from her. You have no right to t-take something that is mine. I will t-tell *Nonna*; I will tell—"

"Pepi." I leaned forward. "Can't I just have a look at it? I love Vanessa's cards. You see"—I rushed on as his face became more mutinous—"cards aren't like letters. When people want to write something very personal to someone else, they put it in a letter and seal the envelope. Postcards are different."

He gave me a long uncertain look. "But I c-can have it back?"

"Of course. It's yours."

He conceded with a shrug and looked suspiciously at Gisela, who was still holding the piece of linen she had been sewing. "Please, Pepi, take this in for me and then run and play. The signorina has come a long way and she is tired. After a rest, she will talk to you."

"I don't want to p-play. I hate p-playing alone. I d-don't like it here; why can't I go b-back to Rome? I want to go to school . . ." His voice had become sing-song.

Gisela caught hold of him. "There is something nice for you in the kitchen," she coaxed. "Marie has made some *cavallucci*."

"If I go and get some, m-may I eat them out here with you?"

"You go and see what Maria says."

He went reluctantly, scuffing up the paths between the flower urns and the laurel hedges.

Gisela said, "The *cavallucci* are honey cakes and Pepi loves them. But they aren't out of the oven yet, so he will have to wait for them. Maria will keep him amused. Here is the card."

I took it.

Do not forget me, darling Pepi, because I shall always remember you. And sometimes you will see me. But you must tell no one.

I turned the card over. On the other side was a very rough drawing of a little boy sitting up in bed staring at a transparent Vanessa—a ghost girl . . .

"It came through the post?"

Gisela shook her head. "I found it this morning pushed under the door of Pepi's playroom. He was at breakfast so I saw it first."

"Someone came into the house . . ."

"Oh, no. His playroom opens out onto the garden just at the side—" She pointed, past the little pavilion. "Someone could have crept up the terrace steps and thrown it into the room and it just happened to fall on the floor."

"But who could get past the gates?"

"No one, without Paolo seeing. But there is a way in through a thick hedge on the far side of the grounds."

"Who would know that?"

She shrugged. "Oh, anyone. You can see the tower of the villa from a long way. We are on a hill."

"Can we be sure that Vanessa wrote this?"

She stared at me. "But of course."

"Not necessarily. It's like her writing, but it is more untidy."

"Perhaps she was in a hurry."

"And the drawing is bad."

"If she was trying to . . . to . . ."

"Smuggle?"

"That is the word. To smuggle it out, and was in a hurry, she would not have time to draw carefully."

Gisela could be right, yet I had to warn her of the possibility that someone was playing the role of Vanessa. I said, "Doesn't it occur to you that she may be dead?"

"*Gran Dio*, do not say such a terrible thing. She must not be . . ." She crossed herself.

I said as gently as I could, "I'm sorry if I upset you. Perhaps I'm exaggerating. Let's not even think about it. Instead, we'll believe that she sent this to Pepi in order to let us know that she is alive but cannot contact us herself."

"But you cannot believe the signorina is . . . not . . . alive," she insisted.

"I don't know what I believe," I said unhappily.

Outside our little center of shadow cast by the crescent of bushes, the sun was fierce. But I felt cold and I looked over my shoulder as if someone stood there who might be visible only to me. A bird swooped across the face of the sun casting a swift shadow and I looked up sharply, watching the dark wings in flight.

"A hawk," Gisela said. "I do not like them. They are unlucky to me and to my family."

I knew that she was full of superstitions and this was not the time to indulge her. I said, "Oh, they're birds of prey, but then everything preys on everything else."

She hadn't listened. "I am getting frightened," she said. "I think someone is keeping the Signorina Vanessa a prisoner and that one day he will demand—" she questioned the word, flicking her fingers.

I said in English, "Ransom?"

She didn't understand the word but she sensed that it was the right one and nodded. "La Signora is angry with her and she may not wish to pay the money they will ask for the signorina's return. If she does not . . ."

"All right," I said. "But even if that's so, someone is befriending her, someone who delivers her cards for her."

I took a long drink of coffee. It was fragrant and very hot, but it didn't touch the deep place inside me where cold fear lurked. I put down my cup and picked up the card again. The drawing was certainly not as good as those I had received in London, nor had the writing quite the same impetuous touch. But Gisela could have been right. Vanessa had probably dashed it off in a hurry before someone came back and found her trying to make contact with the outside world.

"I am beginning to trust no one," Gisela said; her large dark eyes scrutinized me, her lips were down-drawn like a child about to burst into tears. She said, "I am afraid when I am in the house, though I know Maria and Paolo and his wife can be trusted. But—" She stared into the distance, saying softly to herself, "*I muri hanno orecchi.*" The walls have ears.

So Gisela had the same sensation of being watched, being listened-to, here at the Villa Sapphira as I had at Malimbrosa. But she had charge of Pepi, and heightened tension, nervousness on her part and her native superstitions would react badly on the sensitive little boy. I had to reassure her somehow.

I said, trying to put conviction into my voice, "I think perhaps we're making too much of all this. Perhaps the signorina is having a love affair and—" My voice was drowned in a series of sounds that were part cries and part screams.

Gisela started up and ran toward the oleander avenue. Pepi's tricycle was gone.

"*Pepi* . . ." her voice rose. "*Oh, Dio*, which way? Which way?"

The cries came again and we turned simultaneously, looking beyond the villa grounds.

"He has gone into the woods," she cried "and that is something La Signora had made me promise that he must not do; not alone, that is."

We began to run. We tore round the twisting paths between the lawns and the cypresses and skirted the little lake and raced downhill toward the woods. All the time we shouted his name, first one of us and then, as breath gave out, the other took up the call. "Pepi" . . . "Pepi" . . . The hot still afternoon, the golden air rang with our voices as we tried desperately to let him hear us.

We entered the woods and stumbled over twigs and mounds

of tufted grass, through the heavy shadows and the streaming sunlight brushing aside branches laden with copper-green leaves. We separated a little. "Pepi . . . Pepi . . ." Gisela's voice was high with breathless panic. She sounded like some strange bird separated and lost in a fantasy spring migration. I could see her green skirt flowing past the trees. And then suddenly I lost sight of her. "Gisela, where are you?"

"I've found him." Her voice came from somewhere to my left. "I've . . . found . . . him . . ."

I tore my way through the low growing branches of the trees toward the sound and saw her crouched on the ground with Pepi in her arms. The sunlight made arabesques of light and shade of their two dark heads. Pepi was grasping and sobbing, making little hiccuping sounds that were probably words if anyone could have understood them.

Gisela scarcely noticed me as I reached her side and leaned panting against a tree. She was murmuring "*Povero bambino*," stroking his head, his face, wiping away his tears with her fingers.

"He says that he saw the Signorina Vanessa. He says—"

"I did see her. *Zia* Juliet, I *did*. Her hair was all wet and . . ." Shudders began to shake his body. "She made a h-horrible face at me. Sh-she has never made a h-horrible face at me before."

I knelt by his side. "Pepi, listen carefully. Was Vanessa very near you?"

He shook his head.

"Then you couldn't be absolutely certain it was her, now, could you?"

"It was Vanessa . . . She . . . she s-she spoke to me."

"What did she say?"

He turned his face into Gisela's shoulder and I listened hard, translating as he hiccuped the words in Italian. Vanessa had said, "Be careful, darling. Someone is going to hurt you. But you must be brave. You mustn't let anyone scare you out of your wits, must you?" He sobbed that he had run toward her but that she had told him to keep away. "Just remember that I shall always love you." And then, it seemed, she had gone very quickly through the woods.

"But Pepi," I said, "you know that Vanessa would never try to frighten you by telling you someone was going to hurt you. You can't have heard what she said—at least . . . not properly."

"I . . . h-heard. She did s-say . . ."

"Then," Gisela cried "the signorina has gone mad; quite mad."

"All right. All right." I gave her a warning look. Pepi watched us too closely. "Which way did she go?"

He pointed. "To the D-Dead Land."

I looked into the distance and beyond the lavish emerald green and saw a brown haze.

"It adjoins this wood," Gisela explained. "They stopped the fire before it destroyed our woods as well," she continued. "But it cannot have been the signorina Pepi saw there. There is no one living for miles around."

I didn't want to admit—and perhaps be drawn into an explanation—that I already knew the Dead Land. I asked cautiously if anyone lived there.

"Only a young couple who come out from Rome for weekends. They have rented a villa there. It's very dilapidated, but they apparently have not been married long and are very much in love." She smiled dreamily at the thought and then, remembering our recent scare, held Pepi close to her.

I got up and shook fallen leaves and twigs from my skirt. "I'm going to telephone the signora. She must be told."

Gisela lifted Pepi into her arms. He clasped his hands round her neck and buried his face in her shoulder as if he were exhausted and wanted to shut out the huge, frightening world.

"Perhaps," Gisela said as we walked back to the villa. "La Signora will not believe you. Pepi does make up stories, you know. Sometimes to amuse himself, but they get—they get—"

"Out of hand?"

"Out of hand. Yes. And then he frightens himself."

"I think he was telling the truth. I must telephone, anyway. If there is someone who is frightening him . . ."

"Someone? You speak as if it could be a stranger. But how would a stranger know about the Signorina Vanessa . . . about her loving Pepi so?"

The one who was impersonating her would know; would know everything; could possibly wear her clothes; write her cards; copy her style of drawing; lead me on fatal trails . . . But I didn't say all this to Gisela.

"I . . . d-did . . . s-see . . . Vanessa . . ." Pepi was murmuring into Gisela's shoulder.

She began to talk to him softly. "*Caro*, listen. I think you saw a lady and because you wanted so badly for it to be the signorina, you told yourself that it was her. Do you remember me telling you about my uncle Costello? He was a shepherd in the Abruzzi mountains and every Christmas he would come down into the town to play music on his pipes. But he died and I loved him so much that I used to wake up at night and see him standing at the foot of my bed. I believed that God sent him just to show me that he still lived somewhere. So—"

It was too late. Pepi got a message she hadn't intended. He struggled out of her arm, fighting against her so fiercely that she had to put him down. He stood, furious and terrified, his face white. "But Vanessa is not d-dead. Not . . . *not* . . . *not*. You are so stupid, Gisela. P-people cannot write postcards from heaven. It is wicked to t-tell me that she is d-dead. Your Uncle Costello died, but Vanessa l-loves me; she w-would not die . . ." He looked back the way we had come.

I reached out and took his hand and as he tried to drag away, I held on to him tightly, like a little prisoner. So, unhappily, we made our way back to the villa.

We took Pepi to the kitchen where Maria sat him on the edge of the big table and fed him honey cakes, warm from the oven. I asked Gisela to get through to the *palazzo* for me and as soon as Alberto answered, she gave me the receiver.

I was put through to *Nonna* Allegra's apartments immediately and I told her what had happened, leaving out only the arrival of Vanessa's card.

Her voice came calmly over the wires. "Of course, you were quite right to tell me, but you mustn't be upset about it, Juliet. You see, you don't understand Pepi as I do. He is highly emotional and over-imaginative. His fondness for Vanessa was an obsession. What happened is quite obvious to me. He saw someone walking in the woods and because she was fair, he implanted Vanessa's image on to this completely strange girl."

"If you had been there and had seen him you'd have understood how real it was to him."

"Of course it was real. Hallucinations always are."

I burst out, "I don't believe . . ."

She interrupted me. "Pepi is capable of being frightened by his own shadow."

"But *Nonna*—"

She was impervious to my protests. "I understand my grand-child far better than you, Juliet."

It was a steel-hard rebuke, shutting me out; stressing my alienage.

"And now, will you please let me speak to Gisela? She has strict instructions not to let Pepi out of the villa grounds."

A little boy, imprisoned for the sake of his future value to Malimbrosa . . . I called Gisela and she came reluctantly, saying, "Pepi's tricycle. We forgot it. I must go and fetch it . . ."

I took her right hand and curled her fingers round the receiver. "The signora," I whispered. "Don't be frightened. She doesn't believe me, either." I left her and made certain that Pepi was safely with Maria, who was so fat that I wondered how she ever managed to get her shoes on. But there could be no face kinder than hers and I knew Pepi was safe.

I went down the terraces and across the garden, walking out of patches of wonderful mauve shadows into the marigold blaze of the sun. It was late afternoon when everything, every rose and peony and flame flower, seemed to lift its head a little higher as if searching the pitiless ultramarine sky for rain.

I paused when I reached the wood, trying to remember how far to the left Gisela had gone to find Pepi. In the end, a clearing helped me and I made my way through it and saw the tricycle flung against a tree. I hesitated for only a moment, then I left it where it was and looked ahead of me. The sepia landscape of the Dead Land in the distance had a sudden irresistible pull. I had no idea, when I reached it, how far I would be from the Villa Artemis, nor had I any wish to see the place again. But a compulsion urged me on, like a sleepwalker toward unseen danger. Somewhere around here there was a girl with bright hair obviously resembling Vanessa in so many ways that, seeing her from a distance, both Pepi and I had thought we recognized her; a girl cruelly sealing a small boy's love and terrifying him in just a few brief sentences called across a distance he must not diminish. I was quite certain that Vanessa would never have willingly frightened Pepi. So, the girl in the woods must have been the same one whom I had seen in the Via Veneto, and whom I had followed. A girl wearing Vanessa's opal earrings. The impersonator.

Had she come here by car? Had she walked from Isolesi? Or did she, too, live in the scarred stone villa? And, if so, her reason for being here and the words she had spoken to Pepi made terrifying sense. He was to be, as she had put it, "scared out of his wits." The reminder that "Vanessa loved him" was purely to assert her identity. It must have been she who had flung the card into Pepi's playroom; she who was everywhere —here, near enough to Pepi to watch him and play on his fears; near enough to me in Rome to send me searching for her in a place where only my own swift reflexes had saved me from death.

I walked carefully through the thick green woods, toward the beige tapestry-tinted distance that was the Dead Land. I paused now and then to look over my shoulder, to listen for the crack of a twig, the rustle of last year's leaves as someone stalked me. There was no sound.

At last I came to the first of the brown trees. Their dry, bare branches interlocked with those of the rich green chestnuts and I no longer trod on leaves and moss but crunched over dead wood and brown fern skeletons. I went cautiously for some minutes before I saw the villa. I had no intention of going up to it and risking something else hurled, this time with probably more accuracy, at my head. I stood concealed by a thick scarred trunk and watched.

The house looked deserted. There was nothing to indicate that anyone was there, no car stood in the drive, no shutter was slightly ajar. I wondered whether there were still bread-crumbs on the window ledge.

The minutes passed slowly. Coming here had served no purpose. Either I went up to the house and tried to find out whether a girl with bright hair lived there, or I returned as quickly as possible to the Villa Sapphira. I wasn't even tempted to the former but a reluctance to give up this abortive watch kept me pressed against the tree, eyes on the house without knowing what I expected to see. Little waves of heat swept over me; I wiped my palms on my dress, ran the back of my hand over my forehead. The only thing my walk had revealed was that, as the crow flew, the Villa Artemis was not very far from the Malimbrosas' summer home.

I was growing impatient and bored. Waiting was never a pastime I enjoyed, particularly waiting for something I couldn't even explain to myself. I had actually half turned to go back when the door of the villa opened, and a girl came out. For a moment she stood poised, looking about her. Then she closed the door and came out from the porch into the strong sunlight.

My reaction was purely involuntary. I neither stopped to think, nor did I quite realize what I was doing until I found myself running, stumbling over the rough ground.

"Vanessa . . ."

My progress was so slow that she had disappeared round the side of the house long before I reached the track that led to the house. I was scrambling over the bank, the blackened bracken tearing my nylons, scratching my hands and arms, when I heard a car start up. It must have been parked in the shade behind the villa. I saw its long dark nose, then the girl at the wheel. I scrambled over the bank as it turned toward Isolesi. I knew the girl hadn't seen me. The girl . . . Vanessa? I still didn't know for I had not seen her full face.

I crossed the track and walked up to the villa. I was no braver now than I had been a few moments ago, but I had a hope, which I firmly translated into a certainty, that the villa would be empty until the girl returned. All the same, I moved cautiously, creeping up to a shutter which had some broken slats. I peered through into a dim room. I could see some very plain furniture, a scatter of magazines, and a table just beneath the window.

I tried to see what was on the table and went so close to the worn shutter that I scratched my nose. But at least I saw, on the table, some pens, a block of notepaper and some cards. They were unusually large and grayish white in color. *The kind of cards Vanessa used when she sent drawings to her friends . . .*

A shadow suddenly hung above me. I wheeled round and let out a startled breath. It was the hawk again, poised in the sky. I relaxed, leaning against the stone wall. Brittle chips of dead wisteria wood caught in my hair and as I tore them out, fear and doubt chased through my mind like torturers. The cards were no proof that the girl was Vanessa, but if she were not, then their presence on that table was not coincidence.

Vanessa—or her impersonator? If I could only have seen her face close to. But I never had. Distance had always carefully divided us.

I knew, however, that whatever the consequences, I had to tell *Nonna* Allegra about the Villa Artemis. I had to convince her that I, too, had seen a girl who looked from a distance like Vanessa. I must corroborate that part of Pepi's story.

From that moment on, I would have to feel my way, perhaps even tell her about the cards, about the apartment in the Via Campisolo. It would mean breaking faith with Vanessa's demand for secrecy, and what did I know of the consequences of such a thing? If Vanessa were alive . . . but I could no longer be certain. In those moments in the Dead Land, as the sounds of the girl's car receded, I was in a kind of limbo beyond logical thought. I knew things I could no longer keep to myself.

I turned and fled down the uneven drive, across the track and into the tangle of burned undergrowth. My flight disturbed no birds, no wild things, in the unnourished undergrowth; I doubted if my feet killed even the most microcosmic insect. I ran out of the Dead Land and into the living one where the light was green. When I saw the bright, Renaissance-planned garden of the Villa Sapphira, I stopped running, faint with relief and flung myself onto the moss and fought for breath. I lay staring up at the over-weighted trees and faced the fact that it was imagination that made cowards of those to whom it was given. I stared at the prisms of light made by the leaves and the sun and asked myself what I feared. There was an easy answer. I feared for my life. Everything was dovetailing into a macabre pattern, the only trouble was that I couldn't see the basic threads. I didn't know whether Vanessa was alive.

I had, however, discovered by my visit that afternoon to the Villa Sapphira that Pepi, as well as I, was in the way of something so important that my life and his sanity were mere hazards to be put aside.

18 ❧

I WAS BEGINNING TO UNDERSTAND how the seemingly unplanned moves *Nonna* Allegra made with her jade knights and bishops occupied her restless fingers as she gave her mind to the gist of what was being said to her. Behind the movements of her hands there was absolute attention.

She was listening to me now as I sat in the carved chair on the other side of her desk and told her in detail about what happened that afternoon at the Villa Sapphira. I withheld the rest of my story. For Vanessa's sake, I didn't want to tell too much yet. First of all, *Nonna* Allegra's detective, or the police, must find out whether it was Vanessa or someone impersonating her who lived in the deserted villa.

"So," I finished. "Someone very like Vanessa is staying at the house in the Dead Land."

"But you did not see her face?"

"No. But Pepi did."

"I'm afraid his is not a story I can believe. And, Juliet, whoever the girl is, unless she is quite a monster, she would not go around terrifying small children."

"But she *did*."

She lifted her head, a jade bishop in her hand. Her eyes in their deep sockets burned with sudden anger. "I have already tried to explain to you, Juliet, that Pepi imagines things."

I refused to be intimidated. "All children do, but—"

"In his case the fantasies are dangerous. If you want it put to you more clearly, I am afraid that the child is a little unbalanced."

"I don't believe it." I sprang from my chair, courtesy forgotten. "Surely you can tell the difference between a child with . . . with . . . senseless tendencies and one who has been deliberately frightened."

"Yes," she rapped at me. "I can."

For a frozen moment our eyes were fixed on one another. We had become antagonists. I thought with a thudding heart, She's going to turn me out as she turned out Vanessa. She will not be crossed or argued with . . .

Allegra looked away first. She spread out her hands and looked at the two rings with the clear blue diamonds. "Then I must tell you what I do not want to be known outside our family. I have twice taken Pepi to a doctor. He has examined him and he tells me that the boy is a hysteric. For the moment we are doing nothing and hope that he will grow out of this . . . this . . . dementia. If he does not, then he will have to have psychiatric treatment."

It struck me that if Pepi had had a proper home life, with parents, with someone other than a peasant girl from the mountains to look after him, his fancies would probably have been curbed by the knowledge that he was loved. Perhaps it was a need for the right kind of attention—not the coddling and the over-anxiety, but for the companionship of children of his own age, and a sense of the security of a love that didn't see him merely as the heir to something that must appear to him as big as the world.

"After what you have told me of your own observations, I must, of course, report the matter to our detective." Allegra had risen and was looking at me without anger. "I will send Pietro Alderno, who is an investigator employed by us, to the villa you mention. I will tell him to find out all he can about the people who rent it. He is clever, he will work tactfully."

I did not know whether this was a concession to my insist-ance, to pacify me, or the need of an anxious family to have anything that might lead them to the solution of their mystery looked into. Whichever it was, I was grateful that at least she believed me and I thanked her.

"In fact," she said "I will telephone Signor Alderno now. Wait. You shall hear what I say to him."

I leaned against the tall chair and looked at the little chess board. I couldn't play the game; I didn't know whether she perhaps played right hand against left hand—and which was winning; the knights and the bishops seemed to be all over the board. Allegra dialed a number and I heard her ask for Signor Alderno and then, when he came immediately to the tele-phone, she gave him clear instructions. He was to go to Isolesi, the town, and then to Grottochiara, the village, and find out what he could about the people who lived at the Villa Artemis. "It is in the woods," she explained, "in a place the villagers call 'The Dead Land.' There was a fire there last year—" She waited and I saw her nod her head two or three times. "You will find your own reason for making these inquiries, our name must not be mentioned. Then, you will find another reason for calling at the villa. I doubt if they have running water or even electricity there, so perhaps you could represent the corpora-tion . . . Good . . . Good . . . You will go there tomorrow and make your report to me before six o'clock in the evening. And, Pietro, if you can manage to get inside the place, all the better." She replaced the receiver abruptly and gave me a dry, unamused smile. "Does that please you, Juliet?"

I murmured my gratitude and she waved it aside. "It is just possible that I, too, would like to know who this girl is who looks like Vanessa. And now, I have to see Bruno to give him his orders for tomorrow."

I was dismissed as she pressed a switch and spoke into the house telephone.

THE FIRST THOUGHT IN MY MIND when I woke next morning was that the Lyangenti ball was to be held that evening. I faced it with a mixture of dread and excitement. I longed to go; I looked forward to wearing the most beautiful gown I would ever possess; I wanted to see for myself what these functions, so glamorized by gossip columnists, were really like. And, despising myself, I wanted most of all to be with Philip. I lay in the seeping pale-pearl light of Vanessa's blue room and hoped that something would happen that would cure me once and for all of this terrible obsession.

An appointment had been made for me to go to a hairdresser just off the Via Veneto late that afternoon. Until then, the day was mine.

The first thing I did when I went out was to telephone Martin from a hotel lobby. To my utter and helpless fury, he saw the whole affair at Grottochiara as of no more significance than had *Nonna* Allegra.

"You really are a rotten detective," he said laughing at me. "The next thing is, you'll be seeing symbols in the sky. Do you really think anyone would be silly enough to hide Vanessa almost on the doorstep of the Villa Sapphira? Oh, come off it! And, since it seems she's in need of help, would she wander in the woods and drive a car freely into the village? If so, what's to stop her going to the police?"

"And if the girl isn't Vanessa?"

"Ah, that's different. But let's drop your vague suspicions for my more practical approach."

"Which is? . . ."

"The first thing to be done is to find the whereabouts of that three-panel screen in the drawing."

"There must be hundreds of screens in Rome."

"But not one with those hideous gargoyles and that very unusual scrollwork down its sides. I've been looking through books with photographs of the rooms of great houses."

"And you've found the screen and it happens to be in the Vatican!" My voice was derisive. He could laugh at me; I could laugh at him.

"No, I haven't found it, but I think we might if we worked on the idea together."

"And if it's in a public place where tourists go, what help would that be?"

"One step at a time. Perhaps someone, a guide maybe, saw a girl like Vanessa sketching there, and saw the man who came to get her and can describe him."

"It's an idea," I said grudgingly. "But how do we find the place?"

"I'll go on looking through the books I've got hold of. It's just a hunch, but it may turn out to be the one we need. Can we meet tonight?"

"No. I'm going to the Lyangenti ball."

He gave a low whistle. "Make the most of it, sweetie. As far as we know, only Cinderella went to one."

"For all *you* know, she might have spent the rest of her life dancing."

"We'll leave fairy tales. Do you think you can come down to earth sufficiently tomorrow night to have dinner with me?"

"I'd love to."

I came out of the telephone kiosk and looked for a taxi. I was going to find out if Artello were at home.

I had to walk the length of the Via Veneto to the taxi stand. And all the way I kept wondering if I would see the girl again; if she were following me. I might turn a corner and find her on the opposite side of the street; or I might be in a store looking for presents to take home to friends, or climbing the broken terraces of the Colosseum . . .

I told the driver to drop me at the corner of the Via Margutta and from there I walked, intrigued as I had been the first time, by this artists' quarter. The same little group of children played in the courtyard; the same tired geraniums drooped over the stones. I climbed the outside staircase to the top and found that Artello's door was closed. I knocked and a voice bellowed "*Vieni*" without coming to see if I were a friend or the rent collector.

This time the studio seemed less large. I supposed that was

because no one had been in it on my first visit. Now it was filled with the enormous bulk of a man with the Titian hair that is seen sometimes in the north of Italy. As I stood hesitating, I remembered the illogical caution of the southern Italians. "Never trust a man with red hair." Then, as he turned, I felt that I would trust him more than most.

Artello, at the potter's wheel, lifted clay-covered hands in mock dismay. "Signorina, forgive me, I didn't know that I was to entertain a lady." He held his hands under a tap and wiped them on a dirty piece of rag. He had a huge mouth and a charming smile.

"I am Juliet Holdroyd," I said, "a friend of Vanessa's. I believe you were, too."

He said cautiously, "Vanessa—?"

"Perhaps you knew her by the name under which she took her shop in the Via Prassodi. Maria Cyrena."

"That's right." He made no effort to dissemble. "I only learned who she really was when the police called and questioned me." He gave a wry look to his extended hand and put it behind his back. "Not quite clean enough to shake hands." He nodded in the direction of a dilapidated sofa. "Do sit down. The springs sag a bit, but you're very light-weight, aren't you, so you won't be too uncomfortable. I had a woman of fifteen stone here recently and down went her bottom, into the springs and up went her legs. You'll have coffee?"

I said I would and marveled that he could utter all those sentences without seeming to take a breath.

"I'm afraid I'm disturbing you. We could talk while you work, if you like."

"I enjoy an excuse not to be working. If I were industrious I'd be rich." He disappeared behind an archway of peeling plaster. I heard the rattle of cups and the burr of a grinder and then the smell of good coffee well made. There was a terrible noise of bumps and thuds coming from overhead.

"I'm sorry about the din above us," he shouted at me. "Kids play on the roof. Are you English?"

"Yes. I came here to stay with Vanessa and found that nobody knows where she is."

"I gather her family has been looking. Do you know them? Do you take sugar?"

I shouted back that, yes, I knew the Malimbrosas and that, no, I didn't take sugar.

"Good, because I seem to have run out."

The coffee was served in thick mugs but it was just as I had always dreamed of making it and had never managed to. Artello sat astride a chair, sipped loudly, and said, "You want to know what I know about Maria? Well, it's precious little. She came to me for drawing lessons—I'm really an artist you know. Pottery is a necessity because that's what the tourists like to take back. My paintings fetch a great deal more, *when* they sell—perhaps you'd like to see them."

"I'd love to, but later. Vanessa—Maria—"

"Of course." He was quite unoffended. "Well, she had a gift for the lightning sketch, impressions rather than anything with detail. That was her trouble, she was as indolent as a cat when it came to taking trouble. But everything she did, however few the strokes, had a kind of living quality. Oh, *Dio*, I hope she's still alive."

I looked at his face, half hidden by the mug. "Is there anything you can tell me—the smallest thing—that will throw any light on what's happened to her?"

"You're asking me exactly what the police asked. And some detective the family employed. No, I knew nothing about her, really, except that she was vivid as a flame."

"When you last saw her, did she seem happy?"

"Happy? You never knew with Maria. At the time I thought she was just a girl from an ordinary home, setting out to make her own way in life. A rebel. But Renata, that's the girl across the landing"—he tilted his head toward the door—"said that Maria's clothes came from the top places. She said, 'That girl has me puzzled. You don't wear Balenciaga suits or Galitzine dresses in a small shop on the Via Prassodi.' "

"She never gave the impression of being in trouble of any sort?"

"Not trouble." He stroked his chin. "But the last time she came here she picked up two paintings of mine to show in her shop and I had a feeling that something was on her mind." He paused narrowing his eyes.

"Did you ask her what was wrong?"

"Yes. And she just said, 'One day I'll get even with you men.' And then she laughed. But I had a feeling that she might just as easily have burst into tears."

I said, "Perhaps there was someone she was having an affair with . . ."

"Oh, I'm sure of that. A girl like her doesn't go out and about alone in Rome." When he laughed he showed a row of huge white teeth. "I once tried to get her to link up with me—you know, as one does."

I nodded.

"And she gave me a push and said 'I'm booked. Though heaven knows why. He's a rat! He's as two-faced as the moon in a mirror, but he magics me. And that's the hell of it.'"

"You never met this man?"

"No."

"No name?"

"No name." He added brightly, "She said something about you, too. At least, I suppose it was you. She said that a friend of hers was coming from England to stay with her. So it doesn't seem as if she were planning a disappearing act, does it?"

"And that's all you know?"

He said slowly, staring at me as if I were in some way the stimulus his memory needed, "Now I come to think of it, there was one small thing. Odd that I'd forgotten. But when I called at the shop with a new painting she might be able to sell on commission, I saw an English newspaper on her desk." He grinned at me. "I'm multilingual, the result of tramping round Europe for fame and glory. The paper was open at an article. It was called 'Concerning Rome.' Maria had told me that she knew quite a number of English people, so I asked her, without really being particularly interested, if she knew the man who'd written the article. She answered me with a laugh. 'Oh, that's my demon lover.' "

He stopped speaking, and I urged, "And—then?"

He spread his hands. "Nothing more."

Concerning Rome by Philip Cornel . . .

"So the police don't know about that?"

He shook his head. "I've a feeling that I mentioned it to the family's detective, though."

He waved his mug. "More coffee?" I shook my head "I've a very bad memory," he said, "but I'm sure I told the detective."

"And what did he say?"

"So far as I remember, nothing."

That seemed to be all Artello could tell me. Until the story broke that Maria Cyrena was Vanessa Malimbrosa, her life to the people around the artists' quarter was just something to be accepted without questions and probings. I had really learned nothing from this meeting that I did not already know, except that the rumors and whispers that Vanessa had been in love with Philip were now, for me at least, confirmed without any doubt.

I wandered absent-mindedly round the studio, looking at Artello's angry, flaming pictures, the green-bronze pots. I said I would come again and at last reached the door.

"I'd like you to sit for me sometime," he said, standing on the dark landing with me. "Your hair is luscious and I like gray-green eyes."

His glance traveled over me with such frank appraisal that I said quickly, "I'd be a disappointment. I get cramp if I sit still too long." I thanked him for talking to me, and escaped before he began a verbal survey of my good and bad points.

So *Nonna* Allegra must have learned of the affair between Vanessa and Philip, and yet she welcomed him to Malimbrosa. Why? Because she no longer cared what had happened to her granddaughter and was interested only in Philip's involvement with Irena? It presupposed her knowledge of Vanessa's possible love for Philip, although I only had *Zia* Romola's word and Artello's observations for that. But they added up, and the sum total so horrified me that I lagged in the street and was too late to grab the last taxi at the Piazza del Popolo.

I stared at the retreating taxi, unable to emerge completely from my absorption with Vanessa. Suppose *Nonna* Allegra felt that she had become a nuisance . . . And there I stopped, my thoughts refusing to function further. It was outrageous and quite unthinkable. Whatever had happened to Vanessa had been entirely without her grandmother's knowledge. The web of danger and intrigue could have been spun by Philip, but certainly without the help of Allegra Malimbrosa.

19 ✄

I MET *Nonna* ALLEGRA IN THE GALLERY as a clock in one of the rooms struck six. She called me as I was entering my bedroom.

"Oh Juliet, Pietro Alderno telephoned me ten minutes ago. He has been to the Villa Artemis and he tells me that it's quite empty except for a few pieces of valueless furniture. He managed to trace the owners of the place and found that they are an elderly couple who have rented the villa to a young Sicilian and his wife. But they gave it up some weeks ago and it is now unoccupied."

"But the girl I saw . . ."

She shrugged. "Someone could have been looking at the place with a view to buying it. The old couple want to get rid of it, but I gather it's in a deplorable state and nobody seems interested." She walked a few steps toward the elevator as if the whole affair were at an end. "So you see how right I was. You only saw the girl's back and so far as Pepi is concerned, I have tried to explain to you that his mental outlook is shadowy; he lives on fantasies. And now," she said, "just forget Vanessa and set your mind to enjoying yourself tonight. Philip will be calling for you about nine o'clock."

Hours later, walking along the gallery after going to my room to fetch my evening bag, I heard the clock strike nine.

There were voices in the rotunda below and I looked over

the balustrade and saw Philip talking to *Zia* Romola. Neither of them had glanced up and seen me so that I was able to stand there and watch him. He was quite unlike a fictional hero. He didn't wear his evening clothes with that shy, boyish charm which some women, though not I, found so touching. He was completely at ease and I stood with my somersaulting emotions, wanting the evening's festivity as desperately as I wished it were over.

I needed effort to move toward the stairs and down them. I went slowly, holding my long gown away from my feet, hand on the marble balustrade. I was almost happy in the certainty that I looked my best—my hair piled up in swathes round the top of my head, the golden necklace my only ornament so that nothing detracted from the perfect white folds of my dress. I also knew that I needed all the self-assurance I could find to get me through the evening.

Nonna Allerga had joined them in the rotunda and nobody noticed me until I had reached the last curve in the great staircase. Then, as if sensing someone behind him, Philip turned.

His scrutiny was cool, deliberate and all-embracing.

"So the nymphs have flown and the goddesses have descended from Olympus." The mockery in the compliment robbed it of floweriness. He watched me down the last few stairs, and in the lights from the chandelier, his eyes were brilliant.

His comment had set the seal for the evening. He obviously intended to play his role as my escort with a kind of "I'm going to pay you outrageous compliments but don't dare believe a word of them." Well, and I would play up to that; my flippancy would be my only guard against his magnetism; I would use laughter to combat the extravagance of my illogical longing for him.

Romola had turned, too. "She looks lovely, doesn't she, Philip? But, *cara*, have you no wrap? No evening coat?"

I said that I hadn't and that since it was a warm night, anyway, I wouldn't need one.

"Wait." She darted into the room behind the screen and came back with a cloak of some heavy blue silk. "I had a feeling you would not have brought anything suitable with you from London, so I found this. I haven't worn it for years, but cloaks are always elegant." She slid it round my shoulders.

I caressed the thick silk and saw that it had, over the gentian blue, a kind of patina of silver. "*Zia* Romola, it's lovely . . ."

"I am so glad you like it. You really could not go without some kind of wrap."

I thought with amusement: people at these functions just don't. Whether the night is hot or cold, you parade the beauty of an evening coat as you parade your jewels.

"Shall we go?" Philip asked.

"You will have a wonderful time," *Zia* Romola said.

Nonna Allegra merely nodded and lifted her hand a little as though to bless an evening that certainly would be no blessing to me.

The Villa Lyangenti stood some way along the Via Venti Settembre. From the street, all that could be seen of it was a tall tower behind high forbidding walls. We drove under a stone arch and into a huge courtyard. Lights blazed from a house that looked more like some of the churches I had seen in southern Spain. The bell tower was illuminated and from the ornate pediment over the open doors, light blazed down onto the arriving guests.

Philip parked the car, turned off the engine, and said, "I must warn you, dancing isn't a hobby of mine."

"That's all right. You can be my escort just as far as our hostess. Then you can escape. I'll be perfectly happy."

"I'm not escaping, my dear, nor are you. Like it or not, you're stuck with me for the evening." And with that gallant comment, he got out of the car and came round to open the door for me.

The villa had an enormous square hall, the whole of it of white marble, cold and austere, with statues in the alcoves. I was sent ceremoniously up the grand staircase with what seemed to me a hundred other women, chattering and laughing and calling to each other. There was a queue for the mirrors that stood along the walls and I gave up any attempt to reach one. My compact showed me that my hair was in place, my lipstick neither too bright nor too pale, my eye shadow sufficient. Then I turned and went down again wondering how I was ever to find Philip, if he wanted to be found.

It seemed that he did, for he was waiting by the marble bust of a man crowned with laurels.

He took my arm and led me toward a line of guests to be greeted by the hostess, the Principessa Theodora Lyangenti. She was one of the most forbidding people I had ever seen; very tall and thin, with her black hair dressed in severe uplifted puffs, rather like the classical Japanese style. Her gown was black, very plain and probably fabulously expensive. She wore one jewel at her throat; a great diamond which glittered as she turned to take my hand. I was quite certain as she flashed me her formal smile, that she had no interest in me whatsoever and that the whole sumptuous affair was, to her, as organized and heartless as a Malimbrosa enterprise. She was a *principessa* and the ball was a necessity in order to keep herself in the society columns of the continental newspapers.

Philip and I danced with the polite restraint of strangers. All round us was movement and color; jewels glittered and as the dancers passed the great banks of flowers along one side of the room, the women's skirts brushed the petals of the lilies and the tiers of azaleas.

The other side of the room was open to the terrace. I could see that the great glass wall had been folded back so that the illumined garden became one with the house.

Once, when the band stopped playing, Philip was greeted by a broad, stocky man who was introduced to me as Carlo Gianni, "one of the great Roman editors." When he introduced me, Philip said, "Miss Holdroyd is English. She has a certain claim to fame, for she spends her days walking the halls of Westminster—the place, you must know, where the British are misruled."

Signor Gianni kissed my hand, asking in surprise, "You are a politician, signorina?"

I laughed. "I'm merely a secretary and Signor Cornel exaggerates."

Gianni's smile broadened. "That is the charming weakness of our profession. We so often elaborate on the truth. I could not believe that you were yet a Member of your House of Commons. You are far too young and elegant and your face is too unlined. Let me beg you, signorina, never to age yourself prematurely by fighting for principles."

I laughed again. "If I had to speak in public, I would first see that the planks of the platform were loosened so that I could fall through just before I had to open my mouth."

"And that," said Philip, "is a load of humility. The signorina is perfectly capable of talking, and holding her own, I can assure you." His smile belied the acidity of his words. He said, "Shall we go into the garden? It's rather hot here." He turned to Gianni. "Join us. We're going to snatch a table before there's no place left to sit on but the grass."

"I will, when I can find my wife," Gianni promised.

I knew that the eyes of older women seated on little chairs that looked too fragile for them, were on me. I thought, That's what comes of wearing a Francesca Guiscarda dress. And walked by Philip's side into the garden.

Just before we stepped down from the terrace, he looked back. Curious, I turned, too. I recognized the swirl of an apricot chiffon skirt, and saw the gleam of Irena's rubies. Irena and Leo had arrived.

I had a feeling that just before I had turned my head she had glanced our way and that a look had passed between herself and Philip.

I said deliberately, "Irena and Leo have arrived."

"Yes, I've seen them. Come along, or there won't be a table left. I know these balls. Too many people and too few places to sit."

Behind us, the men spun the women around, colors lay almost too richly under the glitter of the chandeliers, the music was playing a quick-step and although the sound was slightly too brassy, the surroundings gave it glamour. Ahead of us lay the garden, sweeping away into a space that seemed incredible in a city as crowded as Rome. And then I remembered that I had heard that the Roman landscape gardeners of the Renaissance were both architects and artists, using every subtlety of evergreen, marble statue and water, creating vistas and the illusion of space.

The moon was high and ilex and cypress stood against the silvered sky. We walked down terraces and through a magnolia avenue, past pedestals on which marble men with faces like Caesars turned their sightless eyes upon us.

A mass of little white tables and chairs were set out on the lawns and all of them seemed already occupied. We found one at last at the corner of a winding path in the shelter of a box hedge and in full view of the moon riding high over an outspread cedar.

Philip said, "I have a sympathy with waiters in this crush. If you'll stay here, I'll fetch our drinks. What would you like? The champagne is flowing."

"Oh, champagne, please."

I watched him melt through the crowds and leaned back in my chair. I wondered dreamily how long the trees had lived and whether Catherine de Medici had walked among them, or the Borgias. Perhaps on this very spot someone had opened the tiny clasp of a ring and tipped poison into an enemy's cup. What did they drink out of in those days? Metal goblets? Sometimes, I had read, if the ancient Romans were very rich, they drank out of cups made of amethyst which, so it was said, had a magic protection against drunkenness.

PHILIP WAS A LONG TIME GONE. Somewhere behind me I could smell roses. I got up and looked for them. I found them, just behind the box hedge, white as paper in the moonlight.

A hand on my arm made me start and all the fears of the past few days flew back. In a panic moment it flashed across my mind that Philip had laid a trap to get me here and I had fallen with a crash into it. A voice said softly in my ear, "*Bella* . . . ah, *bella carissima* . . ."

I swung round, jerking my arm away from the hand. The young man was dark and very young—probably not more than eighteen. He was also happily drunk. He said in Italian, "You are alone?"

I answered him deliberately in English.

"Only temporarily. A friend has gone to fetch us drinks."

He exclaimed with delight, swaying gently in front of me, and spoke back in English, "It is so crowded—it is always too crowded at the *principessa's* parties. Your friend will be a long time. So, you and I . . . You like me, yes?"

"I like you, no." I stepped back from him. "And isn't it rather early to be drunk?" I was careful to sound bored.

"My name is Rudi," he said. "It is true, is it not, that English girls only pretend to be cold?" He touched my face and I slapped his hand. He giggled with delight. He was like some artless puppy quite certain that I was playing games with him.

I said, "Oh *do* go. I don't even like you."

I had said the wrong thing. His eyes glistened and he grabbed me and drew me toward him. I tried to jerk my face away. "Don't be so damned silly."

His mouth came down on mine.

A hand grasped my shoulder and wheeled me round.

My wild thought was, This is the trap—here in a Roman garden . . .

The young man gave a yell, lost his balance and reeled back, toppling with arms and legs flailing into the box hedge. Little leaves covered his face as he lay there staring stupidly up at me so that he looked like a handsome and bewildered clown. I breathed freely again. It was no trap. Philip's fingers released me. "I shouldn't try that again," he said to the boy and began to walk to the table.

"Help him up, Philip."

"Not on your life. He got down there, let him find his own

way onto his two feet. And you don't help him either." Philip pulled me back as I bent to give the struggling boy a hand.

Clutching at branches, he got to his feet and called after us, "What's the matter with you? I am careful about the girls I choose. This one wears no ring so she is not yours."

"I haven't had time to buy one," Philip retorted. "Now hop off."

The fall must have sobered the young man, for he gave me a long, sad look. "I do not understand, signorina, why you marry such an Englishman." Then he vanished with the speed of a sprinter.

I picked up the narrow tulip-shaped glass on the table before me. The champagne was dry and beautifully cooled.

Carlo Gianni and a woman with a fuzz of black hair and magnificent shoulders joined us.

"My wife," he said.

She gave me a wide, friendly smile. "I hope you enjoy this sort of thing. For myself, I'd rather be at home with my feet up. Sometimes I wonder if I am pleased that my husband is such a famous newspaper editor." She was a splendid, uncomplicated woman and she gave him a smile which belied her doubts.

More people joined us and the animated conversation flowed sometimes in Italian, sometimes in English as a courtesy to me. The laughter and the champagne shut out everything except the fun of the moment. I was enjoying myself.

There was a story about someone's great grandfather who ran away with a gypsy and, by some twist of fortune and a few bloody wars, produced a son who became a king, I was sitting back absorbing the vivid details, when a woman behind me called across the table.

"Oh, Philip, what's this we hear?"

The conversation stopped abruptly. I looked round and saw a girl with a small, weasel face and fountains of diamonds in her ears, holding the hand of the man with her and leaning across toward Philip. She seemed surprised at the silence which met her. "Do you have to be so mysterious?"

"Not that I know of," he answered.

The girl said, "An engagement needs a party—or didn't you know?"

He said quietly, "I had my engagement and my party six years ago."

The girl was obviously quite insensitive, for the silence merely added to her curiosity. She looked round the table and her glance lingered on me last of all. "But we've just heard from Rudi Sanrienzi that you and—"

I leaped in to reply before anyone else could. "Your friend Rudi was a little hooked on moonlight. It sometimes plays tricks with the imagination."

"He'll learn," Philip said.

The girl's earrings danced against her face. "You mean there isn't—"

"No," I said, "there isn't," and kept my face toward the girl, my expression bright with laughter.

Signora Gianni changed the subject neatly. I reached out for my champagne glass and took too big a gulp. I could smell a drift of jasmine scent from the girl behind me; I could see the flash of rings on the hands of the women at the table; the moonlight beat on my face making it so naked that I kept my hard, bright smile.

The girl said with a laugh, "Oh dear, so I nearly wasted my congratulations. Sorry." The smell of jasmine lessened as she drifted away.

The conversation soared round me, a little too animated, as if everyone in the party wanted to eliminate the memory of the weasel-faced girl's embarrassing interruption. Without looking at Philip, I knew that his head was turned away, perhaps in boredom or anger. I glanced at the people streaming out of the house and into the garden and saw Irena standing in a patch of light. I was certain, then, that the conversation had neither embarrassed nor angered him; he had scarcely bothered with it. He had seen Irena.

Soon after that the group scattered and Philip and I were alone.

"If you want to dance . . ." he began.

"But *you* don't, and I'm perfectly happy here."

"I doubt that." He turned and looked directly at me and I wished that it were his face on which the moon shone and mine that were in shadow. He continued "I think I should take you back to the ballroom just to show people that I don't expect to monopolize you."

"And you mind what people think? Of course. I'm so sorry."

"What are you apologizing for?"

"Keeping you away from . . . people you . . . want to be with."

"Stop being a little ass."

"I'm trying to be understanding." The word sounded smug and slightly pompous. I rushed on, "What I mean is, in all fairness, why should you have to spend your entire evening with me? People don't—"I rose and gave an airy flick of my hand. "I'm going for a walk. I'll do a kind of circular tour and go back to the ballroom. We'll meet up again later."

"All right. Go and commune with nature if you wish. But there's little nature has been left to do for herself here. You'll find that nothing has been allowed its freedom to be natural. It's one of those gardens where the owner's will has dominated and even the trees have been lopped and bullied into particular shapes."

I walked away from him without looking back. I was giving him a chance to go to Irena.

Trees, bushes, lawns, were exactly as he had said, forced into scrupulous perfection. The garden was beautiful in the way a painting is beautiful, because of the art of the designer. There were no beds of flowers, no wild patches, but it had a certain ordered loveliness and the smell of history.

The path curved sharply and I realized that I had come to a dead end. I turned, took two steps and bumped into Philip. He held my arms so tightly that I winced.

"I've lost my way," I said tamely.

"You never said a truer word."

"Why don't you join your friends?"

"I'm not mad keen on dancing. Remember?"

"Why did you follow me?"

"Curiosity."

There was a stir in the bushes and, like a leprechaun, the young drunk, Rudi, looked up at us, grinning.

"Oh, not you again," I cried.

He was sitting cross-legged in the bushes and he bowed from the waist. "Don't let me interrupt."

"You're not," Philip said, and before I could move, he bent his head and kissed me.

His grip and his mouth were entirely without gentleness. If, to the dizzy Rudi or anyone else who had seen us, we looked like lovers, it was one of their minor illusions. Philip was doing, apparently only for the malevolent delight of a tipsy boy, the very last thing he believed I wanted from him and he was doing it with a cold, deliberate forthrightness.

It was insane to feel anything but hatred for him, yet as I fought him, to Rudi's giggling delight, a wild thought flashed through my mind. *Who knows where the thunderbolt will fall?* It fell on me in a moonlit garden.

He let me go so suddenly that I stumbled and clutched at a bush which swayed with my weight. As I found my balance, I realized that at some time during the last few seconds, Rudi must have been sober enough to decide to disappear. I didn't even look Philip's way, but as I passed him on shaking knees down the path along which I had come, a woman appeared, walking alone along another path that ran at right angles. She was tall and her hair was like a dark crown upon her head. It was Irena and she looked straight ahead of her as if Philip and I were invisible. Yet the bushes were low and thinly spaced so that she must have seen our outlines come together in a mockery of love.

I was filled with shame and fury and my heels crunched the path with a violence as if I were trying to destroy something I trod on; my blood pounded through me with such force that I was quite certain my face was flaming red. I put my hand to my cheek. It was cold. Once, I glanced behind me and saw that this time Philip wasn't following me. I swung round a corner and came to the lawns with the crowded tables. I marched past everyone and saw people turn and look at me. They probably thought that I had been abandoned by some man who had picked up a prettier girl. My fury must have been too obvious —and they were not to know that it was fury with myself for the incredible paradox of my emotions.

When I reached the ballroom, I hesitated. I didn't want to go in and watch the dancers, nor did I intend to hide myself away in the powder room upstairs. I escaped into the silver darkness and walked round the house. It seemed hopeless to try and find a place where I could sit alone; people were everywhere, laughing, chattering, voluble groups or silent couples. And then, walking blindly into a dark corner, I found a little arbor. There was a faint scent of roses. I sat down gratefully on the iron seat, lifted my head and took in deep gulps of the soft air.

Ruth Warren came back to me like a level-headed ghost, from the past. "And the third time it happens, it is emotional suicide."

I fought a battle with myself staring from my dark corner onto the moon-dazzled garden. I was young and free; I was independent and, I hoped, proud. I reached out my arms, resting them along the cool back of the seat. I tried to breathe evenly, calmly; to lay the fantasy of infatuation once and for all. I closed my eyes and thought, *I am free . . . I am free . . .* But underneath the avowal, the demon of real knowledge, stirred and spoke. *I am possessed.*

I heard it and listened. Then, my rational mind argued, there was only one thing for me to do. I must leave Rome. I had not found Vanessa and I had been no help to Pepi and what Romola had told me that first evening, "Vanessa is dead," was beginning to seem a reality. So far as Pepi was concerned, the young weep bitterly and forget quickly. Only escape from Rome could save me from this helpless emotional entanglement and from the threat to my own life. Let the police search for

Vanessa; I had proved too amateur for the job. Leave Rome . . .

"You'd better contemplate the stars from Malimbrosa." Philip's voice was low and amused. "Come along. The party's over."

"This is becoming a kind of game with you, isn't it? 'Find Julie' . . ."

He said, "If you think I enjoy playing hide-and-seek, I don't. But it's late and I want to go home."

"Late?"

"It's past two o'clock. If you'd like to stay till dawn, you can. We'll find Irena and Leo. They'll look after you. But I have a long day ahead of me tomorrow and I've missed far too much sleep in my life, as it is."

Time must have passed quickly as I had sat fighting my private battle to the final conclusion that I would leave Rome, but I knew that the festivities at the Villa Lyangenti had lost their fascination. I, too, wanted my bed.

We walked together through the clusters of people back to the glittering chandeliers and the rhythmic beat of music and found our hostess. As she took my hand she remarked with complete disinterest how delighted she had been to meet me. I was quite certain that she had forgotten my name and, so far as she was concerned, I could have come from Outer Mongolia.

Wrapped in Romola's sky blue cloak, I walked ahead of Philip to where his car was parked. Once, I turned and looked back toward the house. I would never again be asked to such a party and yet I hadn't made as much of the occasion as I might have. I had let the glamour and the excitement pass me by while I fretted, like an exile for a forbidden city, for an impossibility. Why couldn't I take the moment and enjoy it? And what was it in my makeup that caused me to be so involved with the people and the things that could destroy me? The answers were almost too simple. There was nothing complicated about me; I was as ordinary and predictable as anyone else and I happened to care for my friends. If they needed help, I'd help them if I could. My weakness was that I also possessed a large slice of impressionability that drew me to people who were bad for me . . .

A car swung out of the parking line. Philip grabbed me and dragged me back just in time. "Do you have to walk right under some poor innocent's wheel?"

I said crossly, "He must have seen me. He could have waited."

He laughed. "Drivers in Rome don't wait. And, thanks to me, you'll live to fight another day."

"Fight?"

"For Vanessa," he said, and opened the door of the long dark Lancia.

20

IT WAS A FEW MINUTES BEFORE I became aware that the streets through which we were passing were unfamiliar. I leaned forward staring ahead of me. "Is this a short cut back to the *palazzo?*"

"No."

"Then where are we going?"

"For a drive."

"I thought you wanted to go home and catch up on some sleep."

"I have impulses."

"So have I, and mine is for my beautiful, comfortable bed."

"Then it's a clash of wills, isn't it?" He lifted his hands slightly from the wheel.

I capitulated because I knew I had no choice. "All right. You're in command of the car and at two o'clock in the morning I don't feel like a fight."

"Good."

I stole a sideways glance at him. His face was strong, but not sinister . . . However much he was involved in Vanessa's disappearance, this was not a dangerous moment for me. The whole of Malimbrosa knew that I was with Philip . . . And then I wondered how much I could trust Vanessa's family.

"Where are we?"

"This is the Janiculum." He stopped the car, got out, and came round to open the door for me.

Cool air fanned my forehead. I beat back the little spurt of fear that he had not brought me here either for my pleasure or my good, and we climbed the hill to a high ridge. Rome lay smudged with late moonlight and lamplight, cupolas and monuments like shadows painted on starred silk. I had never felt before as I felt as I stood by Philip's side, tired and calm and utterly fatalistic, as if whatever happened would happen anyway, not even fearing him.

For an age we stood silently side by side, and when at last Philip spoke it had the impact of a shock on the still, undisturbed night.

"Five years ago," he said, "Marian and I stood here and watched the dawn."

"Marian?"

"My wife."

I could only have murmured "I'm sorry," which would have sounded like an inanity, so I stayed silent, looking out toward the outline of the Victor Emmanuel monument, which the Romans affectionately called the "Wedding Cake."

"We had been married just a year," Philip said.

I drew the cloak closer round my shoulders, rubbed my hands down the smooth silk, and knew that he still needed no comment from me.

"After a marriage such as ours, nothing is ever deep again. Life is just compromise. One seizes opportunities, material and emotional, takes the moment and moves on to the next."

I hugged my arms beneath the cloak. "Living without feeling! How empty that must be, like living in a vacuum."

"On the contrary, freedom from emotional involvement gives a most marvelous sense of space in which a man can breathe and live. I had to shut up the past in an airtight compartment. It is like another world which I must look back on with discipline, or else I'm lost. That's why I'm able to enjoy the present in a totally different way. Even now, I'm finding it very good."

"Just standing here—"

"Yes."

"But you remembered—Marian—"

"Deliberately. That's why I came to this place. I wanted to test my strength, and I know now that I can relegate the past to its right place. It had meaning and depth, but it is over. The present has to be lived, and I find that good." He turned and looked at me. "You in your white dress and blue cloak and your hair . . . I'm a very ordinary man; I like my sensual pleasures." He paused and added, "Don't be alarmed. I never take them without permission."

"And nothing is ever serious?"

"Not any longer."

A few minutes crept by, then Philip spoke again and the light had gone out of his voice. "There are times when we shut ourselves away from hurt with a wisecrack or a piece of bravura."

"Bravura?"

"We say, 'I'm strong again' and believe we mean it. That's when we get kicked into the pain of realizing that we aren't strong at all; that it's all as I said, 'bravura.' "

"So you can still feel?"

"I suppose so."

"So all you've been saying is contradictory."

Under the lamplight his expression was of someone brought back from a long way off.

"Oh, no. I have everything nicely planned. I look on the past as from a very great distance with only a remembered sadness. It was brief and perfect and is over. Tonight is the first time I have allowed myself nostalgia—it is too destructive an indulgence. The present, for me, is delightful and the future good. I want nothing to upset that balance, do you hear?" He swung round on me with such force that I stepped sharply back. His hands gripped my shoulders. In the lamplight his eyes looked angry. "Why the hell did you come to Rome?"

"You know the answer to that." I tried to outstare him, but it was I who looked away first.

He said abruptly, turning from me, "You're right. What I said just now was contradictory. For a few moments I no longer felt strong; I was no longer certain that I had conquered feeling. I made a mistake in coming here."

For a flash, he was very human. His wife's death still hurt. I said quietly, "Let's go back, Philip," and reached to take his hand.

He avoided me and stood staring out onto Rome and I wondered with whom his thoughts were; Marian? Vanessa? Irena?

He said in a low, bitter voice, "This isn't the place for us."

I had a feeling that he had suddenly remembered that I wasn't just a woman standing quietly on the Janiculum which had reawakened a sadness he believed was over. We were deeply disturbed enemies, he and I—Vanessa had made us so.

I walked away from him down the hill to the car and it was some time before he joined me. We drove in absolute silence back to Malimbrosa.

Leo opened the door for us. "Irena and I have only just returned. Come in." He looked at Philip. "I've brought Brett McArlan back with me. I'd like you to meet him."

"The American engineering genius?" Philip said. "I don't miss opportunities like that. Three o'clock in the morning or not, I'm going to pin him down to an interview before he leaves Italy."

"Come and make the appointment, then," Leo said, and turned to me.

"I'm going to bed," I said. "Goodnight, Leo. And thank you, Philip, for tonight."

He gave me an odd look. "For which particular part of it?"

I did not answer, but turned and went up the half-darkened staircase.

The burr of men's voices from the *salone* followed me across the hall to the elevator. The ormolo clock struck three as I entered the blue bedroom. I undressed, got into bed and lay on my side telling myself that I was tired and would sleep. But every time I touched the borders of it, some incident out of the evening crept into my half-comatose brain and slapped me awake again. Although the room was lofty and fresh-smelling, I had a sudden need for air. I got up, slid into a robe, pushed wide the shutters. The moon had set and it was too early for dawn; there was a chill in the air and all the day's heat had seeped out of the stone balustrade so that it was cold as I leaned against it.

There was no sound from below. Leo had either taken his visitors to his own apartments or, more likely, they had had a drink together and then left. I was quite certain that Philip had got his appointment to interview Leo's American friend.

And Philip himself? I had an irrational urge to go to the roof garden and look across the low buildings to his high apartment. But to have done so would have been indulging in one of those adolescent urges I had told myself long ago I had grown out of. I closed my eyes, willing Philip out of my mind . . .

> Weave a circle round him thrice
>   And close your eyes with holy dread,
> For he on honey-dew hath fed,
>   And drunk the milk of Paradise.

"Holy" was ludicrously inappropriate unless attached to the gods. Leaving that word aside, the words were appropriate for both Philip and me. He already stood within the circle that made him invulnerable. He had drunk the magic potion of perfect happiness with the dead Marian. For me, I had to find the way to weave my own circle in order not to commit what Ruth had called "emotional suicide."

Engrossed in my paradox of fantasy and reality, I was at first only vaguely aware of voices in the *salone* below. The shutters must have been pushed back and a window open for I could not only recognize the voices, but I could distinguish certain words. Irena and Philip were talking. Or no, not talking— arguing.

I heard Philip exclaim, "Dear God, you should know what you have to do."

Irena made some long, wild protest, the words running into

each other so that I could not distinguish them sufficiently. There was a pause, and then very clearly I heard her cry. "Philip . . . Oh Philip, try to understand . . ."

I turned and fled into my room, pulled the shutters to and half closed the windows, muffling Irena's weeping.

21 ✄

I CALLED AT JUTURNA'S AGAIN the following morning. I doubted
if I would be contacted again through them after the last
horrifying, abortive attempt on my life. On the other hand, it
could have been that Vanessa herself had sent me a message, in
desperation, but someone had intercepted it and put his—or
her—own plan in motion. If that were so, and Vanessa knew
nothing about it, then she might try to contact me again
through Juturna's. Next time, if there was a next time, I would
take Martin with me.

The assistant in the shop looked surprised to see me again,
shook his head and said no one had telephoned or called to
claim the earring. I really must take it to the police. He spoke
severely. He wasn't much older than I, but he looked at me as
if he were a reproving father.

I said quickly, "Please don't think, signore, that I intend to
keep the earring. In fact, to prove I'm completely honest, I'll
give you my address. I'm staying at the Palazzo Malimbrosa."

The surprise on his face was almost comic. His manner
changed; I was no longer a nonentity who had spun him a yarn
about some extraordinary coincidence in finding an earring
belonging to a long-lost friend. Malimbrosa was the "Open
Sesame" to trust and obsequiousness.

I could see, however, that something was beginning to puzzle him and realized that I was on dangerous ground. I wondered, as I had on my first visit, whether the two names, Vanessa Malimbrosa and Maria Cyrena, were vaguely linked in his memory. The tiny diamond star he wore on his lapel winked at me. I felt that jewelry was probably his life and his world. For such a man, events in newspapers would become forgotten almost as soon as they had been read.

But even if the names Vanessa and Maria were actually registering, it didn't matter. I was finished with secrecy, although I had no intention of explaining anything more to him.

I asked him to contact me at the *palazzo* should the owner of the earring telephone him again. But perhaps, before that happened, I would have had a chance to tell *Nonna* Allegra as much of the story as I knew. If Vanessa were no longer alive, then I could not harm her and whoever was impersonating her must be found either by the family's detective, Pietro Alderno, or the police.

All the same, as I left Juturna's, I had a sensation of sick depression. Like someone on a cliff edge, with a demon at her back, whichever way I jumped my life was threatened—and I didn't want to die. My only safety was in escape from Rome.

Mixed with my fear, however, was an intense curiosity. If Vanessa had been killed—deliberately or accidentally—who was impersonating her? And was she being hired to play the part? And whom did I menace?

I walked blindly along the street, sometimes bumping into passers-by and murmuring an apology without really seeing them. I was wrapped around in the helplessness of my own despair. I wondered whether caged birds, with the inherited memory of the freedom of their species, felt something of what I did as they sat and looked through the bars of their cages.

As I walked, I wavered in my decision.

I was ashamed of what I saw as my weakness in planning an escape from things too strong for me. I had a half-desire to stay and fight, but the more logical wish for self-preservation won. I would go back to England and *Nonna* Allegra must not be given some vague, carefully polite explanation. She must be told of everything that had happened to me since my arrival.

I was passing a tourist office in the Via Cola di Rienzo and a group of people were climbing into a coach. On an impulse I went into the office and bought a ticket for what was called "A Lightning Tour of Rome." The description depressed me—nothing in Rome should be flipped through like a series of color pages in a magazine—but I needed to be freed for a few hours from my own thoughts. So, with none of the delight with which, in England, I had looked forward to sightseeing, I climbed with the rest of the tourists in and out of the coach. I stood silent and awed on the jagged steps of the Colosseum; I threw coins into the Trevi fountain and made my mechanical wish that I should return; I looked up at Michaelangelo's God creating Adam among the marvelous painted groups in the Sistine Chapel. And in every place, I looked for the girl with the bright hair . . . Vanessa or her impersonator.

On our return I asked to be put down outside the Excelsior Hotel and walked up the Via Veneto to the *palazzo*. I was quite prepared for *Zia* Romola to remonstrate with me when she heard how I had spent my morning. But, as it was, I lunched alone in the great dining room with its heavy black oak furniture. *Nonna* Allegra and Irena seldom had lunch in the formal dining room, but I had hoped that *Zia* Romola would be there.

When Nunzia entered to remove the little dish of creamed shrimps, I turned to ask her if the Signorina Romola were out and saw, to my surprise, that her eyes were red-rimmed.

"What is it?"

She shook her head, set a crimson and gold plate with little pieces of breast of chicken and a salad on a matching dish before me, then, with her head averted, asked, "You will have wine, signorina."

"Don't bother, I'll help myself."

But she began pouring, and the bottle shook against the crystal goblet.

I asked quickly, "The signora isn't ill?"

She shook her head. "No. She is lunching in her room with the Signor Leo. But I do not think they will eat much, they are too distressed."

"What has happened?"

She gave me a sharp look. "We who work here, signorina, are pledged not to gossip about what goes on. But we cannot help knowing."

A feather of fear brushed over me, but I said matter-of-factly, "And as I'm staying here, I can't help knowing, either."

"It is the Signora Irena."

"She is ill?"

"She has gone."

I picked up a fork and flicked at the chicken slices. Then I put the fork down and gripped my hands in my lap. "What do you mean—gone?"

"She has left the *palazzo*. Bianca, her maid, helped her pack and she has taken some luggage and a little jewelry, but not very much. Bianca is in the kitchen; she has wept herself sick."

"If she is just taking a holiday, why is everyone so upset?"

"It is no holiday, signorina. She went very quietly and gave me a note to be handed to La Signora only after she had gone. Bianca said that there was a letter for the Signor Leo also in their apartment and La Signora telephoned him sometime this morning when she read the one I handed her, and he came home. But I must not talk any more, even to you signorina."

"Nobody shall know we have talked at all," I assured her. "Don't worry. But thank you for telling me."

When the door had closed, I wished there were a dog or a cat around to whom I could slip the chicken which I felt would choke me.

Last night suddenly became vivid to me. All my senses flashed back to the moment when Philip had taken hold of me and played the game of lovers for the sake of a silly, tipsy boy; I saw again Irena passing along the path at right angles only a flash of a moment later.

Remembered time slid forward to the early hours of this

morning and the sound of Irena's distressed voice in the room below me, of her sobbing and of Philip's impatience.

I felt searing stabs of conscience that Irena had been a witness to that brief seemingly passionate scene in the garden of the Villa Lyangenti. She must obviously have misunderstood. But even if I could have gone to her and explained, what would have been the use? She might have thought I was protesting too much. I hated Philip all the more for what he had done, not only to Irena but to me—for making me feel guilty of something that had not been of my choosing. But deeper than the hatred was my helpless emotion, my infatuation, which must be killed at all costs—and quickly.

Nunzia returned with a water ice. It was one that was a particular favorite at Malimbrosa, taken from a recipe from Sicily and flavored with jasmine. I ate half of it and then escaped from the oppressive dining room. As I went along the gallery to my bedroom, I wondered if Zia Romola had heard me and would come out and call me into her apartment and give me her version of what had happened. But the gallery was silent and deserted.

I went to the bed, turned down the quilt, and lay on the silken sheets reaching for old Luciana's diary. Set in the past, it would be a release from the present. I felt for the book and my fingers touched only the base of the bedside lamp. The diary was gone.

Up to that moment I had wanted it half-heartedly, but its disappearance made my need for it compulsive. Filipa, the maid who looked after the private apartments, could have tidied my room and put it away somewhere. I got up and began a systematic and fruitless search of drawers. Then I thought that perhaps Zia Romola, who had changed the flowers in my room that morning, could have supposed that I had finished with it and had taken it back to the cellars, or even decided to read it herself. Certainly, she hadn't minded my having it, and there was little likelihood of someone's having deliberately removed it from my stranger's eyes. My first half-hearted wish for it had become an urgency. I picked up two English paperbacks I had bought at the kiosk in the Via Veneto, but neither interested me at that moment. I tossed them down and wondered if there were anything downstairs in the library that might hold my attention for an hour or so.

Only my footsteps disturbed the siesta silence of the great house; the rotunda was deserted. From the dome, red king and green jester glittered in the sunlight from the hidden windows; the parma violet columns were cool as I touched them.

I went round the coromandel screen into the room beyond. Almost all the books in the glass cases were volumes in tooled leather and gilt edges and all of them were written in Italian. It was enough effort for me to speak and understand the language; I had no wish to spend the next hour trying to read its difficult classical literature as well. I needed something easier to digest; something like the diaries which were written in Luciana's simple, direct Italian. There had been a small pile of them in the cellar chest and I could go down and fetch another.

I went through the door leading to the kitchen quarters. There seemed to be no one around and those servants who were not sleeping through the siesta hour in their rooms were probably in their sitting room at the far back of the house.

The passage was very dark with rooms leading off it, and at the far end were the huge kitchens I remembered as a child.

I knew my way to the cellars and didn't bother to turn on the lights, but there was a small strange sound somewhere ahead of me like the retreating footsteps of someone wearing slippers. I could also smell the hint of a scent Irena used, dry and exotic and made by Guerlain. But I had been told that she was no longer here . . . I stood still and called her name incredulously. "Irena?"

No one answered me. I walked down the stone passage toward the door to the cellars. The explanation for the scent was obvious. Irena was gone and Bianca had not been able to resist spraying some on herself. She was probably nervous of being caught using it and, hearing someone approaching, was slipping away ahead of me.

I came to branching passages and remembered to turn left, past some more closed doors, and found that the huge thick door to the cellars was open. I flicked on the light over the worn stone staircase and climbed down. There was a second switch at the bottom and I pressed it. Nothing happened. I looked up and saw by the staircase light that the bulb was missing. Someone had been here since I last came, the light had failed, and the bulb had been removed and not replaced. It wasn't important because the reflected light from the sun outside the grille faintly illumined the first cellar. I went through the arch into the next one where the chest full of books stood and put my hand to the switch. Again, there was no light. But it was too dim to see if here, too, a bulb had been removed.

One failed light was understandable; two were a suspicious coincidence. I looked into the connecting cellars with their vaulted ceilings that, exaggerated by the dimness, seemed to stretch away into absolute infinity; the ordinariness of it all, with the great trunks and chests, the discarded furniture, the bits and pieces that were reminders of a family with too many possessions, was replaced by the sensation of a prison alive with tormented ghosts. I no longer wanted to search for another of Luciana's diaries, so I went back to the first cellar and turned to go up the staircase. My foot was on the first step when the light went out and the door began to close.

I shouted, racing up, stumbling on a broken step, but by the time I reached it, the great door was closed. I hammered on it with my fists, but I made no impact on the enormous thickness —the place had been built to keep far stronger hands than mine from escaping. I decided that my feet might make more sound and I kicked the door, all the time shouting myself hoarse. Nothing moved and at last, exhausted, I leaned against the wall and tried to tell myself that no one had deliberately locked me in.

The door had closed through my own carelessness. I remembered now that it was too late, that when we had come here as children, Gisela had always secured the door with a huge hook

and an iron ring on the side wall. It must have been luck that
the door had not closed on me when I had come down here to
look for a snuff box to replace the one *Zia* Romola had broken
. . . Or perhaps it was bad luck for, had it happened then, she
would have known where I was, and it would have taught me
to be cautious the second time.

I ran my fingers over every inch that I could reach and
found nothing but rough, aged wood thick as a tree trunk,
unyielding as steel. I gave up shouting and hammering when I
realized that the door, like the vaulted stone arches above me,
would be soundproof. The ancient Romans who had once
lived there would not have wanted to be disturbed at their
feasting by the cries of their prisoners.

There was a tea chest underneath the grille. I crossed to it
and tried to pry the grille open. I might have known that it
couldn't be moved from inside.

Then I began to shout. My voice hit back at me, muted by
the thick oleander bush outside. I pressed myself against the
grille, listening to the roar of the traffic passing outside the
high wall of the *palazzo*. I could not hope that my voice would
carry above that din and, even if someone heard it, they would
think it a cry from the street, a child calling its mother; a
woman shouting at a man; a sound distorted by the roar of the
cars. I faced the fact that no one from outside those walls
would come to my rescue.

The clammy cold pressed about me. I knew that nothing
that was stored here was ever needed. Nobody wanted the
dresses of long-dead people, nor old books, nor boxes of objets
d'art when the rooms upstairs overflowed with them. Neither
from inside nor outside the great terracotta palace would
anyone come to find me in the cellars.

Suddenly a thought occurred to me. Perhaps that was why
the light bulbs were missing. Perhaps thieves, knowing of the
treasures, had entered and rifled the chests. It was a far more
comforting thought than the fear that someone had deliberately shut me in.

I felt my way through the arches to the cellar where I had

found the little snuff box. Only the thinnest filter of light reached it, but it was enough to show me that the chests were still crammed with snuff boxes and fans and painted miniatures. Nobody had broken into Malimbrosa.

I returned to the comforting light of the first cellar and stared up at the grille and tried again to mock at my fear. There was nothing calculatedly sinister about the door closing on me. Why on earth should I think I was important enough for anyone to harm? In view of what had already happened to me twice, my optimistic question was a fantasy. Someone had most certainly wished to harm me.

I had to find out if the diary had been put back in the chest. I lifted the lid and tried to see the volumes in the dark and could not. So I took the top ones, a few at a time, to the grille and looked at them. The 1955 diary wasn't among them.

I might have searched the whole chest in case the particular little volume had, for some reason, been hidden at the bottom of the chest. But it was no longer of much importance. Only my escape mattered. *Keep thinking . . . keep thinking . . .*

My heels clattered as I walked through the cellars, looking for something with which I might batter the door down. I found a thick mahogany pole, but when I took hold of it, I had to use both hands to drag it from the wall. I trailed it as far as the stone steps, and then its weight defeated me. I let it drop with a tremendous crash and hoped the sound would penetrate the rooms above and that someone would hear.

Time crawled; fear also crawled like spiders over my skin. I wore a sleeveless cotton dress and I began to rub my arms to warm them. Through the chinks in the thick foliage of the oleanders, I could see that the sun burned over Rome, but the vaults had the chill of two thousand years. I knew that water flowed underneath the city, breaking out into the beauty of its fountains. In all probability there was a stream beneath the foundations of the Roman villa upon which Malimbrosa stood and the stones over which I stormed and fretted were impregnated.

When the siesta was over, would the family wonder where I

was and search for me? And, if they did, would they think of looking here? They would probably not even wait dinner for me. They would say, "Juliet is out with that young Englishman and she hasn't bothered to tell us. That is just another example of today's bad manners." . . . "Juliet is bored here. Her surroundings mean nothing to her; it is young men she wants." . . . I could imagine some such comments over the dinner table. I was quite certain that no one would suggest that I might be huddled beneath them with the great stone arches as silencers between us.

The enforced inactivity was intolerable. Somehow I had to get a message through to the world outside and the idea came in a flash of memory as I sat on the box underneath the grille and stared at the clutter around me. I leaped down from the box and went to the chest that had held the clothes which had once so delighted Vanessa and me. Kneeling on the rough, cold stone, I tore at the tarnished brass locks and lifted the heavy lid. The smell of dust, stale scent and moth deterrent rose in a cloud as I riffled through the clothes to find what I knew was there.

It lay at the bottom of the chest, a sunshade of faded rotted silk. I dropped it on the floor and then searched the tea chest which I knew from our childish explorations contained small but heavy objects. I unwrapped them from the layers of paper which protected them and at last found a small metal statuette that was thickly rusted. I seized it and with the sharp edge of the base made a cross on the stone floor. It worked. It left a clear brownish-red stain. With a sense of desperate triumph, I then went to the box where the books were kept, tore out a fly leaf from one of them and with the edge of the statuette wrote in rust-colored letters; in Italian: "I am locked in the cellars. Juliet."

I wrote the same message on the other side in very large writing. Then I impaled the note on the end of the ferrule of the sunshade and climbed onto the box underneath the grille. I chose the widest opening and carefully pushed the stick through. I was terrified that the paper would become caught on a branch of oleander and because of this fear, I worked with a patience rare for me. I probed and pushed the tip of the sunshade with its precious message through the bushes and saw at last that it had reached beyond the oleanders. Then I eased the message off the ferrule and pushed it forward until it lay in the center of the path.

I wrote three messages on three fly leaves, pushed them all through at points as far away from each other as I could, and then waited. Malimbrosa must never be untidy. At some time or other, someone would glance out to open a shutter or close it and would see the pieces of paper; a servant would be sent to throw them away and huge rusty writing on at least one of them would be noticed . . . And if not? If nobody looked out of the windows tonight, then in the morning Francesco, the gardener, would come to tidy up the terrace and sweep the path round the house. Tomorrow morning . . . And by my watch it was only four o'clock in the afternoon.

I faced the worst. If nobody saw the pieces of paper on the path within the next few hours of daylight, I would have to spend the night in the cellar. And for that, I would need warmth. I would have to take out piles of ancient clothes from the old trunk, sleep on some, wrap myself in the rest. If by any chance anyone found me while I was sleeping—*if* I could sleep in these cold, one-time prisons—they would find a strange sight, a sleeping girl lying on faded silks and satins, covered by rotting velvets and old lace.

The fear that lay beneath my practical efforts to save myself had made me thirsty. I went through the maze of cellars, under the great arches, to the place where the wine used to be kept. *Nonna* Allegra had decided many years ago that it should be stored in a small stone room on the kitchen floor because she had suspected at that time that one of the servants had explored the chests of snuff boxes and fans and miniatures and had stolen some. That was years ago and the present staff were too trusted for the cellar ever to be locked. Neither food nor wine was stored there now. There was, however, just a chance that a bottle of something could have been overlooked.

I had to feel my way to the farthest place where the racks stood. I ran my fingers along the wooden slats and had one semi-hysterical thought. With nothing to eat and only wine to drink, they'd probably find me lying dead drunk on my pile of rotting silks. They wouldn't; the racks were empty.

I went back to the first cellar and a fear struck me that a wind might spring up and blow my messages into the bushes. I went to the grille, climbed onto the box and peered out. The pieces of paper had gone.

I had been frightened from the moment when I found the door locked against me; now I knew real terror. Someone watched; someone guessed that desperation would make me resourceful and had been on the alert for whatever I would do in order to try and get help.

I climbed down from the box so carelessly that I slipped and fell. I lay huddled on the floor, my face in my hands. My heartbeats seemed to spread up to my throat making me breathless. I thought, *Fear can kill*, and tried to get a grip on myself.

I was certain now that whoever hated me was at Malimbrosa. Luciana's diary had probably been taken from my room in order that I should come down to the cellars to look for it or to choose another. The light bulbs had been removed except for the one at the top of the stairs which had been left in order to allay any suspicions I might have until I was too far from the door to save myself before it closed on me.

Who? Who knew that I had gone to the cellars? Who had watched me, perhaps, from behind the coromandel screen, perhaps from a half-open door? Anyone, from Allegra herself to the servants. But only one person knew that I had Luciana's diary and that, if it were gone, I might look for another. *Zia* Romola.

Yet one could not think of Romola and hatred. She liked me; she had been kind.

The cold of the stone floor was creeping into every limb; I was in that state of physical and mental chill that was beyond shivering and the sudden thought that flashed into my mind terrified me even more. Had Vanessa written her postcard from this one-time Roman gaol? "While I wait . . ." But if there had ever been a strangely carved screen down here, it was gone now.

Could there perhaps be another door somewhere in this maze of cellars? I had never noticed one and I doubted it. The powerful senators in Caesar's time would not risk two possibilities of escape.

I had planned to leave Rome immediately but, as if there were someone with whom I had some macabre telepathic communication, he—or she—had forestalled me.

22 ✗

"*Signorina . . . Signorina . . .*"

I scrambled up from the floor, my legs half-atrophied by the damp, glacial stones, and limped toward the steps, shouting my lungs out.

"*I'm here . . . I'm here . . .*"

The blood began to flow again through my semi-petrified limbs and I raced up to the top of the steps and hammered on the door.

I heard the clang of metal against metal with a relief so great that I burst into tears. The door swung open and I saw Nunzia's startled face.

"Signorine . . . Oh, oh, what happened?"

I fell into her arms. "I came down here . . . to look for a book . . . and I was locked in . . ." The sudden sweetness of freedom was so overwhelming that I turned away from her, leaning against the wall and hiding my face. "I'm sorry," I said. "I've been rather scared." The understatement was almost ludicrous and I laughed in the middle of weeping.

She put a warm hand on my arm. "Do not apologize. We never come down to the cellar, you could have been there for . . . oh, *Gran Dio*, for days . . . For myself I would have died of fear before I died of starvation."

I controlled my voice and asked "How did you know I was here?"

"The signora went to her office and as she opened the shutters, she saw some pieces of paper on the path. She dislikes untidiness and sent me to pick them up. I read your message and then I took the papers to her. She is waiting for you, signorina, in the *salone*."

ALLEGRA SAT IN A HIGH-BACKED CHAIR and held out her hand to me with an unfamiliar gesture of warmth. "Juliet, how did this dreadful thing happen?"

"I went to the cellars to find a book to read—*Zia* Romola said I might—" I carefully kept from mentioning the diary.

"But the library has hundreds of books."

"I know. But I . . . I thought I'd like to look through some really old ones." It sounded lame and I was relieved that she accepted it. I had a feeling that although Romola would have no objection to my reading old diaries, Allegra would not be so casual.

"How did you get locked in?"

"I don't know. The door just closed."

"But it cannot close on its own. When the place was used as a wine cellar for food storage before the days of refrigeration, there was a special device fitted to the door so that it could not possibly shut by itself from the outside."

"*Nonna*, that door *did* close. And, what is more, there is only a light on the staircase. The rest of the bulbs have been removed."

A strange expression crossed her face and was gone before I could actually interpret it. Fear . . . anger . . . suspicion . . . It could have been a little of all three.

"Someone has been very careless," she said. "The light bulbs had probably worn out and someone removed them without remembering to put fresh ones in their place. And one of the servants must have passed the door and seen it open, and presumed that nobody was there, and so closed the door."

"But the staircase light worked and just before the door closed, someone switched it off."

"Of course I will question the servants, but none of them is going to admit to doing this. It could have had very serious consequences and they will be afraid. But tell me, how did you manage to get your messages onto the path?"

I told her and she looked at me with a glimmer of admiration. "That was very resourceful of you."

"I suppose desperation stimulated my mind."

"You look pale, *figlia mia*. Do you feel faint?"

"No, just cold and . . . afraid."

"There is absolutely nothing for you to fear here."

"Someone shut that door on me."

"I've told you: a servant's carelessness."

"Or someone's deliberate act."

A look of irritation crossed her face. "You have had a very bad fright, Juliet, but you must not let your imagination run wild. I shall, as I have said, question the servants. But so far as you are concerned, you must forget the whole distressing matter."

I knew, as she spoke, that this was not the time to tell her the rest of the story. What had happened to me in the cellar had had, to her, a completely logical explanation. It was I who was being illogical in my suspicion of some evil motive. How much less would she believe the rest of my story! I had no one to corroborate it—not even Martin for everything that had happened to me had been when I was alone.

There was the perfect moment for everything and I had to wait for it. It could come today, tomorrow—all I knew was that it must come soon . . .

I was pinning my faith on someone other than myself forcing the issue. The jeweler telephoning Malimbrosa with news of another message for me . . . perhaps speaking to *Nonna* Allegra herself. I realized that some outsider must force her to see that I was not a victim of an over-active imagination. If I showed her the earring in my handbag and told her it was Vanessa's, she would believe that I had merely picked it up in the Borghese Gardens—an extraordinary coincidence that she would accept and then shrug aside. In that moment of silence in *Nonna* Allegra's rich room, I willed that the jeweler at Juturna's would telephone a message and confirm some of the salient facts that I would tell her.

"And now, *cara*, you would like some tea."

"Please."

"I suggest you have some sent to your room. Or better still, have it on the roof garden and let the sun warm you."

I said quietly, "Thank you, *Nonna* Allegra."

I rose and then hesitated, remembering the scent that had lingered ahead of me as I went to the cellars. "Irena?" I made a query of her name.

Her eyes were points of black light in the heavy lidded sockets. "What do you want to know?"

"I wondered whether perhaps . . . perhaps she would have tea with me. I would like to talk about last night's ball. I'm sure there were a lot of famous people there and . . ." I was trying to be devious.

Nonna Allegra's face was cold. "But you very seldom see Irena, do you? She has her own life and her own friends. Why ask now? Oh, don't try to search for some explanation. I am fully aware that Nunzia served you at luncheon and that you noticed her red eyes and that she told you that Irena had left us."

"That's true, but it wasn't Nunzia's fault—"

"You do not have to defend her. She is an excellent servant. I have no intention of dismissing her because she has discussed something with you that you would have found out anyway. But I hope you did not gossip with her."

I shook my head.

She said wearily, "And you will discuss it with no one, Juliet. Certainly not with that Englishman you know from the embassy. It is a matter that must be kept inside the family. I cannot stop the servants talking among themselves, but they are under a written promise not to discuss our affairs outside Malimbrosa."

And how long I wondered, before the whole of Rome rang with it?

I took the elevator to the roof garden, found a chair and dragged it into the sun. I needed warmth; I needed light and I wanted, above all, to stop being afraid.

Lying in the long garden chair, I wondered again if my terrible enemy were at Malimbrosa, a servant or someone secreted in the *palazzo*—an unknown resident. It was a wild thought but Vanessa had told me of the many empty rooms on the top floor where no one ever went. Even so, the idea was too crazy to contemplate. Of course no one hid in the house . . .

Tea came on a silver tray with a set of Rockingham china and little homemade *amaretti* that were crisp outside and soft and tacky inside, the way macaroons should be.

I drank two cups of scalding hot tea and felt better. I lay watching the bees search the flowers and a spotted yellow butterfly hover among the roses. Behind me the waters of the little fountains fell singing into the marble basin and a bird rode on a draft of wind between the terrace and the Borghese Gardens.

My eternity in the cellars seemed like some too-real dream. Here in this serene golden world of sun and sky and flowers, I felt that *Nonna* Allegra must be right and only my own imagination had seen some malevolent meaning in the closing of the cellar door and the missing light bulbs. I leaned back and closed my eyes and the afternoon sun burned purple and crimson against my lids.

I had no idea how long I lay supine and half in a dream, relief at my freedom softening the suspicion and the fear that nagged at me.

Quite suddenly I was aware that I was not alone. I opened my eyes slowly and squinted at someone tall and darkly dressed standing between me and the sunlight.

It was *Zia* Romola. In her hand she held a little tooled leather book. I sat up, startled at the twisted violence of her expression and a thought snaked through my mind that it could have been

she, after all, who had shut me in the cellar and was now mad
with fury at my escape.

I covered up my alarm and said in a friendly voice, "*Zia*
Romola, come and sit here. I . . . I'll get another chair for
myself." My eyes traveled to the book in her hand.

As I rose, she reached out and gripped my wrist. "You
know. You've read the diary . . ."

"Know what?"

"You've read the diary," she repeated.

"As a matter of fact, I haven't. I've only dipped into little
bits of it. Why? Is there anything I shouldn't have read? If
there is, I can assure you I've no idea what it is."

I waited and the silence between us was filled with the sound
of the fountain and the burr of distant traffic. The garden
scents were delicate, like a perfumier's banquet.

"Please." I broke the silence and tried to dispel the hypnotic
stare of her eyes. "Sit down."

I doubted if she heard me. She stood, skinny as a sapling in
her dark dress, her neck thrust forward; her black, streaked
hair falling from its knot. The irrelevant thought flashed
through me that if I were as rich as she must be, I would have a
personal maid.

She flung the book down on an empty chair. "You're trying
to spare my feelings, that's why you say you haven't read the
diary, isn't it? *Isn't it?*"

"I've told you, I only glanced through it. I was going to read
it this afternoon, only I found that it was missing from my
room."

"*I* took it. I brought fresh flowers for you and I saw the
diary. I just happened to pick it up and look through it. And it
was then . . ." She gave an odd little choking sound as if the
words would not come, swallowed twice and whispered,
"Then that I turned a page and read—"

I waited, watching her.

"No one knew that my grandmother kept diaries and after
she died and her room was cleared of possessions, the books
were just stacked away without anyone looking at them."

While Romola was speaking, she was staring down at the diary as if it were a burning brand of the devil that she must exorcise with the terrible fury of her eyes. "My grandmother would sit in her chair, nodding and smiling, and we thought she was just senile. She said so little; she lived, we thought, just to eat and fall into a semi-sleep while we talked. And all the time, all the time, she watched and saw and understood. She saw what I, with my good eyesight and my younger brain, never saw . . ." She raised her head and looked at me with near hatred. "You're lying, aren't you? You've read the diary all through, haven't you? You know . . ."

"I'm not lying. Why should I?" My voice was raised in exasperation. "Go on, tell me, why should I lie to you?"

"Because you think it better to pretend you do not know."

I had had enough tension for one day. I slapped the side of an urn with my hand in a gesture that was a wild, outward and visible sign of my bewildered inner state. "Why don't you either tell me what I'm supposed to have found out or let the matter be? We're getting nowhere with these vague accusations that I've seen something I shouldn't have done."

The fury left her face and she said wearily, "I'm not angry about the possibility that you've seen what *Nonna* Luciana wrote. I'm angry because—" she darted to the book, picked it up and thrust it at me. "August eleventh. Read it."

I turned the pages and found the date. Then, before I read, I glanced at her doubtfully. "You really want me to?"

For a moment I thought she was going to snatch the diary from me. Then she said, "Yes. Read it. See how my dear Mamma has destroyed my life. Destroyed . . ." She turned away and stood with her back to me. But although she looked out on to the Borghese Gardens, I knew that she saw nothing of it.

AUGUST 11TH, 1955

This morning, the past came back with all its bitterness.
Allegra sat with me and our conversation turned to old hap-

penings. She recalled when Marco Gimignano had come to tell Allegra that he wanted to marry Romola. At the time, I had not known why he had suddenly disappeared from Rome. Today, all these years later, as we sat talking, I learned the truth. My French daughter-in-law stepped in and stopped a love match, for I am certain that Marco loved Romola. But a Malimbrosa does not marry an artist without family or prospects unless the man consents to forget his artistic ambitions and become a cog in the Malimbrosa machine. This is what Allegra had dared to suggest.

The outburst had taken up a whole page and its reverse side. It was continued under August 12th.

I reminded Allegra that I had protested at the time that Marco would never agree to what was almost a command. But that she had refused to listen to me. Today, as she sat admitting it all, remembering without any sign of guilt, I said, "Do you not realize that Marco probably still hates you for what you did?" And Allegra just smiled and said, "Ah, but you never knew, did you, Mamma, that I put all the responsibility onto Romola. I told him that she had asked me to put the proposition to him; that she would only marry him on condition he forget art and join the Malimbrosas." She sat there in my quiet room and looked proud of herself. She said, "He was such a foolish young man that Romola was better without him. He did not even question what I told him; he just walked out and we never heard of him again." My hearing is very much worse these days, but I can lip-read and I knew I had not misunderstood what Allegra had said. All those years ago, two young people had let Allegra run their lives. Marco was wrong in not going to Romola, but the young are impulsive and proud and he had no intention of being dominated by a mother-in-law."

I turned another page.

I lay awake again last night thinking of what Allegra had told me. How I condemn her, pity her and, yes, admire her because her mind runs on the single track of her own supremacy. In the middle of the night I prayed for Romola. But it is not my prayers she needs, it is for someone to love her. It is so far in the past, but it is that which makes the present and the present makes the futuer.

The entry ended.

Romola had turned and was watching me. "Well, so you know a little of what has happened in this palace which so many envy us for."

I said. "And now . . . Vanessa has disappeared. Another . . . tragedy . . ."

"We must forget her," she said. "If I had married, I would have had children. I have told you. The women of the family are not barren; my dead sister Teresa gave birth to Pepi, but she was herself always delicate. I am strong. I would have had what Mamma wanted. Sons . . ."

"For heaven's sake, why didn't you and Marco go away together?"

"Do you think I wouldn't if he had asked me to? But I wasn't given the chance. He believed what Mamma told him, that *I* wanted him to give up art for commerce." She broke off and her face had a terrible sadness. "Mamma did that and then, all those years after, could still boast of it to *Nonna* Luciana. *My father's wife—*" The words were stressed slowly as if she were trying to renounce her own blood relationship to Allegra.

"And you never saw Marco again?"

"Never after his talk with *her*. It's as simple as that. I was so ignorant. I was still walking on the sun and the moon and the stars. But when I telephoned his studio one morning, he was gone." She brushed her hand over her eyes and moved from the strong sunlight into the shadow. "I only heard of him once more—he had a great success in some exhibition of his work in New York."

And in the years between, what a lot of love could have been given her . . .

I laid the book on the chair. "You can't blame *Nonna* Allegra entirely. If Marco had had any strength of character he would have married you and taken you away from Rome, away from family influence."

She shook her head. "You do not understand. The Malimbrosa tentacles are long and Marco knew it. Mamma is a powerful adversary."

I said feebly, trying desperately to give her a shred of comfort, "At least you were loved."

Her burst of laughter was so bitter, so harsh, that it shattered the peace of the garden. I had a feeling that the flowers shuddered.

"Poor Romola," she mocked. "So rich and wanted by no man, not even for her money. At least that was what I thought. When I was so upset that Marco left Rome without telling me, Mamma said 'Do not fret. He is not worth it.' " She drew in her breath with a little hiss. "And I have that Frenchwoman's blood in my veins."

I forgot my own tensions in my pity for her. I could not tell her that in spite of her protests, I doubted if Marco had loved her very much, otherwise he would have faced Romola with her mother's mercenary project and demanded whether it was true that she had imposed the conditions. In her youth, Romola could have had a certain haggard beauty which might have temporarily attracted the young artist.

Zia Romola said, "I am going to show her the diary. I will say, 'This is what you did to me. Now that I know, I will hate you for the rest of my life.' " She looked down and saw my hand on her arm and drew away from me. She didn't want my sympathy, only my listening. Her face was blank with hopelessness. "But however much I will hate her, it will not hurt her. She is impervious to people's opinions of her. It will be I who am the fool, the gossiping one. All my life I have lived under the shadow of her scorn: only at the clinic where I work am I somebody. I am the rich signorina who has given money for the sick and who goes there to do the work any office girl could do. Do I enjoy it? No. Do you know why I go to that place of suffering and sickness? It is to get away from the Malimbrosa dominance; to dominate myself; to be looked up to. I, who cannot bandage a limb or lance a boil, I walk through that splendid clinic I have paid to be built, opening doors, taking messages—and seeing those I serve look at me with grateful eyes . . ." She reached out and tore at a white rose. Petals scattered and I saw a tiny ooze of blood at the tip of her finger where a thorn had pricked her.

As I watched her, my own guilt spread over me. Because of my curiosity and my smug argument that things that had happened a long time ago could no longer be important, I had brought this misery on her. And there was nothing I could do to compensate for it.

"And now." She stood very upright, with a kind of desperate triumph. "You may as well know what else is in the diary."

"I don't want to read it," I said. "I'm going to ask one of the servants to put it back in the chest." I realized that I hadn't yet told her that less than an hour earlier, I had been shut in the Malimbrosa dungeons. "Something happened—"

"Something most certainly happened, Juliet,—something that concerns you vitally."

"Me? . . ."

She nodded. Her face was set with a bitter amusement. "I had to give my solemn word to Mamma that it would never be mentioned. It was to be blotted out. But this will be the way I shall make her suffer for what she did to me. You shall read for yourself what the diary says about *you*. Look at the entry for July. *Look*, Julie."

I turned the pages.

"So Odette has consented at last and Juliet is coming to Malimbrosa."

Odette, my mother's name. A memory flashed through my mind of myself as a child of eight listening to my mother's angry voice on the telephone and her cold words when she returned to the room: "You will never go to Malimbrosa again."

Romola said, "I will leave you the diary. Perhaps when you have read the pages about yourself you will also have something to say to my dear Mamma. And you can say that I told you to read it. Why should I care? I'm the one who can't keep anything to myself, the one with a peasant's gossiping mind." She walked away from me as she spoke.

I cried, "Don't go. Please don't go."

The rustle of her taffetta underskirt ceased. "And Juliet—" I waited. "When you read what is written there, perhaps you will understand a very great deal."

"What? . . ." Something in her expression frightened me and the single word came out as a whisper which I doubted if she had heard until she answered me.

"You will perhaps understand why your mother refused to let Mamma have you to live here after that holiday you spent with us as a child." She walked under the blue sunblinds and into the house.

23 ✄

I SAT DOWN AND BENT OVER THE DIARY.

*If only Roberto had lived, how different life would have
been. He was the wild, the independent one, and the cleverest.
His mother's favorite child, for whom she had her most
splendid dreams and who defied her and nearly broke her
heart, that is if Allegra has a heart that feels. Perhaps it was just
pride and the crushing of her ambitions that actually nearly
broke her. Today is the ninth anniversary of the night he was
killed in the air crash at Geneva. And with the news had come
another shock for Allegra. Some months earlier, Roberto had
married a girl called Odette Rivers who lived in Cambridge. I
said to Allegra, "Then this girl is your daughter-in-law. You
must ask her to come here." And Allegra sat, looking like a
dead woman and said, "Never. I will never acknowledge this
marriage. Although he is dead, I will never forgive. Roberto is
not my son. Always remember that, Mamma. Roberto is not
my son; nor is he your grandson." I argued with her; I tried to
make her see that he had kept his marriage from her because he
knew that she would never forgive him. He had married in
England, away from his own country, from family approval. I
knew why. It was because he loved this girl Odette and he did
not intend to have arguments, criticisms, protests, tainting his*

*love. Later, when their marriage was secure, I am certain that
he would have told Allegra. But not until he could bring
Odette here and say, "Look we have been married one—
two—years and we are still in love. This is proof. Even you
cannot shake that." And today, on the anniversary of his death,
his daughter Juliet has come to Malimbrosa.*

I read the entries over three times, checking my own translation, and the facts remained. My mother, Odette Rivers, had
married Roberto Malimbrosa. Some time after his death, she
had married the man I had known as my father, that huge,
happy man with the big voice and the sensitive hands that could
mend a bird's broken wing as gently as if he touched thistle-
down.

I let the book lie in my lap and stared stunned and unblinking at the radiant sky. I could say it to everlastingness: *I am a
Malimbrosa,* but I doubted if I could ever really believe it. *I,
Juliet Holdroyd, am really Juliet Malimbrosa. I am one of
them . . . as Vanessa, as Pepi . . .*

I had walked as a shy, enchanted child through my Terracotta Palace, never dreaming that I had a certain right to be
there. *I belong . . .* Or did I? Of what value was it to keep
repeating that I belonged to this family if the Malimbrosas did
not want to acknowledge me? "This will be my revenge on
my dearest Mamma." That I learned who I was. And a revenge
could only be leveled at someone to whom it could cause pain.
So, Allegra had never intended it to be known. The threads
were becoming untangled. Surprise, shock, excitement, were
stimulating my brain. I began to see at last why I was deeply
involved.

Now I was certain that the things that had happened to me
might only partially have been because I was anxious about
Vanessa; there was another fact involving me far more person-
ally. Everything that had happened to me since I came to
Rome was because my father was Roberto Malimbrosa. They
—whoever "they" were—knew, and because of it, I was in as
much danger as Vanessa and Pepi.

My destruction must have been planned as soon as I had been seen in Rome. "They" flattered me by believing that I would react quickly to Vanessa's disappearance.

I thought bitterly, *How well they must know my character!* My headstrong ways, my impulsiveness, and my affection for Vanessa that would not let me remain indifferent to her disappearance.

Was she dead? I got up and went to the terrace edge and looked over Rome. Wherever I went from this moment on, I would be half-looking over my shoulder. I could, of course, go to the police. But that would render me even less safe. For someone watched me and would see that I was silenced before I reached the safety of the law. I knew now, with even more certainty, that I must leave Rome. I could argue that I was behaving like a coward; perhaps I was. But I could also argue that I had no intention of being foolhardy. I loved my life and I didn't want to risk losing it. I had already planned to tell *Nonna* Allegra everything before I left, to warn her that Pepi was in danger, too. Or did she already know? How much was she involved? At least, I would have my triumph in my marvelous exit line. "Goodbye, *Nonna*—and I have an actual right to call you that because, you see, I know that I am really Juliet Malimbrosa."

It was understandable that my mother had kept my real name a secret from me. She had let my birth be known to the Malimbrosas and had been ignored. So, proud and angry, she had decided in turn, to ignore them. Yet, I realized now that all the time tabs had possibly been kept on me. Vanessa could have been deliberately sent to my school; we had been brought together by the headmistress who had known my mother. Even my invitation as a child to visit Rome was almost certainly a deliberate curiosity on Allegra's part to find out what Roberto's daughter was really like. And after she had seen me, she must have approved of me. I could make a guess at the reason for the telephone call from Rome to London all those years ago. "I want Juliet." And Mother had refused her arrogant demand. So much . . . too much . . . to digest. Too much in one shaken afternoon that had begun with my near incarceration in the pagan Roman cellars.

I thought suddenly: And I said nothing to Zia Romola about Irena. We had our own sudden shocks and, in our absorption, we had forgotten her.

I TURNED AND RAN TO MY ROOM, picked up my bag, flew down the staircase and was too quick even for the watchful Alberto to open the doors for me. I flung them wide, half looked back, saw him in the hall and left them for him to close. The wrought-iron gates opened for me and I was in the street.

It was not far to the airline offices and there was no need to hurry. Yet I walked down the Via Veneto towards the Piazza della Repubblica as if my life depended upon it, which, I decided grimly, might certainly be the case. As I went up the semicircular flight of steps to the offices, I thought someone called my name and I turned and stumbled. A woman helped me up. No, I was not hurt, thank you. I smiled at her as if I hadn't a care in the world and crossed the covered way and entered the building. When I looked back there was no one around whom I recognized.

There were a number of people waiting for the clerks to attend to them and when one of them was at last free I handed him my airline ticket and asked if I could have a place on an earlier flight. "The earlier the better."

He gave me a half-grin as if wondering what I was running away from, consulted books, made a telephone call and returned to tell me that all flights to London were fully booked for the next three days. There might be a cancellation. He could, perhaps, telephone me? I said, no, I would book on the flight leaving in three days' time, but I would probably call the following afternoon to see if there was a possible cancellation.

And, I thought as I left the offices, between now and then I would have to have a very long talk with Nonna Allegra.

Back at Malimbrosa, there was a message for me from Martin, reminding me that I was seeing him that night.

As I bathed and changed, I knew that I couldn't tell him about Irena's flight from Malimbrosa nor about the discovery of myself as Vanessa's cousin. I wanted to; I so badly needed to talk to someone, but it was a family matter and the Malimbrosas hated gossip.

As I crossed the gallery to the elevator, Romola came out of her apartment. She had obviously been listening for me.

"You've read about your mother, Julie? You know . . ."

"Yes."

She shook her head like a mechanical doll. "I went to see Mamma. I wanted to have a terrible quarrel with her, but I could not. I find I cannot be hurt any more. I allowed her to tell me that no man would let a woman go if he loved her, and I said nothing. I am so weak with her!" She leaned her head back and closed her eyes. "But *you*, Juliet—"

"What about me?"

"I told her you had read the diary and she brushed the news aside. *Nonna* Luciana was senile; she imagined things. Mamma said the diaries must be burned; they were probably full of dangerous lies. But it is no lie, Juliet. Of that I am certain. You are Roberto's daughter. But I must not know about it because I am a gossip and I will let the secret out. For her own reasons Mamma does not want anyone to know." She opened her eyes. "Juliet, *cara*, there is nothing, *nothing*, we can do. I am so sorry."

"Please don't be," I said. "I have my mother's pride. I will go running to no one for recognition." I touched her hand, which was all she would let me do, and left her.

Martin sat at the wheel of his car, grinning at me.

"I like you in yellow," he said.

"It's the color of the sun. Didn't you know I was a sunworshiper?"

He kissed my cheek. "That's just an apéritif."

With dinner to follow and then love-making as the final

course? He would soon find out how adept I was at avoiding that.

Over a drink I told him that I had booked my flight home in three days' time. He said, stunned, "But you've only just come! And I thought you had a mission here. Finding Vanessa."

"Not any more. I'm running into too much personal trouble. If Vanessa is still alive, she'll contact someone else. And if, as I'm beginning to be certain, she is dead, then what's the use? You don't believe it, I know, but whoever has . . . has done this to her wants me out of the way, too."

"Because you walked into a wrong apartment and trespassed on someone else's land? Oh, come off it! Why make melodrama out of situations you brought upon yourself? Stay in Rome and have a good time."

I gave up the argument and looked about me. The cave restaurant was lit by a hundred candles illuminating the murals depicting Roman scenes, chariots and horses and bathing pools. Martin was ordering dinner. Scampi . . . *Pollo in Padella*. We would choose an ice or a savory later.

I said, "I've told no one yet about my leaving."

"Well, I'm not going to ring up and give you away, but you can't just walk out."

"I'll tell them tomorrow night."

"And by the way, I've got some news for you. I think I know where that screen is."

I sprang to sudden life. "You do? Well, where? When can we go and see it?"

"Hold on. It's on private property and you can't just walk in. I doubt, after all this time, if it'll help at all."

"At least we could go there."

"Suppose you let me see this place and make inquiries as to who lives there?"

"Where is it?"

He said, "Across the Ponte Margherita and I don't intend to tell you any more in case you go rushing there and fall down a drain pipe and accuse someone of putting it there for that specific purpose."

"You won't be serious."

"Not about that," he said, and lifted his wine glass to toast me.

When he suggested after dinner that we should go back to his flat, I said complacently that since I had only two more nights in Rome, I wanted to see something of the city. Martin gave in with a good grace. "As you say, there are two more nights. Come on. I'll take you to see some night life."

It was the same as night life anywhere else, dancing in dim rooms with a lethargic band playing; too expensive drinks; too many people; too little air.

We returned to the *palazzo* as the clock was striking one and Martin kissed me under the lamp by the gates.

"Tomorrow," he said, "is another evening. Save it for me."

"If I can. But *Nonna* Allegra may want me to spend the time with her."

"Why should she?"

"I'm her guest and it'll be my last evening but one," I said, and pressed the bell by the tall left-hand gate.

As I went past the oleanders and up the steps, I heard Martin's voice calling out that he would ring me.

I was thinking, as I reached my room, that he still didn't know that I was the daughter of Roberto Malimbrosa, nor of Irena's escape. These were things that I could tell no one, yet. I knew, too, why I hadn't told him of my grim experience in the cellars. He would have dismissed that in the same light-hearted way that he had dismissed my near plunge to death in the Via Campisolo.

I went to bed and slid immediately into sleep as if nothing that had happened that day had been startling enough to keep me awake.

24 ❧

I HUNG ABOUT THE *palazzo* the next morning, making myself as obvious as I could, hoping that *Nonna* Allegra or *Zia* Romola would send for me. Neither did so and I had no hope of seeing Leo, for he left for his office long before I appeared downstairs. So far, he was almost a stranger to me and I knew that I would leave Malimbrosa knowing no more about him than I already did.

I padded around the house, listening for someone's approach, frantic to know how *Nonna* Allegra would act when she next saw me. She would know now that I had read Luciana's diary. But doubt had now crept in. I could visualize that gaunt, hard face with its hooded eyes looking at me coldly or even with amusement. I could imagine what she might say.

"Poor child! What you read was a senile old woman's wanderings. I believe your mother knew Roberto at Cambridge, but their relationship was casual and unimportant. I am most certainly not your grandmother. It is still only a courtesy title so far as you are concerned, because we let you use it as a little girl."

I grew more and more nervous, watching the clocks in whatever room I had wandered, waiting for someone to break the silence. And all the time imagining what *Nonna* Allegra would say to me, putting words into that long, thin mouth; painting, in my mind, the expression in her eyes that would accompany her amused or pitying comments.

Just after eleven o'clock I could bear the tension no longer and escaped from the house, walking down to Doney's to sit at a table under a tree. I ordered coffee and then changed my seat so that I could look across the street with some wild, and half-frightening, hope that Vanessa would appear again.

"Good morning, Julie. May I join you?"

I looked up and saw, with dismay, that Philip had stopped at my table.

"Of course." I removed my handbag from a vacant chair and he sat down. "Is this a chance encounter?"

"Perhaps."

"I thought you worked for a living."

He said with amusement, "I'm also, to a certain extent, a free agent and all foreigners to Rome find themselves at some time or other at a table at Doney's."

The waiter came with my *caffelatte* and took Philip's order. I felt perfectly certain that his appearance was no coincidence. He had come deliberately to find me.

I said, "You've heard that Irena has left Leo?"

"Yes."

"Do you know where she has gone?"

"Why on earth should I?"

The quiet casualness of his question annoyed me. "Because it should be of particular interest to you."

He looked at me and immediately I became over-interested in unwrapping a little oblong of sugar and dropping it into my coffee.

"What are you going to do when you've got tired of sitting here?"

"Take a look at Rome."

He raised his eyebrows mockingly. "No more searching for Vanessa?"

I shook my head. "There is too much I don't understand and I'm not very good at playing amateur detective."

"I agree with you on that point."

"What do you know about it all?" I turned on him sharply.

"What do I know about what?"

"Vanessa."

"Why should I know anything?"

I sat very still and watched the waiter set coffee before him. When he had gone, I said, "Don't expect me to believe you don't know what I'm talking about. I'm quite certain that you know more than you tell about Vanessa's disappearance—*and* about Irena's. It's all because of you—" I stopped, appalled at my outburst.

"What the hell are you talking about?"

"Surely it's clear," I said in a tight, hard voice.

"No, by God it isn't. Come on, *what did you mean?*"

I was in a safe place, with people crowding around me; I said with the absolute bravado that has nothing to do with courage, "You know why Vanessa disappeared; you know why Irena has left Leo . . ."

"And if half of your accusation is correct, what then?"

"Why?" I turned to him suddenly, my heart somersaulting as I met that direct, dark gold look. "*Why? . . .*"

He asked, "Are you so seized with common curiosity that you want me to tell you?"

"You are involved, that's why I . . . I want to . . . know."

"Like hell I'm involved." He seized my wrist. "Oh yes, my persistent Julie, I'm involved and you can learn how. Come on—"

"I haven't finished my coffee."

"You can drink a gallon after I've finished with you." He was dragging me from the table with one hand; flinging money down on top of the bill with the other. People were watching us. I could scream for help; I could fight him off, for he wouldn't dare be violent. I did neither. I went with him seemingly meekly, inwardly scared. But the fact remained, I went, like some silly goat after whatever it is goats can't resist.

"Let go of my wrist," I hissed at him.

He held it all the more tightly.

"Where are we going?"

"You'll see."

I said with the last spark of bravado left in me, "But suppose I don't want to?"

"Then it's too bad, because you going to do what I say."

"Oh, no . . ."

But his fingers were more gentle on my wrist and we walked together down the Via Veneto in absolute silence. At the corner near the Excelsior he stopped, opened the door of his parked car, and thrust me in.

I was not in the least brave. On the other hand, I felt a stir of irrepressible excitement at what I was going to see, to hear, to find. I made one last belated attempt to argue with him. I said, as he got in behind the wheel, "You don't have to take me anywhere. You could just explain here and now what you want me to know."

"Proof," he said, "is more effective than a million words." And he started the car.

"Do you always do precisely what you want, regardless of other people's needs?" I nearly added, "Like *Nonna* Allegra, moving her jade pawns on her chess board."

He said with sudden fierceness, "Do you think I want to take you anywhere? Well, get that straight, I don't. But neither do I enjoy this permanent state of accusation you seem to be in with regard to me. God knows why I should care. Perhaps it's because your attitude is an offense to my vanity."

"Yes, I can quite believe you're vain."

"We'll leave your analysis of my character. Now, do you mind not talking for a while? I prefer to have all my wits about me when I'm driving in Rome. I can't cope also with an angry young woman."

"You don't have to. You can let me go."

"Not on your sweet life. You've asked for involvement and now you're going to get it."

I said unhappily, "I can't argue that point with you because I don't know enough."

He gave a shout of mockery. "Go on. Don't be shy. It doesn't become you."

I tried desperately to control myself, to hold in my fury and my fear and my incredible love.

We had reached a point where neither of us had anything more to say without it being an unforgivable intrusion. I was uneasy. If all this time he knew where Vanessa was, then he must have had some iniquitous reason for keeping the knowledge to himself and for taking me to her now. But more than anything else, it meant that Vanessa wasn't dead.

So, WE DROVE INTO THE COUNTRY in unbearable, angry silence and I began to wish I had made a scene when he grabbed my wrist and dragged me from the table at Doney's. I watched without any real interest as we drove through the Porta San Sebastiano, along the old Appian Way. In more pleasant circumstances, I could have been intrigued by the odd mixture of the ancient and the modern, of the crumbling stones of some building that had its origin at the dawn of Christianity, the modern garages and the queer little glimpses of old tramlines between the long, untidy bursts of grass.

We came to a town and Philip said, "Albano."

I looked out at the sheer drop at one side into the great stretch of the Campagna. A heat mist threaded with gold lay over the fields and the snow-white houses.

"Are we stopping here?"

"No."

"How communicative you are," I said. "I hope you are enjoying the drive."

"A car gives me a sense of freedom." His resentment and anger made a kind of black aura around us. I saw two coach loads of tourists and envied them their obvious energetic interest.

The next place Philip deigned to point out to me was Velletri, where we shot down a narrow street with pollarded trees. After that, there were vast stretches of vineyards with neat rows between beautiful, healthy-looking vines trained against strong wires. Some way beyond, we came to a straggling village. After the neatness and well-being look of the vine country, the village seemed to lie sadly and poorly in the glare of the sun. Dust was everywhere, on the grass, on the houses, although I wondered how it got there when it seemed that there were no cars except ours to churn it up from the street.

Philip drew into a small square of peeling, decaying houses and a milling mass of children and animals, most of whom stopped and stared at us as if we were people from another world descending on their lost village. A few old men sat under a plane tree and at the far end of the square, a woman was keeping flies off a baby in her arms with a whisk made from strips of newspaper tied to a bamboo handle. Another woman stood on the other side of the chipped water pump that dominated the square and watched us. Her hair was thick and graying, her skirt was full, like a seventeenth-century peasant's, and she was wiping her hands on a torn apron. She was very brown and I guessed that she was tanned by work in the vineyards.

"Take a look across there at the second house on your left."

"Where the woman with the red skirt is standing?"

"That's right."

"What about it?"

"You wanted an answer to a question."

I stared at him. "You don't mean . . . you *can't* mean that Vanessa could be living there." I turned and looked at the house and the woman again. "It's almost falling down," I said. "Broken shutters and all those children . . ."

"And what do you think it's like inside?"

"Dark, stuffy, over-crowded . . . Philip, do you mean that *that* place answers my question?"

"One of them."

"I don't believe you. Vanessa *couldn't* be there . . ."

"Oh, for God's sake, stop this obsession with Vanessa; you sound like a schoolgirl with a crush."

I said angrily, "If you had a close friend—someone you really cared about—and had come hundreds of miles to stay with her only to find that she had disappeared, wouldn't *you* care about what had happened to her? Or no, perhaps you wouldn't; you'd kiss your hand to her shadow and say 'Nice knowing you.'"

He turned off the engine of the car, took out a cigarette, and said, "You don't smoke, do you?"

"No," I snapped, and sat looking at the house, at the woman who had seized one of the smallest children and bundled her inside.

"I thought you were bringing me here to this place—what is its name—?"

"Ruorento."

"—to answer a question, and my question was 'You know why Vanessa has disappeared.'"

"I'd call that a statement, not a question."

"All right, then, but it was because I said that, that you grabbed me and marched me to your car. So, now we're here, why pretend—?"

"I never pretend."

Something very steady and quiet in his voice checked my angry indignation. "Then," I asked almost humbly, "Why?"

"You've forgotten the second part of your accusation. You also said, 'You know why Irena has left Leo.'"

I looked hard at the tilting, ramshackle line of houses and was afraid of what Philip was obviously intending to tell me. I wanted to shout at him, "I know why. I know everything. Romola listens outside windows and told me. I don't want to hear your side. I want to go back to Rome." Instead I held my lips tightly closed and shut my eyes.

"That house you've been looking at," said Philip, "is the one where Irena was born."

I opened my eyes with such suddenness that the sunlight

dazzled me. I stared at the peeling plaster and the broken shutters, the none-too-clean children of the house. It was incredible that such patrician beauty, such grace of movement, had come from this travesty of a home. One of the children playing outside screamed; a bigger child slapped her . . . Irena's home. Oh no . . .

Philip broke through my silent protests. "I can't think why I'm going to trust you with Irena's story. I had no intention of doing so—"

"Then why are you?"

"There are times when, driven by sudden pleasure or sudden irritation, even I act on impulse. And you can guess which drove me to bring you here."

I stared at the deeply tanned woman who was shouting to a neighbor and wondered what had happened in the history of that tatterdemalion family to produce one almost perfect jewel of a woman.

"Irena asked me to find out, if I could, where she was born." Philip sat back, totally at ease, and watched a lean puppy trying to play games with a leaner cat. "There are people in this world who have no interest in their roots. Irena has. She needed to know to whom she belonged, particularly as the Malimbrosas never really accepted her. Even Leo—"

"He married her without knowing?"

"Oh, he's proud of her—she's a marvelous shop window— but how deep his feelings go has yet to be proved. I have done what I have because Irena guessed something of her background and a crisis has arisen in their married life where she realizes that Leo must know the truth, and choose."

"You're talking like someone out of another century," I jeered, delighted to be able to find something that I could actively hate. "As if it mattered where she was born; as if Leo or anyone else would turn her out because she didn't have a golden rattle given her at her christening . . ."

I hadn't managed to rouse him. He said, completely unperturbed, "How do any of us know how another will behave in a given circumstance? You were probably brought up as I was, as all our generation has been, to believe that all men are equal. Well, you're in Italy and you're living with a family whose standards haven't altered much in three hundred years. Just try to use your imagination."

He was right, of course. There was no one standard of outlook in the world. I said in a small voice, "I'm sorry. You're right, of course. But, about Irena—"

"She came to see me some long time ago and said, "I must belong somewhere—everyone does. You can't separate a root from a plant. Where is mine?"

"But surely, she knew the name she had before she married. All she had to do—"

"My dear girl, if it had been as easy as that, why do you think she asked my help? It has taken a long time and much searching. There was so little she remembered."

I looked across at the upper floor of the broken house where clothes hung out to dry on a crooked balcony. An old woman came out and felt them and then stood and looked into the square, scratching her nose.

"Her mother," Philip said following my glance. "One of the things Irena remembered from her childhood was that stone figure on top of the pump. If you looked at it close to, you'd see that it was carved like a horned god."

"Pan. If that's all you had to go on, there are probably dozens around Italy."

"That's right. But when I found this one I went to the local priest and asked him what happened in Ruorento during the war, whether the children stayed. I discovered that the suffering had been terrible and that one woman whose husband had been killed in the war had given away her youngest child, in order to save her from starvation. Then I visited the woman."

"I—see—"

"No you don't," he said curtly, "because in that lay the whole mystery. She had no idea to whom she gave the child. Refugees were pouring through the village in carts filled with family possessions. In the confusion, Irena's mother, who had three older children, threw the little girl into the back of one of the carts as it passed. The people in the front had no idea that she was there until they stopped some way from here and found her crying."

"And that's all she remembers?"

"When the woman tossed her into the cart, Irena's arm caught against the corner of some small piece of furniture. The mother says she saw blood gush from a wound and she had had a last-minute panic and had rushed after the cart, but she never caught up with it. Irena has a scar on the upper part of her right arm."

"And the family who owned the cart?"

"Irena doesn't remember them. She says she dimly recalls being lost somewhere—the owners of the cart probably had enough trouble without having a strange child foisted on them. But a woman found her lying in a street and took her to her house. She said they were good people and they looked after her."

The picture of Irena floated across the golden light, her lovely voice drifted like a silken dream thread through the harsh shouts of the children. I couldn't believe the story Philip told. I said, "Why should it have been Irena? Do you think she was the only child to have been tossed away during that awful time?"

"There's one thing that proves her parentage. I asked Irena's mother whether she had let her take any particular treasure with her—bracelets or a little gold cross or a toy. She said that her husband had once given her a pendant. He had won it in some sailors' gambling joint in Hong Kong. She hadn't thought much of it but Irena had loved to play with it. So, she had hung it on a piece of string round her neck. I've seen it. It's of a rare jewel jade carved in the shape of a lotus. I doubt if the people who found her in their cart realized its value—they might even never have seen it. It could have slipped under Irena's clothes and lain next to her skin."

"You've seen the pendant?"

"I've told you, yes. Irena still has it."

I said slowly, "So it's all true."

"What do you think I've been doing, telling you a fairy tale?"

"When you talked to Irena's mother, didn't she wonder why? Or did you break it to her that her daughter had married a Malimbrosa?"

"I came as a journalist asking questions about what happened to them here during the war. You must remember, I'm trained to question. It was a pretty phoney reason for the interview— the war has been over too many years—but they're simple people and they had no suspicions that I might have an ulterior motive in my questioning."

I reached in my handbag and pulled out my sunglasses. I had been staring too hard into the light and I was beginning to see little flashing stars of color wherever I looked. "Are you going to tell Irena?"

"I told her."

In the salone *beneath my bedroom, with the windows open . . .*

"And that's why she has left Leo." I turned on him. "How could you? Isn't it sometimes better to be in ignorance, oh, not that Irena herself would mind—what does it matter, anyway, where anyone is born? But for the sake of *that* family, the Malimbrosas."

"And doesn't it occur to you that truth can be salutary—it either kills a thing or gives it new growth."

"In this case, it has killed a marriage. You should have left her in ignorance. What good have you done?"

"Perhaps a great deal, or perhaps I have done harm. Time will tell. And anyway, there was one thing she had never faced and I had to make her see."

"What was that?"

"That we belong not to those who bear us, but to ourselves and to those who love us. In Irena's case, it's right that she has no ties. She was given away—thrown away, if you like. She has no moral duty to anyone in her past."

"Except those who took her in and looked after her."

"They are both dead."

I said, slowly, "According to you we only belong to ourselves . . ."

"I added, 'and to those who love us.' "

"That means our parents."

"It all depends. I think not in Irena's case."

I sat looking down at my hands. And in my case? For all my life until yesterday, I believed that my stepfather was my real father and I had loved him. I could understand how my mother had felt.

How easy to have let the bitterness go after my father's death; to have brought me up believing that the man I saw and whose company I enjoyed every day, was my father by right of birth . . . I understood at last.

"You're very quiet."

"I was thinking—" But I didn't tell him my thoughts. I sat watching him restart the car and turn round the square. "You're not going to that house, are you?"

"No. I've done with that. We're going back to Rome."

I glanced through the rear mirror. The woman with the dusky skin came out and watched us go. It was possible that she recognized Philip's car, but she only gave us a very brief glance and then crossed the square with what looked like a bundle of old clothes under her arm. Irena's mother had lost interest in us.

"If those children we saw playing outside the house were hers, however many must she have?"

I heard Philip's first real laugh of the morning. "I gather they're her grandchildren."

I sat with my face turned toward the car window as we drove through Albano.

There would, of course, be no divorce; Irena must be made to return to live with Leo under the shadow of the Malimbrosa arrogance . . . Allegra's peasant daughter-in-law . . . their secret would be well kept and there must be no deviation from Allegra's plan.

And Philip? He was still the unknown quantity, the x I could not place in the equation.

I tried to forget that he was sitting next to me. By keeping my face turned away I could almost believe that I had neither interest nor feeling for the man at the wheel. I tried, instead, to remember the vineyards round this area where once, with Vanessa and Gisela, we had driven as children and Gisela had told us about these particular vines where the hyacinth-colored grapes produced a rich, dry, stinging Velletri wine . . .

We were approaching a small *trattoria* isolated among the trees and overhung with wisteria. "I'm afraid I can't stay long enough to give you a slap-up lunch. While Rome sleeps this afternoon, I shall be working, but I thought we needed a drink, and if you don't mind, we could have something quick and simple."

I was all for a light meal.

25 ❧

We sat on a terrace screened by wisteria and ate new-baked bread and cheese and olives and drank wine. We were in the shade and I put my sunglasses back in my handbag. As I did so, I felt the card Vanessa had delivered to Martin for me. I didn't give a thought to whether I was wise or not; I acted on impulse and drew the card out and handed it to Philip.

"This came for me when I first arrived." I watched him and said, "Turn it over and look at the drawing."

He studied it for a long time. "A carved screen, there must be thousands. Vanessa's seated on a very ordinary straight-backed chair and there's something to her left. I can't see what it is."

I took the card from him. "It looks like some kind of painting."

"An icon such as you see in Russian churches. But the congregation usually stand with their lighted candles during a service and only the old sit on benches built around the sides. So, why the chair?"

"Unless it is in a private house."

"A private chapel . . ." He turned the card over. " 'While I wait.' Wait for whom?"

You? I thought, and watched his face. But his expression told me nothing.

"So," he said, "all we know is that she was expecting some-one to come and fetch her."

"But why wait in a chapel? Why not at her apartment? I think she drew that place deliberately hoping I would find out where it was and who owned it."

"It's possible. When did you receive this?"

"It was put through Martin's mailbox for me. He found it when he returned from London. Vanessa obviously sent it to him because she had no idea where I would be staying."

He handed the postcard back to me and looked at his watch. "I've got a column to write this afternoon, so we'll have to get going."

He had so easily dismissed the card that the full force of my suspicion of his involvement returned. Our journey to Irena's home village had solved nothing of the real problems between Philip and me. In fact, he could have been offering me some alternative interest in order to keep my mind from dwelling on the things that more importantly implicated me.

As we walked out of the *trattoria* he put out a hand and lifted my hair. I felt the soft breeze on the nape of my neck.

"You have very beautiful hair," he said.

We climbed into the car and drove on to the ancient Appian Way. We made wonderful time until we reached the city, and then every traffic light seemed to hold us up and I sensed Philip's curbed impatience. He was capable of great control yet something of his inner disquiet seeped out and puzzled me. His life seemed to me to be without much anxiety; his role was planned; his payment assured. He was self-contained, arro-gant, curiously gentle in patches. Could it be that conscience tore at him in a paradox of violent ambition and rejection of feeling?

Our conversation was vague and desultory and when the car stopped at the *palazzo*, I said, "I'm going to meet Martin tonight. He thinks he knows the place Vanessa drew on her card. We must try and find it."

"And what will that prove?"

"I don't know."

He changed the subject abruptly. "I shall be calling tomorrow evening to see Leo."

"You're going to tell him the story you told me!"

"I shall tell him exactly what I think he should know." He had opened the car door for me and something in my expression made him say, in the tone of someone saddened by me, "You have a lot of growing up to do, haven't you, Julie?"

"It all depends," I rapped back at him, "what you mean by growing up." Then I said less angrily as I stood by the *palazzo* gates with him, "Thank you for taking me to Ruorento. Whatever you choose to do, I shall never mention it to anyone."

"No," he said, "I don't believe you will. I wish you were as wise about other things."

I turned my back on him and heard him get into his car. I didn't look over my shoulder at him, although I wanted to.

Nonna Allegra was crossing the rotunda as I entered. "Ah, Juliet. I hope you enjoyed your morning."

"It was interesting. I'm sorry I wasn't in to lunch. I should have telephoned—" I was horrified to realize that every minute had so absorbed me that I had forgotten all about it.

She said, "Phillip told me you would probably be lunching with him."

So, when he had come upon me at the table outside Doney's, he had, as I suspected, intended to find me; had perhaps even watched from his parked car to see where I went.

I said uncertainly, "I've got to ask you. Is there any news of Irena?"

"There is no news, but that is unimportant for the moment. She will come back."

"Did you say that, *Nonna*, when Vanessa disappeared?"

Anger flashed across her face but she checked it quickly. "You forget, I had not seen Vanessa for some time when she disappeared; I no longer acknowledged her as my granddaughter."

"Why, *Nonna—why* . . .?"

"That," she said, "is my affair, my child."

"I'm sorry." I wondered what would happen if I said, 'I read *Nonna* Luciana's diaries. I know who I am.' But suppose, after all, Nonna Luciana had been so senile that her fantasies became facts in her mind; suppose she had begun to like me and had willed things to be true that had no truth in them? . . .

Nonna Allegra said, as if she believed she were following my thoughts, "Leo will find Irena—and without the aid of either a private detective or the police."

Scandal being unendurable, particularly following so quickly on top of the Vanessa affair . . . I looked at the thin, arrogant profile.

"You will rest this afternoon, Juliet?"

"Perhaps." I smiled at her. "Or I may go shopping." (And some time today or tomorrow, *Nonna*, I will have to tell you that I am leaving Rome.)

"If you are short of money, you must tell me."

"You have already been very generous. That lovely dress, the necklace . . ."

She waved my words aside. "That was nothing. You had better insure the necklace as soon as you return to England. It is quite safe while you are here."

Quite safe? When somebody could slip in and lock me in a cellar without anyone in the house knowing? Or perhaps it wasn't an outsider . . . the thought didn't make the fact less sinister.

"Don't, please, be too independent to ask if you need money, Juliet. Your mother was proud. I hope you haven't inherited that from her."

"I'm afraid I have. But thank you all the same. There is one favor I would like to ask. May I use the Dauphine this afternoon?"

"Of course."

I DROVE THROUGH THE THREE O'CLOCK HEAT to Grottochiara. Old Paolo was standing outside the lodge smoking a cheroot.

He opened the gates and greeted me with delight. I stayed and had a few words with him, met his wife who came running out of the house to take my hand and nod and talk in quick, almost incomprehensible Neapolitan. It was good for someone to come, to see the child. Was I, by any chance, intending to stay? Her eyes moved to the back of the car and saw no suitcase there. I said this was a brief afternoon visit for I did not have the courage to tell her that I had come to say goodbye to that small, thin chicken of a boy. Then I left them and drove to the house.

Through some grape-vine which could easily have been nothing more mysterious than the telephone in the servants' quarters at Malimbrosa, Gisela knew of Irena's break with Leo.

She said, "I have not yet dared to tell Pepi. After Vanessa, it was the Signora Irena he loved most. She was coming here next week to stay for two or three days."

I said, remembering *Nonna* Allegra's conviction that Irena would return, "Perhaps she'll be back by then."

Gisela shrugged her shoulders. "He should have shown her more clearly that he loved her. He was so cold, so aloof," she added passionately. "Not even if he had picked her up from the streets, should he have behaved as if she were—were just a—" She sought for words.

I said softly, "A valuable asset."

I had spoken in English and Gisela didn't understand. She looked at me for a translation. I said, "Never mind; all we can hope is that she comes back, *if she wishes to*. Where is Pepi?"

She pushed open the shutters and I saw him sitting in the canopied swing with Maria, who was reading to him. I narrowed my eyes against the sun and played with a fantasy. *Where are the children? Bring in the children—bring a dozen; a hundred; a thousand. Make these vast gardens ring with their voices; make them hold out their hands to Pepi* . . . I blinked and the fantasy scene I tried to create was stillborn. There was only one bored little boy in the garden.

I said, "Does he still have nightmares?"

She nodded. "He had a terrible one last night. Maria and I stayed up with him for a long time."

"Vanessa—?"

"He screamed that she was in his room, that she kept saying: 'I am dead, but you will always see me, *caro*, because you love me. I will haunt you with my love and people will think you are mad.' At least it was something like that, but Maria and I could only get the words out of him in broken bits in between his terror."

I said, "If the Signora Irena returns to Malimbrosa and comes down here next week, you must tell her. Or even tell the Signor Leo."

She shook her head. "It will make no difference. They will say he dreamed it all. And I am afraid he must have."

She sat watching me, obviously wondering whether to tell me something, and then made up her mind. "Maria and I sleep at the side of the house, on this floor. We thought it would be better for Pepi to have his bedroom near mine downstairs—I do not know that La Signora would like me to do this, but Pepi is too alone upstairs. If he stops having these dreams, then I will move him to his own room again."

"So, as he sleeps on this floor, his room must open out onto the garden."

She nodded. "There is a door leading to the terrace. But every night it is locked and he gets air from the little window above it—" She made a kind of drawing of it with her hands.

"A transom," I said. "Yes, I understand."

"So, nobody could possibly get in and frighten him. The door was secure in the morning. You see, it *was* a dream."

An obsession about Vanessa, the only one in the Malimbrosa family who had given him the gaiety and love that he needed . . . Even so, I walked round the terrace with Gisela and looked into Pepi's bedroom. The lock on the door was one of the burglar-proof kind. No one could have walked in; no girl with bright hair who was impersonating Vanessa.

Pepi saw me and scrambled from the swing and ran to meet

me. I hugged him and asked what the story was about.

"King Arthur of England and the Round Table," he said. "It's all lovely. There's a beautiful lady in it called Elaine and there's a wizard called Merlin."

"And a magic sword called Excalibur," I said. "Yes, it's a marvelous story."

"I like King Arthur best."

The once and future King . . . Just as you will be of an empire not of people but of plastics and chemicals—if someone will ever let you reach your manhood with sanity . . .

"Why do you look so sad, *Zia* Juliet?"

I said, "I'm frowning. I've got the sun in my eyes," and laughed and took his hand and raced him through the too-hot afternoon as far as the distant lawn where the white peacocks spread their tails and shrieked at us, and the air was honey-scented.

I had come to say goodbye to Pepi, but I hadn't the courage. He had lost Vanessa, Irena might never come back. I had to let him have a week or so to get over that and then I would write him long letters from London, promising that I would come to Italy again. That way, it would be easier for him to face the loss of another adult who cared for him as a little boy and not as a business asset.

I LEFT THE VILLA SAPPHIRA without even telling Gisela that I was flying back to England in two days' time. I said "goodbye" with the lightheartedness of someone returning soon.

Halfway down the hill toward Nemi, I stopped the car, got out and made my way across the woods in the direction of the Dead Land. I had planned nothing; I just walked between the sepia trees, looking for the Villa Artemis.

When it came in sight, I stopped. I had no intention of rushing into more danger, but I watched the ugly little house, waiting, perhaps, for someone to arrive or leave. Like a blind date. I had no idea who or what I would see. The house looked closed and neglected and I turned back after about five minutes because the silence and the stillness had a ghostly touch. I had taken careful note of the way back, finding certain formations of trees and tangled brown glades to guide me.

There is a kind of silence, a quality perhaps, that seems peopled with living things, breathing at you. Yet the whole forest appeared isolated so that my presence was almost a desecration. There were no green branches on which birds could establish their owner-occupier rights in song; no rich earth for the animals; no color . . . and then I saw a patch of emerald and garnet and dived toward it. It was a silk scarf and it lay in a small glade. A quiver of alarm ran through me as I picked it up. I knew that I had passed through this particular glade—I had noticed the strange shape of a certain tree, its branches twisted to make the odd outline of a horse's head— open mouth, flaring nostrils, mane . . . And there had been no scarf in the glade then. I dropped it as if it were alight and it lay splayed over the dead bracken.

Someone was there, someone watching me, and the soft, lovely square had either been tossed down as a warning to me to keep away or to lure me to the Villa Artemis to enquire if someone living there had lost it. Either way, it was a pretty, silken threat.

I had never in my life before felt violent enough toward anyone to want a gun, but only with one in my hand would I have had the courage to walk up to the Villa Artemis. As it was, I began to imagine noises in the woods, the crackle of dead twigs, the rustle of dried fern fronds . . . I looked round and saw no one. Every bit of me, bent on self-preservation, wanted to run as hard as I could back to the car. Instead, with an exaggerated casualness, I retraced my steps without too much haste and breathed freely only when I touched the door handle of the blue Dauphine. I drove quickly away, without looking in the rear mirror to see if anyone came out from some hiding place to watch me go.

If I told Martin, he would probably laugh at me and ask me

if I thought I was the only one who went to look at the Dead Land. I knew, though, that had other people been there, I could not have missed seeing them. The distance from the glade where the scarf had lain to the track that led to the Villa Artemis was so short that I would have to have seen whoever had passed that way—*had she wanted to be seen* . . .

Pepi hadn't dreamed that he had seen Vanessa; nor was he living in moments of hallucination. Someone was pretending to be Vanessa—someone so like her that, across the width of the Via Veneto or in the dimness of a bedroom, she could be mistaken for Allegra's granddaughter, someone chosen for her likeness, to be a tool for whoever wanted my generation of the family out of the way.

As I drove back to Rome, I stored the incident up as one more proof to give to Allegra that Pepi's sanity was being threatened; that Pietro Alderno had slipped up when he had said that no one now lived at the Villa Artemis. Oh, I had such a lot to tell my own grandmother . . .

26 ❧

FOR DINNER WITH MARTIN the following evening, I wore the yellow dress that he liked so much, and because I was early, I decided that I would go to the airline offices and check my plane ticket.

There were voices in the *salone* and Philip came out into the rotunda as I was crossing to the door. I caught a glimpse of *Nonna* Allegra hovering inside the room and I had a strong feeling that Philip—or even both of them—had been waiting for me.

I flicked a casual look at him and said, "Oh, hullo. I'm just going out to dinner with Martin."

"At six o'clock—in Rome?" His eyes mocked me. "Or do you mean a late lunch?"

"It could be that. We like to sit over our drinks for a long time."

"Fair enough. May I give you a lift to wherever it is you're going?"

"No, thank you. I have other things to do first."

"What?"

"I have to check my air passage back to London."

"But, good heavens, you've got plenty of time for that. Or are you tired of Rome?"

I said vaguely, "I just want to be certain that everything is in order."

"Then I'll take you."

We were at the door. Alberto let us out, eyes lowered, like an actor playing at being a butler. We went down the steps together and the gates swung open. I had no idea how it happened, but we strolled like lovers, hand in hand. Immediately we were outside, I stopped on the pavement. "I'd like to walk, if you don't mind."

He laughed. "Why should I? You're free. Where are you dining, by the way?"

It was asked so casually that I replied with equal casualness, "At Ostuni's."

"Good food," he said briefly. And then, as if it were an afterthought, "I've just seen Leo. He has been coming home early from his office since Irena walked out on him. I think he always hopes he'll find her back in his apartment."

"You didn't tell him?"

"What? About Irena? Yes, I did."

I asked icily, "And *Nonna* Allegra, too?"

"No."

"You—*didn't*—?"

"When I say No, I don't mean Yes," he said with a flash of anger. "But I suggest you don't question me any more. I haven't the slightest intention of giving you the satisfaction of knowing what Leo's reactions were."

We stood on the pavement in full view of passers-by as if we were preparing our strategic positions for a fine old war.

"Doesn't it occur to you that Leo is very influenced by *Nonna* Allegra. She'll get the truth out of him and then, *don't you see*, if Irena comes back, *Nonna* will make her life a misery. She'll take every opportunity to mock at her urchin daughter-in-law."

He looked at me coldly. "Have you such an opinion of your hostess?"

It was a terse rebuke. I fumbled with my handbag, furious at putting myself in the position of inviting censure. Suppose I

said, "I have every right to criticize her. She's my grandmother. Or perhaps you knew . . ." And then I thought, But
is she? Who am I? Who was my father? A Holdroyd or a
Malimbrosa?

"We look," said Philip, "as if we're hanging around waiting
for a moment when nobody's looking so that we can rob the
house. Either let me take you where you want to go, or let's
say goodbye."

"I'm not keeping you."

He raised one eyebrow at me and moved toward his car. "I
could wring your charming neck."

As I walked down the Via Veneto toward the airline offices
in the Piazza della Repubblica, Philip drove past me and
made no sign. Well, why should he? Except that, unreasonably, I had had my head turned to watch for him, expecting at
least a casual flick of his hand.

I doubted if I would see him again. And after a time it would
no longer hurt. For a few moments, however, I felt such a
deep loneliness that I could easily have turned round, fled to
Malimbrosa and hidden myself, weeping, in Vanessa's blue
room. With an effort I forced myself to think of Martin and of
the place across the Ponte Margherita where Vanessa had sat
and drawn a picture of herself while she waited.

It no longer seemed important that Martin had found the
place. Too many weeks had gone by; too much had happened.
I felt suspended between two beliefs. One, that Vanessa was
alive and that I must do exactly as she had asked and tell
neither *Nonna* Allegra nor the police of my involvement. The
other, the greater conviction, that she was dead and that
someone was impersonating her. I could keep on asking myself
why and find some sort of answer—but I had never been very
good at guessing games.

OSTUNI'S RESTAURANT OUT ON the old Appian Way was very
grand. I remonstrated when Martin asked me if I liked caviar.

"As a matter of fact I like the Black Prince's ruby in the Crown jewels, and I like film star clothes, but I don't expect to have them. Let's be reasonable. I'll choose scampi."

"If you like caviar then you're going to have it," Martin said.

"I love caviar," I said in a small voice.

He gave the order and shook me further by asking for champagne. "In another day you'll be gone and that's a good enough excuse for me. I'm extravagant. Didn't you know?" He laughed at me across the soft lights of the table. "I see you're wearing the yellow dress. Is that because I said it's my favorite?"

"As a matter of fact, yes."

"Thank you. That's what I call a charming gesture. Do you like me?"

"Idiot, of course I do."

"And forgetting the first word, that's quite a charming answer."

His gaiety was, as usual, infectious, and a magic recklessness descended upon us until I said, toward the end of the meal, "You know, I'm not certain if we're being wise in going to this place where you say the screen is. Where is it by the way?"

"In a small private chapel."

"What a strange place for Vanessa to wait for someone."

"It is, isn't it?"

"I thought it would be in some *palazzo* open to the public. But wherever it is, I don't see now that we can do any good by going there now."

"I'd like to," Martin said, "just to satisfy my curiosity. The place is attached to a villa which was bought by a White Russian just after the first world war, in 1918. He had the little chapel built there. Nobody uses it now; it's more or less locked up—"

"So how did Vanessa get in there to wait?"

"That's quite a question."

"And another question is, how do we get in there?"

"We'll have to wait and see. You never know, I may have learned how to pick locks."

"If we could find out who owns it—"

"It goes with the house," he said, "which is now let out into apartments. No one seems particularly interested in the upkeep of the chapel, though."

"Martin, don't let's go."

"Are you afraid?"

I picked up my glass and gulped champagne without the delicacy that it deserved. "Yes, I am."

He leaned across the table. "Don't be, Julie—not with me around. And, you know, I still think that those other two occasions when you thought you'd been attacked have perfectly reasonable explanations—"

"That's what everyone to whom I told my stories was meant to believe. I wasn't going to be shot at in the Borghese Gardens; no one was going to be seen around, in the Via Campisolo, when I—I—"

"Julie, stop it."

"Sorry." I looked across at the flame leaping from the banana flambée on the trolley by our side. "I'm not particularly brave."

"Oh, you're brave all right, or you wouldn't have gone into that strange apartment looking for Vanessa in the first place. Snap out of your apologies and eat. You can't keep a flambée waiting."

While we ate, Martin steered me into a happier conversation. He hoped he would get a chance to come to England next Easter and he hoped, too, that this would be the beginning of something good between us.

Easter was a long way off; I could only think of tonight and the little Russian-built chapel of some long-dead member of the Tzarist court.

"What is the name of this chapel?"

He said, "Santa Paschal."

"It could be a trap."

"I doubt if anyone has been sitting there waiting for us since that first postcard," Martin said matter of factly. "Shall we go?"

"I suppose so. Though I don't see what good it'll do."

"Nor do I. But when we've had a look round, we might go to Tivoli. It's about the best finish to a farewell party that I can think of."

We drove back to Rome past the Colosseum and across the Ponte Palatino. In the distance was the Janiculum Hill where I had stood in the starlit hours with Philip. I didn't want to remember that it was there, and turned my face away.

Martin took a right-hand turn and the car threaded its way through narrow streets until we came to a cul-de-sac. It was very dark, but ahead of us I could see a large building with shutters drawn across most of the windows and a huge nail-studded front door over which two lights burned. At the side of the building was a little round Byzantine chapel.

I said as he stopped the car, "It looks as if it would be very charming inside. *Can* you pick locks?"

"Perhaps we'll be lucky and find the door is open."

It would be interesting to see inside, but it couldn't help in any way. It was all over and out of my hands. I had failed and I wished we hadn't come and that we had driven straight to Tivoli after our splendid dinner.

I glanced at Martin. The lamplight shone onto his fair hair, his eyes were bright with excitement. He had never before seemed to me the kind of man who enjoyed looking in old churches.

"All right," I said, "let's go."

There was a huge iron ring for a handle. I turned it and it didn't yield. "Of course," I said, "the place is locked up."

"Not enough muscle, that's your trouble," he said, and seized the handle and twisted it. The door opened.

The chapel was very small and round. I had expected to find complete darkness, but four candles burned in sconces on the many-branched iron stand to the left of the mosaic columns that supported the little domed roof.

A girl stood in the faint light. She was slim and not particularly tall. She wore a blue dress and her hair was an aureole of gold. The candleglow behind her gave her a luminous beauty that was quite false, for she wasn't in the least beautiful, just arrestingly different . . .

It was Vanessa.

"Come closer, Julie."

I ran to her and seized her hands. She flung me away from her with such unexpected violence that I nearly tripped over a flagstone.

I said, "I thought—I was afraid—that you were dead. Oh, Vanessa, this is so wonderful—" I turned to Martin who was standing behind me, smiling. "How did you find her?"

"He knew where I was," Vanessa said.

I turned round, frowning, not understanding. "Then there's nothing terrifyingly wrong. You aren't in danger?"

"No dear, *you* are."

Suddenly she reached to a stone ledge and picked something up. She raised it and the light from a powerful torch flashed in my face, dazzling me. I put up my arm to shade my eyes. "Don't!"

"I want to see what you look like when you're afraid."

"Why should I be? It looks harmless enough in here and there's a perfectly good escape route." I glanced over my shoulder. The door was closed and the little airless chapel smelt of incense burned long ago and lingering in the carvings and the cracks of the stones.

"It's a good place in which to talk," Vanessa said. "We shan't be disturbed."

But as I went toward her again, she backed from me.

"What *is* all this?" I checked my movements and stood rigid. "If you aren't in trouble, why did you let me think you were? Or—*are* you?"

"Not now that you're here," she said.

Instead of finding comfort in what she said, a whisper of fear brushed through me. To counteract it I laughed, and the sound was harsh, as if I had a sore throat.

"Let's come to the point. Martin—" I turned to him.

He gave me his wide, friendly smile, walked past me and put his arm round Vanessa's shoulders. "Go on, *carissima*, tell her. Tell Julie why she has to be removed."

"I've already noticed that your vocabulary is bad," I said to him. " 'Removed'—as though I'm a discarded painting in an exhibition."

"Then let's be more explicit." He was still smiling, and I saw how meaningless it was—just a stretch of a mouth in an otherwise expressionless face. "Shall we say 'disposed of'?"

Anger was my only weapon against fear and incredulity. "Like wealth—or garbage? Don't be damned silly."

"He isn't," Vanessa said.

But this wasn't Vanessa; this was her uncanny double; her impersonator. I said, "How did you manage your extraordinary likeness to Vanessa. Was it plastic surgery? And where is—"

"Would you like proof?"

"Yes."

"Then do you remember this?" She reached again toward the ledge where the candles burned, picked something up and held it out to me, palm upward. The torch in her other hand shone onto the companion to the opal and ruby earring in my handbag.

I leaned toward her and she smelt of some perfume that had sandalwood and flowers in it. The same scent that Irena used.

I turned away from the palm with the glittering jewel. "That's no proof. You could have stolen it."

She tossed the earring back onto the ledge of the sconce and said in beautiful, perfect English, "Once, when we were having coffee at Fortnum and Mason's, you said, 'I'd love to be able to afford that pearl bracelet I saw downstairs.' And I said, 'When I inherit my share of Malimbrosa, you shall have one like it.' Remember?"

She hadn't needed to give me proof. Nobody else could be like her, her face was unique—tilted, pagan features; blazing hair . . . Vanessa . . .

I blinked in the stark light of the torch and turned away. I had to get air. I had taken three paces before Martin caught me and turned me gently round again. "Face to face, Julie," he said.

It could have been a nightmare, or a hallucination, but it wasn't. It was real. Martin had brought me here knowing perfectly well who would be waiting for me. Even so, it hung in the logical part of my mind as an unbelievable fantasy.

Vanessa, my enemy; Vanessa training her torch onto me as if she were preparing some third-degree. Vanessa. I should be laughing and insisting 'Look, the joke's over. Let's get down to facts.'

But the facts were there, in the charming mosaic chapel with the heavy black shadows and the four burning candles. I gave a thought to Byron and his words that had become a cliché

> . . . *for truth is always strange;*
> *Stranger than fiction.*

Truth; that I was here with someone I had believed to be my friend, and a man who had been my gay companion. It was then that my eyes, becoming accustomed to the deep shadows, saw the screen. The carvings were intricate, the three little gargoyles looked over the top of the three panels as if at their own reflections. Beyond, I saw the glimmer of gold. The icon that had been faintly drawn in on Vanessa's card. "While I wait . . ." *For you, Julie . . .*

27 ❧

I WANTED DESPERATELY TO SIT DOWN because the stone floor
under me felt like quicksand. But I was rooted and sinking, not
because the stones had changed their constituency, but because
my legs were shaking. I knew at last that this wasn't black
magic, or even a black joke; it was more like a black, perverted
miracle. Vanessa, whom I believed dead, was alive. Vanessa,
my friend, turned . . . turned what—Accuser? Accuser of
what? Judge? Judge of what? What had I done for the atmos-
phere around me to be charged with such hatred?

And again, my fear made my tone and my words burst out
over that hushed place in a spurt of anger. "I must have been
very dumb all these years. I thought we were friends . . ."

"We were," she said almost gently, "until I found out."

"What?"

"That you were my cousin."

"How do you know?"

"You don't sound surprised."

"You can answer my question first."

"*Nonna* Luciana's diaries. I read them all, but I doubt if
anyone else had. They thought that *Nonna* Luciana was stupid
as well as deaf. She wasn't, but she knew *Nonna* Allegra, so she
kept her counsel." The torch moved slightly and I saw Vanes-

sa's face. She was looking puzzled. "*Why* aren't you surprised?"

"Because I read the diary, too."

"Well, good for you! I thought you'd be far too polite to read something so private."

"I asked permission of *Zia* Romola."

She shook with laughter. "That's marvelous. And she had no idea what you were going to discover?"

I didn't bother to tell her that *Zia* Romola knew, too.

"And you've learned it all too late to benefit." She shook back her hair and for a moment I thought that one vivid strand of it had become caught in the candle flame. The light dipped and rose again; her hair fell, unsinged, into place. She reached up and drew Martin's face down and kissed him.

"All this time, my darling, you played the good friend to Julie and she never guessed. How I would have loved to have been invisible and watched you!"

"For goodness sake, come to the point."

"I have." she snapped. "Surely you must know now what it's all about?"

"Start telling me." My voice was over-loud, like an armor protecting me from my own fear. "Give it to me, episode by episode. The earring you dropped—"

"You knew that all our jewelry came from Juturna's, so I guessed you'd get the message and go there. That's why I rang them and they sent you to the apartment in the Via Campisolo."

"Don't tell me you live there."

"We rented it temporarily for just the purpose for which it was used. To get you there. But you have very quick reflexes, Julie. I held my breath when you flung yourself back from that door that led to nothing."

She was so calm that she made my blood run cold and still and rigid as stone. I could not see her face clearly behind the brilliance of the flashlight.

I heard my own voice in a whisper. "And—and the Villa Artemis?"

"No one ever came to the place after the Sicilian couple left. The woods would be enough to put anyone off buying it. And so I used it. There's a good, secluded copse where I can hide the car. I have to be near Pepi, you see. You *do* see, don't you?" she insisted.

I remained silent.

"It won't take long to demoralize him," she went on. "When I've done with him, he'll be a mass of nerves, unable to cope with life, and certainly unable to run the Malimbrosa Industries."

"You *did* go to his room; he *did* see you in the Dead Land."

"The first was intentional. When *Nonna* turned me out, she forgot to ask me for the keys to the *palazzo* and the villa. They proved useful. I could walk in at night and play 'ghosts,' to scare Pepi."

"A little boy who always adored you."

"A child who will inherit too much," she lashed back at me. Then she gave a brief laugh. She was entirely at ease, unhurried, savoring her macabre enjoyment. "But that time when Pepi saw me in the Dead Land was an accident. I came to the villa early to . . . to plan something. And I wanted some coffee. There's only a damned primitive water pump at the Villa Artemis. I managed to get the water up and then as I tried to unhook the pail, I tipped it over my head and drenched my hair. I was walking in the woods to try and dry it."

"There's someone else in all this elaborate intrigue of yours," I said. "The man who walked behind you in the Borghese Gardens—"

She interrupted me. "If only you'd been able to see Martin full face! He looked marvelous in his dark wig. But then, we wouldn't have let you."

"You must be insane."

"For the sake of millions of lovely lire, I don't care what you call us." She must have seen my almost imperceptible steps backward, for she said sharply. "The door's locked behind you, Julie. And no one will hear you if you scream."

The present made nonsense of the past, of all the times we had spent together, talking the hours away in my London apartment, exchanging confidences, shopping, finding the same things to laugh about. This Vanessa turned enemy . . .

People's characters didn't change that much. Of course they didn't, but given certain circumstances, unrealized good or suppressed evil could surface and shock . . . *had* surfaced and shocked for Vanessa when she learned who I was.

I said in a voice I hoped sounded braver than I felt, "You quarreled with *Nonna* Allegra. How do you imagine what you're doing now is going to make things right for you?"

"Because no one will ever know we have met. And, after your disappearance (incidentally with some of *Nonna's* jewelry or whatever precious objects I can find to take and discredit *you* with stealing), *I* shall comfort her in her disillusion about you."

"But I don't intend to disappear."

"You can't help yourself." I saw the small movement of her head and looked where she was looking. There was nothing there that I could see except thick, black darkness.

"No one will ever be able to trace that any of us came here. You didn't notice, did you, that Martin has even had a false license plate put on his car. I doubt if you'll ever be found—that is, until they pull the place down some time in the far future."

"Put that flashlight out," I said.

She switched it off. The candlelight lit up her tilted, Pan-like features. "I guessed, when I read the diaries, that after my quarrel with *Nonna* Allegra, you would be sought out and invited to Malimbrosa. That's when I decided to invite you first."

"The shop—?"

"A temporary amusement. Also, I have a sense of the dramatic, I'm an actress *manqué*. The place in the Via Prassodi just helped to deepen the mystery. Only three people knew about it—Martin, of course, and silly *Zia* Romola, who listened

· *287*

at key holes and overheard too much, and—Philip." She ran a hand over her cheek, feeling her soft, pale skin. "I had a proposition to put to him, that's why I asked him to come to Frascati and take me to dinner. I usually get what I want with men, and *Nonna* Allegra liked him. So, I suggested that if he would use his influence to get me back into her favor, I would marry him. I dangled millions of lire before what I hoped were his enchanted eyes. We would be so rich, I said. I knew that he was ambitious and that women meant nothing much to him, so I felt quite sure that he would fall in with my plan. Of course, I had no intention of going through with the marriage—I'd use him, pay him for his trouble and then wave him away—Martin is my kind of man." Again the caress, the soft kiss on his lips.

"And . . . and what did . . . Philip say . . . ?" I held my breath, hoping that he had agreed, hoping that I could hate him once and for all.

"He wasn't very polite. He said he still liked his life, he wasn't prepared for hell on earth. I wanted to slap his face for that, but I held on to my temper. He might still be useful to me—and he could also be dangerous."

All the time she was speaking, I was edging backward at a snail's pace, one foot moving, I hoped imperceptibly in that half darkness, behind the other. I had to keep Vanessa talking until I reached the door. Please, heaven, Martin had left the key in the lock; please heaven, too, that someone was passing on the way to the adjoining apartment block and would hear my shouts . . . *Keep them talking; play for time*—the first adage in a desperate situation.

I said, "So Philip refused. But he must have known you'd try someone else, since you're so obsessed with money."

"Oh, Philip knows," she said.

It was an ambiguous answer. I said, "He knows? You mean he's part of the plan? . . . a liaison between you and *Nonna* Allegra?"

She said softly, "So you like Philip? A lot of women do, but it doesn't get them anywhere. And you'll never know, now, how much he is involved, will you? That's one thing I won't tell you—appetites should be whetted with doubt; it adds to the stimulus of life—*while* you live."

"Oh, don't be so dramatic."

But that was something typical of her nature. *Keep her talking* . . . though for what reason in this little enclosed place with the thick walls and no one on my side?

"The cellars at the *palazzo*. You couldn't have shut me in."

"Oh, couldn't I? There's a door between the *palazzo* and the garage. It is always kept locked, but I have the keys. The door leads to a passage where the cellars are—it's rather isolated from the rest of the house so there was little fear of anyone seeing me, especially at siesta time."

"How did you know I'd be around at that time?"

"I've waited every afternoon for you," she said. "I knew that sooner or later I'd catch you on your way out—the English don't much go for *siesta* when they're on holiday and there's a lot of sightseeing to be done. When I heard you coming, I planned to call for help. You'd have come running and seen the cellar light on and gone down . . . Only you walked into the trap without any effort on my part. By the way, how did you get out?"

I didn't give her the satisfaction of an explanation. Instead I just said, with as much snap in my voice as I could manage, "You're ingenious! I suppose you sent Martin to me in London."

She nodded. "It was a careful scheme—a long investment, you might say, for our future—Martin's and mine."

"And if *Nonna* Allegra never forgives you?"

"Oh, she will. She may hate the idea, but the future of Malimbrosa means more to her than anything else. If there's no other way for the family's continuance, then she'll have me back."

"You forget Pepi."

"A hysterical child? *Nonna* is bright; she knows perfectly well that he won't be an asset *that* way to the family future.

There's only me. I shall marry Martin and he'll take my name, and through us, Malimbrosa will go on as *Nonna* is obsessed it shall. Once this—"

"If you think you are the family's only hope, then you've got a surprise in store for you—"

"Why must you be so blind? *You* won't survive."

The idea that time was my friend was fading, but I clung to it—a piece of seaweed can seem a lifeline when there is no rock at hand . . . She had switched on the flashlight again and I had a wild hope that someone might see the light through the few high windows . . . someone might come . . .

I was aware of the windows without actually looking at them. Vanessa and Martin could both have overlooked that risk and if they noticed, then the flashlight and the candles might go out and I'd be at their greater mercy in the dark.

"There's a plan," I said, "involving Irena—"

"Irena and Leo? Don't be silly. He can't give her children; it's a medical fact—" She stopped. It seemed suddenly to occur to her that she hadn't let me finish what I had intended to say. "What did you really mean just now about a surprise?"

"Philip," I said. "Philip Cornel. You had no idea, did you, that they—" If I told her, Irena also might be in danger from Vanessa's megalomanic plan; telling would help no one. . . .

"Why don't you finish your sentence?" A fourth voice spoke from the darkness.

Vanessa suddenly gave a shout of laughter and my blood ran cold.

A man stood some way away, watching us. Deep shadows cut into his face like weals; his body had the alert litheness of something ready to spring. Philip . . . Philip, too. Waiting until they called him, but because of what I had begun to say, unable to resist facing me with what I knew? An unholy triangle of two men and a woman and I, Juliet Malimbrosa, in the center of the vortex.

Vanessa's hair flew round her shoulders with the speed of her movement; she blew out the candles and the smell of smoldering tallow stifled her Guerlain perfume.

There was action everywhere. I fled toward the door and was caught and dragged, fighting, back into the center of the chapel. I turned in terror and Vanessa's flashlight beamed in my face. I saw then that behind her was a heap of torn-up flagstones, a long black hole. My grave, of course, the final horror of the night—the grave for the last Malimbrosa who stood in the way of what she wanted, the rich prize, the wealth, the power and the glory. As Martin swung me round and imprisoned me in his arms, the flashlight went out, then on again. I had one swift sight of Philip's face. Behind his head, for that second, the icon glowed—halos of rich, dark gold; copper-colored faces . . .

I tore at Martin's arms and heard Vanessa scream. "Over here . . . Over here . . ." I felt the disturbance of air as she came to me. Then Philip was there. Something crashed to the ground; then a flashlight beamed on and off again . . . Philip cried, "Damn it to hell! This bloody light—"

Three against one . . . I fought like a fiend to keep my balance against the power that was dragging me across the stone floor. I bit the wrist that held me, then a fist hit me and I fell to the ground. I had one strange blinding thought. The dinner . . . "For her last meal, the condemned woman dined off caviar and champagne . . ."

I hit the floor with a crack that seemed to burst open my skull.

28 ✖

SOMETHING STIRRED. I was beyond knowing what it was—a shadow across my eyelids; a whisper in my ear. In the swinging limbo of returning consciousness, I could not for some time distinguish sight from sound.

When I did, I realized that it was not some cold Byzantine stone that cradled me, but Vanessa's lovely bed. I felt its familiar softness before I opened my eyes, and when I did I saw dark, gentle eyes watching me. A perfume hung over me in a faint, expensive wave. Vanessa's . . .

A vague terror zig-zagged through returning consciousness. "Vanessa—" My voice was a whisper in order not to anger to still more fury the thousand small hammering devils in my head.

"Lie still," the voice above me said, "and don't talk."

Not Vanessa, But Irena . . . Fear was laid like a half-manifested ghost.

"I want to talk—that is, if everyone will whisper. Don't shout—please—"

"Just be quiet for a while. I'm here with you."

I said, stupidly, "You're back?"

She was at the windows, closing them quietly.

"How—?" I began.

"I'm told not to talk to you until you're strong enough."

"I'm quite strong enough."

She moved to the bed and I saw that she wore a long green robe girdled at the waist. In my reeling state, I thought of a picture in a schoolbook of Guinevere standing before the castle in fabled Camelot. She, too, had worn a green robe and her hair had fallen in waves upon her shoulders.

In my mind was a murmurous jumble of thoughts, like little floating pains which I hadn't the energy to gather up and analyze. I had been somewhere in a dark place and three people had wanted me dead . . . But where; and who? I had to clear my mind before I went to sleep again. Irena touched my cheek with a smooth hand and I leaned my face against it.

"Go to sleep, *cara*," she said softly, and as I closed my eyes, not because I wanted to but because I could no longer keep them open, I felt her lips against my temple and her soft hair brush across my face.

In and out of the vague fabric of my dream, there rang a name like a bell, tolling. Vanessa . . . Vanessa . . .

When I opened my eyes again Irena was talking to Nunzia.

The devils in my head were a little less rampant. I lifted myself up in bed and said in a clear voice, "Tea. I want some tea," and the sound of my voice seemed to shatter my temples. I slid down again onto the soft pillows.

The door closed very quietly behind Nunzia and Irena came to my side, saying on laughter, "That's a very English demand. Nunzia has gone to make it for you. And—"

"And don't tell me not to talk," I whispered. "How did I get here?"

"Philip carried you—"

"Philip . . ." I struggled up, fighting the enveloping bed-clothes. "Irena—you said—"

She laid a hand on my shoulder. "I was told that I was not to excite you. Please, Julie, just lie still. *Please*—or Mamma will do what she said she would do and send for a nurse—"

"I don't want a nurse. I want to know what happened."

"You hit your head when you fell in the Chapel Santa Paschal."

The Chapel . . . Vanessa . . . Martin . . . Philip. Three people in a dim place, each like an outmaneuvering army converging on me.

Slowly, painfully, memory crept back. "I didn't fall. Someone hit me—"

"Mamma will be here directly. She'll tell you everything. But not before I tell her you're well enough." She turned as the door opened. "Your English cup of tea."

It was beautiful—fragrant and hot and the cup was one of the green and white Rockingham set. Irena poured out for me and I seized the cup. But my hand shook so badly that I couldn't lift it.

"This is silly," I cried. "I'm all right now. Why can't I just lift a simple cup?"

"If you do, you'll burn your mouth. Leave the tea for a moment or two."

I said, looking at her, at the lovely robe, the cloud of hair, "So you came back."

"Yes."

"Why did you run away?"

"You know that. You went to Ruorento."

A bit of memory crept back. "Philip told you he had taken me there? How *could* he?"

"Please, no excitement . . ."

"Irena, how *could* he?"

"We'll talk later—"

"We'll talk now. You must see that I can't rest until my mind is clear as to what happened. Go on . . . go on . . . Why did Philip tell you that I knew?"

"That was something between you and himself. Perhaps, by telling you my story, he hoped to understand you better."

It wasn't an easy answer to work out and I left it. "But you —and Leo. Tell me, please. It's all right between you?"

"We hope so. We have to leave that to time; things don't suddenly become solved. Leo and I have never been very close and what Philip discovered was an obstacle."

"It couldn't be. Not these days." I lay frowning, thinking

slowly. "What can it matter where anyone was born? That sort of idiocy went out years ago."

"It matters to the Malimbrosas," she said. "That's why I went away. Leo had to choose, either to find me, or let me go . . . He came to find me."

"Philip knew where you were?"

"Oh, yes."

This time my hands were steadier. I managed to lift the cup without help and drink the tea.

"*Nonna* Allegra—"

"We hope she will never know. The old are set in their ways; what she has not been able to forgive all her life, she can never forgive now. To her, I still have a past that is wrapped in mystery. I know she consoles herself by believing that perhaps I have illustrious forebears." She smiled. "That is the way she would put it. And it is better for her—for all of us—that she can keep the illusion. The truth would shock her too much. You cannot tell her that the world has changed since her ideas took shape. In business she is of the present; in her private life she is of the past."

The devils were leaving my head. I lay back on the pillows. "And Philip?"

"What about him?"

"You and he—"

She moved away from me. "We have talked too much."

I reached out and caught her hand. "Philip—" I said again.

She gave a small sigh of resignation. "He helped me very much. I can never be grateful enough. He made me see that my roots were here, with Leo. You see, I love my husband and I want him to love me."

"But he does . . . he must."

"Perhaps, let us say, that he has proved that he needs me. It is a beginning."

Her voice soothed me as I think she intended it to do but as she sat by my side, I kept remembering what *Zia* Romola had said. *To Irena and Leo Malimbrosa, a son.* But not his son . . .

I put my hands over my face and turned my head away

from her. I think she thought I wanted to sleep because she took the bed tray and quietly left my room. I lay with my eyes closed. The passing seconds were full of names of places and people, all of them slowly becoming linked in my mind with one colossal betrayal—one name. Vanessa . . .

How could I ever have believed in our friendship? How blind was I? Or how clever was she? Perhaps it was neither; perhaps it was the torment of seeing the Malimbrosa fortune slipping from her grasp that had changed her from a spoiled but charming young friend into a nemesis of hate.

And Philip . . . My mind was not yet capable of concentration. I opened my eyes and stared up at the moulded ceiling. What about Philip? What about Martin? The Via Campisolo and the Dead Land; the Chapel of Santa Paschal? . . . the names fled in and out of my mind like the swifts that darted among the ruins of Rome. I tried to hold on to a single thought and follow it to a conclusion, but I could not. Everything was interwoven and I needed someone to guide me, to pause and clarify. I knew too much, and too little; I needed the Götterdämmerung in my head removed by calm and ordered speech.

I lay, though, with a strange awareness of the inevitability of the past upon the present. The things that had shaped today had begun years ago, before I was born—in Cambridge. My mother and my father perhaps meeting on a daffodil-haunted lawn behind King's College, and because of it, I was born and lived and nearly died at the age of twenty-two . . .

A restlessness seized me and I got up, struggled into my robe, and went to the window. I wanted to see the world, alight and alive, outside; a vista might snap me back to a normality which the hyacinth walls of Vanessa's room was failing to do.

"And what are you doing out of bed?"

If I moved quickly the hammering would increase in my head, and so I turned like a slow-motion film, holding on to the dressing table.

Nonna Allegra came toward me. She, too, wore a long robe, but her hair was an immaculate white sheath round her head.

She put an arm round me, led me back to the Venetian bed, and pulled the silk sheets over me.

"I'm all right now," I protested. "Please, let me get up."

"Tomorrow."

"What is the time?"

"Twelve o'clock. Midnight."

Only that. I breathed a sigh of relief. By morning I would feel fine. I said, "Vanessa—you know she's alive? She was there in the Russian chapel with Martin and Philip."

"We'll talk about it later."

"Now," I said, and my voice was fierce. "*Nonna*, what happened?"

She walked to the desk, picked up an orange silk scarf and ran it through her hands. "I blame myself. I blame myself . . ."

"Vanessa is alive," I said again.

She sank down in the blue chair by the window. "I know." Her hands were spread out over the dark silk of her robe. Without the hard glitter of her rings, they looked less old, softer. "After all that happened, I owe you the truth." She paused, and said with difficulty, "Vanessa had been forging my signature to checks and so I could not allow her to remain here. On the other hand, a scandal was unthinkable with all its dreadful publicity. Like any other large concern, we have our enemies, and even if we had not, there is our name . . ." She rose from the chair and sat at the dressing table, looking not at herself in the mirror but at the reflected room. "It would have been useless to have sent Vanessa out of the country where I could not have kept in touch with her. I could not trust her, if she were out of my influence, not to write to her friends, to put some exaggerated case to them and so start gossip. So there was only one way out. She must seem to disappear, but I must know where she was. I took an apartment for her under an assumed name—Maria Cyrena; I had new clothes for her—all the old we stored away—"

"I saw them at the Villa Sapphira."

She did not seem to hear me, but continued in her deep, flat voice. "I gave her my word I would make over a large sum of money to her if she would remain in hiding for a year. But she had to stay in Rome—people don't look for a missing person right in the shadow of her own home. I told Vanessa that when the time was up and the search accepted as a failure, I would arrange that she left Italy for good. She agreed because the alternative was as unthinkable for her as it would have been for me. A court case and then prison . . . Vanessa could not have borne that."

I watched her gaunt reflection and the tired, hooded eyes. "You know, don't you, that I read *Nonna* Luciana's diaries?"

She rose and stood at the foot of the bed, gripping the carved wood with her hands, leaning on it for support.

"It's true, Juliet. My son married your mother and you were born after he was killed. I never met your mother, but I wanted to know you. That was why I sent Vanessa to the same school that you attended, why I asked the headmistress to bring you together. That is why, also, I arranged for you to come out here with Vanessa for your holiday. I wanted to adopt you, but your mother refused, and that was the end of the affair."

"So, if you kept in touch with Vanessa, you knew that I was coming out here."

She shook her head. "She didn't tell me. But then you came . . ." She began to walk to and fro across the room.

I said. "You weren't going to tell me who I was, were you, *Nonna?*" Then, as she turned quickly, moving her hands in a swift protest, I added, "You told *Zia* Romola that it must be secret, that no one must ever know that I was . . . *who* I was . . ."

"That is wrong, Juliet. It had to be secret until *I* told you. Romola is indiscreet; she has to be taught to hold her tongue although, as you now know, she cannot do even that! I was going to tell you in my own time and my own way."

Still autocratic; still the one who must make the moves—the manipulator.

She brushed her hand across her eyes. "But I never dreamed that such terrible things were happening. I knew Vanessa was spoiled, willful, extravagant—but evil . . . oh, no, I never knew."

As she spoke, the cloak of power, of pride, seemed to slide from her. She faced her failure to understand and to cope with her granddaughter. She held her hands, bereft of rings, in front of her and looked at them. "You should have told me about the things that were happening to you. You should have trusted me, Juliet."

"Vanessa's card stressed that I wasn't to. I thought of kidnappers who kill their victims if the police are informed. I was afraid for Vanessa; that's why I told you nothing."

"And all the time you should have been afraid for yourself."

"Oh, I was that, too. And, *Nonna*, I still don't know how Philip was involved."

"You showed him a card with the drawing of a screen on it. The place was featured recently in a magazine article on unknown churches in Rome and Philip recognized it. He is a newspaper man; he has intuitions about things—perhaps he knew Vanessa better than I ever knew her. He was also in my confidence because I needed someone to watch her. Leo is away so much, and couldn't. Romola mustn't and Irena—" She shrugged her shoulders. "She didn't even know what was happening."

Because she was an outsider in the family. I had a feeling that perhaps the incidents of the last few days would change all that and give Allegra a new trust in her daughter-in-law.

She continued, "Philip was interested in knowing why Vanessa sent you that cryptic card when he knew perfectly well she was in no danger and that she was remaining quietly under her assumed name in an apartment I had taken for her in a suburb of Rome where no one knew her. When she went out she wore one of the dark wigs which I had bought for her, and dark glasses."

(Except that time in the Via Veneto when she stood waiting

for me to follow her . . . I remembered that she had carried a large handbag. Big enough to hide a wig in and put it on again when she had thrown me off her tracks . . .)

"So when Philip heard that you were going to Santa Paschal with Martin Kean, he got there first. It was not a last minute rescue—he was there, waiting and listening. He had to hear everything."

"Where is Vanessa?"

"The police have to find them both. God help me, the thing I most dreaded is now inevitable."

Headlines in a newspaper . . . I said, "You could try Villa Artemis in the Dead Land at Grottochiara."

"Philip told them about that and the police are on their way. If they are not there, they will not be far from Rome. Vanessa has no passport. I saw to that."

"And Martin?"

"The Regina Coeli when they find him."

Rome's prison . . . I said, "I suppose I shall have to give evidence." There was dread in my voice. "What can I say that has any proof? What, that need not be just all my imagining? The judge could think I'm making the story up."

"There was a witness in the Russian church. Remember?"

Philip . . .

Before I could question her about him, she went on. "There are ways in which we can prevent unpleasantness for you over this. I will take control, Juliet. Do not worry." She came up to the bed. "You were fretting to know the whole story, were you not? But now that you do, you must rest." She leaned down and her huge dark eyes burned. "You must believe me, *figlia mia*. I intended to tell you the truth before you returned to England. It was just that I was finding it difficult. Pride, Juliet, my pride that had to admit to rejecting you for so long because I could not find it in my heart to forgive my dead son his secret marriage, nor your mother her refusal to let me take you, as I have taken Pepi, to be brought up here at Malimbrosa. You will, perhaps, forgive me in time."

I reached up and drew her closer to me. My lips touched her

dry skin. She understood that this was forgiveness, and she smiled.

"Tomorrow," she said, "we will talk. There are so many plans to be made."

"Plans?"

"Malimbrosa is always open to you, Juliet. You have no parents now. I want you to look upon us as your family—as indeed we are—and this house as your home."

A feather of caution touched me. "*Nonna* . . . please. . . . understand. I must go back to England, to my home and my work. It is so beautiful here but I love my life in London."

In the moment's silence I knew that my grandmother was fighting to try to understand what I felt she could never fully grasp. Her eyes were on me, deep-set, puzzled, and I could almost read her thoughts. Here was a beautiful house and money to enable me to live in luxury; here was a new found and legitimate family. Yet I was choosing to return to long hours of work in Westminster. . . .

I took her hand again. "But I want to come back here often and see you."

I was relieved to see her smile. "Of course, you have your own life, *cara*. Just come to Malimbrosa when you can. It will make me so happy."

When she left me, I lay thinking and drowsing and thinking again.

For a time I slid into a dream that I was again following Vanessa in the Borghese Gardens and that the man behind her turned round and I recognized Martin's face under the dark wig. I awoke and pulled myself out of the distress of my dream and lay wondering how he could have been there in the gardens in office hours, and why.

The answers were clear. He had slipped out of the embassy and walked between Vanessa and myself to give a certain greater credence to the illusion that she was held prisoner. When she had turned her head, he had known it as a signal to stop and light his cigarette and give her time to drop the earring onto the seat.

· *301*

So simple; so much a story built up by them like a game . . . a bright game under the Roman sun with a black horror as its finale.

I felt suddenly that I wanted to escape from this room. My head no longer reeled and I could stretch my legs and feel them firm and able to carry me. I wanted to get up and I would have liked to have flung a robe round myself and gone downstairs without bothering to dress. But it was all too formal, even for a granddaughter to wander through its great rooms in a robe and roughened hair. Irena had been gentle; *Nonna* Allegra had been kind; but there was nothing cozy about Malimbrosa.

I was careful not to bend too much as I put on nylons, slid into my dress, found shoes into which I need only slide my feet. My hair was the difficulty, for my head was too sore for me to use a comb, and so I smoothed the long, ruffled strands with my fingers. I put on lipstick and gave a last look at the pale anthracite color of my skin. I looked awful.

As I walked out to the gallery, I heard the elevator. Late though it was, I intended to allow no one to send me back to bed. Even if the *salone*, the library and all the rest of the rooms were deserted, I would prowl around and perhaps old Riccardo, the night watchman, would get me a sandwich. I didn't dare go into the kitchen myself.

The elevator stopped and the gate opened. My expression must still have registered some state of shock as I looked into Philip's deep topaz eyes, for he snapped his fingers lightly.

"Come out of your trance, Julie."

"You're the last person I expected to see!"

"And *you*," he said, "always seem to be in places where you shouldn't be. Why aren't you in bed?"

"Because I only had a bit of a crack on the head, and I'm better now." I smiled brightly at him, my voice firm. But my legs were unsteady and I reeled a little.

Philip reached out and led me to a seat inside the elevator. He sat me down and stood leaning against the gilded panel, not looking at me. "So you're better and you want to talk. Right.

Do you remember what I said when we first met?"

"You said quite a number of things, none of them particularly flattering."

"I misquoted a Spanish proverb. 'Glory on horseback, disaster sitting behind.' "

"Yes, you said that."

"Then why didn't you listen and take warning? You utter little fool." The softness of his voice didn't disguise the violence. "You thought you could be so clever."

"None of this has been a game. Can't you understand? Vanessa was my friend and friendship involves trust. She didn't want anyone but Martin and me to know what was happening."

"You can say that again!"

I reminded him wearily, "I had a bang on my head, so you might at least treat me gently."

He turned and looked at me, his voice still quiet, but his eyes were fighting mad. "Gently? I do not want to treat you anyway at all. I want no involvement with women, you understand?"

"You needn't worry. I'm going back to London and I have no intention of trying to involve you—whatever you mean by that."

His hand, which had reached to take a cigarette from a leather case, stopped in mid-movement. "You don't need to run away from Rome now. You're safe."

"Oh no, I'm not."

"Now that Vanessa—"

"I'm not talking about Vanessa, I'm talking about myself."

He didn't ask me what I meant and if he had, I could not have told him. I had to get him out of my blood and here, in this small solitary cage under the cupola with its red king and green jester was as good a place as any.

I said, "I've seen Irena."

"I thought we had begun to discuss you and your reason for leaving Rome."

I wished he wouldn't look at me. I said vaguely, "Oh, that's very personal. But about Irena . . . Suppose she and Leo adopted a child—or an army of children?" I watched him closely.

"I haven't the least idea what they intend to do."

"But you—"

"You seem to be dodging about among personalities." His tone held amusement. "Now me? What have I got to do with Irena?"

Something in his brilliant glance made me nervous. An inner trembling was now added to my sore head and my shaking legs. If I'd had any sense I would have gone, without another word, straight back to bed. But I might not get another opportunity to find the last bitter piece of this gigantic puzzle. I would probably never see him again after tonight and so I could be daring in what I said; I could force the truth from him and then leave Rome able to hate him.

I knew what I had to say. What I could not control, however, was the hectic rush with which the words poured from me. I felt rather like some prisoner pushing a great wall down in order to escape. Escape Philip Cornel . . .

"*Nonna* Allegra talked to you one day, didn't she, about the future of Malimbrosa? *Zia* Romola overheard her. *Nonna* was saying that there was only Pepi and he was a little weakling. *I* don't think he is—" I digressed in order to give myself time for the final assault on what was, after all, his private affair. "*I* think Pepi is just lonely and that he'd be fine if he could live a normal life. But that's beside the point—" I lost my courage; the rest was too monstrous to say.

Philip was implacable. "Go on . . . So the signora talked to me. *So*—?"

"She said—at least *Zia* Romola heard her say—she wanted Irena to have children—a son . . ."

"That's true." He waited, watching me, and then said, "Let's have the rest, Juliet. What more did Romola tell you she'd overheard?"

I should have waited until I felt better before I made this onslaught into his privacy. The devils were back, playing leap-frog in my head. Philip was no longer looking at me so that he couldn't have seen my involuntary frown of pain. He was staring out at the caryatids which upheld the staircase as if the swirls of their marble robes fascinated him. Then, without waiting for me to answer his question, he said, "The signora talked to me about Pepi being the last accepted child of the line. She said, 'Providing the man were strong and of good character, I wouldn't mind by whom Irena had a child so long as it could be brought up as my son's. And also provided that nobody outside myself and the people involved knew.'"

"And—you—?"

He heaved himself away from the gilt wall. The caryatids no longer held his attention; he was looking down at me in exasperation and resignation. It was obvious that I was being too curious, but he was humoring me because I'd had a blow on the head. "I just said that I couldn't imagine Irena consenting. It was no use telling the signora that she was being outrageous. Malimbrosa is her adopted religion. For it, she would sacrifice anything, including herself. I knew that I couldn't influence her, but I said that Irena had pride and independence. She said, 'You like her very much.' 'Like' is a nonentity word, I said, 'I *care* for her.' After that, I left because there could be no argument between us. She saw morality as something to be adapted to the family's needs."

For a long moment there was absolute silence; the gallery, the great staircase, the walls of the rotunda, all seemed to be infused, like humans, with breath. I could sense the tension which I knew had to snap. It did.

Philip burst out, "What are you looking at me like that for? *Me?* Good God, you don't think she was hinting that I would sire a Malimbrosa child, do you? And don't tell me that isn't in your mind—" Temper flared in his eyes and for a moment I was afraid. Then the fire went out of him. He sat down by my side and turned my face round to meet his eyes. The strength of his fingers was like burning brands on the sore side of my head. "Julie, look at me. I said, *Look at me.* That's better. I hope I'm jumping to the wrong conclusions. For all saints' sake, what's been in Romola's mind all this time? Not that it matters; she has never liked me because she has a blind love for Vanessa, as if Vanessa were the child she never had. She was always hinting that Vanessa was in love with me and why was I so blind? It was she who was blind. Vanessa has never loved anyone but her own wild self in her whole life. I'm ready to guess that Romola is at this moment in her apartment weeping herself into exhaustion."

I said, "I'm sorry—"

"*You're* sorry?"

"That I . . . I said what I just did."

"I don't blame you; you don't know me well enough. But I can assure you here and now, that my sole interest in Irena was to find her roots for her. I did that."

I leaned against the back of the elevator. There was nothing more to say. From fretting to know the final truth, I had now moved into a sense of utter finality. Somehow I must keep the torn flag of pride flying. I must seem to accept that this was the end of my involvement with him with a remark of such casualness that he would never know how deep the hurt went.

I said, "I told you I'm returning to England. I'm leaving tomorrow. I want to get on with my life."

"Your life is wherever you are."

"Oh no, not necessarily. There are things we want to escape from." Some magnet drew my eyes to his face. His expression was angry and urgent and gentle all at once.

"I've told you," he said violently, "I want no involvement with women."

"And that's fine with me. I—"

"Instead," he continued, as if I hadn't spoken, "here I am, involved. Get up."

"For you to throw me out of here? Thanks, but I'll walk, and I'll go in my own time." I rose to my feet and wavered. "I . . . I can't stand . . ."

He reached out and held me. "Like this, you can." He bent his head and kissed me with a sudden and marvelous gentleness. When he raised his head, he still held me. "I've fought you ever since I first met you. I've tried to dislike you. I kissed you at the ball the other night hoping that I would hate touching you. I've tried to tell myself that you madden me. God help me, you do—"

"That . . . makes . . . us . . . even."

He said, "But I've lost the battle, Julie."

I kept to myself the fact that I had lost mine from the moment I saw him. Instead, I said faintly, "Am I supposed to understand?"

"Of course. There's too strong an attraction between us for either of us to pretend. I can't fight you any longer, Julie."

A most extraordinary sense of calm flowed over me like a healing wave. I put up my hand and touched his face, feeling the uncompromising contours, the dark, drawn eyebrows, the firm mouth.

"Perfection is never given twice by the gods," he said. "I'm not an easy man. You have a strong personality; you would find it hard to put up with me."

"I know it all, already." The devils in my head were dancing now and the pain was excruciating and wonderful.

"So, I can only give you something less than perfection," Philip said.

I closed my eyes and rested my aching head against him. "I don't want perfection. It's a myth, anyway. There's no such thing as a faultless relationship. That's a matter of one being the all-giving and the other, the receiving—and both liking it that way . . . One acting as a mirror in which the other admires himself—herself. There must be times when we want to breathe different air."

"I shall want to breathe it often."

"And so shall I. We're not doormats."

We had to give and take freedom. It was gloriously inappropriate that we clung together, time and place forgotten, in a gilded cage.

ABOUT THE AUTHOR

─────────────────────────────

ANNE MAYBURY *is the author of such successful books as*
The Minerva Stone, The Moonlit Door, I Am Gabriella, *and
many others. Though she now lives in "a flat above the trees
of Kensington Gardens," she was inspired to write Gothic
novels by a 1640 house which she inhabited for many years.*